VIOLETTE MALAN

SHADOWLANDS

VIOLETTE MALAN—
A bold new voice in fantasy
from DAW Books:

The Mirror Lands:

THE MIRROR PRINCE
SHADOWLANDS

The Novels of Dhulyn and Parno:

THE SLEEPING GOD
THE SOLDIER KING
THE STORM WITCH
THE PATH OF THE SUN

VIOLETTE MALAN

SHADOWLANDS

DAW BOOKS, INC.
DONALD A. WOLLHEIM, FOUNDER
375 Hudson Street, New York, NY 10014
ELIZABETH R. WOLLHEIM
SHEILA E. GILBERT
PUBLISHERS
http://www.dawbooks.com

Cover art by Paul Young.

Cover design by G-Force Design.

DAW Book Collectors No. 1596.

DAW Books are distributed by Penguin Group (USA) Inc.

Book designed by Elizabeth Glover.

First Printing, August 2012
1 2 3 4 5 6 7 8 9

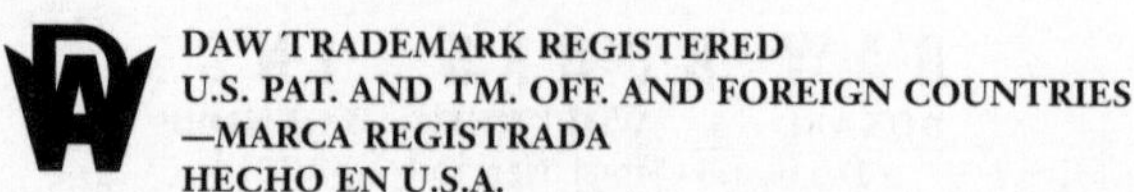

PRINTED IN THE U.S.A.

For Paul

Acknowledgments

As always I want to first thank my editor and publisher, Sheila Gilbert, and thank my agent, Joshua Bilmes. Really, without them I wouldn't need to thank anyone else. There are also people who work alongside them, however, who also need my thanks, people like Debra Euler, Josh Starr, and Marsha Jones at DAW. My thanks also go to my good friends Shari Cohen and Steven Serber, for lending me their house, and their neighborhood. And to Barb Wilson-Orange, for helping me again with my proofs. Thanks to Vaso Angelis who helped me out again, this time with some Greek phrasing; to Jerie Shaw who pointed me at Dr. Paul Ekman's books; to Robin Gibbings for her advice on Australian mines (any errors are mine); and to Jim C. Hines for advice on a more delicate subject. Brian Baird of Computer Depot in Kingston helped me with the fix on the major tool of my trade. Thanks to Samantha Milks and her online book club, whose questions about *The Mirror Prince* helped me clarify some of my ideas for this book.

Special thanks to the staff of Hair of the Dog Pub and Restaurant. If you're in Toronto, stop by and enjoy yourself. I always do.

Three people purchased the rights to have characters named after them at three entirely different silent auctions. The first is Jaiden

Corey Wayne Mattice, by his parents, Corey Mattice and Teresa Lucas. I had to fiddle with the name a little to make it fit, and I hope Jade Enchanter likes the book when he gets old enough to read it. The second is Yves Crepeau, who I'm sure won't mind being a bit of an Outsider. He's not alone, however, as I've made Wai-kwong Wong an Outsider as well.

Prologue

THE SMELLS, SCENTS, AROMAS in the place humans called a bar were almost overwhelming, even when Foxblood was in his Rider form. There were food smells—though these weren't so varied as the humans seemed to think—and the smells of perfumes, of sweat, of strange drugs, of sickness and decay, both from the foods and the humans themselves. He and his kind had learned to mask their own scents the same way, though these humans weren't as sensitive even as Riders.

There was so much *dra'aj* here, and soon, soon he would take some. For now, it was enough to know it was here waiting for him. He'd imposed control on his Pack, so he couldn't relax it in himself. Part of him longed simply to herd all these humans into one place and hold them against a day of shortage. But it was too soon to think of doing such things. The risk was still too great. Not that humans could be much of a threat, but until he knew what the Riders were planning, until he knew where the Horn was, and who now held it, Fox and his Pack had to be patient, to watch and be wary.

They could afford to wait. It wasn't as if there would ever be any shortage. This pool of *dra'aj* was unspoiled, untapped. Even the Riders didn't know about it. Not all humans had the same level of the vital energy, but there were billions of them. An unending resource. The Hunt could live off them forever.

And human *dra'aj* was different. Less, perhaps, in each individual, but oh, what there was, was choice, tasty, and lasting. Fox looked at his hand, turning it over to study first the palm, then the back. It stayed a hand. That could never be done with the *dra'aj* of the People.

It couldn't hurt to taste a little now. Just a little. That one, that fair-haired woman with her strange blue Moonward eyes in her rosy Sunward face, that walked toward him now, stepping out of the path of the waitress. She would do.

Fox reached out and grabbed the human by the wrist as she passed him by, spoke the words, drained her, and watched the hands of others reach out to help her as she stumbled and went down.

Chapter One

I LIKE SUBWAYS. The more crowded the better, as far as I'm concerned. Having all those people around mutes my awareness of them, makes it less acute, until all their psyches, their truths and untruths, their fears and worries and lies, just become so much white noise in the background of my mind. Like the sound of a freeway on the other side of a hill. It's always there, but after a while, you don't notice it anymore.

Today there weren't many people in the car with me, but fortunately any city large enough to have a subway, even Toronto, is populated enough to make me feel comfortable. That is, until the couple that got on at Broadview decided to sit down on the bench seat that was at ninety degrees to mine. *She* felt safer sitting close to another woman. *They* were avoiding the two teenagers who were doing their best to look hard as nails as they hovered around the door in their oversized clothing, their studs and plugs, and their tattoos. I'd brushed against them myself when I got on at Woodbine. [The taller one was worried that someone—his father?—had been acting strangely lately, quiet, distant, and apathetic, not at all like his usual raving drunken self; the shorter one was having an imaginary conversation with his girlfriend in which he was getting the upper hand. For once.]

I shifted in my seat, but just enough that the woman's knee stopped touching mine. I'd had to learn not to overreact to casual physical contact. We were crossing under the Bloor Viaduct and almost everyone in the car automatically looked out the window at the Don Valley, as if even the few minutes we'd spent in the tunnels had starved our eyes for greenery.

I hadn't moved far enough. The woman's knee kept bump, bump, bumping against mine as the car swayed along the track, slowing as it entered Castlefrank Station. I shifted again, and focused my eyes on the headline I could see across the aisle. I could have sworn it said "High Park Vampires Claim More Victims," but that couldn't be right. The *National Post* wouldn't print something like that. Besides, there aren't any vampires. Other things, maybe, but not vampires.

Not even that distraction was doing much good. With direct contact any distance I had was gone and, white noise or no white noise, I learned more about the woman than I wanted to—and about her boyfriend too, since *they* were touching. Really strong emotion blanks out what I read, but the woman had been living with her worry long enough to get some distance on it, so I was getting good clear images, continuously, almost like watching a movie. She believed her boyfriend was having an affair, and she was honestly grieving. That's rare. Most people would have been angry, and trying to figure out how they could turn their belief to their best advantage. You know. Revenge. Payback. A new living room suite.

I could set their minds at rest, I thought, and the idea made me smile. I glanced at the subway map over the nearby set of doors. *I probably shouldn't.* Oh, but I wanted to. Indecision made me grit my teeth. Sherbourne, and then the big station at Yonge and Bloor where the east/west line connected with the original north/south one. I was going past it, to the junction at St. George, to go south on the University line. The announcement came, that neutral female voice: "Arriving at Sherbourne. Sherbourne Station." I stood up and took a good grip on the nearby pole.

"He's not cheating on you," I said. I hitched the strap of my bag more firmly onto my shoulder as I stepped away. "He's lost the money for your engagement ring and he's working a part-time job to save it up." I turned to the guy, as open-mouthed as the girl. "The money's in the—" [running shoes?] I shook my head. "In a box, a blue box. Hall closet."

I moved quickly past the teenagers. I felt the whoosh of the doors as they slid shut behind me, but barely heard the noise of the train as it started moving again. That's how loudly my heart was beating. I could feel my lips stretched out in a grin so big my teeth were drying, and I was closing down my face fast before I remembered that I didn't have to worry about that kind of thing anymore. I didn't have to control the expression on my face if I didn't want to. I was buzzing with adrenaline, exhilarated and guilty at the same time, shifting my feet in what were almost dance steps. I'd done it. No one was going to be mad at me, and no one was going to punish me for reading someone I wasn't asked to read.

Hey, maybe I should have told the tall kid his father wasn't ever going to be a problem for him again.

I took a few steps farther away from the edge of the platform, but though I turned to face the train, my couple was already out of view. We'd been sitting in the front car, and the last car was just passing me as I turned. A man was standing at the door at the end of the car, a dark silhouette against the lights behind him. Suddenly all my half-guilty giggles were quenched and I was left shivering, icy cold. I caught a whiff of rotten meat, far stronger than the usual garbage bin smell you sometimes got from a subway tunnel. The man was leaning forward, pressing his face against the glass so hard his features distorted into a twisted rubber mask. He was still standing like that when the train disappeared into the tunnel.

Suddenly my fear melted away as a rush of hot anger swept through me. I was *done* being frightened—been there, and not going back. Not for some squirrely guy on the subway, not for anybody. I actually took a step forward, my hands forming fists, even though the train was gone.

He'd been trying to catch my scent. As stupid as that sounds, that's exactly what he was doing. I realized that no one else around me had felt the cold, smelled the old meat. I squared my shoulders, but decided not to wait for the next train after all. I headed for the stairs, and the sunlight and taxis I would find on the street. Always have cab fare; that was something Alejandro had taught me in Madrid.

As soon as I was up out of the tunnels I pulled my mobile from the outer pocket on my shoulder bag and hit the speed dial. "*Soy yo,*" I said when Alejandro answered, as if he wouldn't know. "I just saw something odd on the subway." I described the man I'd seen as well as I could. "He seemed to be trying to pick up my scent." There was silence on the other end of the phone.

"Stay where you are, I will come."

I smiled and rolled my eyes at the same time. He was bored, and I should have known he'd want to come to the rescue—again. Still, I hesitated, looking around me for the taxi rank.

"We talked about this," I reminded him. "I need to start doing stuff on my own. If it's someone who works for the Collector," I said, using my private term for the man who had taken me from my parents, "he might just have been trying to figure out what I am, without knowing it's *me*." I cleared my throat. "I got the feeling he was curious, not that he was tracking me."

"But if he sees *me* with you, and he does come from our friend, then he will know for certain who you are." I knew Alejandro would understand. "Still, I do not like it. If he were entirely human, you would not have read so much from him."

"I'm getting into a cab now," I said, as one pulled up in front of me. I tried to sound confident and secure, but maybe there was a little pleading in my voice. I needed to do this job alone, and he knew it.

"Good luck, *querida*," he said. "Call immediately if you should need me."

I used the taxi ride to push the subway man and his strange behavior to the back of my mind. I had to focus on the job I was heading for. By the time I got out in front of the glass-walled Christie Institute on University Avenue, I was calm again. I'd been able to check my hair and makeup in the cab, and changed out of the flats that were sensible subway wear into the Stuart Weitzman pumps that went better with my Nuovi Sarti suit. The flats went into a little felt pouch and joined two impressive looking folders in my shoulder bag.

There was a security desk masquerading as an information kiosk across the spacious terrazzo floor of the lobby. I already had the room number I needed, but the uniformed guard "helped" me find the office by phoning up and making sure I was expected. The place was air-conditioned, but only just. Or maybe it wasn't warm enough outside yet to make you really feel it. I'd been under the impression that this was a medical facility, but I was fast figuring out that it wasn't the kind where patients had appointments.

I was met at the elevator by an older blonde woman in a taupe slacks suit with a matching cami top and red, mid-heel, open-toed shoes, who showed me into an empty office and took my order for a glass of iced water with a slice of lemon.

After waiting twenty minutes past the time of my appointment, an olive-skinned man with a nose almost as big as Alejandro's came in. He stopped short in the doorway, seemed about to frown, and then came forward with his hand outstretched to take mine. His hair was black—real black—and still had some curl even though it was cropped short enough to show off his beautifully shaped head. His shirt looked like silk, and his suit cost at least twice what mine did.

Alejandro had taught me a firm, short, handshake for business purposes, to minimize actual contact, but this time the images I got from the man were more fragmented than usual, and I held on for a second longer, concentrating to get everything I could. [A long life; the suit was made for him; someone named Harry was dying, but not of the disease the Institute researched; he knew about a lot of dying people.] At least here in North America I wasn't expected to kiss people on both cheeks.

"Good morning, Dr. Martin," he said. "I'm Nikos Polihronidis, counsel for the Institute." I'd expected something Mediterranean, but his accent was pure second-generation Greek Canadian. This wasn't the Human Resources person who'd contacted me, and I wondered if I should be worried. He looked at me pretty narrowly, even though his dark eyes now twinkled a bit, as he took the chair behind the desk and glanced at the cleared surface with faint surprise. I wondered if I had better get another work outfit, especially if I had to come back here. This guy would know my suit if he saw it again.

And he *was* worried, now that he was seeing me, about whether I could do the job.

"I was expecting someone older." He leaned back in his chair, right leg crossed over left, elbows propped comfortably on the armrests. "Though, of course, you come with impeccable recommendations."

I should have, considering all Alejandro's work, and all the people he knew in high and useful places. I smiled as though I thought I'd been complimented. Alejandro had made me up to look older, literally painting an older woman's face on top of mine. Even close up, all anyone could really tell was that I was wearing makeup. I lifted my left eyebrow, but kept the rest of my face neutral. "This isn't your office," I said. "You'd never have that print in here if it was. *Your* office is . . . something more traditional, but not conventional, if I had to guess." As if I was guessing. "And I'd put money on a corner office. Your firm acts for the Institute, but you donate your time pro bono."

His smile made the temperature in the room drop; the twinkle completely disappeared from his eyes. I was relieved to find my hands steady, and my heart rate calm. Apparently I didn't find him intimidating. Unlike the last person I worked for, Nikos Polihronidis couldn't starve me, or lock me in a closet. Or take away my teddy bear.

"I suppose that was a demonstration."

I tilted my head to the side. I certainly wasn't going to explain. They'd wanted a psychological profiler, and according to my curriculum vitae, that's exactly what they got.

"Please don't profile me again." He looked at me in silence for several minutes, eyes narrowing once more. I imagined this was how he looked at clients when he was deciding whether to take them on.

"How much were you told about this case?" he asked finally.

"You have a candidate for a senior research position," I said. "He looks very promising on paper, but several of the current employees have gotten a 'bad vibe' from him."

He inclined his head a couple of centimeters and brought it back up.

"Also, the HR person who contacted me has heard some disturbing rumors."

"And were you . . ."

"No. I specifically asked *not* to be told. Psychologists can be just as susceptible to finding what they're looking for as the next person."

Again the shallow nod. It looked as though that was all I was going to get. Finally I asked what stage of the application the candidate had reached.

For a minute I thought I was going to get the freezing smile again.

"All of the senior people have given their opinions, some in writing." He raised his eyebrows at me.

I held up my hand. "No, I didn't read them and, again, I'd prefer not to be told."

Again with the cold smile, as he glanced at his watch. I'm sure Alejandro would have been able to tell exactly what kind of very expensive watch it was.

I stood up when he did, and followed him down the carpeted hall and into a wide conference room with a floor-to-ceiling, wall-to-wall view of downtown Toronto, complete with CN Tower, and the blue expanse of Lake Ontario. Even from here you could tell the water was cold. Even in June.

There were three people standing in the room when Nikos Polihronidis and I came in, helping themselves to coffee and pastries from an elegant wheeled tea table off to one side. It didn't go with the room, and I wondered where it came from, though I wasn't curious enough to touch it. I was introduced as a consultant, and there were handshakes all around.

I sat where the lawyer indicated, diagonally across the table from the applicant, back straight, knees together, ankles crossed, my eyes looking at the notes I was taking with Alejandro's Montblanc fountain pen. The notes were because, as Alejandro put it, "verisimilitude is the watermark of reality." In other words, if I wanted to be mistaken for a psychologist, I should do the things people expected psychologists to do.

Oh, and I should probably avoid real psychologists.

On my left was the CEO, a compact British woman in her midfifties [once an Olympic class swimmer]. Mr. Polihronidis sat a little farther along the same side of the table as the applicant, and made himself as unobtrusive as such a striking-looking person could. Immediately on the CEO's left was the assistant head of the HR department, a young man with an MBA [thought he'd be head of HR, if he told what he knew]. He was the one who'd actually contacted me.

I settled in, listening and taking notes, waiting my turn to speak.

I found it interesting, since I'm not sure I could have told he was lying without my special talent to rely on.

Most people don't realize it, but you have to learn how to lie. And, for most people, this learning process happens when you're a child. You get taught—at first—to keep a certain kind of blunt opinion or observation to yourself, and not to repeat private information even when it's true, and someone has asked you to tell. Eventually you learn not only these lies of omission, but lies of commission as well. You not only *don't* tell your best friend's mum that her mashed potatoes taste like wallpaper paste, you tell her they're the best mashed potatoes you ever had.

Like everyone else, I'd also had to learn how to lie. Unlike everyone else, I didn't pick up these lessons slowly as I grew up—though I do vaguely remember my mother coaching me in keeping things to myself. At least I think I do. The man who took me from my parents had a more forceful method of training me to stay quiet until he told me to speak, whereupon only the precise truth would do. But how to actually lie to people? That's something I've only learned in the last couple of years. Luckily, it hadn't taken Alejandro long to teach me what he called the lie circumstantial, and the lie direct.

About forty-five minutes into the session, after a break to refresh our coffee, it was my turn. I'd known everything I needed to know from the handshake, but again, verisimilitude.

I asked him the questions Alejandro and I had worked out ahead of time, in the measured, calm voice I'd been practicing.

"Dr. Weaver, can you tell me about your team at present? How many people work with you, for example, and what is your team structure?"

"Can you tell me about your process for delegating work?"

"I'm assuming you have ongoing research, what will be done to complete that?"

"It is a little unusual for a person of your seniority to be relocating. Why are you leaving your current position?"

"Dr. Weaver, what will you do if you don't get this position?"

I did my best to act like I was listening to the answers—took notes and everything—but of course I already knew the reason for the "bad vibes" I'd been told about. The only thing I found unexpected was that the images had come to me with an overlay of cold, and a smell of old meat. Something about Dr. Weaver was reminding me of the man on the subway.

Oh. I almost smiled when the images finally fell into place. I was associating the smell with predators. That actually made me feel a bit better, since it was now even less likely that the man on the subway had anything to do with the man who took me.

I really would have preferred not to shake hands again at the end of the interview, but there was no way for me to get out of it without being obvious about it.

I fidgeted, helping myself to another pastry, until the Institute people came back to the conference room. The CEO resumed her chair, glancing at her legal counsel.

"Well?" Mr. Polihronidis said to me.

I shrugged. "I think you'll find that it's come to light he's had multiple affairs with both his research assistants, and his graduate students." I pretended to check my notes. "It might be interesting if it could be determined how much of his work is actually his own, and how much he's just taking credit for." The looks on their faces when I said this was a revelation. "In any case, the questionable sexual behavior will be the real reason he's looking for a new position."

"His present employers have given him excellent references, both written and verbal." There was no hint of protest in the CEO's voice; she was merely stating a fact. "They're a bit cool, perhaps, but then, he's always been known as an arrogant, unpleasant man."

"Given the current political climate with respect to sexual harassment in the workplace," I said. "I would suggest that there is some sort of agreement in place, that if he takes himself elsewhere they won't prosecute him." Nikos Polihronidis' eyes hardened.

"And they obviously can't stand in the way of his taking himself elsewhere," the HR guy said. "Hence the good references." He looked toward the CEO. "Do you think there was any threat of legal action?"

I didn't really listen to the answer. I found myself thinking about the kinds of things Alejandro had had to do over the years to keep his own secrets. The relocations, the disguises, the false papers, and now, the whole network of fake Internet information. Suddenly, I realized they were talking to me again.

"You *are* certain, aren't you?" the CEO was saying. Not like she doubted me, but as though she was summing it up in her head.

I nodded. "I'll put my detailed reasons into the report: body language, micro-expressions, and so on. Right now I can tell you that the changes in his demeanor when he spoke about his subordinates were very significant. If he were an employee, you couldn't fire him on the basis of my findings, but you could certainly use them to investigate further." I stood up. I wondered how far I could go. My talent had given me more details than I could have reasonably received from the answers to my questions—no matter how well trained I was pretending to be. "You might think about interviewing current and past clerical staff as well. Often, no one pays them much mind and, like servants in a big house, they see more than their employers are aware of, and keep silent because they have more to lose by speaking up."

"You mean he's been boffing the secretaries as well?" The HR guy really needed to toughen up. This was nothing compared to some of the stuff I'd seen.

"I don't think so," I said. [No.] "But they'll likely be able to name names. I wouldn't ask his own assistant directly, but the administrative assistant likely works for the university, not for him. She'll be less loyal, and just as likely to know something."

It wasn't quite as simple as that, of course, but as Nikos Polihronidis himself escorted me to the elevators, I knew that they were going to do exactly as I'd suggested, and that things would turn out exactly as I'd predicted. And that there would be referrals in my future.

We reached the elevators, but my escort didn't push the button right away. He was looking at me in that narrow-eyed evaluating way he'd used earlier, but now the twinkle was back.

"I have to say, I was skeptical about hiring you," he said. "All you did was ask him the questions any HR suit would have asked, but you saw something in his answers none of us had seen."

"You'd seen them," I assured him, making a mental note to come up with cleverer questions the next time. "That's why you called me in the first place, right? 'Bad vibes?' And it wasn't just *what* he answered; it was also *how* he answered. You're a lawyer. You know better than most that people will always give themselves away if you give them an opportunity to talk, and if you've been trained in what to watch for." I shrugged, hoping he wouldn't question me too closely about what I'd just said. "You still have to check that my interpretation is valid."

"I think we both know it will be. Please send your report directly to me, by the way." He handed me a business card, pushed the elevator button, and shook my hand again. This time he was the one who held it a little longer than necessary. [More fragments, like a jigsaw puzzle pieced together; the signet ring was his father's. The father had been murdered by a neighbor when Nikos was thirteen. Everyone—including Nikos himself—thought it had been an accident.]

Just as the elevator doors were closing, he said, "Your eyes are the color of caramel."

I went down in the elevator thinking of dark curly hair, warm hands, and sandalwood aftershave.

I'd planned to have the security guard in the lobby call me a cab, but now that it was over, I felt high as a kite, like I could float all the way home. Or at least to the nearest subway stop. I was so buzzed I didn't even think about phoning Alejandro—I wanted to see his face when I told him. The strange guy on the subway wasn't even a blip on my radar.

I'd done it. The first time I'd ever done a reading for money, the first time by myself anyway. All the rehearsing, the small practice jobs I'd done with Alejandro in the last few months, had paid off. I could do this. I could make a living—for myself, not just for others. Part of me *had* wanted him to come with me today, but all along I knew it wasn't a good idea. We wouldn't have looked like two colleagues; we'd have looked like a performer and her handler.

I didn't want the kind of clients who were looking for a psychic. All my papers, my degrees, my letterhead, my Web site—all said "psychologist," and that's how I needed people to see me. That other label was just too risky—as I'd already learned the hard way.

The irony is, I really am psychic. It's the papers and the degrees that are fake. Mind you, I'm not a telepath. I don't read minds, though I realize it might look that way. What I do is read truths about people, sometimes truths they don't know, or aren't consciously aware of themselves, usually about whatever it is that's on their minds right now. Like I said, strong emotion can distort what I read, that's why objects are easier (people's rings and watches are a godsend) or relatively calm people like the couple on the subway. Worried, but not hysterical. When the read's good, I see whole pictures right away.

Otherwise, what I get is fragments, images, sights, smells, sounds. Usually, experience fills them in for me, gives me a coherent picture. But sometimes, without a context, there's no telling what I'm reading. When I was with the Collector, I was always given the context for the people he loaned me out to—usually businessmen, occasionally politicians, once a Cardinal of the Church. With the couple on the subway, the context was the fact they *were* a couple. Given that much, everything else fell into place.

This talent didn't give me as much trouble when I was a child as you might think. Somehow, my parents weren't freaked out when they noticed that some of the things I talked about I couldn't possibly have known. They didn't shush me and pretend that there wasn't anything weird about me. I realized later, when I was more grown up, that they must have known what I had. I don't think they were psychics themselves, but maybe they'd had some other gifts.

I remember my mother, before I was taken, teaching me how to hide mine—at least I think I do—as if she knew that what I had could bring the wrong kind of attention. But she never got a chance to finish teaching me.

The Collector took me when I was four, or maybe five. I'd had a real blind spot when it came to him, at least at first—no context, you see? He'd told me he was only looking after me while my parents were gone, that they were coming soon. I don't know, maybe part of me had known all along what was going on, that my parents weren't coming to get me [not dead, though], that this hard, cold man was the only one who was keeping me safe. Like all kids, I fantasized about a rescue, about getting away from him, living my own life, maybe finding my parents, but mostly I knew that if I wanted to go on being safe and looked after, I should meet the people he wanted me to meet and answer the questions I was asked afterward.

I even got to where I was happy to help out. Sort of.

But, of course, I got older and better at what I did, and more knowledgeable and experienced about the world and how things worked. I got good enough, finally, that I could read him as well as I could anyone. His own specific talent couldn't block me out anymore. I thought I had him fooled for a while into thinking I hadn't caught on to him, but then I realized he was going to get rid of me anyway when I reached the right—or the wrong—age, just in case.

And I mean get rid of me, not give me a handshake and a farewell dinner. Considering how much I knew about him and his business, to say nothing of everyone who had ever used me, it kind of made sense.

That's when I really started looking for a way out, and found Alejandro.

These memories took me quite a way down University Avenue, and I was starting to think I should have asked the guard at the Institute about the subway after all. I didn't turn back, though. I was still feeling the heady buzz of success—I found myself smiling more than once—and besides, I'd been kept indoors for almost fifteen years; I had a lot of outside world to catch up on.

I had some things to learn about walking around outside, though, such as there was a reason I had a pair of flat shoes in my shoulder bag. There didn't seem to be any benches I could use to sit and change my shoes, however, and I felt a little shy of just propping myself against a lamppost or something and going ahead. I caught sight of the elevated sign that meant a subway entrance, but debated, as I walked toward it, what I wanted to do. Part of me wanted to get home as quickly as possible and start celebrating with Alejandro. Part of me was reluctant to go back underground, as if the strange [smelling] man [predator] might be down there waiting for me. I managed to convince myself that it was a nice sunny June day, not too warm for my suit, and I was enjoying feeling like a regular person, and maybe even catching a few admiring glances from my fellow pedestrians.

But to go on walking, I'd have to change my shoes. Luckily, my problem was solved by the appearance on my left of a wrought iron fence. The palings were well over eight feet high, with a design detail that gave every seventh upright a wider, leaf-shaped base just large enough for me to sit down on.

I was maneuvering my shoes back into my shoulder bag—the space they'd formerly occupied having somehow vanished—when a dog's head suddenly appeared, thrust through the foliage that grew along the inside of the railings. My life hasn't exposed me to many household pets, but I knew what I thought I should do, and I was already extending my hand, palm out, when I caught a whiff of old meat, and felt that now familiar chill.

The world seemed to slow down. A disembodied voice yelled, "Don't!" and my brain sent the signal "pull back," but it was a long time getting to my hand. The dog's head, with its liver-colored markings [what big teeth, what big eyes] stretched out as if it knew I was going to back away, and its teeth seemed to grow larger as they reached for me. A hand came out of nowhere, clamped down on my still outstretched arm, yanked me to my feet, and then we were running down the sidewalk.

The images I got from him made me run even faster. I didn't look behind us to see if the dog was still a dog. I just ran.

I knew who my rescuer was long before he had us sitting in one of the booths of the Second Cup at York and Front Streets—I'd known the minute he'd touched me. What I still couldn't be sure of [strong emotion combined with that odd fragmentation I'd picked up earlier] was how Nikos Polihronidis had managed to be where he was, when he was.

Other than by following me.

I'd managed to get a couple of other things from him along the way [*much* older than he looked; bitten/touched by a Hound once] but what had made me run as fast as I could was the image of bottomless, ravenous hunger in his psyche, and the echoing emptiness that hunger left behind.

And I knew what that hunger was, though I'd never encountered it myself. *The Hunt.*

"You were being followed," he said now. He wanted something from me, and that's why he'd been on the spot to save me. The calm exterior hid hard images of anger, fear.

"By something besides you, Mr. Polihronidis?" I thought that would provoke him, and I was right.

His face tightened even as he waved his hand in a pretty good imitation of a casual gesture. "Better make it Nik." He picked up his espresso and put it down again. "You could have knocked me over when I saw you come into the office," he said. "You're the girl with the Rider, aren't you?"

I blinked. I hadn't seen *that* when he was touching me.

"We've seen you together." He jerked his head toward the bulk of Union Station, just visible at the end of the street. Where the crossroads was. And the Portal. "I can see his *dra'aj*, and yours for that matter, so don't try to say you don't know what I'm talking about."

I straightened up so fast my spine cracked. Reading people's *dra'aj*, seeing what their talents were, that's how the Collector found people like me. But I wasn't in any danger from Nik. "Wouldn't dream of it," I said.

"That was a Hound following you," he said, clearly expecting me to know what he meant. I nodded. Once.

That was why we'd run several blocks down University, past a fire truck which was trying to close a hydrant that people Nik knew had managed to open. Moving water, apparently, would throw the Hound off the scent. My scent. I'd picked up that much in jolts and fits and starts, as we were running.

Just the idea of the Hunt was enough to set anybody running, but something was making no sense.

"What's the big deal?" I asked. "The Hunt doesn't prey on humans." Okay, so he'd been bitten, but he was still alive.

His smile gave me a hitch in the back of my throat, as if I was about to cry. "Maybe they didn't, maybe that's the way it was, once. But *doesn't*, isn't, *can't*, and *once* isn't *now*." He reached across the table, but I moved my hands to my lap before he could touch me. He'd read so oddly that I wasn't sure I wanted to read any more. I was still seeing jigsaw puzzles and rag rugs—as though the fragmentation wasn't in my images, but in him.

"They can prey on humans, all right," he said, drawing his hand back. "They're doing it all the time now." He licked his lips. "More every day."

"They're killing people?" Why hadn't I heard something about this? Had it been on the news?

Nik shook his head, but he wasn't saying no. "It's not that simple. People *are* dying, yes, but—if it was only a few . . ." He shook his head again. "We need to talk to a Rider, about the Hounds. Can you set that up for us?"

"Why?"

A flicker of anger hardened his face. "Because you're human, like us."

"No, I meant, why do you want to talk to a Rider?"

"Because they did this. They brought the Hunt here. It's their responsibility. We can't," he swallowed. "We can't fight them off ourselves." His voice shook a little, the assured lawyer of the Christie Institute almost gone.

"If people aren't actually *dying* . . ." My voice dried up, and Nik squeezed his eyes shut.

"The Hunt takes our *dra'aj*," he said. "It's worse than dying. It makes us empty. We don't live, we can't even want to die."

I got it then. I got what it meant. Nik had been bitten. That's why he felt all fragmented.

"But you're okay," I said.

He shook his head, impatience getting in the way of what he was trying to tell me. "There's a fix, but it has to be renewed, and now, with so many new ones, we can't keep up with the demand."

New ones? "Those people in High Park," I said. "Wandering around without a clue why they were there? Half starved?"

He nodded.

"Not vampires." *I knew it.* "Not some kind of flu. The Hunt."

He winced, looked as though he was going to say something, and then shrugged before nodding again.

Part of me wanted to take him home right then and there, even though I wasn't sure what Alejandro could do to help him.

But another part of me wasn't thrilled by the idea that here was yet another person thinking of me as someone he could make use of. Even his saving me had more to do with getting me to help him than it had with me personally—or impersonally, for that matter.

And speaking of personal, I admit I was disappointed that all that stuff about my caramel eyes hadn't meant anything after all.

Most of my life I hadn't been allowed to make my own decisions. Since my rescue, I'd been learning how—but this wasn't about me. It was about Alejandro. I couldn't make decisions for him.

I stood up. "Okay, I'll ask my friend, but I can't promise anything. I've got your card."

"I'll go with you—at least let me walk you to the subway," he added when I shook my head. Before I could say no again, his mobile rang. I paused when he answered it, holding up one finger. Somehow I couldn't just walk away.

I watched the color drain out of his face. "It has to be me," he said.

"I'll have to take her." He glanced up at me. "Wait until I get there." He snapped the mobile shut and stuck it back in the breast pocket of his jacket.

"Would you come with me?" he said. His voice trembled, as if he was keeping a tight rein on himself. "You need to—" he broke off and took a deep breath. "I need you to show you someone, for a profile. Please?"

"What, now?"

It was fear I was reading from him. Fear and anger and grief. "Please."

I think it was the please that did it. Not very many people had ever bothered to say "please" to me.

Next thing I knew we were in a cab, and heading to an address on Spadina north of Bloor. Nik spent the ride on the phone, but traffic was with us, and in practically no time we were running up the steps of an old, double-fronted Victorian house, and in through the heavy glass-inlaid doors, past ground-floor offices, all the way up to the second floor. Two women were waiting at the spacious landing at the top of the stairs. One was wearing slacks and a short, military style jacket; the other had a flowery print dress. Both were clearly secretaries.

"Is she in her office?" Nik asked the one in slacks. "How long since you first noticed it?"

"She seemed a bit odd yesterday morning—"

"And you waited until now to call me?" As if he realized that losing his temper wasn't going to get him anywhere, Nik took a deep breath and let it out slowly. "Sorry," he said. "Just tell me what happened."

"She kept saying she was okay," Print Dress said. "Maybe just a bit run-down. But then yesterday she had no dictation, and today she canceled all her appointments."

"You have to speak to her a couple of times to get her to respond," Slacks added. "Then, instead of jumping as though she was startled, she just turns and looks at you, as if she knew all along you were there, but just didn't care. We thought—" she broke off and looked at the other woman, who nodded at her. "We thought it sounded like the High Park flu."

"You know," Print Dress chimed in. "What the people caught

down in High Park. Those people the police found there after dark. And when you didn't call in after your meeting at the Christie—"

Because he'd been following me. I began to feel a little sick. Not vampires in the park, no. But maybe the Hunt.

By this point both of the ladies were staring at me a little wildly, and only relaxed when Nik finally said, "This is Dr. Martin." Neither of them raised an eyebrow when I followed Nik into another office.

"Elaine?" I hadn't known his voice could get so soft.

The woman was smiling, but it was just lip movement.

"Hey, where'd you get this bruise?" There was a purple-blue mark like a stain on her lower arm.

She pulled her hand away, but you could see it was just a reflex. "I don't know. On the weekend, maybe. I went out with Sue and Vicki."

That would fit the coloring, I thought. The bruise had only just begun to fade. Nik turned and looked at me, and I found myself stepping closer.

"Dr. Martin, this is my friend and law partner, Elaine Serber."

Elaine was doing an excellent job of pretending to be well. But there were signs that would have told any good observer that there was something wrong. The left sleeve of her blouse wasn't ironed; her face had been completely made up except for blush and mascara; her hair was not artfully tousled, it actually had not been brushed that morning.

She stood up and put out her hand to shake mine, but she was just going through the motions. It was like shaking an empty glove. [Tables with glasses; beer; a dark-haired man with long, pointed nose and sharp teeth (?); jigsaw, the pieces loose, shifting and shuffling like cards; there were pieces missing, important pieces; she was related to Nik, very distantly.]

Oh. The images suddenly clarified. Elaine was like Nik, fragmented, but also *not* like him. Where Nik was a puzzle in a frame, glued together and whole, Elaine was like a puzzle that had been poured out of the box onto the floor, pieces flung and tossed everywhere, some facedown, others piled two or three deep, and—like I said—some pieces missing entirely.

And I knew how it had happened. I saw her with her girlfriends in the bar, the look of the man who had taken her by the forearm as she'd passed him on the way to the bathroom. And I knew that he wasn't a man, but a Hound.

"What do you see?"

For a second I was so startled by Nik's voice that I almost thought he knew that I was reading Elaine. Then I realized that he just meant could I, the psychological profiler, see what the problem was.

"She's almost completely affectless," I said, dredging up what jargon I could remember. "There are no micro-expressions in her face. None at all. As though she's been wiped clean. You sometimes see this in the severely depressed. Sometimes rape victims. Look." I nodded toward her. "She's not even reacting to what I'm saying."

"That's what the Hunt does to us. This is what they're calling the High Park flu."

"You said you could help her?" I still had her by the hand. I was afraid that if I let go, she might fade away completely. [Pieces; rage; cold; static; a couple of hitches like catching breath, a refocusing of attention; Nik would help her.] I didn't know whose hand was trembling, hers or mine. "I think you'd better hurry."

He squeezed his eyes shut, his upper lip in his teeth. I couldn't think what the holdup was. Finally, he nodded. "Come on, I asked the taxi to wait."

It was easy to get Elaine downstairs and into the taxi, she held my hand and didn't resist or protest in any way. Nik gave the driver another address, and I was a little surprised when we pulled up in front of what was obviously a hospital. We took a side entrance, an elevator up two floors, and exited into a sunny lounge. There were three people sitting in comfortable padded arm chairs. A man holding the hand of a woman who had fallen asleep nodded at us as we passed, and smiled. Another man, still wearing a straw fedora, was sitting forward in his chair, staring at his clasped hands.

The nurses' station turned out to be a young woman in paisley scrubs with a laptop on the low table in front of her.

"Eva," Nik called softly as they approached her.

"Hey, Nikki, whatcha got?"

"Couple of visitors for Harry."

"Oh, that's great." A frown ghosted over her face. "They do realize . . . ?"

"Oh, yeah, they're not family, legal stuff."

“Okay.” She went back to her computer.

Nik led us down the hall into a double room, where only one bed was occupied by what I greatly feared was a corpse.

“Harry?”

My breath caught in my throat as the man’s eyes opened. They were the only thing about him that showed any life at all—more life, I realized with a jolt, than Elaine’s did. Harry’s lips moved and, concentrating, I could just make out what he was saying, more by reading his lips than because there was any real sound.

Is it time? was what he’d said.

“Only if you’re ready,” Nik said. “If you’re sure. Here she is.” He moved Elaine closer to the bed. “Her name’s Elaine.”

Not you? And the lips moved as if they would smile, but the muscles had forgotten how. *Prettier.*

“She sure is.”

Ready.

“Two blinks if you’re sure.” The papery eyelids fell, and rose, fell and rose again. “Elaine, take Harry’s hand. Go on. Hold Harry’s hand.” Nik put his own left hand on the old man’s shoulder.

“Hold on,” Elaine said. Her voice was the thinnest thread.

“That’s right, babe, hold on.”

Thank you.

Still holding Nik’s forearm, Elaine took hold of the old man’s hand with her free hand. At first, I thought nothing was happening. The papery eyelids had fallen shut, and the man’s shallow breathing slowed and slowed until finally the chest fell and did not rise again.

“Oh.” The sob was so alive, so vibrant, that I didn’t realize it had come from Elaine’s mouth until she fell to her knees. She rested her cheek on the old man’s hand, and looked up with eyes that focused.

“Oh, Nikki,” she said. “Oh, my god, Nikki.” And she burst into tears. Nik lifted her into the bedside chair, and handed her the box of tissues on the bed stand before joining me where I stood at the foot of the bed.

“I know Elaine, I can help *her*,” he said. “But what about everyone else?” His abrupt gesture took in the whole of the city outside the windows. “There are too many out there that I—that *we* can’t help.

We need the Riders. They've got to help us. They've *got* to. It's not going to stop here."

I didn't say anything. I just nodded.

Later, Nik Polihronidis eased Elaine's bedroom door shut. She needed sleep right now, and he needed to let the rage he'd held off all day surface; if he didn't let go of it, it would suffocate him. In a bar on the Danforth, for god's sake. No one was safe. He stopped himself just in time from pounding on the wall. *That* wouldn't help anyone. He knew it wasn't his fault. Just because he'd been away for a few days; just because he'd gone to his meeting without checking in at the office first. It wasn't his fault.

But he'd promised his sister to keep her children safe. And Elaine was the last, the very last of her descendants. He squeezed his eyes tight. And now there wouldn't be any more.

Nik took a deep breath and went over to where Elaine's iPad sat on a small table next to the couch. He'd have to find her another infusion of *dra'aj* soon, within a week or so—newbies had so little control, it could dribble away pretty fast. It would take some juggling, but he could manage it.

So long as they could count on some help against the Hunt.

He pushed his hands through his hair, forgetting that it was cropped short. That was another thing. He'd almost blown it today. He'd almost scared off Valory Martin. He glanced at Elaine's bedroom door. More than anything else, more than anything *he'd* told her, it was what happened to Elaine that had convinced Valory. Nik's hands formed into fists and he forced them open. If Valory managed to persuade her Rider friend, what had happened to Elaine might be the saving of all of them.

That didn't make him feel any better.

Chapter Two

"BUENO, AQUÍ ESTAMOS, SEÑOR. *Señor, hemos llegado.*"

It was a moment before Stormwolf realized the driver was speaking to him. The language was no difficulty. He had only to listen carefully, and he could recognize the true tongue that underlay any of the human languages. It wasn't the Spanish, but the taxi ride itself that distracted him. The speed of it, the apparent recklessness of his own and the other drivers. The moving landscape outside the windows, and his own internal awareness that though they were moving, they had not Moved. He was not sure he liked traveling in cars.

Among the lessons and instructions the High Prince had given him was one about taxis and fares. Wolf extracted the correct bill from his wallet, returned a reasonable tip from the change he was given, and stepped out of the vehicle. With an abrupt wave of his hand, the driver indicated the lane before which he'd stopped, and then inserted his taxi back into the stream of traffic with a screech of tires and a blast of horns.

The lane was wide enough for automobiles, but it was also steep enough to require shallow risers in the cobblestones as it angled away from the larger street. Smooth plastered walls three and four stories tall rose to either side, with individual houses indicated by the scattered doorways and ornately grilled windows. Two six-sided glass lamps hung from wrought iron stanchions at strategic spots along the wall. Stormwolf had no trouble visualizing people on horseback passing through the place.

His destination was in the angle where the lane veered to the right, a wide double entrance, with thick wooden doors showing signs of weathering. A large ceramic tile with the number "15" in blue on a white background was inset into the stone to the right of the door. Even if he had not been given the address, however, Stormwolf would have known he was in the right place. Even here in the street the house smelled of Rider, though faintly enough to tell him that his prey was not at home.

Wolf drew in a sharp breath. He must stop thinking that way. The Rider Nighthawk had once been Warden to the Prince in Exile. But he was not prey. He was merely the first person the High Prince had told Wolf to find.

Nighthawk's trail was clear. Wolf followed the scent along a twisted path of lanes and alleys, some of which were narrow enough that the stones under his feet were chilled, the sun never having found its way down to them. Finally, the trail led into a larger road, with cars parked on one side, along to a square where mature trees thrust themselves up through the cobbles to give shade, and then into a bar on the opposite corner.

But there was no Sunward Rider in "El Caracol." Crowded as it was, Wolf could not be mistaken. Instead, the spoor led down the short hallway to the privies, and out a back door next to the grills in the kitchen. He was not surprised when he found himself headed back toward the house, although through different laneways. As he crossed through another square, this one open on one side where the land fell away, he paused, glancing over the parapet at the view of a large palace brightly illuminated across the valley.

The Rider's trail was still clear, but others crossed it here. A smell/not smell. And there was something familiar about another, something Wolf felt he should be able to place.

He looked around the square. A few people were admiring the

view of the palace, two held small boxes to their faces. One man stood apart, looking at his hands with a faint air of puzzlement. The smell/not smell seemed to emanate from him. Wolfe shook himself. He was on scent, and had a trail to follow. He could not indulge his own curiosity. He glanced once more at the palace, then followed Nighthawk's spoor into another alley, this one so narrow he had almost to turn sideways to fit himself into the space. Just as the alley was widening, a noise gave him enough warning to freeze where he stood. He eyed the long blade that glittered in the darkness. A *gra'if* blade, forged by neither human nor Rider.

"Well, now. You are not what I expected, Moonward one," came a voice out of the darkness at the end of the blade. "Tell me why I should not cut your throat."

"I am—"

A skittering sound from above them, a moving shadow, and the sword left Wolf's face as a Sunward Rider who could only be Nighthawk leaped away from him into the next patch of light, allowing a winged lizard with the head of a dog to land heavily between them. Wolf's belly clenched in recognition, icy cold, as he saw the dog's wings wither and shrink, its legs lengthen and grow talons even while its tail sprouted barbs.

"Stump!" he called, but the Hound did not acknowledge him. Was this the explanation of the elusive smells? The tail swung toward him and without further thought the umbrella in Wolf's hand became a *gra'if* sword, and he pulled his *gra'if* dagger from the scabbard under his left sleeve. Like it or not, with the other Rider here, he would have to kill it. "Do not look it in the eyes," he called out as he shifted to avoid the swinging tail.

Nighthawk grinned at Wolf's advice and, ducking under the monster's reaching talons, thrust at its breast with his own sword. It reared backward, giving Wolf a chance to slice its left hamstring with his dagger as he cut its flank with the sword. Nothing to do now but kill it. The beast hissed at the pain, and morphed into a leathery wyvern with two clawed feet and wings covered with patches of leather, fur, and feathers. It staggered. The cut hamstring had morphed along with it.

The alley was not wide enough to allow the beast to turn easily—or so Wolf thought until he saw that Nighthawk had been knocked to the ground. Wolf sheathed his dagger and leaped forward, grasping the thing's tail above the barbs, and with his sword hacked repeatedly at the base of the monster's spine. The skin under his hand became scaled, the beast flickered into a monstrous snake, turning its horselike head toward him and wrapping its tail around one of Wolf's legs. The slit-pupiled eyes narrowed, seeming to search his features.

Wolf tightened his grip on the sword and shifted to keep his other leg free. If only he could keep it from biting him, he might yet be able to damage it enough that it would at least release him, and perhaps take another form. The head moved closer, and Wolf gritted his teeth against the sudden pain in his leg as the thing constricted. The creature moved in two impossible directions at once, falling to the ground in pieces. Wolf staggered back, sword still poised. Beyond the two writhing halves of the snake he saw Nighthawk, blood dripping from his blade, scrambling out of the way of the beast's death throes.

The snake sprouted sudden wings, became wyvern, flickered into leathery griffin, flickered again into the claw-footed dog. Wolf, leaning against the wall, his chest heaving and the sweat dripping into his eyes, turned his head away before he saw the final change. When the noises had stopped, he looked again, and found the cobblestones bare. He shivered.

"What was it you said?"

Wolf shook his head at Nighthawk. He couldn't tell whether he felt triumph or horror. *I had no choice. It would have killed him.*

"When it attacked," Nighthawk coughed. "I thought . . . you called out something."

Wolf took a deep breath, trying to slow the pounding of his heart. What had he said? "Jump," he said finally. "I told you to jump."

"You are not . . . a creature of the Basilisk Prince . . . I take it." Nighthawk's breathing was only now slowing. "Else you would not have aided me against that." He gestured at the empty space between them. "I knew I was being followed . . . I thought you were with the Hound." He looked down at the blood evaporating off his sword and frowned. "Don't look so gobsmacked, boy. It's dead and we're not, and that's as it should be." Another deep breath. "Who *are* you, then?"

Wolf's heart had stopped racing, and his own breath was steady enough for him to speak. "I am Stormwolf. My mother was Rain at Sunset. The Chimera guides me. I am the . . . the emissary of the Dragonborn Prince." Wolf stumbled over the words. It was the first time he'd said them.

"The *Dragon*born Prince, you say?" The other Rider took a step closer, his brow furrowed. "And who might the Dragonborn Prince be?"

"You *are* Nighthawk? Once Warden of the Exile?" Though by now Wolf knew perfectly well who the other Rider was. "Known here in the Shadowlands as Diego Rascón?"

"I am. My mother was Flies by Moonlight, and the Dragon guides me."

Wolf drew himself to formal attention, saw the other Rider's eyes narrow, the tip of his sword lifting. "Then my mission is to you. You have mentioned the Basilisk Prince. The Rider who gave himself that title is Faded, and his *dra'aj* returned to the Lands. The Exile, known here in the Shadowlands as Max Ravenhill, has resumed his rightful place as Guardian of the Talismans. Those Talismans have spoken, and a High Prince has been named."

"Evidently someone who is Guided by a Dragon." The tone was dry enough that Wolf compressed his lips before speaking.

"She is the one named Truthsheart, once your fellow Warden. Here she was called Cassandra Kennaby."

For a moment there was total silence. Nighthawk's *gra'if* blade lowered. "And you have some proof of these assertions?"

In answer, Wolf undid the collar and top three buttons of his shirt, pulling the garment open. There, in the center of his chest, just below the hollow of his throat, was a black-and-silver-and-dark-red dragon, the Seal of the High Prince.

Nighthawk stepped closer, his *gra'if* blade now hanging loosely at his side as he reached out with his free hand. Wolf gritted his teeth as the Sunward Rider placed cold fingertips on his skin. Hawk blinked and took an abrupt step away, though his smile was wide. Wolf rebuttoned his shirt, wondering what the other had seen.

"It is hers," Hawk said. "And she sent you here? To tell me this news?" The Rider's smile was dancing in his eyes.

"To tell you *first*. After you, I am to go to the one called Graycloud at Moonrise, who may point me to others of the People."

Suddenly Nighthawk was in front of him, clasping his shoulders and kissing him on both cheeks. Wolf stiffened, but managed not to pull away. "Well, now, this calls for a drink."

But Wolf looked carefully around him as he followed Nighthawk back to his home. Where there had been one Hound, there were usually more.

Perhaps even the one he was looking for.

Alejandro was in the back garden when I got home, his head tilted to one side, apparently staring intently at a honeybee crawling into a deep pink flower. He stood with his hands open, his arms lifted slightly from his arched torso. You could almost feel the sunshine of the bullring. I was suddenly reminded of the first time I'd seen him.

The man standing in the salon of the Collector's apartment in Prague didn't look like a retired matador in his mid-eighties. He was way too young, with a ruddy complexion, and strawberry-blond hair just showing some gray. But the way he stood looking out the window, head on an angle, fist on one hip, sure, you could see him in a *corrida*.

"Mr. Martin?" I said.

"Mar*teen*," he corrected, putting the emphasis on the second syllable. Then he turned and smiled at me. "I know, you expected someone older. I'm sure your . . .?" He raised his brows and looked expectant.

"Uncle," I supplied. That's what I called him, the man who'd taken me from my parents.

"Of course. Your uncle can explain my transformation should he find it necessary."

"Of course," I agreed. "Pleased to meet you." Even though I'd been told not to—it wasn't him I was supposed to read, but something he brought with him—there was something so intriguing about this younger-than-expected man that I went right up to him with my hand out. His was warm, and smooth, and strong and suddenly I was overwhelmed with images, with colors and sounds and faces and places, the sound of trickling water and the smell of green leaves and sunsets and underneath it all the way his mind—more his *being*, really—was feeling out the space around him, locating himself in relation to the salon, to the building, the street, the rest of the city, the Vitava River—the planet for all I could tell, shouting I AM *HERE*, in a way that just wasn't human at all.

The next thing I knew, I was on my knees. Then he was helping me to my feet, and I could still feel the buzz of his psyche and I knew what he could do, what made him the thing he called a Rider. I knew how much he'd loved his human wife, and his human children, and how he'd stopped being a soldier when all the honor had left the profession, and finally, finally, here was someone who could help me, someone who could get me away before my "uncle" killed me for knowing too much about him. If only he would—

"Will you get me out of here?" I said. "He's going to kill me—not this minute, but soon. Can you—will you, with that thing you do?"

"That thing I do?" He might have been asking me if I took sugar.

"You know, 'move' me, relocate me. Please."

He searched my face with his brown eyes. "I must find a missing child; he was to help me."

Now I knew why I was in the room. "You have something of hers? Can I touch it?" I put out my hands.

His eyes widened as he, too, began to understand why I was in the room. He pulled a ring off his pinkie finger and laid it into my palm.

"Her mother's stepbrother has her. A farm in the Extramadura," I said. "Just outside of Campanario. Old, no one uses it anymore, but the name's Hellín." I opened my eyes. "He thought he didn't get enough in the will."

"She lives?"

I nodded. He took me by the shoulders, and there was a rush of air, and my ears POPPED! and the light was coming in a totally different window from a totally different angle.

And I was free.

I could feel his hands on my shoulders again. "*Querida*, what is it? What has happened?"

Maybe it was because of what I'd seen in Elaine, maybe it was because my triumph of the morning now seemed so distant and so unimportant, maybe it was the memory of the day my life changed, but suddenly I started to cry.

There was a light SNAP! of displaced air as Alejandro Moved us from the patio right into the living room. He sat me down, and had an afghan around my shoulders and a hot mug of green tea in my hands while the tears were still drying on my face. I could hear him moving around the kitchen with that peculiar inhuman speed and grace that he showed only when we were alone.

Alejandro is a Rider, one of what we humans call "Faerie." Specifically, he's what we'd call Trouping Faerie, the kind that, according to legends, dash around in groups riding beautiful horses, wearing bright armor, and making humans fall in love with them. It didn't work out that way for Alejandro, though. Long ago he fell in love with a human woman, and stayed here in what they call the Shadowlands for her sake, and the sake of the children they had together. He's never gone back. I don't know how long ago it really was, but parts of his story sound an awful lot like some of the fairy tales and ballads I've read about demon lovers.

He says he can't go back now. There's been some sort of civil war in the place he calls the Lands, and the Portals between our two worlds have been shut ever since. The Prince who lost the war got banished to this world, which I guess is why the Portals had to be closed, so he couldn't just go home.

According to Alejandro, there are other Riders hiding here, along with Solitaries like Trolls and Ogres, and Naturals like Water and Tree Sprites. All of which make up what he calls the "People." Some had reasons like Alejandro's not to go home, some just didn't like the idea of living under the rule of the Prince who won the war. Most keep a low profile here, as human technology catches up with magical abilities, but I've met the Water Sprite named Shower of Stars, who lives in the fountain of Cibeles in Madrid. One night, when it was pouring rain, she came out on a bar crawl with us. She liked the *mejillones a la vinagreta* the best.

Then there are the people like me, humans touched with the blood of the People, who have inhuman, or supernatural skills. All the most famous mages in history—Merlin, Cagliostro, Rasputin, David Blaine—have some Rider blood. The greatest of these now living is the man I call the Collector.

"Tell me," Alejandro said now, coming back into the sitting room with a teapot on a tray. "I cannot read your soul as you do mine," he said when I didn't answer right away. "So you must tell me."

I inhaled deeply, taking in the steam from my tea, before looking up at him. "Alejandro, could the man I saw on the subway have been one of the Wild Hunt?"

He straightened abruptly. "Were you bitten?"

"No, I wasn't, but—"

A wave of cold passed through Alejandro where he stood, and tears sprang back into my eyes. He was afraid. He'd never been afraid before. I stood to go to him, the afghan slipping from my shoulders to the floor, but even as I moved I felt warmer, and he shook his head, holding up his hand.

"It is well. Sit."

He seemed sure, so I sat down again. Alejandro's complexion had regained its natural ruddiness. His coloring—a dark strawberry blond—was a little unusual for a Spaniard, but then, he wasn't really a Spaniard, was he? He wrapped his long square fingers around his own large mug of green tea as if he still felt a chill.

"You told me they didn't hunt humans."

Alejandro propped himself on the arm of the couch, eyes narrowed in thought. "The Hunt feeds upon *dra'aj*, and while humans have it, the quantity is so small that I would not have thought it would tempt a Hound."

Okay. I relaxed against the back of the couch. That explained everything. *Dra'aj*, roughly speaking, is the life force, the magical essence that makes the People what they are—Alejandro says that they don't *do* magic, they *are* magic. *Dra'aj* informs everything about them, and the Lands as well. Like he said, humans also have *dra'aj*—some of us enough to give us a talent that certainly looks like magic—but the amount we have is negligible, just a shadow of what the People have.

Oh. Shadowlands. Now I get it. But Alejandro was talking again.

"You have already learned that what humans know of the People is based on scanty information, most of it at best skewed, and at worst plainly wrong. How we see ourselves . . ." Alejandro gestured to himself. "How we are in reality, it is not at all how humans see us."

I nodded. "You said we only know the People through these sporadic visits, before the Exile," I said. "That it was like understanding another culture through tourism. Like not all Spaniards dance flamenco, or not all Japanese know karate." I knew about that kind of thing; I'd been watching television and movies in the last couple of years. "But humans use this kind of shorthand when they think about each other, so they did that with your people as well."

Alejandro took a sip of his tea. "And, of course, human tales are human-centric, are they not? So when your stories tell of the Hunt, they usually describe them as preying on humans whereas, in reality, even when they have been here in the Shadowlands, they were brought to hunt People, Riders in particular."

"I think that's changed." Suddenly a group of images I'd had for a while fell into place. "You met one when you were in Granada last year, didn't you? One of these Hounds." I remembered that weekend clearly. It was the first time I had ever been left alone. No guards, no minders. I'd been so nervous I'd almost begged to go with him, but I thought that if I once started doing that, I would never stop. *Now* I felt I understood something that hadn't been clear at the time. Like I said, I can see the images and not know what they mean, exactly, if I have no context for them.

"No, not a Hound, but one of the followers of the Basilisk Prince." Alejandro studied the surface of his tea, as if there was something else in the cup. "I was passing through the Albaycin."

I knew what Alejandro had really been doing. Walking around, basking in the familiarity of a place that—at four in the morning at least, when there'd be few lights on, and fewer cars—hasn't really changed for hundreds of years. He'd done that more than once since we'd found each other. Now, for the first time, I wondered what he was going to do for ancient walking routes here in the new world, and whether he'd ever been here before.

"I heard the sound of fighting," he was saying. "Not fists, *that* I would have ignored. I heard the sound of blades. When I tracked it to its source, I found two Riders, a Sunward like myself, and a Starward. The Starward still had the smell of the Lands upon him, and so I went to help the Sunward, thinking him a hidden one like myself. Together, we killed the other Rider."

I waved at him to continue, carefully so as not to slosh my tea. "How did you know he wasn't a Hound?"

Alejandro shook his head. "The Hunt are a different kind of being entirely—you must understand that not many meet with a Hound and live to tell of it. They can take the shape of certain animals, but most often they change their form constantly, shifting from one grotesque shape to another, as if shape is no longer in their control. In Granada," his gesture was dismissive, "the Rider we killed threatened us with the Hunt as we confronted him." Alejandro lifted his mug to his lips and took a swallow, his eyes narrowing as he thought. "From this we concluded, Nighthawk and I, that the Basilisk Prince has found a way to make the Hunt obey him, perhaps even the Horn itself. Another reason, if we had none already, to avoid him."

"The guy on the subway wasn't like an animal, and he didn't change his shape," I said, nodding as the pieces fell into place. "He was just a regular-looking guy. Well, except that he had his face squashed up against the glass. But there was a dog later, with the same chill and smell. And the guy who helped me, he called it a Hound."

Alejandro's eyes narrowed still further and this time they were aimed at me. "The first man could have been a Rider, I suppose, leading the Hunt. But your 'helper,' he was human?"

"Sure." I hesitated, and Alejandro waited. He was nothing if not patient. "Well, maybe it's not that simple." I shivered. It was all just too creepy. "His name is Nikos Polihronidis, and he's definitely human, but he *has* been bitten by the Hunt." I didn't want to say the word *eaten*, though that's what stuck in my mind. "They took his *dra'aj* and it fragmented him somehow."

Alejandro lowered himself onto the couch next to me. "It did not kill him?"

"No, but it . . . it emptied him, broke him into pieces like, well, like a jigsaw puzzle."

"And that is what you saw when you touched him?"

"Yes, partly." I screwed up my face, reaching for the words that would explain everything and coming up short. "He has *dra'aj*, he's been put back together, but it's not his own *dra'aj*."

"He has taken it from someone else?" Alejandro's face had gone like stone. "*Vampiros.*"

I waved my hands. "No, no! You've got it wrong. Nik hasn't sucked the life force out of anyone, he's not some human version of the Hunt." I thought about how to explain it. "He—*they*—they get their replacement *dra'aj* from people who are dying anyway." I made a motion with my hands like a flower opening. "They capture it as it's released. Their emptiness draws it in."

Alejandro's face had relaxed, but he really hadn't liked what he'd heard. "I am relieved to learn that it is still only the Hunt who can take *dra'aj* by force."

"Nik says it's been happening to humans for years, but usually in isolated incidents of a few people here and there. Lately it's been happening more and more, and to larger groups. All these news reports about people wandering around, lost and confused? Like the people in High Park? Nik says that's the Hunt."

Alejandro looked off into the distance, his brow furrowed. "Perhaps in the absence of their usual prey, they have had to turn to humans."

Somehow I didn't feel sorry for them. I chewed on my lower lip for a second, but I couldn't see any way other than to just say it. "Nik wants you to help him. He says Riders brought the Hunt here, and you have to do something about it now."

"Offer ourselves to be fed upon, you mean?"

I looked down at my teacup. Alejandro's sarcasm was a little unexpected. "I know not everyone is part of your *fara'ip* . . ." I stopped when Alejandro lifted his hand.

"*Querida*, I did not bring the Hunt to the Shadowlands, no matter what this Nik might think. And I am only one Rider. What does he—or you—think I can do?"

Truthfully, that had already occurred to me, back when Nik first spoke to me, but I'd had a little more thinking time since then.

"Okay, sure. But there *are* more of you. What about this Nighthawk?" I was still connecting the images around him. "He's got something to do with this Exile, with the Prince who lost the war," I said. "He's a guard or something."

"A Warden. That is what they are called." Alejandro bent to pour himself fresh tea, and held up the pot, glancing toward me. I shook my head. "When Dawntreader, the Prince Guardian and Keeper of the Talismans, was exiled, his *dra'aj* was bound, so that he could not use it to return, or even to Move himself from place to place here in the Shadowlands."

"But that would have made him vulnerable to humans, so they sent these Wardens along with him, to keep him safe?"

"Exactly." Alejandro smiled. He loved it when my ability helped me understand quickly.

"But there's something more," I said. "He did something else to the Guardian, the bad guy did, something that makes you a little nauseated." Alejandro's nose wrinkled. "You might as well tell me."

"Somehow the Basilisk Prince removed the Exile's memories."

I shivered, but I was nodding. "It makes sense," I said. And it did in a horrid way. "Talk about making sure that your enemy can't turn the tables on you. I mean, he didn't just exile the guy from his home, he exiled him from *himself*." I rubbed my arms as another chill ran up my spine. "So if this Basilisk guy sent the Wardens in the first place, why would he send someone to attack the one in Granada?"

"They were searching for the Exile, but, in fact, he was at that time here in Toronto."

"In Toro—Ah, but he's not here now. And everybody knows it, which is why it's safe for *us* to be here." Except that after what I'd seen today, maybe it wasn't as safe as Alejandro had thought. I licked my lips. We were only here in the first place because of me, because something the Collector had once said made me think my family might be here.

"Precisely. The Banishment was ending—it may even be ended by now. After we destroyed the Rider who had been sent to menace Nighthawk, he sent a message to the Warden who was here, closest to the Exile, warning her of what was afoot and in order to save him from those who would capture and make use of him, she was forced to take him through the Portal to the Lands."

I nodded. "Okay. So then what happened?" Alejandro frowned. "Oh," I said. "No one knows." He inclined his head with his red eyebrows raised in the way that meant "precisely."

"So Nighthawk can't help us?"

Alejandro shrugged. "He is Warden to the Exile. That is his duty." He stood up and walked from the couch to the TV cabinet, from the TV to the front door, from the front door back to the couch, where he stood staring narrowly at something in the air in front of him. As usual, all his movements were quick, graceful, precise.

"In the face of what you have told me, it may be I have made an error in bringing you to this city." Alejandro pressed his lips together and shook his head. "If the Hunt is here, perhaps with the followers of the Basilisk Prince, and preying upon humans . . ."

I put my empty cup down on the coffee table and went to him, put my arms around him, and rested my forehead on his shoulder. I wouldn't get much from him now; over the time we'd been together I'd touched him so often I already knew practically everything there was to know. But if there was anything recent, anything different . . .

[A flash of turquoise in the sun, his *traje de luces*; a sharp angle of blade, his *estoque*, poised, dark brown eyes narrowed as he sighted down the bull's neck for the spot to place his thrust; where were the other *toreros*? Why was Alejandro alone? Where was I?]

"Oh, no, you don't." I backed away far enough to look him in the face, but kept hold of his arms. "You're not going to stick me somewhere safe and take on the Hunt by yourself." He opened his mouth and I stopped him with a lifted index finger.

"So you've been bored, huh? You're actually disappointed the Collector didn't send someone after me. Living with me's just not exciting enough for you, huh?" My eyes felt hot, as if I was going to cry, though I couldn't have told you why. "Well, listen to me." I jabbed him on the chest with my finger. "I'm going nowhere. And you're not taking on the Hunt by yourself, no matter what you think."

Alejandro looked at me from under his brows, but a smile was forming on his lips.

"We find help and we fight, or we run together," I said, making it clear that I was emphasizing the *we*.

"You would help me fight the Hunt?"

I swallowed, my mouth suddenly dry. My life with the Collector was fresh in my mind today, and I have to say part of me wanted that safety, that security back. But then I remembered Elaine, and I looked at Alejandro, and the glint of adventure and daring in his eye, the glint that had appeared there the day that I met him, the day that my life had changed.

"*You* saved *me*," I said.

"Ah, so this is now my fault." But he was smiling as he said it. He looked at me carefully, and he must have seen what he was looking for in my face, because he nodded. "Very well. But we need to know more. Is it only the Hunt? If there are Riders searching through the Shadowlands, followers and henchmen of the Basilisk Prince," he shrugged, "it was they who likely brought the Hunt with them, and they are dangerous in themselves. Perhaps it is best if I go—"

I pressed my lips together, took a deep breath and let it huff out, more exasperated than angry. "I'm sorry," I said. "But I've really had more than enough of being protected."

Alejandro's smile was very soft. I had the feeling he'd had this discussion many times in the past. "You are free now," he agreed. "And that means free to risk yourself."

I kept my voice quiet, afraid that otherwise it might shake. "I'm really not saying all this just to prove how brave I am," I said. "Not even to myself. And it's not that I don't understand how dangerous things can be. I've seen the worst there is in human beings." I patted his hand with my free one. "I know you had to rescue me, but—"

Alejandro laughed and swung me around, shaking his head. A lock of his reddish-blond hair fell forward and he brushed it back off his face. "I was merely your instrument. I could not have saved you if you had not reached out for me. You knew what I was, and you were not afraid. If you had been the cowed, enslaved child he thought you to be, he would have been able to dispose of you." He believed it, I could tell.

"So," he said, clapping his hands. "We do not run away, we gather intelligence, and look for reinforcements. This Nik, you say he wishes to meet with me?"

I looked at the clock on the mantel. "He'll be here in about half an hour."

Alejandro smiled. "You were so sure of me, then?"

I smiled back. "I guess so."

I let Nik in the front door and showed him into the dining room. Alejandro stood in the kitchen, watching us from the pass-through.

"Valory has told me how you helped her, and I thank you." He tilted his head. "There have long been rumors of humans who hold themselves apart from the rest of their kind. Long-lived humans, with a strange origin, and even stranger appetites."

I could almost hear the words that vibrated in Alejandro's mind.

Vampiro. Hombre lobo. I could only hope Nik wasn't that good at reading people.

"We call ourselves Outsiders." Nik's tone was dry as the tundra in winter. I guess he was.

Alejandro gave a slow nod, picked up a tray of coffee, cups, and heated milk to carry it into the dining room. "I have met one of you before," Alejandro continued as he set down the tray. "She was not disposed to converse with me."

"'Not disposed to converse with you.' That's about right." Nik sank into the chair I'd pulled out for him, his eyes on Alejandro. "None of you have ever been of any real use to any of us."

Alejandro spread his hands. "I know of no reason for this animosity."

Nik turned his head away, lips compressed to a straight line. But turning the way he did meant he was looking at me, and I saw his face soften. Maybe he remembered he was here asking for help.

"*You* brought those things here. You *Riders*." The word came out hard, but maybe not as hard as it could have. "The Hunt. You let them loose on us." He tapped himself on the chest. "And when we came to you for help, you sent us away."

"I assure you, it was not I who brought the Hunt here, nor have I ever been approached by any of your kind for help." Alejandro frowned at his cup of *café con leche*. "This is not to say that I might not have refused them help, if I felt I had no reason to give it."

"But you'll help now?"

Alejandro was quiet for long enough that I could hear the ticking of the clock in the living room. Then he nodded.

"Why?"

"Because it is Valory who asks me."

Chapter Three

NIGHTHAWK HAD THE TYPICAL COLORING of a Sunward Rider. His hair and sharply pointed beard were a deep auburn, his eyes amber, and there was a sunny golden tinge to his skin. Wolf was Moonward himself, and he hoped this would not bring any trouble with it. Given the High Prince's attitude, it was unlikely her fellow Warden had any strong Ward prejudice. Still, it was not unknown for fights, even wars, to erupt between Sunward, Moonward, and Starward Riders.

The variations in skin, hair, and eye color that Wolf had seen in the Shadowlands meant that neither he nor any other Rider in any way stood out among the humankind on the basis of coloring. Height was another matter. The High Prince had warned him that Riders in the Shadowlands took some pains to make themselves appear more human, and that meant shorter.

Wolf looked around him and decided that the Sunward's study suited him. It was a small room, with a single window on the house's interior courtyard. The walls were lined with bookshelves, and the furniture consisted of an oak desk made untidy with papers and open books, a swivel chair, a drinks table, and two comfortable armchairs upholstered in soft, well-worn leather with a round pedestal table between them. The deep blues and reds in the rug that covered the center of the tiled floor glowed in the light from two shaded lamps.

"Truthsheart is a Healer, and after the Great War, a Healer is what the Lands need." Hawk's satisfaction was evident in his tone and the glow of his expression. "And she has lived here, passing herself as human. That is needed also, now that the Portals are to be open again." Hawk shot a glance at Wolf. "They are to be open again?"

"That is more than I can say. My mission is to find others like yourself, those who were left behind or who went into hiding when the Exile began," Wolf said. He had another goal—almost more a hope—but he had not even told the High Prince of it.

"So you bring to all the message you have brought to me?" Hawk rose again, pulled a bottle out of a small cold box, and took two short, tapered glasses out of a cupboard. He poured out two servings from the dark bottle and passed one to Wolf.

"I am also to give warning that followers of the Basilisk Prince have been escaping into the Shadowlands, and all here should be wary of them until they are found."

Hawk stopped with his glass halfway to his mouth and fixed Wolf with a sharp glance from his amber eyes. "But if the Cycle has turned, it will have turned for them as well."

Wolf shrugged one shoulder. "Better to say the Cycle *turns*. The process is not yet complete. The Basilisk's followers may fear to accept the new Prince." Wolf took a sip of the liquor, raising his eyebrows in approval. "Do not doubt, however. The Cycle *is* turning, I have seen it with my own eyes," he said. "Solitaries and Naturals both are welcomed to the High Prince's court, and into her *fara'ip*. The works of the Basilisk are being undone. The *dra'aj* of the Lands spreads in abundance, the High Prince has manifested her Guidebeast—as indeed have others. I myself have seen her Dragonform, and the Phoenix of the Guardian Prince. And some among the Wild Riders have manifested as well."

A tension Wolf had not even noticed left Hawk's shoulders, and the older Rider smiled, an expression so sweet and warm, that Wolf found himself smiling back.

"I long ago gave up any hope that I would survive to see such wonders," Hawk said. "A new Cycle, my old comrade made the

High Prince." He pressed his lips tight, and shook his head in slow arcs. "And she sent you first to me?"

"And then to the one called Graycloud at Moonrise."

"Who will be of great help to you. Most of the ones who remained behind are known to him. His name is now Alejandro Martín. He was living in Madrid, but he has taken his human ward to North America, to a city called Toronto."

Toronto. "I know of the place. I am to stay there," Wolf said, touching the chain around his neck. "The High Prince has given me instructions to find her home."

"I have been there." Hawk nodded. "The Royal York Hotel. The crossroads are very near to it." He drew his brows down in a vee. "I could telephone Alejandro, give him the news myself."

Wolf considered. He knew what a telephone was, and in theory he knew how to use one. The High Prince, on the other hand, was well versed in such things.

"Truthsheart did not give *me* this option of announcing my news by proxy," he said. "I can only conclude she did not wish me to do so."

"Then she had her reasons, and we will respect them." Hawk gestured with the bottle and Wolf reached out with his glass. "Still, I could find out exactly where he is, save you some time."

But when Wolf had agreed, and he had watched with interest as the call was placed, they found that Alejandro Martín was not to be reached so easily. Hawk spoke into the instrument nevertheless, leaving something he called a "voice mail."

"If you do not hear from me before you go, check at the concierge's desk of the hotel for a message from me. In the meantime . . ." Hawk drummed his fingers on the tabletop, looking about him with a distracted air, before rising and pulling a mass of folded paper out of a drawer in the desk. Wolf leaned forward with interest. This might be some of the writing Max the Guardian had told him about—proper writing, not just the bits of words he'd seen on signs.

But it was only a drawing. "This is a map," Hawk said, tapping the paper. "Humans use these to picture their land, and to give directions." He looked up. "You know how the land is here? All of a piece, one single place?"

Wolf nodded. "I came through the Portal in Rome," he said, "and arrived in Madrid by train, to see as much as possible and acclimate myself." He said nothing of the fact that he had been here in the Shadowlands before, in another form. Only the High Prince herself needed to know that.

But Hawk was already unfolding another of the maps. "There are two others of the People here in Spain that I know of. Not all of them have chosen to make themselves known to me. But you may start with these until Alejandro can direct you to others."

Wolf noted the use of the human name. He watched with interest as Hawk showed him how the map worked. He would not need it to return to Madrid, of course, since he could Move directly to the crossroads in the Atocha train station, having been there already, but Hawk showed him on the map how to find the fountain of Cibeles from the station.

"In the fountain you will find a Water Natural, Shower of Stars by name." The Sunward Rider unrolled the second map. "A Solitary, a Troll, lives here," his finger tapped the paper, "just to the north of the city, in Segovia, where there is a great aqueduct."

"How did a Natural come through a Portal?" Wolf asked, his finger on the map of Madrid.

"That I cannot tell you. I am not on such terms with her that I might ask such a question. Nor do I know what decided her to remain here." Hawk emptied his glass and got up to pour himself a refill. He squinted one eye at Wolf before nodding and refilling his glass as well.

"You will return, then," Wolf said, not really asking.

"Oh, yes," Hawk replaced the bottle as he answered. "I would see the Lands again, and my fellow Warden, and the Exile, now that he is no longer my charge. And who knows?" Here Hawk smiled again, his eyes twinkling under his dark auburn brows. "I might be able to manifest my own dragon, to go night flying along with the High Prince."

Wolf found himself smiling back. "Look for the Princes' court in the Vale of *Trere'if*." He sipped his wine and sighed as he lowered the glass.

"You like the *fino*? You must take a few bottles with you when you leave Spain. The true *fino* is not found very far outside of Andalucia."

Once back in Madrid, with the image of the map in his head to orient him, Wolf had no trouble finding the fountain of Cibeles. Unfortunately, the fountain itself was in the center of a roundabout, and the traffic swirling through the lanes like water in a whirlpool never stopped, and rarely slowed. A half-familiar movement in the corner of his vision made Wolf look to the left and then to the right, but he saw nothing. On the other hand, no one seemed to be taking any notice of him. The sound of Movement would be covered by the noises of the traffic. Wolf focused once more on the fountain, picked out what looked like the perfect spot and—

He was standing in the spray in front of the goddess' chariot, his hand on the rump of a stone lion.

"Nighthawk sends me," he called out. At first nothing changed, and he wondered how long it would take for some human to notice him standing here. He had been warned that in this world moving water only concealed the People from others of their kind, not from humans. Just as he was beginning to think he had better Move back to the sidewalk, the spray thickened, obscuring the cars and buses, the crowds of humans, and the buildings, until even the sounds and smells of the outside world faded, and Wolf found himself standing in a cool green room with iridescent walls, sparkling in spots with a sapphire luster. A small woman, sitting cross-legged on what passed for a floor, smiled up at him.

Wolf looked around him. He appeared to be completely underwater, but he had no trouble breathing, and no difficulty standing on what seemed to be a liquid surface.

"I am Shower of Stars," the Water Sprite said. "Sit. You bring a message from Hawk?" Like most Sprites, Shower of Stars was much smaller than a Rider, though fully formed, except for her feet, which were hidden in the water. Her skin was a pearly gray-blue, her long hair slightly paler and rippling of its own accord as though it floated in a current. Her eyes, like those of all Water Sprites, were a brilliant emerald, with no whites. Her clothing, like her hair, was in constant, rippling motion, and Wolf wondered if this was because she was the Natural of a fountain, and not a pond.

"I am Stormwolf. My mother was Rain at Sunset. The Chimera guides me."

"I do not know your mother, though there is water in your ancestry, Wolf of Storms, son of Rain at Sunset. Welcome. What news?"

The music in the Water Sprite's abrupt and tinkling manner of speech felt familiar, but Wolf could not quite place why. He took a deep breath and repeated what he had already told Nighthawk. He stumbled a few times, but on the whole found it easier going the second time. The Sprite had fewer questions to ask, but that was likely because she was not personally acquainted with the new High Prince.

"Go back," she said in answer to his own final question. "Pleasant to experience once more the full *dra'aj* of the Lands, the presence of the High Prince."

With a little shock Wolf realized that if Shower of Stars had experienced the full *dra'aj* of the Lands before, it meant that she had lived through more than one Cycle. He frowned. There was something about *that* thought which also eluded him, something that felt important, but nothing more followed, and he had other, more pressing concerns.

"If I may ask," he said. "How is it that you plan to pass through the Portal?"

"You tell the High Prince. She sends a Rider to bring me. Someone with strong water connections—stronger than your own, Stormwolf."

Wolf nodded. "I believe there is such a one, a Singer who has *fara'ip* with the Water Sprite, Tear of the Dragon."

"A Singer, who has the history of the People in her care? Ideal. More so if she has *fara'ip* with one of my kind already."

"Nighthawk gave me your name," Wolf said now. "And that of the Troll, Mountain Crag. Are there any others that you know of to whom I might pass the news I have been given?"

The Sprite's emerald eyes narrowed in thought, but she ended by shaking her head.

"Once I knew of more." She shrugged, causing clothing and hair to ripple even more. "But I have been long in my fountain. Ask Graycloud. He knows."

"I have his name also," Wolf said. "I thank you. May I, uh . . ." He gestured at the walls. How was he to leave?

Shower of Stars' laughter was the tinkling of water from her fountain. "You may Move from here, Rider, since I will allow it."

A moment later, and Wolf was standing once more on the sidewalk. He was not surprised to find that his clothing was quite dry.

The Troll, Mountain Crag, was even more matter-of-fact about Wolf's news than the Natural had been. Following Hawk's directions, Wolf had found the Solitary in a pleasant bar, dark and crowded, within sight of a great two-tiered aqueduct that towered over the mountain town of Segovia. The Solitary had made himself look like a bull of a man, short, thick across the shoulders, with a massive head covered with thick graying hair, gray-pupiled eyes under shaggy eyebrows, and hands like hams. He seemed a working man, and Wolf was not surprised to gather from the talk around them, that "call me Jenaro" was a mason who was well-established and well-known in the region.

"Good news, I would suppose, for them as cares about it," the Troll said, tossing back the small glass of beer in front of him and signaling to the barman for another. A miniature loaf of bread and a plate of sizzling sausages roughly the size and shape of the Troll's fingers, though much redder in color, appeared in front of them. "A new High Prince, a Dragonborn at that. I'm glad to know of it." He popped a sausage whole into his mouth and followed it with a piece of bread torn from the small loaf. "Though, in answer to your question, Younger Brother, I don't think I'll return to the Lands. I came here before the Basilisk ever thought to raise his war banners, before the Banishment of the Guardian Prince. That these events have passed to the old Cycle mean less to me than they might to others." A broad grin disclosed a mouthful of squared-off teeth. He gestured out the bar's open doorway at the massive blocks of the aqueduct. "And besides, where else will I have so magnificent a bridge?"

The old Troll's eyes narrowed at Wolf's question about others, just as the Water Sprite's had done.

"To the west, across the great water," he said. "That's where Graycloud has gone, that's where you'll find *him*." He grinned again, and Wolf steeled himself not to back away as a shadow of the Troll's real shape seemed to pass in an instant over his human form. "A Sunward Rider, if you care about such things. He's been the longest tenant here, if I may speak in those terms, having lived in the Shadowlands longer than any of us. There was one of my kind in China, many years ago, but we've lost touch. Alejandro can tell you of others there may be."

Wolf tossed back his glass of *fino*. Nighthawk was right; he'd have to procure a bottle or two before he left.

(Flicker) Flat. Black and white. Smell of fear sweat, exhilaration. Layer upon layer of greasy meat and pastry, tobacco and other burning grasses, alcohol, perfumes, burnt sugar. And here, in the hidden recesses of the upper stories of the building, the dust of ages. Sound of pigeons cooing, flapping of wings, pittering of rodent feet. (Flicker) Louder, nearing, claws on concrete, paws, footsteps, claws. (Flicker) The smells recede somewhat into the three-dimensional background. Color.

Foxblood could understand, pretty well, what his Pack mates said to him when they were in other shapes, but the whole Hunt found it easier to think and speak to each other when in Rider form. The great scaled lion that approached Fox now, way too fast for the concrete floor, scrabbled to a stop only just in time.

"Control yourself," he told it, waiting as patiently as he could for Claw to turn back into a Rider.

"Easier said than done, as you should know better than most." He must have just taken human *dra'aj;* nothing else could have made him so cocky. Foxblood took a step toward the other Hound.

"Though you're right, you're right, as usual," Claw said, cringing, his shape flickering into that of an actual dog for a second. They all knew who was Pack Leader here. "We should control ourselves, absolutely. And we will, for sure. Once we have plenty of the new *dra'aj*." A line of saliva trickled from Claw's mouth, and he wiped it away with the back of his hand. "Like you said."

"Tell me," Fox said, stopping himself just as he was reaching for the other's throat.

Claw ducked his head again, and pretended he only meant to look around him, sniffing. As if he didn't know as well as Fox did that except for the others guarding the stairwells, they were alone.

"Stump's missing."

Fox's hand went involuntarily to the cell phone in his pocket—another thing, like the pocket itself, that only existed when he was in Rider form. A great way to keep in touch with the rest of the Pack, since they couldn't Move.

"Who reported it?"

"Badger. She reported in on time, says she hasn't heard from him."

Fox frowned. There'd been a Five of the Pack in the place called Europe. Did this mean there were only four now? Impossible that a human could have killed Stump. Far more likely he was in a *dra'aj*-induced stupor and had simply lost track of time. Possible, but not as likely, that some Rider had got him. Fox considered who to send. He had two Fives of the Pack here with him, but it was still tricky, very tricky, for them to move like humans did. No. He'd have to rely on those already in place.

"Tell Badger it's her job to find out what's happened, not just report it." Fox deliberately waited until Claw had ducked his head and was turning to leave, before he reminded his Pack mate that they had other business.

"What about the girl?"

"Lost her again." This time the other Hound did cringe away, and even lifted his arm, partly to bare his belly in submission, and partly to block a blow to the head. Fox's hands (paws) formed fists (hooves), but he held back.

"How?" His throat quivered with the need to howl.

"The scentless ones, they got in the way, drew her off, and muddied the scent."

Fox rubbed at his lip again. "So why don't these humans Fade once we've fed on their *dra'aj*?" He looked at Claw. "Catch one, bring it here. And tell Badger that when she's learned what she can, she's to gather her Five and come to us here. And, Claw—"

A commotion at the entrance made Fox curl his lip back from his teeth. He was gesturing at Claw to deal with it when the two from the bottom of the stairs appeared with a Rider between them. Neither of them had been able to hang on to their own form, and even Claw flickered as he backed away. The Rider was Sunward, and his *dra'aj* shone from him like the sun through clouds. No wonder the others hadn't been able to control themselves. The surprise was that they hadn't simply drained the stupid Sunward fool before he got to the top of the stairs. Fox ground his teeth together, gripped the armrests of his chair, and held his shape.

The strange Rider approached, and inclined his head. "I am

Longshadow," he said. "My mother was Lightstorm, and the Simurg guides me."

Fox blinked, and his mouth fell open in a grin. This Starward one thought he was a Rider! For a moment the blood pounding in his ears blocked out all other sounds. In an instant Fox saw his advantage and took it.

"From the Lands, huh?" he said. "The Basilisk sent you back to collect his doggies? What if they're my doggies now?" He hadn't returned the courtesy of giving his own name and Guidebeast, and Fox wondered what the Starward would do about it.

"You will not have heard, then." If Longshadow was offended, he hid it well. "The Basilisk has Faded. The Lands have a High Prince, and the Cycle is turned."

Fox pulled his lip back. Well. That was news indeed. "And those with him?" He wouldn't ask straight out about his brother; Riders didn't seem to be able to distinguish one member of the Hunt from another. But he had to know what had happened.

"Some are Faded as well. Some follow the new Prince."

"And those who don't?"

"Some of us have given *dra'aj* oaths." He cleared his throat. "Some of us have gone too far down the Basilisk Prince's path to follow the High Prince now." The Starward Rider rubbed at his lower lip. For the first time, Fox saw the tremble in his hands, the sweat on his brow. Saw, and *smelled* it for what it was.

The Basilisk's path, is that what they were calling it? Fox smiled, and even Claw flickered into his Rider form long enough to bark out a short laugh. That was a path they knew all about. That path brought you to the Hunt. If Stump was really lost, then Badger would need someone new to complete her Five.

"We don't care about Princes here," Fox said aloud. "But we can get you what you need."

The Sunward licked his lips, his eyes flicking from side to side as he tried to watch the Hounds around him. Finally he nodded.

"Claw." Fox crooked his finger at his Hound. "Take our new Pack mate and show him where he can feed. Feed yourselves while you're at it. Claw!" The three Hounds stopped their circling of the Rider at the whip in Fox's voice. "I'll want to see our friend Longshadow later, so make sure you look after him. And make sure you look after those little jobs I've given you, before you eat your dinners."

He waited until they were all at the top of the stairs before he stopped them again. "And, Claw? Find the girl. Follow her, but don't get caught. She smells like Rider, and I need to know where she fits in this Hunt."

Claw scampered away, changing into a dog, a dragon-shaped wingless thing, and back to a Rider before reaching the doorway.

Fox relaxed enough to let his Rider form change, and melted back into the shadows of the concrete cavern to think. As soon as Longshadow had completely turned, Fox could question him about Stormwolf. He *had* to find out what had happened to his brother. Had he Faded with the Basilisk, or would Fox have to fight him now for the leadership of the Pack?

On the other hand, the Horn was obviously gone—lost or broken—and there might be other potential Hounds among the abandoned followers of the Basilisk. Maybe even another Five. Maybe more. And as for those who weren't changing, they might still be allies—as long as they didn't have the Horn.

Hounds or allies, Fox could increase his numbers. A must if the plan that was forming in his mind was going to work. He'd need a way to persuade this new High Prince that coming after them would be too costly. That it would be easier to just let the Hunt keep the Shadowlands for themselves.

What *was* this human girl? If the old Rider valued her as much as it looked, maybe he could use her to make the Riders listen.

Wolf stepped through the crossroads into a quiet darkness smelling of cooling metal, of diesel exhaust, of cold stone, of cleaning fluids. There were no sounds, no people, and precious few lights to be seen, and yet this was the right crossroads, this was Union Station in Toronto. What could it mean? In both Rome and Madrid the train stations that sat on the crossroads had been full of light and sound and humans.

All he saw in the semidarkness was a large empty room, numbered exits and entrances, silent escalators waiting to take absent people to the other levels. Wolf shut his eyes and shook his head before opening them again. There was no hidden message here, no unexplained tragedy. It was simply that the station was closed. Like so many things, paranoia was a useful servant, and a poor master.

Wolf set out into the concourse, away from the crossroads and the Portal, so tempting, from which he imagined he could smell the air of the Lands. He had no excuse to go through. Nighthawk, the old Warden, would carry word to the High Prince that Wolf followed the trail she had set him, and that the Water Sprite, Shower of Stars, had requested aid to return to the Lands; he would carry word even about the Hound. All of which left Wolf free to come to Toronto.

He followed the instructions the High Prince had given him and walked through the arrivals concourse toward the closest exit doors. As he walked, Wolf caught the scent of the guardians of the place. One such guard he avoided simply by stepping into the nearest shadow, and used the time it took for the guard to pass on his round to fix his mental image of the place, lest he should he require it again.

Unfortunately, as he neared the glass doors of the exit three men in uniform, holding cups from which came the hot, bitter smell of coffee, barred his way. One man was taking bites from a pastry that even from Wolf's hiding place in the shadows smelled sickly sweet. Another had an apple in the pocket of his uniform jacket.

"Nirmal should go home if he's just going to sit in the locker room staring at the walls," Pastry was saying.

"Leave him alone," Apple said. "He's just got that High Park thing that's going around."

"He can't afford to miss another shift," No Food added.

Wolf waited. Finally Apple drifted away to the east and disappeared behind a wide marble staircase. Wolf glanced to his right. He would have to go that way, as it appeared the remaining two could go on talking about the illness of their comrade for hours.

Swiftly, silently, Wolf darted through the shadows to a set of double doors that had been left ajar and into a food market that smelled of cleaning fluids not quite masking spoiled food. Somewhere beyond the market stalls he thought he could smell outside air.

The exit doors were locked shut, but Wolf used his *gra'if* dagger to cut through the metal of the locks. The *gra'if* glowed slightly in the darkness, but Wolf had it sheathed before it could give him away.

Stepping out, he was faced with a narrow stretch of roadway, another set of double glass doors on the other side. There were streetlights above him, and the sounds and smells of traffic overhead. That would be Front Street. The Prince's home was in the building on the other side. Wolf eyed the parapet, an easy leap.

He put his hand to his chest, touched through his shirt the key the High Prince had given him.

"Go in through the front doors of the hotel," she had said. "But use the east lobby elevators and go to the top floor. The apartment is in the southeast corner of the building, and has a silver knocker in the shape of a dragon on the door."

As if the thought of a Guidebeast triggered his senses, Wolf's nostrils flared. Somewhere here, in this submerged laneway, there was a faint scent of Rider. He turned, intent on fixing this scent in his mind—and his attackers were on him almost before he knew they were there. Sound more than scent gave them away. Too many shadows, too many conflicting odors, had masked their approach. Two of the three grabbed him by the upper arms and were dragging him toward the darkest corner while the third was dodging in front, trying to reach Wolf's feet.

They weren't trying to hurt him, he realized, just secure him, but while they were touching him, he could not Move without bringing them with him. Wolf planted his feet, shrugged off the dark form on his right, flinging out his arm. As that person was still airborne, Wolf spun, swinging the one holding his left arm into the man in front. The impact broke the man's hold on Wolf's arm, and he immediately Moved, first to the shadowy spot in the train concourse he had used earlier, then to a safe spot in the market area, behind the juice vendor.

He could hear the people who had accosted him. They were still outside, the one he had thrown groaning. Apparently Wolf had broken some ribs. The High Prince had warned him that humans were more fragile than Riders, but evidently he had not paid sufficient attention. Instead of setting themselves to watch once more, the two relatively uninjured men helped the third away, and the laneway was once more deserted. Now alert, Wolf Moved back to where he had been attacked, immediately leaping onto the parapet, and stepping down onto the wide sidewalk.

In a moment he was across the street and pushing through the revolving doors of the hotel. He barely took in the vast lobby, as large as the great hall of a prince's palace. Even at this late hour there were a few people about, but Wolf had dressed carefully in a good suit, though the collar of his shirt was open. Only one woman said, "Good night, sir," to him as he passed. He nodded at her, and tried to smile. He must have succeeded, for she smiled back.

He had already dismissed the attack. Young men, he thought, likely trying to rob him. What was occupying Wolf's mind as he pressed the button for the elevator was the faint spoor of Rider he'd detected where they had jumped him.

Later, having settled into the bed of what was clearly the guest room, he dreamed.

He puts his clawed feet to the ground, but they are no longer clawed, and his tentacles, sooty gray, at once scaled and leathery, find no easy purchase. He sees the scent he is following, leading away from him like a ribbon of soft golden silk floating through the air. Reaching away from him into the world. Then he sees them, a Starward male and a Moonward female, and he knows them, smells their *dra'aj* so like his own. They turn and greet him with smiles. They do not see what he is; they do not lock themselves away from him.

Wolf woke up cold with sweat, the sheets damp. Swung his legs over the side of the wide bed, and sat with his elbows on his knees, rubbing his face with his hands, unable to work any warmth into his skin. He thrust his hands into his hair.

"I am the Hound of the Dragonborn Prince," he said aloud, shocking himself with the harshness of his voice. "My mother—my mother was Rain at Sunset and the Chimera guides me. I am Wolf in the Storm."

This was by no means the first time he had dreamed about what he had been before Truthsheart had made him real again. Always the same, the same shapes and smells. Always he had returned home, and destroyed what he found there. Though the dreams were getting better, he told himself as he stood under the shower, washing away the fear that stuck to his skin. At least now they stopped before he began to feed.

As he padded back to the sitting room, passing through shafts of moonlight, he stopped and stood looking around him. There *had* been something new. He had never before wondered, while dreaming, why his parents had not locked their door to him. There was a way, a very simple way. After all, parents whose children could Move still required privacy from time to time.

What did this mean? He could not close the apartment to Moving, or he would lose the use of it himself. But there was something he could do . . . Wolf went to the door of the apartment, wondering if he would remember the Chant. It had been so long ago, but he had heard it many times. He placed his hands on the door frame, wood and darkmetal and paint. It would have to do. He licked his lips, and began to Sing.

Tomorrow, once the sun was up, he would follow the Rider's trail.

Walks Under the Moon lifted her forehead from the neck of the Cloud Horse when Lightborn's silhouette blocked the light from the doorway.

"I thought I would find you here," he said. He was a Starward Rider, as she was herself, and even inside the stable his platinum hair shone.

"I knew you would come." Moon smiled, trying to keep her voice light. "You might have gone without letting me know, but never without a horse." The Cloud Horses that now looked at them with interest from their stalls were Lightborn's special pride, raised by him in this very stable.

He came straight to her, and took her hands in his own. "I would have found you, before I left," he said. "This is not the best time, but I've been trying to find the right words."

Moon clenched her teeth. This did not sound like anything she wished to hear.

Lightborn drew her to a seat on the nearby bench. "I don't want to leave you under a cloud. No, not you my handsome one." Lightborn pushed away an inquisitive muzzle, another horse snorted, and Moon laughed despite the cold feeling in the pit of her stomach.

"There, that smile's more genuine."

"But you *are* leaving, aren't you? I saw the messenger come, and I saw that you were called into your mother's receiving room." She looked at him out of the corner of her eye. The light from the doorway did not seem to touch his dark blue eyes. "And I was not."

"It's a soldier they need, Moon, not an expert on lore. The High Prince's attention has been on Healing the Lands, but reports have come of Warriors of the Basilisk who are not laying down their arms." He paused, his lips pressed tight. "They may even be preparing a stronghold somewhere near the Tourmaline Ring."

"And *you* must go?"

"I go, your sister the High Prince goes; Max, the Prince Guardian, also."

Moon studied Lightborn's face. He still called his cousin Max, and not Dawntreader, the name they had used when they were both children. "And I suppose Windwatcher, and all the others?"

Lightborn hesitated. "It must be one of us who leads, the Princes or someone of their blood. My mother has armed herself also, and if you were a soldier, you would be sent as well."

"And as I am not a soldier . . ." Moon glanced around the stable as she searched for the right words. Her eyes came to rest on the metal that banded her left wrist, metal that shone with a light of its own. "I can Ride," she said. "I bear *gra'if*, and I am, as you said, an expert on lore. Why should I not come with you?"

Lightborn was quiet a long time. Long enough that Moon, touching him lightly on the arm, was about to withdraw her request, when suddenly she found herself facing him, his hands gripping her shoulders.

"Do you think I would take you into danger? Do you think I would risk your life?"

"But *you*—"

"The Princes have asked; I cannot refuse."

Moon shook her head, her smile returning. "You would not."

His eyes shut and he released her. "No. I would not."

Moon nodded. "We have not been lucky, have we?"

Lightborn's laugh was more than half sigh. "No, we have not." He turned to face her and took her hands again. "Moon. This call was so unexpected, we have just begun to talk around this thing between us—I thought we had more time, I—"

Moon lifted her hand, afraid to move too much. "You don't have to say anything. We both of us knew that there was—that there *is*—something between us." Though in truth, she hadn't *known*. Now she *knew*, and she could feel the singing in her heart.

"I am speaking straightly to you now," he said. He drew a small, sparkling object from the breast of his tunic and held it out to her in the palm of his hand. It was a broach, fashioned in the shape of a griffin. Moon touched it, and it turned to nuzzle against her hand.

"We are not Wild Riders, we cannot exchange *gra'if.* Take this instead. When my task is over, when the Basilisk's Warriors have been dealt with, we will wed, you and I."

"Yes, we will." His lips were warmer than she had expected, and his hands more strong.

Sometime later the snorting of the horses woke them.

"I've been thinking," Lightborn said.

"No, I believe it's called something else. Ah!" she rolled away. His fingers were as good at tickling as they were at other things.

"Lovely one, I would like it if you stayed here, in my home, while I am away."

Moon took in a deep breath and released it. "Without either you or your mother here? I don't think so," she said, rolling over on her side to see his face more clearly. "I make people uncomfortable." She tried to make her tone as even as possible. "They don't forget that I was once with the Basilisk."

"You are the one who can't forget."

"Perhaps." Let him think so. "But I can't stay here." Moon's gesture took in the whole of the fortress that lay outside the stables. "Not without you. I will go to my sister's camp. Perhaps I am no warrior, but who knows? She may find some use for me."

"Just you be sure you don't find a use for one of those Wild Riders."

"That entirely depends on how long you will be."

"However long, I will come back."

After, when she watched him Ride away, she fastened the pin to the collar of her tunic, and felt the tiny jeweled griffin move under her fingers. She patted it into place, then lowered her hands to her belly and smiled.

"Yes," she said. "You will be back."

Max Ravenhill, Prince Guardian, was pulling on a pair of *gra'if* gloves when he saw a small knot of three Riders approaching the Prince's pavilion from the perimeter of the camp. Not, as he might have expected, a captured minion of the Basilisk come to throw himself on the High Prince's mercy, but a Sunward Rider walking casually between two of the Wild Riders who had today's watch. And not only that, but a Sunward Rider dressed—

"Well, well," he said. "The man in the gray flannel suit." Too bad Cassandra wasn't here—no one else was going to catch the movie reference.

"My Prince?" It was Wings of Cloud who approached Max with the newcomer just behind him.

Max took a short step away from the entrance of the pavilion. "That's definitely a suit and tie," he said, smiling.

"I don't know if you will remember me, my lord Prince." The man in the suit was older, his auburn hair as carefully trimmed as his sharply pointed beard, and his amber eyes hooded.

"Nighthawk, of course I do." Max stuck out his hand. At least people from the Shadowlands knew what to do when he did that.

Max waved two seats into existence, proper cushioned ones, and waited until Nighthawk was seated before sitting himself. "Stormwolf reached you, then?"

"He did. And you can imagine my joy, not to say my relief, when I heard his news. And the High Prince?" Nighthawk glanced around, but no more than politeness would allow.

"She's away just now, but she'll be pleased to learn you made it back."

"Stormwolf told me of this as well." Hawk accepted a cup of wine with a distracted nod. "So it is not only in the Shadowlands that the Basilisk's old followers continue to make trouble?"

Max sighed. "It's not that we expected everything to go smoothly—we knew that the Lands themselves would need Cassandra's special touch, but there's been more determined opposition than we expected."

"That cannot be easy for Cassandra."

Max shook his head, but in agreement. "It isn't. But she *is* High Prince of the Lands." He fixed his eyes on Nighthawk. "All the Lands, and all the People, including the Basilisk's followers, and even including the Hunt. She must find a way to help any and all of the People who require it."

Hawk's amber eyes narrowed. "Even the Hunt?"

"Even the Hunt, now that we know what it is."

Hawk's gesture was almost dismissive, and Max found himself stifling a smile. Part of the Sunward Rider was reacting with the habit of years, and still saw Max as his human self. Hawk didn't see that he was no longer speaking with his Ward, but with the Prince Guardian. "The Hunt is an old danger, always with us, from Cycle to Cycle if we believe the Singers. A walking hunger," he said. "Their purpose is to destroy, and they cannot be helped."

"A natural danger? You think they're just a part of the Lands like the Abyss or the Blood Desert?" Max shook his head. "The Hunt are *Riders*, Hawk. Riders who became addicted to *dra'aj*, needing more and more, until it changed them utterly."

"*Addicts.*" Hawk sat straighter in his chair. "Cassandra discovered this?"

"She did. She saw the beginnings of it in the Basilisk Prince. The inability to hold his true shape, the uncontrollable hunger."

Hawk was frowning. "What are you suggesting, then? Some kind of 'Hounds Anonymous'? Hello, my name's Incisor, and I admit I'm powerless over *dra'aj*?" He shook his head. "It will not work, and it is too risky; we *have* to kill them."

Max studied the surface of his own wine. "You forget that Cass is a Healer."

"Max, if you know addiction, you know not everyone *can* be cured. We can't take such a chance with the Hunt."

"We already have. The Rider, Stormwolf." Max fixed Hawk's amber eyes with his own. "He was a Hound."

Hawk froze, his cup halfway to his lips. "The Rider she sent to the Shadowlands? Who sat in my home and drank my *fino*? *He's* a Hound?"

"Not anymore."

Head tilted to one side, Hawk raised his hand, index finger extended, mouth open to lecture. But before he could speak, three Wild Riders, one from each Ward, presented themselves in front of Max, far enough away for courtesy, but too close to be ignored. Max looked up and nodded.

"Your pardon, Dawntreader." Since Max was himself, technically, a Wild Rider, they sometimes took the liberty of calling him by his name, rather than his title. "As the High Prince is not here, we have brought this supplicant to you, for judgment."

Behind the Wild Riders stood a pair of Moonwards. At Max's gesture, the older of the two stepped forward. Her jet-black hair was loose and curly, falling almost to her knees, and in sharp contrast to the *gra'if* mail shirt that was all she wore over full green trousers and polished dark brown half-boots. She indicated her companion with a wave of her pale hand.

"My Prince," she said. "I am Falcondream, my mother was Flight of Arrows, and the Roc guides me. This is my son, and the only one of my blood I have left to me. I was among the guard of Windwatcher, and he will speak for me if needed, but I am here to speak for my son."

The younger Moonward Rider resembled his mother in his alabaster skin, and the curl of his black hair. He was dressed, however, in the purple colors of the Basilisk Prince, and he seemed to find it difficult to raise his green eyes from the toes of his scuffed boots.

"Can you look up, and name yourself?" Max tried to keep his voice gentle, but judging from the young Rider's reaction, there must have been some steel in it.

The green eyes flicked up at Max, down, and up again. "I—I'm Visionflight, my mother you know, and the Dragon guides me." The green eyes were dry, but Max thought he could hear tears in Visionflight's voice. *Yeah, and what kind of tears? Rage? Frustration? Or remorse?*

"How do you come to be here, Visionflight?" Max leaned forward, his elbows on his knees.

At first the young one said nothing, until Falcondream gave him a nudge that was very nearly a push.

"I'd like to offer my service to the High Prince." The words were spoken almost too quickly to make any sense. The mother rolled her eyes and let out a long sigh that spoke of her own frustration.

"You might as well tell me the whole story," Max said, now leaning back in his chair, fingertips braced against fingertips.

"I went to serve the Basilisk Prince—" His mother clouted him. "Ow! I mean Dreamer of Time."

"That's all right, Falcondream," Max said. "I'm not offended by anyone calling him a Prince."

In a voice that wavered between surliness and wheedling, Visionflight told a story Max had already heard many times. How he had wanted to serve in the court of the High Prince and lots of Riders had said the Basilisk would be the next one, how he had never risen to any position of importance, and on and on. Finally he wound down, and looked at Max with a mix of hope and defiance in his face.

He's young, Max thought. Older and he'd hide his feelings better. Max propped his chin on his right fist and narrowed his eyes, studying the way the boy stood, the set of his shoulders, the cant of his eyebrows. Finally he sat up. "You're angry," he told the young Rider. "You might be angry because you backed the wrong horse and now you feel stupid. Or because you're afraid that the High Prince won't forgive you. Or maybe because it turns out your mother was right all along." Here Max grinned at Falcondream before continuing. "But it's also possible—just—that you're angry because your mother is forcing you to be somewhere you don't want to be. That you have no love for the High Prince, and don't really wish to serve her."

Visionflight would have thrown himself at Max's feet, but the Guardian Prince stopped him in mid motion with a flick of his fingers. "I can't be sure, but the High Prince can. You'll have to wait until she returns." He looked at Falcondream. "Is this acceptable to you? Truthsheart will know with certainty merely by speaking with him. My own methods are nowhere near as quick."

"If you distrust him, Keeper of the Talismans, he has only himself to blame." From the sharpness of Falcondream's tongue, Max thought he could see a reason why her son had left home to take up service elsewhere as soon as he could.

Max nodded to the Wild Riders and watched them lead the boy and his mother away.

"Are there many like him?" Hawk followed the departing Riders with narrowed eyes.

"Quite a few, I'm happy to say, if I'm right about him. Just ordinary people with no evil in them, who happened to be on the wrong side."

"How will you make sure he doesn't escape? Do you have a Signed room somewhere?" Hawk's question was reasonable. A Signed room, a room whose walls were spelled with darkwood and *gra'if* so that no Rider could Move either out or in, was the time-honored way to keep prisoners.

"It's not possible to Sign a tent," Max said. "Not even Cassandra's pavilion. But those aren't ordinary trees out there." He indicated the woods, dark and thick, that lay behind the pavilion. "That's *Trere'if*, the Eldest of the Tree Naturals. When we need it, he just makes us a nice comfortable clearing that can hold any Rider."

Hawk nodded, but his amber eyes had lost their focus, as if he looked into the heart of *Trere'if* itself. After a few moments his gaze returned. "You set me a good example, Max. Not to judge too quickly, and not to condemn out of hand those who once stood at the sharp end of your sword. If the High Prince has cured a Hound, then I will trust in the skills, and in the judgment of my old comrade."

Max smiled. "I'm sure she'll be pleased to hear it."

Hawk raised his right hand, index finger extended. "But I have other news."

Max let himself fall once again against the leather back of his chair. From the look on Hawk's face, the news wasn't good.

"I sent her warning once before, my lord Guardian, and it seems I'm doing so again." Hawk braced his hands on his knees and took a deep breath. "We've mentioned that some of the Basilisk's Warriors are in the Shadowlands, but you may not know that the Hunt is there as well. And if they are still allies . . ."

Max felt like he'd swallowed a pool of ice. Allies wasn't exactly the word, but—"They can Move the Hunt. Wings of Cloud!" he called, getting to his feet. "Find Walks Under the Moon and bring her here," he said, when the young Wild Rider answered his call. He turned to Hawk. "Cassandra's sister," he explained. "We may need her." He wrapped his hand around the dragon torque at his throat. "You'll have to excuse me. I must find the High Prince."

Chapter Four

CASSANDRA KENNABY, HIGH PRINCE of the Lands, pushed her hands through her hair and sighed, opening her eyes.

"Do you tire? Would you rest?" *Trere'if* sat just within the edge of Trees, where the dappled light that filtered through the moving branches obscured his true form.

Cassandra let her hands drop to her knees. The light in the clearing had not changed since the last time her eyes were open. In this particular clearing, the light would never change.

"I can feel every mar in the Lands," she said, straightening her legs out of the lotus position and getting to her feet. "Like an itch I cannot scratch. I won't be able to truly rest until the Lands are fully restored."

Trere'if was the eldest of the Tree Naturals. Resting here in his very heart, Cassandra could feel the pattern and network of *dra'aj* that connected him to the younger Trees spread throughout the Lands, some dreaming under blankets of snow, some buffeted by wind, or rain, or baked by the hot sun of the tropics.

It was because she was High Prince that these connections were open to her, because she was bonded to the Lands through the Talismans, feeling—when she needed to—the ebb and flow of *dra'aj* as if it were the blood in her own veins.

"If you would continue, there is another place where a wood was cut down, where now only carnivorous grasses grow." For a moment his voice was the rattling of dry leaves in a winter wind.

Cassandra drew her brows together. "I know that place, I have seen it." She shivered. Trees lived so slowly, many, like *Trere'if*, lasting from Cycle to Cycle. The idea that some of these near-immortal beings had been cut down, destroyed forever—she rubbed at her eyes. The damage done by the Basilisk in his fear and his rage was near to overwhelming. It seemed that she had already spent a lifetime following the roots of the *dra'aj* that informed the Lands, like a physician, looking for flaws, for injuries, dangers, thin spots, so that she could redirect *dra'aj* to where it was needed.

"This last place, *Trere'if*, and then I will rest for today."

The canopy above her head parted slightly, just enough, Cassandra noted with a wry grin, to let her pass. She leaped straight up into the air, spreading her wings and beating once, twice, thrice, and she was above the Trees. Feeling them lift high, higher, highest, until the Wood that was *Trere'if* looked small below her. For a moment she had the image—from *Trere'if* himself?—of the black-silver-and-red dragon erupting from the cool green of the trees, and she saw with pleasure how beautiful she was.

Cassandra laughed, and the fire roared from her throat. The wind held her, caressing her wings and belly. In her Dragonform she could see as well as feel the *dra'aj* that made up the Lands. See it as different bands of color, including some that only dragons could see, and Riders had no words for. Below her, the Lands spread like a crazy quilt woven of rainbows and the auroras. Not only the Lands, but all the different People, down to, if she concentrated, their individual threads. She resisted the impulse to look for the thread that was Max. She would see him soon enough.

Then she saw the dark spot *Trere'if* had spoken of, the break in the network, the hole in the quilt where rot and decay had damaged the Lands. Striking her wings, she plummeted, pulling up only when she hovered over the place where the flesh-eating grasses grew.

With her dragon fire she burned the grasses away, her *dra'aj* sending Healing with every searing breath, fresh greenery and even flowers springing up in the wake of her flames. Cassandra drew then upon her Binding, touching the bright colors of the Lands, teasing them to grow until the rot was gone and there was only life. She called along the bands and whorls and loops of *dra'aj* and *Trere'if* answered, sending her the shapes and colors of Trees willing to answer her summons. She felt the surge of *dra'aj*, the playfulness of some of the younger Saplings as they shifted, changed, and Walked toward her as she drew their threads along the paths she created. With them came older Trees as well, to anchor the new Wood.

The Trees left her a place, a dragon-sized clearing where she landed and took on her own form once more. The clearing shrank, until it was a comfortable size for a Rider. The Trees behind her rustled, and Cassandra turned just as a Green Lady stepped from between the trunks and vines.

"Greetings, High Prince," she said. Her skin was smooth and silvered, mottled green here and there, her hair an oddly becoming mixture of mosses and long, tapering leaves. "We thank you with limb, and sap and leaf for the Wood you have made us." The Tree Natural bowed, the Trees around her moved their branches with her.

"You are welcome," Cassandra said. "I will ask among the Water Naturals displaced by the Basilisk whether any will come here, to gladden your groves with their liquid music." *I had better be off*, she thought with a private grin. Much longer and she might not be able to stop talking like a Tree. "Have you chosen a name?" she asked.

"We have," the Tree said. "We are *Feena'en*, High Prince."

"I will tell the Singers," Cassandra said. "And your name will be recorded." Once again they bowed, and a sudden breeze shivered the branches around her.

Cassandra's fingers strayed to the phoenix torque around her neck, caressing the fine pattern of feathers. It was Max's, *gra'if* made from his blood, and at this moment strangely warm under her caress, tingling somehow, as if—a RUSH! of displaced air, and Max was standing next to her. He smiled, as he always did when he saw her, but his green eyes were clouded. She raised her brows.

"Nighthawk has returned from the Shadowlands, and has news you must hear." For Max to speak so formally, the news must be serious indeed.

Cassandra turned to look around her. "Farewell, *Feena'en*, I will not forget the Water." She took Max's hand in hers, and they Moved.

"As I see it," Alejandro began as he handed me an umbrella and picked up his walking stick. "There are two possible sources of danger. The Hunt, and a combination of the Hunt and the Basilisk Prince's Riders. So we must take every precaution.

My stomach fluttered. I grounded the point of the umbrella firmly on the front hall carpet and stood up straighter. I reminded myself that what we were about to do was my idea. "Which do you think is more likely?"

Alejandro shrugged. "We must deal in possibilities, not likelihoods. No one has ever died of taking precautions. And you are my *fara'ip*."

His family, he meant. His chosen family that is, not his family by blood, though the closest we humans have to it is what we call blood brotherhood. In his particular case it also meant "all I have left," which some people might have found scary, or too clingy and controlling. With someone else it might have been, but with Alejandro all I'd ever felt was the love.

As we stepped out of our enclosed front porch onto the concrete front steps, we were greeted by the enthusiastic barking of a small dark gray dog. We found our right-hand neighbor, Barb, standing on her own front steps with an open letter in her hand. There was a crooked line between her eyebrows.

"Can we be of assistance, *señora*?" Alejandro at his most courtly.

Barb looked up and smiled. "Thanks, but no. It's good news, really, though a bit screwy." She waved the letter. "A friend I haven't heard from in a while."

"A Spanish stamp, if I am not mistaken."

With her mind still on the letter, Barb glanced at the envelope and handed it over to Alejandro, who took it with genuine interest. *Postmarked Madrid*, I thought, brushing it with my fingertips. [Pale women with honey-gold hair and gray eyes; flashing blades; weird pen, weirder paper; two letters.] Barb was a little more relieved than her behavior indicated. Apparently, her friend had vanished about three months before without leaving much of a message, and this was the first time she'd heard from her.

"I'll have to let them know at the dojo." Barb stood there tapping the refolded letter against the edge of her hand, her gaze focused in the middle distance. Put together with what I'd gotten from the letter itself, it was obvious she was debating whether to call them. There was no way I could tell her a second letter had already reached the dojo.

"A dojo?" Alejandro recalled Barb's attention by handing her back the envelope. "A martial arts academy?"

Barb waved the letter again. "My friend's part owner. So it's likely they've got a letter of their own, but she doesn't say so." Her forehead creased. "They'll be needing another fencing master, that's for sure." She blinked, suddenly realizing that she'd been doing a lot of her thinking aloud, and with a roll of her eyes for apology and a smiling "seeya later," she disappeared into her enclosed front porch, her small dog at her heels.

Alejandro and I checked our own mailbox (just flyers) and went down the walkway and across the street, angling to the corner so we could walk down Elmer to Queen, where we were planning to take the 501 streetcar. We were meeting Nik Polihronidis at the Union Station subway stop, and Alejandro wanted to use a route we hadn't used before.

He was very quiet as we made our way to Queen Street, and I waited until we were standing at the streetcar stop before I asked him what was on his mind.

"You'd like to apply for that fencing job, wouldn't you?" I said.

"That shows you the limits of English. Anyone would think I were a carpenter." He kept his eyes focused down the street, as if he could make the streetcar materialize by force of will. On the other hand, maybe he could.

I shook my head and smiled. "You've got credentials, haven't you?" The streetcar arrived and we left the sidewalk, crossing the short section of roadway between us and the opening doors. Rush hour was over, and we were able to get two seats together close to the rear doors.

"Alejandro Martín has no such credentials." He tapped himself on the chest. "My fencing credentials are much older, and for a man who has not existed in over a century." He spoke quietly, even though there was no one close enough to overhear us. "The international fencing community is smaller than you think. A psychologist like yourself, my dear, might be created out of thin air, but a fencing master must, at some point, have been seen physically."

Over the years, Alejandro had used more identities than he could readily remember. So I wasn't too surprised that every now and then he'd mention one I'd never heard of before.

"What will you do, then?"

"You mean, what *would* I do, *if* I were going to apply for this work?"

I rolled my eyes. "Fine, what *would* you do?"

"Offer to fence with whoever is currently the dojo champion." His smile was a beautiful thing to see.

"And would that work?"

He shot me a look out of the side of his eyes. "You wound me, my angel, by even pretending to doubt it."

I grinned, and hugged the backpack I had in my lap. "So why is it only what you *would* do, and not what you *will* do?"

He managed to shrug without brushing against me. His eyes were focused to the front again. I thought I was going to have to touch him to get an answer when he finally spoke.

"How can we undertake other commitments until we have discharged the one we have now before us?"

I pressed my lips together and stared out of the window. Other commitments. Alejandro was only in Toronto because of me, to help me find my family. I was a bit chagrined to find out it was only now occurring to me that I'd taken Alejandro away from his life and the place he loved.

I thought about how determined I'd felt when I'd seen that strange man on the subway, and I remembered how exhilarated I'd felt leaving the Christie Institute. I realized that was how I still felt, determined and exhilarated. Oh, yeah, and scared.

"I hope Alejandro knows what he's doing," Nik helped me shift my backpack to a more comfortable spot. "I don't like using you as bait."

"Yeah, well, we've been through that, and if you don't have any better ideas now than you did last night, can we get on with it?"

Nik raised his eyebrows at me in such a way that I knew he guessed how nervous I was. I shrugged and looked away. We were standing just inside the subway station, below street level, with the entrance to Union Station's food court across the lane from us. According to Nik, there were a lot of sightings of the Hunt around Union Station, which had made sense to Alejandro, considering both the crossroads and the Portal were there. There were thousands of crossroads, but only nine Portals. Why they were *where* they were, was something even Alejandro didn't know.

"We need to find out what we're up against, so Alejandro can figure out which of the hidden People is most likely to help us. We already know the bad guys are showing interest in me," I said. "So I'm the one they're most likely to follow."

"Yeah, yeah. And if they follow you, then we'll know who and what they are. I know the plan, I just don't like it."

I bit my lip and eyed the station entrance. Alejandro was already inside. Nik would come in after me. Nik's people—both people *like* him, and people *with* him—were inside as well, and though I didn't know all of them, they'd seen photos of me.

"Got your umbrella?"

I hefted it. As if he couldn't see perfectly well that I had.

"Don't let anyone touch you," Nik said. I remembered what I'd seen inside Elaine and nodded.

"What if no one follows me?" I said.

"Oh, I'm pretty sure *someone* will follow you." I heard the smile in Nik's voice and turned toward him in time to catch it on his face. "In fact, I'd be surprised if they didn't."

I rolled my eyes. It was silly, I know, but I was feeling better as I set off.

Because he was looking for it, Alejandro saw almost immediately that half a dozen men and women were not wandering randomly through the concourse, but were casting back and forth through the crowd in a subtle pattern that left no entrance or exit unwatched. These would be Nik's friends and followers, the ones he had called and made arrangements with the night before. Now that he had noticed them, it was clear they were equally aware of him, and that they were avoiding coming near.

And here came Valory, punctual and precise, from the direction of the subway entrance. She kept her pace steady, just quick enough not to impede the other pedestrians, but slow enough that she didn't gain on anyone. Alejandro was pretending to look at a collection of wallets in the small luggage shop—one of which seemed to exist in every train station and airport in the world. He allowed Valory to pass him and get perhaps twenty-five paces ahead before drifting along behind her, letting his eyes wander as if he were either bored or lost in thought.

Today there was nothing noteworthy or eye-catching in Valory's dress or appearance, no designer suit or four-inch heels—nothing, in other words that should make ordinary people notice, let alone follow her. Valory seemed a perfectly ordinary girl, her chestnut hair bouncing in a ponytail, her angular features striking rather than pretty. Khaki trousers, trainers, peach T-shirt with matching hoodie, backpack slung over one shoulder, mobile in her hand.

The roving pack of watchers changed their pattern slightly, letting her pass unmolested, but incorporating her, making her the center. If Valory noticed them, she gave no sign. She walked entirely without self-consciousness. The years she had spent with the Collector were those in which a young woman normally begins to feel her power over men—something of which, Alejandro reflected, Valory had indeed learned, though not in the usual way, nor with the usual results. She was more watchful, more skeptical than was usual in woman of her age.

Alejandro had been afraid at first that because of her years of isolation, and her singular ability, she would not be able to go out among people, especially in a crowded modern city such as Madrid or Toronto. But the press of people had been no trouble to her; she preferred crowds, in fact, and was probably feeling more comfortable here and now than Alejandro was himself. She diligently followed the route through Union Station that they had outlined for her, starting from the subway entrance, through the shopping concourse into the train station proper, angling into the embarking area, then up into the great hall, down the far stairs—

Alejandro straightened. A man was standing off to one side, leaning against the now-deserted information desk under the central clock. His eyes trailed, seemingly unfocused, over the heads of the people passing, but in reality noting each one, as if checking them off on a mental list, though none received more than glancing attention. But when Valory walked by, the man's head lifted, and his nostrils flared. He turned his head to keep his eyes on her as she passed.

One of the wandering watchers gave the agreed-upon signal, but Alejandro was already in motion. As Valory moved farther away, the man pushed off from the edge of the desk and began to pace behind her, maintaining his distance, but keeping her always in sight.

Rider, Alejandro thought. It was unmistakable, now that the man was moving. Not a Hound. Alejandro did not know all of the People who had remained in the Shadowlands when the Exile began—but he knew every Rider, and this one was a stranger. One of the Basilisk's crew, then, and therefore to be caught in their trap.

This was the part Nikos Polihronidis had not liked, the part that Valory had insisted would work. Mindful of her desire not to be smothered with protections, Alejandro had stifled his own protests. Valory had reached the staircase. Alejandro waited until he was certain the strange Rider was following her out of the Station, and when he was sure . . . he Moved.

In the side of the overpass that lay on the west side of the train station was an alcove, a narrow space with an access door chained and padlocked at the rear. Alejandro had scouted the place carefully, he knew every crack in the concrete, especially the one where water seeped, every ripple of paint on the old steel door, the number of links in the chain, the brand name still faintly visible on the padlock. Ah, he had forgotten the odor of urine (strong) and of vomit (faint). Just as well. He stood as far back in the shadow created by the alcove as he could. Valory walked by the opening, not revealing in any way that she sensed his presence—or perhaps, he reflected, she actually did not. He was not sure, even now, precisely how her talent functioned. Surely, though, she knew he was already there. He called upon his Guidebeast, the Hippogriff, to steady his hands, and crossed himself automatically, grinning when he realized what he'd done.

Footsteps approached and he readied himself. It was not the man who had been following Valory, but a younger, darker-haired man who evidently thought himself too cool to remove his sunglasses, even in the obscurity of the overpass. For a moment Alejandro thought he was mistaken, that this young man was the Rider he'd seen following Valory. But no, the coloring was wrong entirely.

Next came two young girls walking in the opposite direction, one on her mobile, and both giggling. The one nearest him shot him a steady look as they passed. Outsiders. Then a long-legged dog, white, wiry-haired with liver-colored markings, entered Alejandro's field of vision.

He almost missed it, he was letting it go by him, but in the last second it turned to him and grinned, showing all its teeth and he stepped out from his shadow, twisting the handle on his walking stick as he moved, drawing the *gra'if* blade out of the wooden shaft, slashing downward with one smooth stroke and slicing deep into the thing's shoulder. The Hound spun on its paws, paws that were changing to clawed feet even as it turned.

It grew abruptly to five times its previous size, retaining its dog shape, though grotesquely misshapen and scarred as if by burns. This was definitely a Hound, not a Rider—where had it come from? Did the Rider Alejandro had seen somehow send it after Valory?

It leaped upon him, and Alejandro had no more time to speculate, barely meeting its lunge with the cutting edge of his sword. Just in time he remembered the advice Nighthawk had once given him and looked away from its eyes, keeping his focus on the claws, and the teeth. His hands and feet moved automatically with the precision and grace polished by centuries in fields of battle, and the sands of the bullring.

He struck, and the dog shape became a furred and armored lizard, tongue darting from its mouth. Ignore the changes, he'd been taught, and keep striking, no matter what you see. The thing morphed again, and Alejandro raised his blade high, stepping lightly to one side, arching his body as he had done so many thousands of times avoiding the bull's horns in *corridas*. And just as he had done then, he jabbed at the shoulders, weakening the muscles there to make it lower its head. Feeling his own heart racing, and his breath coming short, striving to take air in slowly, to keep his hands steady. If only he himself could transform, if only he had *dra'aj* enough, he could take to the air and kill it from above.

Then he saw it, the dip of the shoulder, the head hanging—just for a split second—at the right angle, and in that fraction of an instant he moved, faster than he had ever done in the *Plaza de Toros*, leaping up from his toes and leaning into the thrust, the full length of the blade passing through muscle, past bone, into the lungs and heart.

He stepped forward as it fell, unwilling to let go of the sword, though it went against every tradition. Only when he felt the sting of a claw against the meat of his calf did he step back, withdrawing the blade. The Hound changed again, and again, almost rippling as its body settled onto the ground. Finally, it took the form of a man and Faded completely, leaving not a mark on the ground, only the blood dripping from Alejandro's blade.

And trickling down the back of his leg.

Wolf peered out through the building's smoked glass wall, realizing that the girl out in the sun-filled square wasn't standing on the faint trail of Rider he'd been following all morning, The trail ended where she stood. It was *her* trail. Impossible. For a moment the world seemed to shift around him, as it did when passing through a Ring. Was he losing his ability to track? Ordinarily, that idea might have pleased him, now that he was no longer a— He pushed that thought away.

Wolf examined her more closely. Trousers the color of sand. A sweater with a hood in an odd shade of orange. Canvas-topped, rubber-soled shoes. A backpack hitched on one shoulder. Not particularly tall for a human female, she was a little too thin, he thought. Her chestnut hair reminded him of the women he'd seen in Spain, where the color was popular. He stepped out into the sun. She glanced toward him, seemed about to smile, but then looked away.

The girl appeared about to take a step back in the direction from which they'd come, at the same time looking around her and lifting the mobile phone she held in her left hand to her face. Between one breath and the next Wolf was behind her, his left arm pinning her arms to her sides, his right hand covering her mouth. She smelled very faintly of vanilla.

"Who are you?" he asked. "*What* are you?"

[The rough heat of a lion's breath, the slash of a scaled tail. A Chimera. A gray-eyed woman, whom he loves, and fears—though not as much as he fears himself. Guilt, old and new; and anger; and fear.]

The images crashed against me—[flash of bright metal; swing of claw] thick, choking, like waves crashing against rocks. I struggled—not physically, though I was sure I was doing that, too—to hold my head, my *self*, up, away from the blanketing tide. [Place after place, beach, hillside, trees, pond, snow, lightning, stonewallrainsunshine-sandrocktidewater; I AM *HERE!*] I'd felt this before, with Alejandro, I knew what it was. But Alejandro, that first time, had shaken my hand and let me go, and this guy, this Rider, this *STORM* was holding me tight.

I focused on that, I focused on the physical, as if I were really drowning. On the arm tight around my body, and the hand against my mouth. On the hard body pressed tight against mine. On the warm cinnamon smell. I squirmed in his grip. A *very* hard body.

The tide started to recede, the white noise of the city rising up to cushion me. I should have felt too warm standing this close to him, but I didn't. It felt *just right*. When it occurred to me I shouldn't be thinking about baby bear's bed at that moment, I knew my psyche was mine again.

The terror of the moment when he touched me faded, helped somehow by his voice. There was music somewhere in it, as if he was reciting verse, or as if he'd just left off singing, and his voice still rang with it. I'd known at once that he was a Rider [I AM HERE!], but maybe at one time he'd been an actor, the way Alejandro had been a soldier and a matador. There was nothing frightening in the warmth and strength of his body, or even in the way his psyche brushed against mine. [His shoes/jeans/T-shirt/jacket were really boots/trousers/mail shirt/tunic.] It was only that the suddenness, the grabbing, the hand over my mouth, had startled me. It didn't, as you might think, remind the little girl inside me of the man who took me. *That* had happened in my sleep.

I stopped squirming. There *was* a hot fury in this Rider, but it wasn't directed at me, it was pointed somewhere else, perhaps at the gray-eyed woman who was so important to him, perhaps at himself. [Umbrella hooked to his belt really a sword.] The lion part of the Chimera was very close to the surface in him, very strong, very hot, but if I just waited for a minute, he would calm down and listen.

My heart still hammering, I tried to relax, drew air in through my nose, willing him to figure out that I couldn't answer his questions while his hand was over my mouth. He was confused [Riders; the trail; the scent; he was worried about his brother], wondering who I was and why I smelled like a Rider, but so faint, so very faint, like a trail almost cold. He'd been sent to find Riders, to give them good news. He was pleased about it [the news], but somehow saddened by it [the sending] at the same time. His hand relaxed.

I was just about to ask him who he was when a bright light flashed in the corner of my vision and sharp bangs exploded all around us. I was shoved roughly from behind, two hands against my shoulder blades [a rescue! Knock the Hound on the ground; save her!]. Before I could speak to clarify things, there was a CRACK! of displaced air, much louder than the bangs of the firecrackers, and suddenly we weren't in the square anymore.

Alejandro could see Valory as he ran into the square. The Outsiders were with her and he started to relax, until he saw she was being held by a dark-haired man—the man in sunglasses!—and the others were trying to get her away from him. Just as he reached the outskirts of the group, he heard—and felt—the shift of air as the dark-haired stranger Moved, and he and Valory were gone.

Nik Polihronidis ran from the back entrance of the train station just as Alejandro raised his sword. "That supposed to help?" The Outsider leader turned his back on Alejandro.

"What happened here? Where's Valory?"

"It took her, the Hound took her."

"I killed the Hound," Alejandro said. "You see its blood on my blade." The blood dripped, falling toward the ground, but never reaching it.

"Oh, like there's only ever one Hound." This from a tall man with a faint French accent.

"Yeah, they're called the Hunt for a reason, you know. They range in packs," said the young girl who had looked at him as he stood in the alcove.

Like Riders. There was something in that thought that bothered him, reminded him of something, but Alejandro pushed it aside, impatient that his mind could go wandering at a time like this.

"Where is she, then?"

"Like I said, it took her. The other Hound." The girl slapped her hands together in a sharp crack. "Like that."

Alejandro shook his head. "The Hunt cannot Move." He looked at Nik, but there was no answer in the other man's face. Riders. Hounds. The one following Valory had looked like a Rider at first, and then again at the end. What did it mean?

"I knew this was a bad idea, I should never have listened to you. *Riders.*" Nik spat the word like a curse. "As if you ever gave a damn about humans."

"Do you dare? She is my *fara'ip*. She is blood of my blood, bone of my bone. Who harms her, harms me."

"Really? 'Cause you look fine to me." The French-sounding one was standing close enough that Alejandro could see his beard forming close under his skin.

"Let me remind you that it was you came to me for help," Alejandro said, his voice as quiet and cold as his *gra'if.*"

A family—mother, father, and two preteen children—came out of the train station entrance. They were each wearing a sunhat, and their backpacks all had a bottle of water in the outside pocket. The parents glanced over, and without other reaction began to herd the children faster toward the entrance to the Air Canada Centre. The kids were talking about what they would get at the official NBA store, and did not seem to notice the gang of armed individuals standing in the open square.

Alejandro made an effort to calm his breathing. All was not yet lost. It had been a Rider who had taken Valory, not a Hound. "This is not the place to take council," he said. He took a handkerchief out of his pocket and wiped off his blade very meticulously and thoroughly before sliding it back into the wooden body of his walking stick.

"Any ideas on what we should do now?" The tone in Nik Polihronidis' voice was like a lash on Alejandro's back.

Alejandro looked at the cloth with distaste, before glancing at the human, right eyebrow raised. "Has anyone a match?" At his simple question, some of the tension began to ease from the air.

The young girl standing behind Nik handed Alejandro a pink plastic lighter. He burned the cloth, making sure that there was nothing but ash left. This gave them all further time to calm themselves.

"So where were you, then?" Nik said.

"I was killing the Hound," Alejandro said again. His tone was even, but he felt the heat underneath it. "You saw the blood on my sword. If you know so much, you know what blood it was." Alejandro narrowed his gaze. "That was no Hound that took my Valory." There was heat in his voice. "That was a Rider. *Hounds do not Move*."

Nik swallowed. "Okay," he said, and Alejandro understood that it was, in its way, an apology. "Okay. So what now?"

It was an honest question this time, and not a provocation, but Alejandro felt no better.

His mobile rang. There were only two people who could have the number. Backing away from them, Alejandro pulled the vibrating phone out of his jacket pocket and looked at the display.

Valory.

It was Dogfang who came to report, changing repeatedly as he approached, unable to keep his Rider form long enough to speak. Excitement, Foxblood wondered, or was he badly in need of *dra'aj*? Strange how quickly they were all becoming accustomed to their stable shapes.

"Go, eat something," he said. "And make it quick. Send me someone who can speak." The other scampered off, first on two legs, then four, then three. Fox looked down at his own hands, as they (flicker) became hairless paws, the claws thick and twisted (flicker) talons dull with age, (flicker) pincers, leathery and cracked (flicker) hands, the fingers long and perfect.

A change in the air, and Hook came in.

"Pack Leader," she said. Her Rider form flickered for an instant, almost like a tic, and then settled down again.

"Where's Claw? Why doesn't he bring the report?"

"He's gone, he is." This came out in a long hiss, and Fox frowned. Hook should be able to control herself better than this. He stood suddenly, taking her by the throat, lifting her into the air and giving her a shake before he threw her to the ground.

"Do you think that's an answer?" he said, letting the growl come out in his own throat. The other (flicker) became something long and scaly, and (flicker) was a Rider again. She stayed on her knees, though, one hand to her throat.

"He's Faded, Pack Leader. The old Rider, the Sunward one who keeps the girl, came with a *gra'if* blade and took him. But not without being marked, Claw—" she grinned, and her teeth were sharp. "He clawed him, for sure."

The first thought that blasted its way through the haze of rage that followed this news was "more for me" but Foxblood did his best to shake it off. That wasn't a useful thought, no matter how true it might be. There was so much *dra'aj* here for the taking that the Hunt would never need to fight and turn on each other for it ever again.

Right now one less meant fewer warriors, not more *dra'aj*.

A thought flashed clearly in his brain. Would they still be Hounds, if their hunger was always fed?

"There's more, Pack Leader."

Fox blinked. He'd almost forgotten Hook was still there. "You know where the girl is?"

"No, not yet," the other Hound said. "But another Rider turned up in the dark last night."

"Sure it wasn't the same one?" At this Hook bristled, and Foxblood grinned. Like any of them could be fooled when smell told them so much.

"He's a Moonward," Hook asserted. "Not the Sunward who keeps the girl. But he's familiar somehow. Like as if we'd smelled him already."

"Another of the Basilisk's ass sniffers?" Fox's hand strayed to his upper lip. If it was in the same condition as Longshadow, okay, but if it wasn't? Maybe this one could tell him what had happened to his brother.

But Hook was shaking her head. "No. Not one of those. Maybe you should look at him yourself, see if you know him."

Fox sat down again. Who could the strange Rider be, with his familiar but unknown scent?

Chapter Five

"WHAT ARE YOU," the strange Rider asked me again.

"I'm human." I grimaced at the squeak in my voice and tried to swallow. My lips felt bruised and my jaw stiff. "I have a Rider ancestor, but a long way back. That's what you smell." I wondered what more to tell him. He *had* been following what he thought of as my trail, but he'd never seen me before today, so he wasn't the one I'd seen in the subway car, and he wasn't the one Nik and the Outsiders had noticed. It was then I started to wonder where Alejandro was.

The Rider's grip loosened enough that I could turn in his arms to face him, though he kept hold of my upper arms. My heart was beating fast, and I could feel myself blushing, but I wasn't at all afraid. He had pale, perfect skin. Pale as almond. Hair black as sloes, eyes gray as ash and still retaining heat. A Moonward Rider, I realized, though I had never seen one. I knew there were three Wards, Star, Moon, and Sun, but so far I'd only seen Alejandro.

The room was so much darker than the sun-filled square we'd Moved from that it took a minute for my eyes to adjust. Now I could see there was scarring around this Rider's right eye [bird claws] that was matched elsewhere on his body. I swallowed. I couldn't remember ever being this aware of anyone physically before, and I was hoping he couldn't hear my heart. He was studying me as closely as I was studying him. I started to breathe faster.

He stepped back from me, and the *pushing* against my psyche was gone. We were standing in the middle of a large rectangular room. A dining table and chairs took up the far end, close to the windows, and there was a fireplace in the center of the long wall on my right, with two wing-backed chairs drawn up to it. A low table divided them, and the one on the right also had a smaller, round table on its other side. A book sat on it, with a slip of paper marking the place where the reader had left off.

Not the Rider, I thought. That book had been sitting there, abandoned, for quite some time.

"You are not afraid of me." His voice growled. "At least, not any longer."

"Well, no. You thought you were saving me from those others—not that I was in any danger from them—in fact, they thought they were saving me from you. You have questions to ask me." I was babbling. I pressed my lips together, shocked at myself, and feeling the blush spread over my face. "You're not going to hurt me." *At least, not on purpose.* But I didn't say that part aloud.

"And how do you know this?" He looked down at his hands then, as if he thought they would turn into something else.

My knees felt wobbly, so I sat down on the arm of the nearest wing-backed chair, letting my backpack slide to the floor at my feet. "I'm psychic, I know things about people," I said. "True things." I was a little surprised that I told him so easily what I took pains to hide from other people. I picked up the book. "This doesn't belong to you. It belongs to a gray-eyed Rider, with honey-gold hair. A Starward." The same one who'd written the letter to my neighbor Barb, I realized with a shock, the same gray-eyed woman I'd seen when I touched him; the one he loved and feared. "She was very sad when she was reading this, but not because of the book. There's a dragon around her, and she's not sad anymore, is she?"

"A Truthreader." The Rider immediately cut his eyes away, focusing on the small figure of a dragon, crudely pinched out of clay as if by a child's fingers, that sat on the mantel of the fireplace. As if he thought that I couldn't read him if I wasn't looking into his eyes.

I took this chance to get a more complete look at him, since I hadn't been able to until now. I knew what he smelled of [cinnamon] and the feel of his palm against my lips [smooth], and the hardness of his arms and body, but not much more.

He was taller than Alejandro, and younger-looking, though I knew that didn't necessarily mean anything. Touching him, he'd seemed very old, and much younger at the same time. It had something to do with a change he'd gone through recently, but none of the images that had poured through me told me any more.

He looked pale in the dim light that filtered through the sheers, but then, I imagined I looked pretty pale myself. His mouth was wide, the lips generous and, just at the moment, turned down at the corners. His ash-gray eyes were wide over high cheekbones, and when he stepped closer, I again saw the scarring around the right one. There was something significant about that, I realized. Most Riders healed without scarring, so for this guy to show marks . . . I found myself half reaching out to touch him again, just to see what I could find out.

I gave myself a shake, and pulled back my hand. What was I thinking?

"What truth do you know about me?" His voice was low, and the growl was still there. The hair rose on the back of my neck and on my arms, and I had to remind myself that I wasn't in any danger.

"You're a Rider," I said. [The gray-eyed female Rider; the letter.] "And just now a messenger. Something important has happened, something that changes the world as you know it. That's the message you bring." *And you're alone*. I caught my breath. He was afraid of going [being] insane. Riders rode together with others, in troops. It was dangerous for them to be alone.

Alejandro—but Alejandro wasn't alone, I thought, nodding to myself. He'd always had his family, his *fara'ip*, as he now had me. But this guy, all he had was the gray-eyed Rider he feared [loved].

"I don't know your name, but your Guidebeast has some lion it in."

"I am Stormwolf," he said. "The Chimera guides me."

I admit, I shivered a little then. Chimeras. Not your pretty fairy-tale Guidebeast.

"I am sent by the Dragonborn Prince."

The air around us changed when he said those words. Maybe it was just the way he said them. As if they were charged with some special meaning beyond the simple words. Special for him, in particular.

"I don't know that one." I swallowed and wondered if I could ask for a glass of water. "I know about the Basilisk Prince."

"The Basilisk is no more. The one known as Truthsheart, daughter of Clear of Light, and guided by the Dragon, is acclaimed High Prince."

I thought about what Alejandro had explained to me, and frowned. Images were trying to organize themselves in my mind, but—

"Would you mind?" I said, I took a step closer to Stormwolf and held out my hand. He hesitated, but he must have known what I wanted, or else they had a similar custom in the Lands, because he took my hand as if to shake it, though all he did was hold it firmly.

I was expecting the warmth, but not how comforting it felt. And I was surprised at how he shut his eyes tight, and turned his head away, like a dog that expects to be smacked.

It was easier this time, but still shocking enough to take my breath away and make me cling to his wrist with my other hand. Most of what I read I already knew. This was the end of the story that Alejandro had told me, the story of the Guardian Prince's exile, and the Warden who saved him by taking him through the Portals. I saw a Phoenix, and a Sword and a Spear and a Cauldron and a Rock—*Ma'at?*—and a Basilisk destroyed in a Dragon's fire. So now all was as it should be back in the Lands. Or would be soon. Everyone safe and sound.

Well, everyone except Stormwolf, that is. Sometimes even I forget that I also see the truths people don't know about themselves—as well as the things they know, but are trying to hide. I'm not sure how to describe it, but there was a part of Stormwolf that cringed away from me, as if I were shining a spotlight on him that was too bright to handle. Even though now he was looking at me, right into my eyes with his outer self, it was another matter inside. Inside, he was still turned away. Inside, he was ashamed.

[Inside, he was a Hound.]

I caught myself before I could pull my hand away, I don't think even he noticed it. He wasn't a Hound now, but he had been one, and part of him thought he always would be. She had saved him, the High Prince, and he loved her for it—though her ability, the *power* that made her able to save him, frightened him a little. He loved her for saving him, and trusting him. But he was also very much afraid the trust might be misplaced, that the Hound part of him might come out and destroy him again—and others along with him.

He was angry, too, at himself, and at her—though he wasn't *ever* going to admit that part—because he still had the skills of the Hunt, and she was asking him to use them. These skills set him apart from everyone else, but they were useful skills. Boy, did I know how *that* felt.

I had a useful skill myself. A skill that set me apart from everyone else. So useful I'd been Collected. A liability, until Alejandro had rescued me.

And I couldn't tell anyone any of this, I realized. I couldn't even tell Alejandro. He wouldn't believe that Stormwolf was no danger to us—he'd chase him away. And a part of Stormwolf would accept that as deserved, and I couldn't let that happen. His wound was too fresh. He needed more time, or he would throw away everything the High Prince had done for him. So I had to lie to my friend, my friend who'd saved me, in order to maybe help save someone else. I told myself Alejandro would understand.

Alejandro. Oh, crap. I felt in my pocket and looked around for my knapsack. "Where's my mobile?"

"He's telling the truth," I said. "We can trust him." Alejandro had met me in the lobby, half overjoyed to see me safe, half furious that I had scared him so badly, even though it wasn't my fault.

"No, not possible that you can trust any of these guys, *mademoiselle*." The tall man with Alejandro, his voice softened by his French accent, gave his name as Yves Crepeau. He was dressed in business casual, as if he worked in one of the glass-walled office buildings nearby and was on his coffee break. Like Nik, he was older than he looked. Much older. I got a familiar jigsaw puzzle vibe from him, so I knew right away what he was. His eyes kept drifting away as he spoke, but not as though he found the hotel lobby interesting. And the whole time he was rubbing his left index finger with his right hand, as if there was a mark there he wanted to rub away.

Nik had sent him with Alejandro, instead of coming himself. That couldn't be good.

"He's not a Hound," I said, frowning at him. "He's another Rider." Here, Yves snorted and the corner of his mouth twisted up. I turned to focus on Alejandro. "And not one of the Basilisk's. He's got news, good news."

Yves had drifted along with us as far as the elevators, but refused to go up. "I don't need to see this fellow," he said. "Just to see you're okay. I'll tell Nik. He says call him if you need him." He looked at Alejandro and pressed his lips together before shrugging.

"Wait," I said. I didn't like his color, and if anything his eyes seemed more unfocused now, dropping away from mine as if he lacked the strength to keep them looking at me. On impulse, I reached out and took hold of his right wrist. He stopped rubbing, but didn't pull away. Again, the jigsaw puzzle feel, but the pieces were starting to scatter. There was something missing. *Dra'aj*, I thought. A moment ago there had been enough of it; now, it was seeping away.

I transferred my hand to his shoulder. "You need help," I said. "Soon. Is Nik nearby?"

"Sure, outside."

Then why hadn't he come in? "Go to him. Yves? Look at me." I waited until he met my eyes. "Go to Nik right now," I said, trying not to shake him.

"I know. You don't have to tell me." He didn't sound particularly interested, but as I watched Yves walk away, I was satisfied. This had happened to him before, many times. He might one day let it go too far, wait too long. But not today.

The elevator came, and we stepped in. As we rose to the top floor, I filled Alejandro in on what I'd learned—not everything, just what Stormwolf had told me about the new High Prince.

Stormwolf was still standing in the middle of the room, as if he hadn't moved since I'd left him to fetch Alejandro.

"So. Moonward one." Alejandro's voice was as sharp as his sword. Oh, crap. I'd forgotten all about this animosity between the Wards. This was the last thing I needed to deal with just now.

"I am Stormwolf." His voice was low, and the growl was back. Again I found myself wanting to step back from him, but forced myself to stay where I was. "My mother was Rain at Sunset, and the Chimera guides me."

"I am Graycloud at Moonrise. Starwalker was my mother, and the Hippogriff guides me," Alejandro said. "I do not know your mother, Moonward one."

Alejandro was formally telling Stormwolf that they'd never met. I guess when you lived as long as these guys did, that kind of thing was necessary.

"Nor I yours," Stormwolf said, which was the response Alejandro expected.

I was beginning to see that this meeting wasn't working out the way I'd hoped.

"So they were wrong, these Outsiders, you are not a Hound. You are some other tool of the Basilisk, no doubt," Alejandro put in. "Perhaps even he who called the Hound I killed."

My mouth fell open as I rolled my eyes. Alejandro hadn't heard a word I'd said to him in the elevator. "He has nothing to do with the Basilisk Prince, Alejandro."

Alejandro turned toward me without taking his eyes from the other Rider. "Perhaps. There *was* a Hound following you, but out of curiosity only, it was not set on your trail." His eyes narrowed. "I did not know it was a Hound until I saw the dog shape. How was it able to retain the semblance of a Rider for so long?" There was no mistaking the accusation in Alejandro's voice.

And there was no mistaking the look of confusion that passed over Stormwolf's face. Anyone would have seen it. Anyone except Alejandro, that is.

"I might ask you that question, *Sunward*." Wolf spat the word out like a curse. "Did anyone see this Hound but yourself?" Stormwolf stalked several paces forward, and Alejandro took hold of his sword cane in both hands, ready to pull out the blade.

"There is no Dragonborn Prince," he said.

"There *was* no Dragonborn Prince," Stormwolf said.

"Wait, wait." I put my hand on Alejandro's arm. "He's telling the—"

Alejandro shook me off with an abrupt jerk. Shock more than anything else made me take a step back.

I could *feel* the force of their conflict, like a fourth presence in the room. This had happened to me before—emotions running so high and so hot that they swept over me like a blast of hot wind in an air-conditioned room, bringing the grit and smells of the outside. For a moment I stood frozen, as if I was still with the Collector, as if I had no option but to wait until the storm subsided. Then I remembered who and where and when I was, and I started walking.

I must have been at the elevator before they even realized I was gone.

What really annoyed me was that I had nowhere to go but the house. We hadn't been living in Toronto long enough for me to have found a place I went to think things over, and I wasn't disposed to just wander the streets, not now that I knew what might be out there. I shivered. Touching him, I'd caught the echo of what Alejandro had killed and it hadn't quite left me.

If we had been at home—and I realized I still thought of Madrid that way, the only real home I'd had since I'd been taken—I would have gone to the Retiro, or to my favorite corner of the Plaza Mayor, and Alejandro would have come, eventually, to find me. I guess that was the real reason I was going to the house now.

I let the doorman at the Royal York's entrance put me in a cab, and concentrated on not picking up too much from the last person who'd sat in the backseat. Just the same, I might almost have welcomed someone else's psyche at that moment. I was glad to be in public, even if only in a cab, with the excuse it gave me to control myself. I wanted to push my hands into my hair and grab tight. I was so frustrated, tears kept brimming up into my eyes. I could feel them at the edge of my lids, and only my clenched jaw and tilted head kept them from spilling over.

I actually pulled out my mobile and found Nik's number, but I didn't call him. I didn't even send a text. Call me if you need anything, he'd said, and then he'd sent Yves instead of coming himself.

Wolf and Alejandro had been focused so closely on each other that both of them had stopped listening to me, stopped paying any real attention to me at all. And yet they were only in the same room together because of me.

That was what frustrated me. Neither of them had been willing to listen, and I was the only person who actually had the answers both of them wanted—at least the Collector had listened to what I had to say.

I stiffened, enough that the cabbie glanced at me in his rearview mirror. The smile I gave him must have looked halfway normal, and he turned his attention back to the road. I shivered and hunched my shoulders as a chill ran its fingers up my spine and took hold of the back of my neck. Was I really comparing Alejandro to the man who took me from my parents? Who used me as a lie detector and a spy? Being with Alejandro was *nothing* like that. Nonhuman though he was, Alejandro actually had my welfare at heart, my real welfare, not just how my health and happiness made his life easier.

So what had come over him this afternoon? It couldn't be it just the Sunward/Moonward thing. Could it?

The cab had pulled up in front of our house and I had to apologize as I searched through my wallet for the fare. I hopped out and went down the lane between our house and Barb's, letting myself in through the gate. I was just resetting the latch when there was a SLAP! of displaced air and Alejandro was there, his arms around me.

"I am so sorry, my dear one," he said. "Please forgive me."

I backed off, my hand on his chest, until I could look him in the eye. "No." My voice trembled, but I had to make a stand. "You're sorry I got so upset. But you're not sorry for upsetting me. You don't believe you did."

Alejandro released me and took a step back himself, squeezing his eyes shut and holding the tips of his thumb and index finger to his brow, as if he felt a migraine coming on.

My anger flared up again and I shook my head, long slow swings from left to right. "You believe I know *you*," I said finally. "So why don't you believe I know *him*?"

"It is not that I do not believe you," Alejandro said. "It is that you may be mistaken."

The calm I'd gained from my trip home vanished in a heartbeat, and I felt all hot with anger and disappointment. I propped myself against the patio table, my arms crossed in front of me. I know my face didn't show very much, but Alejandro must have felt something; he moved away and sat on the edge of the small deck at the back of our house.

"Since *when* might I be mistaken?" Finally, my throat unlocked enough to let me speak. "Am I mistaken about you? Was I mistaken about the Collector?"

He was in front of me, his hands on my shoulders—gently, very deliberately *not* drawing me into his arms, though that was what he wanted to do. I was so upset I actually got a read on him, as if he had another self superimposed on him.

"My dear one, no. *Querida*, no. You are not mistaken about me. You are my *fara'ip*, my own blood. I will never harm you."

Not knowingly—but to be fair, that amendment was only in my own head, not in him. No one can guarantee that they won't hurt you by accident—or that they won't hurt your feelings.

Well, maybe *I* could. But that wasn't important just then.

Alejandro didn't see that by doubting me he *was* hurting me, that his skepticism made me smaller. He took the one skill and talent I had and made it nothing. It wasn't what he intended, no. But this was a clear case where intentions and outcome didn't match, and it's the outcome you have to take responsibility for. I took a deep breath and released it slowly.

"I was thinking about this on the way home," I said. "Do you realize that until now we've never disagreed? That's what makes this so difficult." I shifted under his hands, and Alejandro released me. I crossed the patio on stiff legs and sat down on the edge of the deck. "Until now, *my* observations have always agreed with yours. But now, when what I'm telling you doesn't match what you already think, it's *now* you believe I'm mistaken."

Alejandro sat down on the steps, so our heads were almost on a level, and we could speak more quietly. "I suggest a possibility only," he said. "'What if?' is all I'm asking." He raised his shoulders and turned up his hands. "*What if* you are mistaken? You have explained to me something of what you sense, and you have told me that your observations, or rather your interpretations, your own understanding, is sometimes limited because of what you do *not* know."

Well, I hadn't put it quite like that.

"You will admit that your experience, even of human life, is limited and these—the Outsider, the Rider—they need not think nor feel nor act in the way that you might expect. It is possible that you may misunderstand them."

"You mean the way I misunderstand you? *You're* not a human being." This was the meanest thing I'd ever said, and I wished the words back as soon as they were out. Alejandro didn't turn away, but he shut his eyes tight. He must have had this type of argument before, I realized. Maybe with one—or more—of his own partly human descendants.

"You are my *fara'ip* now," he said finally. "It is too great a risk for us to trust this Rider. We know nothing of him. It is the risk that makes me speak this way."

I couldn't help thinking how lucky it was that I hadn't told Alejandro everything I knew—if he didn't trust Wolf now, he would certainly never trust him if he learned Wolf used to be a Hound. Still, I owed it to him to consider what he was saying. When Wolf had first touched me, I'd been startled, but now that I had the context to understand what it was I felt about him, the contradictions in him . . .

"Alejandro, what Stormwolf says about the new High Prince, all of that is true. I have the context for that—you gave it to me yourself, and I can't be mistaken about it. I'm in no danger personally from Stormwolf—or from Nik and his people for that matter." At least not the kind of danger Alejandro was worrying about. "There's no risk there, I *know* it. It's *you* Nik needs to help him and the others, not me." With luck, Alejandro wouldn't notice that I was shifting the emphasis off of Wolf. "He doesn't even know I'm psychic.

"Of course there's interpretation in what I do; you know there is. But if—" I searched through my experiences for an example. "If a man believes he's getting away with cheating on a business deal and he isn't, I'm going to know, whether he does or not." I tapped the signet ring Alejandro wore on his left index finger. "When I touch an object, I can see who made it, who it once belonged to, and who it belongs to now."

"You knew the name of the Solitary who forged my *gra'if* blade." Alejandro's gaze was turned inward, remembering. He began to nod. "Even though I had long forgotten it."

I felt a smile coming on. "I see what's really there, even if I don't always understand the whole truth of it." I thought about Wolf calling me a Truthreader, but I thought I wouldn't mention him just now. I put my hand on Alejandro's arm. "When I first met you, I didn't know you were a Rider, because I didn't know that's what your people call yourselves. But I knew you weren't human, and I knew what it was about you that was different, the Moving and . . . and—" [How he still hears his wife's voice singing to him in the wind; hears her voice and feels the touch of her hand and that's why he won't go back, won't ever want to be in a place that did not know her.] I blinked and swallowed. Another thing I would never say aloud. "And I know that you would never harm me, or let me come to any harm."

Alejandro rubbed his face with both hands. He'd been doing that a lot more since we'd arrived in Toronto. He wasn't exactly regretting we'd come, but almost.

"I apologize," he said. "I am sorry both that you were upset, and that I contributed to the cause of it." This time he meant it.

"And you believe me?"

"About the message the Moonward one brings? Yes, of course. But you must understand, I trust *you*. Him I cannot trust so easily. Not without knowing him better." Alejandro stood and put out his hand to pull me to my feet.

"But you trusted Nighthawk right away, when you didn't know him."

Alejandro shrugged. "Nighthawk is a Sunward Rider."

I blinked at him as he held the screen door open for me. I'd known about the different Wards thing—I just hadn't realized how big it was.

"But come," he said walking ahead of me toward the kitchen. "There is food to prepare, dinner to eat. And—who knows?—telephone calls to make."

Okay. I followed him into the kitchen. He was letting me get refocused on our normal lives; putting the other stuff on hold. Saying that his problems with Wolf were really just Rider politics, something he hadn't paid attention to in generations—and something I didn't have to pay attention to at all.

I realized I'd been expecting him to reopen the "let's get you somewhere safe" discussion, and I was relieved to know that wasn't going to happen. Maybe I wasn't going to be put at risk again in the fight against the Hunt, but I wasn't going to be sent away.

I thought of the warmth of Wolf's skin, the strength in his hands. *Good*, I thought.

Chapter Six

LIGHTBORN THE GRIFFIN LORD rode half a length ahead of the mixed group of Riders accompanying him, barely gaining on the magenta-clad Riders in front of them. The landscapes flashed by as they Rode, now a soft wooded path, now the cropped grass of a tended lawn, now the hooves of the Cloud Horses plashing hock-deep in cold surf. Lightborn smiled, aware, as always, of the liquid slide of muscle as his Cloud Horse galloped.

"They are heading for the Portal," Windwatcher said from just behind his elbow. "Why?"

Why, indeed? There were five guards at each Portal, which meant these seven Riders had not a chance of taking them out before Lightborn and his Riders fell upon them from the rear.

"Come, my Clouds! Faster!" Lightborn could not let his people slacken their speed. They must keep on the heels of their quarry, harrying them, breaking their concentration, so that they would be unable to Move.

They were close enough now that Lightborn could see two Starwards in with the other Riders. Unusual. It was the Basilisk's Sunward followers—most favored by him and therefore most twisted from the true—who made up the bulk of those who were resisting the rule of the High Prince.

Abruptly, the scene around them changed to a dense wood, and they slowed, some in both parties cursing. Lightborn knew immediately that these were Trees—Naturals—and he shouted out: "I am Lightborn, son of Honor of Souls, cousin to Dawntreader, the Prince Guardian. Hear me, Trees, and help me. Stop these, my quarry, hold them safe for the High Prince's justice."

There was more cursing, but now it came only from ahead of them, along with one long drawn-out sound that was more howl than curse.

"Lightborn, what passes?" Windwatcher was at his right hand in an instant, his Cloud Horse finding the path suddenly easy.

"The Trees assist us," Lightborn said. "Our quarry will be waiting for us ahead."

"The Trees can do this?" The voice came from behind them.

Lightborn glanced around. The young Rider who spoke looked around her, shoulders hunched. There had been an edge of fear in her voice. Windwatcher, his Sunward face ruddier than usual, had opened his mouth to answer this breach of discipline, but Lightborn stopped him with a raised hand.

"A straight question," he said. "And deserves a straight answer." There had always been tensions between Riders, Naturals, and Solitaries—something Cassandra was trying to eliminate. "They can do this, and more. But you will see they only defend themselves, or answer the call of the High Prince, as now."

"And that is lesson enough for today," Windwatcher said. The younger Rider wore his colors, and she was his to discipline. "Our business is now before us."

The path the Trees had left for them widened into a clearing, where their quarry was held. Five were still mounted, kept on horseback more by the vines and branches that twined around them than by their own inclinations. Two had attempted to flee on foot before the trees had stopped them as well. One of these spoke up immediately as Lightborn came into view.

"How can you! How can you side with these Naturals against us?" The outrage in the Sunward's voice had an edge of hysteria. The Basilisk's people had good reason to fear the Trees.

"I speak here for the High Prince." Lightborn dismounted and approached the spokesperson. "I call on you to submit in her name." He crouched down on his heels and put his hand on the vine that wrapped itself around the Sunward Rider. "I am of her *fara'ip*, and cousin to the Guardian. The Trees only keep you from Moving because I have asked them to." Lightborn straightened to his feet, addressing all those held prisoner.

"The Basilisk is no more," he said. "He has Faded, and his *dra'aj* is returned to the Lands. You need not Bind yourselves to serve the Princes, if you have no heart for it. But you must Bind yourselves to do no more harm to others of the People."

"Where will we go?" Still the one on the ground.

"Back to your homes," Windwatcher suggested. "Back to your own *fara'ips*, where you belonged before the Basilisk took you."

"And if we have none?"

Lightborn smiled, spreading his hands. "Begin anew."

The one on the ground struggled to get up and, as if reading his new intent, the vines and branches released him, withdrawing into the shade. "I am Thunder Cat, my mother was Stormlynx, and the Hydra guides me."

It seemed that the others would follow the example of their leader, rising cautiously to their feet as the Wood released them. Lightborn left them for his men to sort out, and allowed Windwatcher to pull him to one side.

"How many?" the old warrior asked.

"You mean 'how many more?'" Lightborn shrugged. "Who would have thought there would be *any*? What keeps them fighting, when the Basilisk is Faded?" He thought about what Moon had said, and wondered how many of those she thought looked askance at her did so because of their own pasts. How many were others like herself—and like himself—followers of the Basilisk's who'd come to their senses and now wished it forgotten.

"Will the High Prince have to examine these?"

"She will, or some other Dragonborn who can read the truth," Lightborn said. "And now what?" Sharp cries and the snapping of branches had him heading toward the edge of the clearing.

"It's the two Starwards," Windwatcher said, snorting his displeasure as he followed close behind.

"Here, here, now. You'll damage yourselves." Lightborn laid one hand on the nearest shoulder and the other on the rough bark of the nearest Tree. "They are afraid of you," he said, addressing the Natural. "They cannot help themselves; the Basilisk trained their minds against you." If anything, the thrashing of the two Starwards increased. "Please, if you would, release these Riders, it is their fear which makes them fight you." Slowly, reluctantly, as if they disagreed but did not know how to say so, the vines and branches withdrew.

Lightborn took a firm hold on the elbow of the Rider nearest to him, concerned that the man still grimaced, his contorted face fixed now on Lightborn's own. He saw out of the corner of his eye that Windwatcher was helping the other one, who also stared, still wide-eyed, pulling back from his living bonds. The one Lightborn was holding cried out, swinging his arms and catching Lightborn himself in the chest with his flailing fist.

"Steady now," he said, laughing. "I'm no Tree." The Rider pulled away, cursing, and Lightborn took a step toward him, only to fall to his knees as his legs refused to hold him. He looked down at the spreading stain of blood on the front of his tunic, heard the sound of raised voices, pounding feet, and screaming. Felt, from far away, hands on his shoulders, heard Windwatcher bellowing for the Healer who would not come in time.

Moon, he said.

As he Faded, Lightborn had the strangest feeling that his killer had not really wanted to hurt him.

Chapter Seven

WALKS UNDER THE MOON felt her heart lift when she saw Max returning with Cassandra—nothing, not even the dark news Nighthawk had been telling her, could displace the glorious secret she had come to share with her sister. At the moment Cassandra seemed paler than usual, her storm-gray eyes looking dark against her ivory skin. She was dressed in her usual blood-red tunic over a silver shirt, black leggings, and boots, with *gra'if* showing at wrists, neck, and forehead. Her honey-gold hair, a shade or two darker than Moon's, hung loose, telling Moon that her sister had recently used her Dragonform.

When will I—but no, Moon pushed that thought away, her hand on her belly. She needed all her *dra'aj* for other things, now. She would manifest her Manticore afterward, when the right moment came. She stood, lower lip between her teeth, as Cassandra approached, Max speaking in her ear. Her sister's face was still as marble until Cassandra met Moon's eyes and smiled, reaching out her hand to her, as she turned to greet Nighthawk, her old mentor.

Moon searched her feelings for any sense of discord. There had been a time when she would have been jealous of the bond that evidently existed between the old Sunward Rider and her sister, but now she smiled, feeling only the echo of her sister's pleasure.

"Let's go inside," Max was saying. Now that the High Prince was back, it seemed that every eye in the camp was turned toward them. Max gestured, and the seats she and Hawk had been using disappeared.

The interior of the tent was full of light, but in every other way more closely resembled a palace than a pavilion. There were carpets and rugs on the floor, comfortable furniture, and even a fireplace in one wall, with a salamander dancing it in. There was a table, but Cassandra sat in her chair by the fire, and Moon took her usual place—at least when they were in private—on the hearthstone near her sister. Food and wine arrived, portions were cut, plates and glasses passed, and Moon saw Max and Hawk exchange a glance.

The lift to Cassandra's right eyebrow showed the High Prince had seen it as well. "So." Her sister looked at each of them in turn, but smiled only at Moon. *Does she know? Can she?* "The Hunt is in the Shadowlands. Stranded there, perhaps, with the fall of the Basilisk Prince?"

Hawk set his plate down on the small table next to his chair. "And joined, perhaps, by Basilisk Warriors who have fled there."

"It lacked but this." Cassandra had picked up a plate of fruit, but now she put it aside. "To have the problem spreading into the Shadowlands already, with all that I must contain and deal with here." Her eyes narrowed, and she shook her head, looking to the Prince Guardian. But Max was clearly thinking of something else. He got up and moved to look out a window that gave not on the camp outside the tent, but the heart of a forest glade.

"The Hunt was taken there to find me," he said. Moon noticed that as he spoke, his hand had drifted down to the spot on his side, low and on the left, where a Hound had once injured him. He seemed unaware that he'd done it.

"And that makes the Hunt our responsibility." Cassandra rubbed her forehead with the fingers of her right hand. "I agree. But who can I send? Who has the necessary experience of both the Hunt and the Shadowlands?"

Max turned back from the window. "I'm afraid that as far as many here are concerned, the Hunt can stay in the Shadowlands as long as they like."

"But surely . . ." Hawk's voice trailed into silence.

"It's different for us," Max said. "We've lived there. It's as much our home as the Lands, though never in the same way."

Cassandra touched Moon on the shoulder. "Dear one, what do you think?"

Moon knew what her sister wanted: the perspective of a Rider who had never been in the Shadowlands and, moreover, who might have a better idea of what some of those who had previously supported the Basilisk Prince might think.

"For those of us who lack your experiences, the Shadowlands is only the place of the Prince Guardian's exile. Nothing more," Moon pointed out. "Many think of it as a mythical place, and of humans as creatures of myth, nothing more." Moon stroked the griffin pin in her lapel. "Though the Wild Riders might enjoy it. They love strange paths, and have long seen it as part of their life task to destroy the Hunt."

"There is your answer, then," Hawk said. "Send the Wild Riders to the Shadowlands. I can work with them."

"We can't." Max drummed his fingers on the arm of his chair. "You don't understand, Hawk. The Cycle has turned, but it's not like pushing a reset button." Moon was bewildered, but it was evident that Nighthawk understood the reference. "Everything didn't just return to normal. Cassandra's busy all day, every day, healing the Lands—not just the parts the Basilisk twisted and perverted, but areas of neglect and decay from the waning of the old Cycle."

"And there are the Basilisk's Warriors," Moon picked up her glass of wine and put it down again without tasting it. "Those who cannot, or will not accept the change."

"I need the Wild Riders to deal with them," Cassandra said. "They are made up of all Wards, and have *fara'ip* with both Solitaries and Naturals. They are the closest thing we have to a neutral force, accepted by all. The only force I can use to both hunt down and protect my People. Until the crisis here is over, I cannot spare them." Cassandra sighed. "Still, it goes against the grain to simply leave the Hunt in the Shadowlands."

Moon saw the same dejection on the others' faces. "What about the Horn?" she said. "If we could call the Hunt . . ."

Cassandra shivered, and Moon put her hand on her sister's knee. For a moment she, too, felt the echo of the Horn, the cold it brought, and the sound so low it shook your bones.

"The Horn." Cassandra lifted her hand to her neck, stroking the Phoenix torque with her fingertips. "Did the Basilisk not have it?

Moon tilted her head to one side, considering. "He was known to give it to some of his trusted favorites to use for him," she acknowledged. "As we ourselves witnessed. Most granted such favor were only too happy to give the artifact back to him when their task was done. Dealing with the Hunt, even in a position of power, is said to be an unpleasant thing." She tilted her head and considered. "The Basilisk had it with him at the Stone."

"I could check there," Max put in. *It would have to be him*, Moon thought. As Keeper of the Talismans, only the Prince Guardian could Move to the Stone.

"And if it is not there?" Cassandra asked.

"Moon, you're the closest we Riders have to a historian." Max looked to Nighthawk. "During the Exile, Moon began researching the ancient Chants by gathering Singers and comparing different versions of Songs."

"Ingenious," Hawk said. "Like a modern scholar, comparing different myth cycles to discover history."

"Exactly. She's not a Singer herself, but she has extensive knowledge of the Songs." Max turned back to her, his green eyes bright. "What can you tell us of the calling of the Hunt?"

Moon sat up straighter on her perch, eager to help, to wipe away the stain she still occasionally felt of being one of the Basilisk's court. The Hunt had not been her major focus; the Basilisk Prince had already been in possession of the Horn when she first knew him. But, of course, you cannot make an extensive examination of Songs for one topic, and not note others as you pass them by.

"I know of seven hundred and forty-eight Songs mentioning the Hunt," Moon said finally, accepting the quince tart Max passed to her, and breathing in deeply as she savored its aroma. "Of these, two hundred and ninety-six tell of the Hunt being Called, seventy-four mentioning the Horn specifically, but only three in any way describe it." She placed the tart, whole, into her mouth.

"Remarkable," Hawk said.

Moon chewed and swallowed. "Is it not? You would think there would be more, and yet, there it is."

Moon caught a look as it passed between Cassandra and Max. Both of them seemed to be stifling smiles, and Moon felt her cheeks grow warm. Apparently, it had not been the number of Songs which Hawk had found remarkable.

"All three descriptions agree that the item is made of bone, dragon bone or griffin, perhaps. Much is unclear as it must be inferred from the context." Moon picked up her wine and this time sipped at it. "The object that I saw was somewhat the size of my index finger." She held her finger up to show them, and turned to Cassandra. "But *you* will have had the most experience with Hounds, my sister, with your Healing." Moon froze.

"Moon, what is it?"

She hesitated, unwilling to add to her sister's burdens, but . . . "You did not know about the presence of the Hunt when you sent Wolf to the Shadowlands. Is it safe for him to be there, alone?"

They were all of Cassandra's *fara'ip*, but Moon looked upon Wolf in particular as her brother. After the fall of the Basilisk, she had needed a quiet place to contemplate the evil she had done during her time as his willing tool. Wolf also—newly returned to his true self from a time infinitely longer, and more evil—had need of the same quiet seclusion. This had made them closer than others with whom they shared *fara'ip*.

Cassandra's head tilted back as her eyes narrowed in thought.

"They do tell alcoholics not to put themselves in drinking situations," Max pointed out.

Cassandra looked more troubled. "You're saying it might be the same for him? His addiction is gone, but I've sent him right back to the same neighborhood, the same gang? Perhaps the same situation in which he became addicted in the first place?"

"He did seem like the perfect person to find stray People in the Shadowlands, but . . ." Max slowly shook his head. "Maybe you need to send someone else."

Cassandra leaned forward, her hands clasped together. "Hawk, I must make use of you for this. You say the Water Sprite in Madrid wishes to return? Very well, you will go, and take the Singer, Twilight Falls Softly, with you, she has a water connection. Then you will find Wolf, and bid him return." She turned her head to catch Moon's eye. "In the meantime, Moon, you will look for the Horn. Let us do what little we can."

Moon hopped up from the hearthstone. "Of course, but I wonder if first—"

The other three were on their feet in an instant, hands on their swords. Cassandra took a step to the right, putting Moon behind her. The unheard-of interruption was no menace, however, but Windwatcher pushing his way into the room, his square Sunward face almost white. When he saw Moon, his color paled to ashes.

"Are you hurt?" Cassandra went to him immediately. "Is there some injury?"

But something in the older Rider's face, something in particular in the way he looked at her, told Moon that Windwatcher was not the one.

"No," she said, but so quietly no one heard her. She touched Lightborn's broach, pinned now to her collar. A moment ago, the tiny griffin had moved under her fingers, as it had done since Lightborn had given it to her. Now, for the first time, it lay still. "No." This time she was loud enough that they all turned to look at her. She heard Windwatcher's murmur, Max's cry of pain, and her sister's liquid chocolate voice responding to them both. Her hands shook as she released the clasp on the broach and held it in her palm. She stroked the griffin with the tip of her finger, but it was cold, nothing more than jewels and darkmetal in her hand.

"Would not stop fighting." It was as if someone else heard Windwatcher's voice. "We had to kill them both in the end."

Good. Moon felt her knees hit the floor. She felt her sister's arms wrap warmth around her. "No," she said. "Let me feel it. I must feel it all."

"I'm not *Healing* your feelings, my dearest." Cassandra's voice was farther and farther away. "I'm—oh, Christ! Moon! You should have told me."

"What is it? What's wrong?" A voice above her head.

"Nothing now, but there will be when the baby comes."

"Baby? What are you talking about?"

Moon knew. Without the support of Lightborn's *dra'aj*, the child, when it came, would take all of hers. Without Lightborn's *dra'aj*, she would die.

So be it.

"Cassandra, you have to do something." That was Max. No one knew better than he did what would happen if Moon gave birth without the child's father there. That was how Max's own mother had died, something for which his father had never forgiven himself.

"Quiet, please." Cassandra pushed her sister's hair back from her face and concentrated until she could feel the Lands the way she had in *Trere'if's* clearing. *Please let it not be too late*. Lightborn was Faded, but his *dra'aj*, if she acted quickly enough, might still be—she narrowed her focus even more, until she could see each individual life thread. There! Like a stitch unraveling, there was the thread that had been Lightborn, already Fading, dispersing into the *dra'aj* of the Lands. Not sure if she could, but knowing she had to try, Cassandra reached out and caught that thread of *dra'aj* and pulled at it, drawing it away from the Lands, coiling it around her own while she looked for and found the thread that was her sister, already showing a branching. The branching that would kill her without Lightborn's *dra'aj* to support it. Cassandra took Lightborn's thread and wrapped it around, twisting all three together until even she could not be sure where one started and the other stopped, and then she released them. She hoped it would be enough.

"Cassandra?" Max said again.

This time she opened her eyes.

"What did you do?" he asked. "Will she be all right?" His face fell. "The baby?"

"No." Cassandra nodded her thanks as Max helped her to her feet. "I think I found enough."

"Enough of what? I don't get it."

"Enough of Lightborn's *dra'aj*." Max still looked puzzled. "Enough so that both mother and child will live."

(flicker) and the world changed. Became shadows and light. Grays and whites. Sharp edges and the lure of movement. (flicker) Color again, but now no perspective, everything flat. Longshadow looked through the other eye, but it made no difference. Still flat. Both eyes open meant two images, not quite superimposed. (flicker) Lost height and color, but, oh, the smells. Richer, so much richer.

The other two were beside him, unchanging, not flickering and one squatted now and patted him on the head. One of the prey, a small one, pointed. "Doggy," it said.

(flicker) Longshadow was bigger, and the eyes and mouth on the small prey widened, until he bit it on the arm, and *sucked* the *dra'aj* out of it, young and hot and juicy, and the prey sat back again, uninterested. He scampered to catch up with his Pack mates. (flicker) Taller, color again, perspective, the rounded arms, and shoulders, and legs and necks. Grabbing and clutching as he trotted through.

Longshadow didn't get his share, stupid to trust the others who ran before him, not waiting, taking before he could get to more than five or six additional prey.

One looked at him with what seemed like awareness in its eyes, like a Rider, like she knew what he was and was not afraid. Longshadow lowered his eyes, suddenly overcome with a feeling that made him want to hide. Not fear, something else. Something that wanted to become anger. This one he caught by the throat and shook until more than her *dra'aj* was taken from her.

He dropped her, belatedly realizing she was the last, the others had finished the humans in the subway car.

"Here's the station," Briar said.

(flicker) Longshadow checked his appearance, and nodded, satisfied, as the train pulled into the station. His suit looked nice, as nice as those of the others. Here, in this place, no one would look twice at them.

I actually had two voice mails. The first was the HR guy from the Institute who'd called to tell me they'd given my name to two other places. The second was one of those two places calling to see when I could come see them. I couldn't help smiling. It's one thing to be told you've been recommended to someone, it's another to have that someone call you so quickly. I made a note of the number, wondering whether I should call back right away, or let it wait a day or two. Was it possible to look too eager?

I'd almost forgotten what a great job I'd done at the Christie Institute yesterday. Everything that had happened since then had pushed it right out of my head. But Alejandro and I had gone to a lot of trouble to set up my new life—and here was proof that I'd be able to have one, even if it couldn't start right away.

So it was with a different frame of mind that I let Alejandro reopen our conversation while I set the table. It was almost four o'clock, only a little bit later than we would have been eating in Spain. Alejandro poured the wine and made sure I could reach the bread before he spoke.

"What more can you tell me, then, of this Moonward Rider?" Once again, I could hear that slight overlay of distaste in Alejandro's voice. "Why did the Outsiders believe him to be a Hound?"

"Couldn't say." I lifted my wineglass to my lips, shaking my head as I sipped and then swallowed. Lying to Alejandro wasn't going to be as easy as I'd thought. Though, technically, I *could* answer without lying. It wasn't my fault the Outsiders had their tenses mixed up. Wolf wasn't a Hound *now*; he'd only been one before. I wondered if Alejandro would define this as a lie circumstantial.

"Though I *can* say they're wrong. Oh, come on." Alejandro had given me a polite look. My temper threatened to flare again—why wouldn't he *believe* me? Was this what all liars felt? "I can't be mistaken about that."

"Perhaps not—"

"*Perhaps* not? I thought we'd settled that argument." That's right, distract him.

"*¡Dios mio!* Have you never heard of a figure of speech?" He pointed at me with his spoon. "As I was *about* to say, perhaps not. *However*, he could still be in league with the Hunt."

I shook my head. "You know what? Never mind. Let's just eat."

After we'd spooned gazpacho for a while in silence, Alejandro cleared his throat. When I looked up, eyebrows raised, he passed me the bowl of croutons. "May I ask?" he said, when my mouth was full.

I gave him a slow nod, and swallowed.

"The Moonward one says that Nighthawk sent him. Why would Hawk not come himself? Or telephone to me? Unless he was not able to." Alejandro stood, picking up his bowl and reaching for mine.

The way he said "Moonward" reminded me that both Alejandro and Nighthawk were Sunward Riders.

"No," I said. "I read nothing like that." But Stormwolf had killed someone, I *had* read that much. I debated whether to keep this, too, from Alejandro. "I'm not saying he hasn't killed—and recently—but not Hawk. In fact . . ." I waited. Something else, an image only half-formed . . . but nothing more came, and I shrugged. "He feels very badly about it," I said finally. "About the killing that he's done."

"That is true of all of us who have killed. Something you would not know, my dear." Alejandro put plates of chicken stewed in white wine down in front of us, but before sitting down, he pulled his mobile out of his pocket and pressed two numbers.

"Maybe I would." He looked at me, the phone still at his ear. "Some of the things I learned when I was with the Collector—learned and reported—could have resulted in someone's death." I'd thought about that a lot, before Alejandro came.

He gave me a look of understanding that had absolutely no pity in it. He held the phone to his ear. His eyebrows drew together and his lips twisted to one side. He checked his display.

"How strange. There is no response. None. As if Hawk's mobile does not exist."

"Still doesn't mean Wolf hurt him."

Alejandro pressed his lips together before answering. "It is not the first time I have called. The Moonward may be truthful in all he says, and still be a danger to us." He put his mobile away and sat down.

"No, he isn't." I speared a piece of chicken with my fork, swept sauce onto it with my knife and lifted it to my mouth.

Alejandro looked at me without speaking, but I knew that he was still thinking, *Perhaps.*

Something else had been nagging at me. Maybe it was a low way to change the subject, but I had to grab what straws I could. "What Nik said is true, isn't it? Riders *did* bring the Hunt here." I knew the answer, but the day's earlier argument made me want to see what Alejandro would say. For a minute he just looked at me, blinking, and then he gave the smallest of nods. He picked up his knife and fork.

"It is more complicated than that, and I must admit, it did not occur to me that the Hunt would be interested in humans. Humans have *dra'aj*, that we know, or we could not breed—forgive me, that can be such an ugly word."

"But you knew about Outsiders?"

"Certainly. But only as I have already told you, humans who feed upon others. They are a relatively new phenomenon, and rare, appearing perhaps only in the last five or six hundred years." Only a Rider would think of half a millennia as "relatively new," I thought. "As I said, in all the years that I have been in this world, I have met only one before Mr. Polihronidis." He drew down his brows in thought. *Alejandro should know*, I thought. He'd been here longer, probably, than any other Rider.

"So how does the Hunt/prey thing work," I said, seesawing the fork in my hand. "I mean, since you guys can Move, doesn't that make you really hard to hunt?"

"Only Riders can Move, though the other People travel each in their own peculiar way." Alejandro put down his fork, and topped up first my glass and then his. "What is known about how the Hunt travels is limited. We know that they cannot track a Natural at all; flowing water is a good barrier to stop them from tracking you—or even from seeing you, at times. The Hunt *can* follow a Rider through a Move, however, even through a crossroads, but only if they are practically on your heels. One thing is certain. They cannot use a Portal unless they have a Rider with them, but that is also true of Solitaries or Naturals."

I took a sip of my wine and watched him. His gaze was turned inward as he thought.

"The Songs of the People also say that when a Hound is on scent, it will not turn from it, perhaps cannot. That is how I know that this morning's Hound was not sent to track *you*, in particular. Had it been, it would not have stopped to deal with me." He tossed back the last mouthful of his wine and stood, picking up his plate.

"But where do they come from?" Leaving my wineglass still half full on the table, I used the pass-through to hand him my own dishes.

Alejandro executed that full body shrug common to many Europeans. "Some have wondered if the Hunt are in some fashion related to our Cloud Horses. They are the only other animals in the Lands that can pass through a Move with a Rider." Alejandro took my plate from me, scraping off the garlic potatoes and the chicken bones into the compost bucket before sliding the plate into the dishwasher. He indicated the bottle of wine, and I refilled his glass.

Alejandro took a long sip before setting his glass aside and looking me in the eye. "And so, is there nothing more you can tell me about this Stormwolf?" His voice calmer, his question now seemed quite reasonable.

I concentrated, trying to re-create the images and feelings I had when Stormwolf had held me in his arms, his hand over my mouth, his breath in my ear. There had been so *many*. It had taken me months to be able to touch Alejandro without being overwhelmed, and Wolf was somehow so much . . . well, fresher was the only word that came to mind. I shivered. "He's undergone some kind of change recently," I said, my eyes closed. My mental image of him was coming clearer as I thought about it. "Some kind of enlightenment, or—" I grasped Alejandro's wrist. "He's here," I whispered.

Alejandro raised his eyebrows and pointed to the front door. I shook my head. "In the alley."

Alejandro made a motion like pulling his two fists apart. I knew he didn't need his sword cane, but I also knew that he would feel calmer, more in control, if he had it with him. I motioned into the sunroom. "Leaning against the table," I said.

He waved me to keep back, but of course I followed him. After all, if Alejandro thought the smart thing to do was Move, the safest place for me to be was within reach. I didn't want to, I knew beyond doubt that Wolf was no danger to us, but if Alejandro wanted to go, I knew I had to go with him. He had one hand on his sword cane and the other on the doorknob when I stopped him again, putting my hand around his upper arm.

"Let's not have a repeat of the scene at the hotel," I said quietly. "Nighthawk *did* send him, remember. He's been truthful with us." Which was more, I thought, than I had been, but I pushed that thought away to where not even I could see it

"The same Nighthawk who does not answer his phone." But Alejandro's voice remained calm.

I shook my head, and stepped past him out to the deck. It was a measure of how much he had taken to heart my earlier anger that he let me.

"Come in," I called out. "The gate's unlocked. You can pull the latch from the outside."

At first I thought he wasn't going to, but then the shadow under the trees shifted, and a pale hand came through the opening in the gate and lifted the latch. The gate swung open and Stormwolf stepped through.

It was me he looked at, as if Alejandro wasn't even there, and his eyes were like ashes that still had coals beneath them.

"I am pleased to see you are safe," he said. "I thought you may have been frightened."

By him, he meant. He was used to people being frightened of him, and almost couldn't believe it when they weren't.

"I know we can trust you," I said. He raised his eyebrows just a little, but I think I saw him relax.

Alejandro was going to make Stormwolf sit outside on our tiny deck, but I'm happy to say common sense prevailed. It was getting to be the time that people were coming home from work, and I could imagine the kind of questions we'd get from either Barb and Jim on the one side, or Shari and Steven on the other, if they overheard us. Both sets of neighbors were pretty worldly, but it was the otherworldly nature of our discussion we needed to hide.

I held the door open and Wolf was past me in an instant—so fast that if I hadn't already seen Alejandro's speed, I would have thought Wolf had teleported directly from our patio into the sunroom. The two Riders bristled, giving each other the unmistakable look that said, "I am armed."

I pulled out a chair for our guest at the marble-topped table, tacitly acknowledging Alejandro's desire to keep him from penetrating deeper into our home. I did the best I could to put my own irritation to one side. Somehow, now that he was here, the fact of Wolf's past became more than just something I knew that Alejandro didn't. It became something I was keeping secret, and now that I had secrets of my own, I was beginning to see how things could be more complicated than whether the person I trusted most also trusted me—or more accurately, my ability.

I could also tell that there was more than one kind of tension between the two Riders. Part was what I'd expected, the issues that came of their being different Wards—pack issues wouldn't be putting it too strongly. Riders usually Rode in groups, and those groups were almost always made up of Riders of the same Ward—and that actually explained the rest of the tension. They also have an instinctive prejudice against and distrust of that rarity among Riders, the loner.

No, neither of them saw the irony in that.

And let's not forget that Stormwolf really was hiding something, even if it was only something he feared about himself, rather than something *we* needed to fear.

Alejandro passed into the kitchen, and through to the inner part of the house. *The phone*, I thought. *This time he's going to try Hawk on the landline.*

I smiled at his retreating back. At least he trusted my judgment enough to leave me alone with our guest. That gave me an idea. I went to the fridge, and got out two beers, giving one to Stormwolf, and going into the front room to hand the other to Alejandro. There was also a jug of sangria in the fridge and I poured myself a glass. Beer was still a taste I hadn't acquired.

"What do you call yourself here?" I said, when it seemed Alejandro was going to be a while. I was trying to give as normal a look to things as I could. Stormwolf was uncomfortable, edgy, and part of that had to do with me. He could place Alejandro—he was here to find him, after all—but he couldn't see what our relationship was, and it didn't seem to be part of their etiquette to ask.

"Edmond Wolfe," was the answer.

I nodded and sipped my drink. Of course it made sense to use a name that was at least partly his own. Even if he didn't pick it out for himself.

I smiled, but he was focused on the beer bottle's label, tracing the letters with the tip of his finger. [He can't read!]

"It says Alexander Keith's," I said, pointing toward the words but carefully not touching either the bottle or Wolf. "That's the name of the man who started the company. And 'India Pale Ale,' that's the type of beer it is."

He nodded without looking at me.

I raised my own glass to my lips, straining for the sound of Alejandro's voice, and trying to determine what it was I was feeling. Was I agitated, or was I only picking up a vibe from "Edmond Wolfe"?

In many ways I was still learning to pay close attention to my own reactions, making sure they *were* my own, and not just borrowed from the people I was reading.

Wolf was even more ambivalent than I had guessed. Outwardly, he seemed calm and at ease. He was leaning back in his chair, his face smooth, his gaze steady. Inside, it was as if he was sitting on the edge of his seat, and shifting his eyes to the exits. It was more than just the underlying awareness of a Rider's physical place in the universe that I was familiar with from Alejandro.

And that's when it hit me. I was used to feeling and reading certain things in Alejandro—or maybe I should say Graycloud at Moonrise—and here I was reading the same things from someone else. I'd never met another Rider before, let alone someone who hadn't spent more time in this world than any human now living. Compared to Alejandro there was a wildness to Wolf, as if he was a wolf in fact. This didn't make Alejandro any less fierce or deadly, it just made his aspect . . . tamer somehow.

This world was not Wolf's natural habitat, no matter how at home he looked in his Italian suit and Spanish shoes. I wondered if this was what the Europeans had felt when they encountered the natives of the Americas. Or maybe it was what the natives had felt.

Wolf's gray eyes were looking back at me now, and I automatically steadied myself, thanking my long training for helping me to keep my face impassive, even if I couldn't stop myself from blushing.

"Valory." The warning in Alejandro's voice as he came up behind me was clear. He wanted me to step away, to remove myself from Wolf's reach. I almost smiled. As if either of them couldn't grab me from the other end of the house before I could stop them.

"I have telephoned to Nighthawk," Alejandro said, pointedly addressing Wolf. "There is no answer, either at his home, or his mobile. His *ama de llaves* has not seen him in some days."

Wolf appeared unfazed. "He said he was going to the Lands, to see the High Prince."

"He did say that," I said.

"And did he go?"

I shrugged. "That's more than I can [yes]—Yes. Yes, he did go."

Alejandro turned back to our guest. "Why did Hawk not call me with the news you bring?"

"Because it is *mine* to give," Wolf said.

"Wolf didn't hurt him," I put in. "On the contrary, Hawk was very happy to hear about the new Cycle, and told Wolf about Shower of Stars and Mountain Crag."

Alejandro's lips pressed together. "Do you bring anything, some talisman from either Nighthawk or the High Prince, to show that you speak for her?"

"Alejandro." I let the tightness in my voice show him how close to the edge I was. He believed me, I *know* that he did. This was just some kind of macho posturing. What a waste of time. "I've already told you he's speaking the truth. We can trust him."

"It is what I should have asked him at the hotel," Alejandro said. Well, I couldn't argue with that. "You are not a lie detector, nor should I use you as one."

My chest felt tight, and I had to blink. He didn't want to use me. Now, if he'd only said that in the first place, we could have saved a lot of upset and arguing.

"It is a reasonable request." Wolf undid the buttons of his shirt and pulled it open.

I heard Alejandro's indrawn breath as I took an involuntary step forward, drawn by the shimmering colors on the almond skin of Wolf's chest. Dark ruby red, the liquid silver of mercury, a black as dark as Wolf's own hair. I hadn't seen a lot of tattoos in my life, but even I could tell this dragon was something no human hand could have created.

Without hesitation, I reached out and placed the tips of my index and middle fingers where the dragon's heart would be—and gasped as I felt it beating, laughed aloud when I realized that of course it was Wolf's heart I felt. I had the context, and the images I read were as clear and bright as the tattoo itself.

"It's not a tattoo," I said. "It's like *gra'if.* Made by a Gorgon for—no, *from* Truthsheart." I looked around at Alejandro. "The High Prince. From her blood, and tears, and breath."

I lifted my fingers from his skin, and looked into Wolf's bottomless gray eyes. "She smells of saffron," I said.

"She does," he agreed.

Alejandro cleared his throat, and, very slowly, I turned to look his way. He took a swallow of his beer, nodding as he lowered the bottle.

Then he made that complicated motion of the upper body and shoulders that is the Spanish shrug. "What can you tell me of the Hunt?"

Wolf blinked. Obviously not what he was expecting. "Why are you curious?"

"I have pledged to help the humans against them. What do you know of them? How is it that the human Outsiders thought you a Hound?"

Wolf had started to say that he knew nothing of the Hunt, but at Alejandro's final question he caught himself, glancing at me.

"How was it that *I* could be mistaken for a Hound?" Wolf was pretending he didn't understand the question, but he was thinking, *What is showing? What is giving me away?*

"I saw a Rider this morning, following . . ." Alejandro hesitated and then inclined his head toward me, unwilling to say my name aloud. "It was only as it passed me outside that it wore the shape of a dog, and only when I challenged it did it begin to change."

Wolf's face shut down, as though he'd suddenly thought of something he wanted desperately to keep to himself. He shook his head. "There was no sign or track of Riders there, other than your own, and that of . . ." Now it was time for Wolf to nod toward me, not wanting to use my name when Alejandro hadn't. "But you," he continued, turning back to Alejandro. "*You* have the smell of this Hound on you now."

I drew myself up. *That* was why Alejandro had felt strange to me when he'd touched me earlier, as if he had two selves. But why hadn't I read it as an injury?

"A scratch, it did not bite me, I assure you."

Wolf shook his head, his eyes never leaving Alejandro's face. "The scratch will not heal."

"Alejandro, let me . . ." I gestured toward his leg.

"*Querida*, you can do nothing that I have not already done. I have had much worse than this in the bullring."

"No, that's not it." I had an idea, and I needed to see where it would take me. "I wonder, if I touch it, could I get anything from it?" Now they both looked at me. Finally, his forehead still furrowed above his red-gold brows, Alejandro rolled up his pant leg, exposing a bandage wrapped around the meaty part of his calf. The blood seeping through the layers of wrapping was fresh. I loosened the clips, and unwrapped the bandage as quickly as I could. I had to admit the wound didn't look all that bad. It was deepish, for a scratch, but even I had seen worse. Still, it should have stopped bleeding by now. I laid my hand along the wound.

[An animal; wings won't open; body distorted, the sickness, the constant, uncontrollable hunger; *flicker*, twitch, tic; moments of peace, moments of control; fear of the Pack Leader; fear of the bright *gra'if* blade –]

"Valory." It was Wolf's voice, Wolf's hand on my shoulder, pulling me back from Alejandro. He had my glass in his hand. I hadn't realized I'd dropped it. He must have caught it before it hit the floor.

"It was the same person," I said. "The one you saw, the Rider? The Hound? The same person." I pointed to his wound. "He's still there, somehow." I looked at Alejandro. "You saw him, just before he Faded away, you saw the Rider."

Alejandro did not look up from rewrapping his wound. "I saw a Rider," he admitted. "I could not be sure." He pulled down the leg of his trousers so the wound was covered once more, and looked up at Wolf. "How can this be?"

The other Rider shook his head. "I do not know," he said finally. "The Hunt were brought here by the Riders of the Basilisk Prince, to search for the Exile." His eyes flicked from me to Alejandro and back again. "Until Hawk and I killed one in Spain," he said, "I was not even sure they had not all returned."

Alejandro glanced at me and I nodded. That had been the recent killing I'd read on Wolf earlier.

"Was it difficult?"

Again a look flashed over his face. Alejandro would see horror, and attribute it to the encounter, but I knew suddenly that Wolf had recognized the Hound that he'd killed. Had thought how easily it could have been him. I couldn't say anything to comfort him, no gesture, without revealing too much to Alejandro.

This lying thing was more difficult than I'd thought.

"I have *gra'if*," Wolf finally said. "And there were two of us."

Again, Alejandro and Wolf looked steadily at one another.

"What can we do?" I said to Alejandro. "How do we fix your leg?"

"He must go to the High Prince. Only a Healer of the People can medicine a wound of the Hunt."

"Nonsense."

"You know it is so. A Hound's bite will not heal."

"But this is only a scratch, the beast did not bite me."

"You can't chance it, Alejandro," I said.

"And you can bear news of this new Hunt, these new Hounds, to the High Prince."

"Should that not be *your* job." But I could tell Alejandro was wavering.

Wolf shook his head. "I have my task already, and I cannot turn from it. The High Prince gave me your name, having known of you, during her time here as Warden. And those I have spoken with confirm that you are the one who will point me further along my way. That is why I came to you, why I am here, now."

I felt an unreasonable pang, but it was only momentary. Maybe Alejandro wasn't the only person Wolf had come to see. Even as he spoke, he was looking at me. But what he'd said had made sense to Alejandro. He was, after all, the oldest resident, and over the centuries, had met most if not all of the expatriates of the Lands.

"Have you seen maps," he asked Wolf now. "Do you know how to use them?"

Chapter Eight

I'D THOUGHT WE'D BE OFF to the Lands right away, but once Wolf had gone it didn't take me long to figure out that Alejandro had no intention of having his wounds looked at.

"Just let me put on some shoes," I said to him. "How long do you think we're going to be? Should we ask Barb to feed Oro?"

But Alejandro only shook his head. "There is no need for us to go anywhere. We cannot even know if she will help me."

"But she's your High Prince." I sat down in the seat Wolf had vacated. I knew that tone, we were in for another argument. "Of course she has to help you—look, she's sent Wolf here to let all of you know about her, hasn't she? Why would she do that if she didn't mean to help you?"

"I cannot believe that you have so quickly forgotten my promise to the Outsiders." A gesture stopped what I was about to say. "I have contacted the others I know," he said. "Asking if they have also seen reports of occurrences similar to what is being called the High Park flu. Some have not yet replied. I am needed here, *querida*, I cannot go to the Lands."

I opened my mouth and closed it again without speaking. Obviously, there wasn't any point in arguing that getting medical attention might actually be of some help. The wound wasn't going to heal, but what could I say? That Alejandro wouldn't go because it would look as though he were following Wolf's instructions? Oh, yeah, I knew where that would get me.

Okay, then. If the direct approach wouldn't work . . .

"How fast is this poison supposed to work? How about if we wait until your friends get back to you, and then go, if you aren't any better?"

That was a compromise he could agree to, but he still wasn't ready to give in completely. "I cannot leave you alone and unprotected. The Hunt has already shown an interest in you—"

"And that's another reason to go, to take the news about the Hunt and these stable Hounds. The High Prince needs to be told about this." I waited, but his face showed no change. I sighed. "Look, if you're worried about me, I could go with you."

"Ay, querida, estoy entre la espada y la pared."

That almost made me smile. The Spanish expression for "between a rock and a hard place" was very apt, considering the number of swords there were around. "It can't be as bad as all that."

He shut his eyes and shook his head. "If you stay, there is the Hunt, and if you go . . ."

I exhaled through my nose, good and loud. "What's so dangerous there?" I asked. "Isn't the bad guy gone, and the good guys in charge? I've met some of the People already; I'm not likely to be spooked. Besides, I've got as much right to go as any other human who's been taken to the Lands, maybe more. I should be allowed to visit the ancestral home of my forebears."

"Ah, but the People you have met have been long in the Shadowlands, and learned to live with humans, to value them, to form *fara'ips*." Alejandro began to pace. "The People of the Lands do not live like humans, in cities. *Fara'ips* of Riders are based on Ward or Guidebeast or even shared philosophy, as with the Wild Riders, who rove freely, always Moving, while others, like the Griffin Lords, have strongholds. And that is only true of Riders." He stopped pacing and faced me. "Solitaries are truly as their name describes them, living entirely apart and may go the whole of their lives without having contact with any one else. Naturals." He shrugged. "They live as they live, how could they not?"

I thought I knew what he meant. I'd met the Natural who lived in the fountain in Madrid. At least, that's how I'd always spoken of her. But the truth was she didn't *live in* the fountain, she *was* the fountain. How would someone like her, but one who had never seen a human being, react to meeting one for the very first time? Still . . .

"There must be some who've met humans before."

"And there are some who believe humans are only myths," Alejandro countered. "And others who might very well treat you as though you were merely an interesting type of animal—a pet. I would not have you exposed to such . . . disrespect."

I don't think that's exactly what he'd meant to say. "But that's *my* lookout, I should think. I mean, if it's safe otherwise, I'm willing to take the chance of being looked down on. And even if it isn't," he opened his mouth again and I interrupted him. "You've just admitted you don't think it's any safer to stay here."

Alejandro leaned back in his chair, crossed one leg over the other and started swinging his foot. "You are right. I must not leave you alone. Please." He held up his hand as I opened my mouth. "That is not what I meant. Though you must be reasonable, my dear one. Surely you see that taking precautions is essential. Even small children are taught to look for cars before stepping into the street."

"Okay." I nodded. "Okay. I'll even concede that extraordinary circumstances call for extraordinary precautions. I just don't want to be kept locked away." My voice shook a bit on these last words, but Alejandro pretended not to notice.

"Very well. If I go to the Lands, you shall go with me."

I don't know if I could have gotten him to agree to more, but just then the doorbell rang. Once again Alejandro got to the door ahead of me, but I knew who would be standing there just the same.

"Val." Nik Polihronidis looked over Alejandro's shoulder at me and smiled, making my stomach flutter. The two men followed me back through the house, but something made me offer Nik a seat in the dining room. Somehow I couldn't sit down with him in the same place I'd been sitting with Wolf. Alejandro went through to the kitchen to make coffee.

"Okay, so that's one less Hound, and one who isn't a Hound, Yves tells me." It wasn't a question, but Nik turned to me and raised his eyebrows.

"That's right," I said.

"So you won't mind telling me how you know?"

Today Nik's suit was a tan linen, with a very faint pale blue chalk line that was picked up by his shirt. He wasn't wearing a tie, but his question had come out just like we were in a courtroom.

My jaw actually dropped open. Crap. I'd forgotten that he didn't know. Alejandro put the tray with coffee cups, sugar, and heated milk on the ledge of the pass-through and came into the room himself, picking up the tray again and placing it on the table.

"*Querida,*" he said. He was leaving it up to me, to handle as I wanted, and the knowledge that he believed I could gave me the courage to do so.

"I'm psychic," I said. When I'd told Wolf the same thing earlier that morning, he'd used a better word. "I'm a Truthreader."

I don't know what I was expecting, but Nik took his coffee from Alejandro, shook his head at the milk, and accepted the sugar without shifting an eyebrow.

"I remember in my village, a friend of my ya-ya's was supposed to have the sight." His voice was quiet, and he spoke with his eyes almost closed, looking back what I knew was quite a long way. He stirred his coffee, and looked at me from underneath his eyebrows. "That was a very long time ago, and I don't remember her being very good."

"Valory is excellent," Alejandro said.

Nik began to nod with the air of someone who'd just made a discovery. "All that stuff at the Christie yesterday," he said. "You're not a profiler at all, that was all stuff you picked up directly."

"He's a much worse man than I told you about," I said. "But you only needed enough to turn down his application."

"What did you see when you touched Elaine—" he held up his hand. "No, don't tell me." He took a sip of his coffee and set it down with great care on the table. He turned to Alejandro. "Okay, so what's our next move?"

I blinked. I should have been relieved that Nik wasn't having hysterics, and pleased that he accepted my talent so easily. So why was

I annoyed? Hadn't I always wanted to be accepted as just an ordinary girl?

Alejandro spread his hands. "I have contacted my acquaintance among the Riders here. Not many of them bear *gra'if*, but we must hope that those who do will be inclined to help us."

"Why should that make a difference?"

"I am not certain it does, but the Songs say the Hunt can only be destroyed by someone who bears *gra'if*—which is much the same as saying 'by a Rider.' Very few of the People can bear it, or will make the attempt."

"What is it? Can we get some?"

In answer, Alejandro laid his walking stick on the coffee table between us. I watched Nik's face, saw his eyes widen as the stick became a sword. The *gra'if* metal glittered as if under moving lights. Nik put out his hand to stroke the hilt, but was unable to touch it.

"I have heard that it is possible for someone who bears *gra'if* to touch the *gra'if* of another," Alejandro said. "Indeed, among the Wild Riders, who have their own tales and legends of such things, it is the custom for those who wed to exchange some piece of it. As you see, those who do not bear it cannot touch it at all."

Nik leaned forward, but I already knew that no matter how closely he looked, he wouldn't be able to make out any details on the blade. "What's it made of?"

"Metal mined in the *Glaso'ok* Mountains of the North, by Trolls and Goblins. Forged using the bearer's own blood by Solitary smiths." Alejandro picked up the blade and set it leaning against the arm of his chair. "No one else knows how it is done."

"Okay. So that's a dead end." Nik drummed on the table with his fingers. "Look, we'll take any help you can give us, any at all, but—and no offense meant—how much can *you* do? Is there any other way you could get reinforcements?"

"Nik, what is it you're not telling us?"

He took in a lungful of air and let it out slowly. "Can I use your Internet?"

Something told me Nik wanted more than a smartphone, so we took him upstairs to the spare room we'd set up as my office. Alejandro had all the latest stuff up there, and it only took Nik a minute to access the CBC News site.

I frowned as the headlines popped up. Seven students from a private school had been found dead, an apparent suicide pact. I looked up at Nik, but he pointed back at the screen. Names were being withheld pending notification of next of kin.

"The poor children," Alejandro said, reading over my shoulder. "Their poor parents."

"The parents are going to say the kids didn't have any reason to do this, and no one's going to believe them."

Apparently, there had been a rise in suicides over the last six months, and not merely among the young.

"They don't mention High Park flu," I said.

"The CBC won't," Nik said. "But wait, look at this." He went to another site and scrolled slowly though a number of pages, clicking on links for related items. Some were news articles like the one we'd already seen, from the CBC, City, and CTV, others had the look of privately exchanged links, articles, blogs, and live journals. They all recounted the same kinds of events. An increase in the number of homeless found dead—unusual in the warmer weather. A husband bringing his catatonic wife into the emergency room. High Park flu—those words came up over and over. Three children drowned swimming off Centre Island while their parents drifted away in their canoe.

"These are all items collected by Outsiders," Nik said. "We've seen this kind of thing before—most recently in 1918, the so-called Spanish flu. So far, no one else has put together what we've seen."

"They don't know what they're looking at," I said. "They don't see the connections."

"Rise in depression, in suicide rates, hell, in PTSDs. And you can see there've been incidents in other places as well, in Rome, in Beijing, in New Delhi, Cairo, New Orleans."

"Where there are crossroads, or a Portal to the Lands," Alejandro said.

"Anywhere the Hunt might have come through," I said.

"Exactly." Nik nodded. "It seems to start here, in Australia." He clicked on a series of articles which were now several months old. "It spread out, though now the incidents seem to be dropping in other places, and rising here." He turned to face us again. "You know the *dra'aj* I have isn't my own."

I nodded. "Not what you were born with, anyway," I said. "But it was freely given to you. Like that old man with Elaine."

"Right, exactly. But it's like I said then, there's only so much available, and there's too many . . ."

He looked at his empty coffee cup as if seeing it for the first time. He gestured at the computer. "We can't help everyone, and there are more every day. How many can we save? Can you see what this might lead to? There's only so many people dying of natural causes at any given time, only so much *dra'aj* available, even in cities larger than Toronto. Even if we could move all the stricken ones to say, Beijing, our organization couldn't handle the influx. Our whole system would collapse. Maybe, if there were no new ones . . ."

He turned to Alejandro. "Do you see, we appreciate your help—hell, we *need* your help, but we're afraid it won't be enough."

It seemed like it was someone else nodding, not me. I rubbed at my mouth, but the numbness I felt was everywhere.

I knew what he wasn't saying. An input of *dra'aj* wasn't a permanent cure. Outsiders were like cups with tiny cracks, tires with slow leaks. They needed a regular supply of *dra'aj* to keep themselves sane and whole. There was a limit to how much they could be expected to do for newbies.

And what was more, Nik had given Elaine the *dra'aj* he'd been expecting to use himself. That's what old Harry in the palliative care ward had meant when he'd said "Not you?"

"You can't kill them all by yourself, can you? Soon enough? You talked about others, but if what you say about *gra'if* is true . . . Can you get anyone else?"

I looked at Alejandro. He was rubbing the back of his calf with his hand. He caught me watching him and looked grim. Then he sighed like a parent who was about to give in, and shrugged.

"Perhaps I can."

We can trust him. Stormwolf blinked unseeing at the ceiling that was lost in the darkness of his bedroom. Valory Martin's words pricked at him like needles, sliding cold through his skin and touching with points of pain at unexpected softness. How could she be so certain? Remembering her eyes on him, he shivered, though the room was warm. The High Prince looked at him with the same eyes, though hers were gray and not the human's warm caramel. Both women had dragon fire in their gazes. Wolf felt he understood the High Prince, even if not completely, but this Valory, what was she?

A psychic, she had said. A kind of Truthreader, he had guessed. Get of a Rider, she had said, and that made more sense. That explained, if nothing else, the so faint smell of the Lands that had first set him, though in error, on her trail.

It now seemed that several times, and in several places, he had made similar errors. There had been the scent/not scent of the man in the open square in Granada, and here, in and around the train station. These were accompanied by other smells, familiar smells, but off somehow, changed. Familiar, but not familiar enough.

Did this mean he had been smelling the Hunt all along? Changed somehow, as the Sunward Rider and Valory had suggested?

He threw off the covers, sat up, swung his feet to the floor, ran his hands through his hair. Had he been so close to his goal all along, and not known it? He drew in a great lungful of air and tried to order his thoughts. Concentrated on recalling the precise nature of these unidentified smells.

The encounter with Stump in Granada. He'd noticed the scent crossing that of Nighthawk, and just before his old Pack mate had appeared.

Twice now in Toronto. Once around the area where Valory's trail had been crossed by running water. And the other . . . where had the other been?

Stump. Stump was one of Badger's Five. So they, for certain, had been left here in the Shadowlands. Who else? Why could he not remember clearly? Wolf gripped the edge of the mattress, letting go as he felt the heavy cloth start to tear in his hands. Badger's was not the only Five that had taken part in the Hunt for the Exile. Some had returned to the Lands with him, at the Basilisk's command. Some had remained. If only he had been able to question Stump before killing him.

Wolf rubbed his face. He was afraid to think. *We can trust him.* How could she know?

He had tried to set aside all thoughts of his life as a Hound ever since the High Prince cured him of being one. But when she decided to send him back to the Shadowlands, one thought had resurfaced, unbidden and unwanted. Was his brother here? Could he and the others be saved, as Wolf had been saved? Now, he needed to remember everything.

The hunger. The need. Wolf squeezed his eyes shut. If he was going to remember, he would have to face even that. How everything smelled, how easily it could be tracked, especially the *dra'aj*, like a heavy perfume that lingered in the air. The tracking he could still do. It was the hunger that made the *dra'aj* smell so sweet. The pain of being without it, the itch that could be scratched only by the shifting, the changes. The consequent inability to be still, as the need for the *dra'aj*, its taste, its scent, its force overwhelming and powerful, swept into you, blotting out the world as it came—

Wolf opened his eyes, tried to slow his breathing.

He had wanted to forget this. Had he succeeded well enough to mistake the scent of his old Pack? Did they smell differently because of his cure? Was the change in him? Or in them? Beyond doubt they were here. What did that mean for him? He pulled his lips back from his teeth.

"He is telling the truth. We can trust him." The irony was so heavy he could taste it. What he had told them was indeed the truth, but certainly not all of it. Valory had spoken with the certainty of the Truthreader, of the Dragonborn. Was Valory Martin right? Could he be trusted? Could she know?

Could *he* know?

This was no part of his work, Wolf thought. The High Prince had given him a task and he should even now be about it, instead of lying here pretending to rest. But those he was to find, those who had chosen to hide themselves, they had been waiting long already; surely a short time more would not displease anyone?

While that same short time could be all he required to learn what he needed to know. The truth of the strange scents, the truth of the Pack, the truth of himself, if it came to that.

Surely the Dragonborn Prince, full of the fires of knowledge, would understand his need?

Wolf got to his feet. In his mind he pictured the room where they had sat drinking beer. He subtracted the bed behind him, the heavy curtains to his right and the window behind them. The thick wool of the carpet beneath his feet, and the hard oak floor under it. He added a wide uncurtained window with cranking mechanisms to open the glass. A cushioned bench, a basket chair with matching cushions. Added a rectangular table made up of a streaked marble top resting on curving metal legs. Stiff woven matting on the floor, with panels of some strange wood composite beneath.

CRACK! And he was standing in the small room at the back of Valory's house. Enough light bled in from the streetlamps outside that, even without Rider's eyes, he would have been able to recognize the room and navigate within it. He held still, waiting to see if the noise of the displaced air brought any response from the Rider Graycloud, but there was no sound from anywhere else in the house.

And *there* was *her* scent. Now that he had a person to connect it to, he no longer smelled only the faint essence of Rider that had first drawn him to her. Now he knew the scent of warm vanilla that was Valory Martin, and no one else. A perfume in his nostrils. He followed it through the kitchen area with its cooking smells, so common here in the Shadowlands, the next room, narrow, with its long wooden table, glass-fronted cabinet full of patterned plates and drinking glasses. He could smell the traces of bone in one, and silver in the other. To his left was the staircase.

I knew that Wolf was in the house before the movement of air told me the door to my bedroom had been opened. He hadn't made any noise that I could hear, but I'd known he was there just the same. I let him get all the way into the room, and close the door behind him before I turned on the reading lamp next to my bed.

I blinked, and not just at the light. For a second I actually couldn't remember whether I'd ever seen a man naked before—and then I realized that of *course* I would have remembered. This wasn't something I could ever forget. I decided not to say anything. *Think about how pale his eyes are*, I told myself. Not dark like Nik's. *Okay, don't think about Nik either*.

He saw that I was awake, but he didn't say anything, just stood there with his brow furrowed, and his lips in a thin line, as if wondering why he was there. I put my finger to my lips, but his eyes only narrowed, and I realized that he didn't understand me. I made a mental note that the meaning of that particular gesture didn't carry over to the People. I signaled him to come closer—that gesture was apparently the same—and tried to keep my eyes above his waist. A girl can be curious, but there's a time and place for everything.

"Can you be very quiet?" I said, placing my finger on my lips again so he'd get the connection, and then patting the air in a downward motion.

He nodded, sitting cross-legged on the floor next to my bed. Fortunately, that meant his lower half was now out of my line of sight. As long as I didn't move.

"What is it you need to ask me?" I figured I knew, but I found I wanted to hear his voice.

"How do you know *what* you know?" he asked me. [The gray-eyed woman with her masklike face; fear and longing.]

"I told you, I'm psychic." He waited, so evidently more was needed. "Alejandro says the Rider that was my ancestor was guided by a Dragon, and that everyone who is can see the truth. Wouldn't that be it?"

Wolf sat quietly for a moment, his gaze turned inward. "The High Prince, Truthsheart, is Dragonborn." [A great beast, black, and silver and the red of dark, dark blood, rises over the edge of a cliff, smoke of eye and fire of breath]. "She is a Healer; she does not read the truth as you do."

"I don't think I'm related to her," I said. "Or rather, Alejandro doesn't think so. I would have to meet her myself to know for sure."

"You will go, then? To the Lands, to meet the Prince?"

"That's the plan."

Wolf nodded, still looking off into the dark corner of my room. "Do you see other truths? The Hunt? How is it they can now hold their forms?"

I thought about the images I'd read in Nik and in Elaine, trying to concentrate. "They're feeding on humans now, deliberately, but I don't know why that would do it. They began because there weren't enough People around." He nodded again, shifting his eyes until he was looking at my pillow. I cleared my throat.

"Will you be able to find everyone Alejandro's told you about?" I asked, trying to get him to look directly at me. "You won't be able to Move everywhere." He'd been able to Move here, of course. And I was pretty clear, I thought, on why he'd wanted to. He wanted to know *what* I knew, not just *how* I knew it. But part of him was afraid to ask me. Part of him thought that no one other than the High Prince herself could know the truth about him and not turn away. If I admitted out loud that I knew, would he run? Never come back again? Because I realized that I wanted him to. In a way, he was the first friend I'd made on my own since Alejandro had rescued me.

It wasn't anything to do with seeing him naked.

"No, I cannot Move to any of the places Graycloud has told me of. They are all new to me, and some distance away." And *that* was something I should have noticed myself. Was Alejandro up to something? "But I have been instructed in the modes of travel in the Shadowlands, and I have sufficient wealth to obtain it where necessary."

He looked at his clasped hands, flicked his gaze up to mine and away again. Suddenly, I got it. Never look it in the eyes, keep striking, no matter what you see. Instructions on how to kill a Hound.

I made a decision, suddenly sure that it wouldn't backfire on me. "It's all right to look in my eyes," I told him. "You can't hurt me by looking at me, and looking away doesn't keep me from knowing things about you." I paused to let him take this in. "I already know everything you're afraid of—what you were, how you changed—and I'm still here, talking to you."

He shook his head, slowly, his jaw tight. Then he looked me right in the eye. I didn't flinch. His breathing got faster. Or maybe it was mine. I could feel my heart beating. I could hear it. Could he?

"I can feel your *dra'aj*." His voice was very rough.

I swallowed, my mouth suddenly dry. "I know. Alejandro can feel it, too. I imagine others can as well."

"Others of my kind?"

"Riders. You're a Rider. Just like any other." I held up my finger to silence him. "Think what you like, I *know*."

"Do you know how many have died because of me? How many Faded, their *dra'aj* taken, the Lands deprived and their spirits lost?" His voice was harsh.

Now it was my turn to shake my head, my eyebrows raised. Some of the tornado of images I'd had of his Healing began to make sense. "No. Their *dra'aj* was returned. Their spirits are at peace." Now I sounded like one of these afterlife people.

He was very still, for what felt like a very long time. Finally, he licked his lips. "I was there—"

"That's right. You were in the Lands when the High Prince restored you, though she wasn't that yet, was she?" I put my finger on my lips. "Alejandro's waking up." He was on his feet before I finished the words. That reminded me. "Oh, and Wolf? Word of advice? In this world you should put clothes on when you leave your home, no matter where you're going."

Chapter Nine

ALEJANDRO CAME DOWNSTAIRS, favoring his leg, as I was sorting through my backpack.

"How does it feel this morning?" I asked.

All I got for an answer was another one of those Spanish shrugs as he passed me on his way into the kitchen. I followed him, reaching out to take his wrist as he poured himself some *café con leche* from the thermos jug I'd prepared earlier. He must have seen me out of the corner of his eye, because he shied away, spilling coffee on the counter.

I pulled my hand back as quickly as if I'd been scalded. Riders are *never* clumsy.

"Alejandro!" I grabbed a cloth and started mopping up coffee before it got onto the floor. I contrived to brush against his leg as I did—and got three images *flick-flick-flick* [doors to the lounge at Union Station; a waterfall in Asturias; his wife's face]. Ah, *that* was it. He knew he had to go, but he wasn't happy about it.

"It is nothing, I am a little tired. I did not sleep well." I turned away to rinse the cloth out in the sink, so he couldn't see my face. He couldn't have heard noises or voices, could he? Wouldn't he have come to check?

I'd been undecided, but at that moment I knew I shouldn't tell him about my moonlight visitor. I had a fairly good idea of what he would think of my having a naked Rider in my room. I hadn't done anything wrong, but I had a feeling that plenty of teenagers had used that argument before me.

"You're not having second thoughts, are you?" Though, at this point, they'd be more like third thoughts, or even fourth.

Alejandro steepled his hands and tapped his lips with his fingertips. Then he reached for his cup. "I wish I did not have to take you, but there is really no safe place for you to stay, between the Hunt, the Outsiders, and the Rider, Stormwolf . . ." He shrugged again. "I am sorry, *querida*, but he still troubles me."

"Which is why you sent him to all the People farthest from us." He looked up, startled. I waved. "Hey, remember me? Psychic? I don't have to be paying attention, I know anyway."

The corner of his mouth twitched, but he didn't smile. "Perhaps you are right, perhaps that *is* why I sent him where I did."

Not that he went, I thought. At least not right away.

"He makes my teeth itch. I cannot describe it any better than that."

It should have sounded silly, put like that, but somehow the mention of teeth made me shiver.

"The sooner we go, the sooner we'll be back."

"If we go too soon, we may be back before we have left." Alejandro took a sip of his coffee and put the cup back on the table. "What? Time passes differently between the two worlds, or it can. But do not fear. We are going. I only hope the information we have is worth the help we are asking for."

"The stable Hounds," I said, nodding.

"The stable Hounds, indeed."

"So let's go."

He nodded, slowly, red-blond hair catching the sunlight that came in from the window. When he looked at me, his eyes seemed gold. "But we will return, will we not?"

Was that what was bothering him? "Our lives are here." I wasn't sure whether I was agreeing with him or reminding him. I'd just been starting to feel that I had a life of my own before all this mess began. I wanted to get back to that feeling. Something of what I was thinking must have shown on my face because Alejandro relaxed in his seat.

"Therefore our fight is here," he said, agreeing with me. He tossed back his coffee and stood up, setting the cup down on the table. "Are you ready?"

For an answer I held out my hands. I'd dressed casually, jeans and a silk T-shirt, running shoes and my backpack. Alejandro took my hands in his.

CRACK! I stumbled a bit, and Alejandro's hand under my left elbow steadied me. We were in a back corridor of Union Station, voices and footsteps echoing off stone floors in the near distance. Fewer voices, and fewer footsteps than I would have expected.

"Give me more notice next time, would you?" I grumbled. "I could have left my bag behind."

"I saw you had a good grip on it."

"Alejandro." I tried to keep my voice as gentle and neutral as possible, but I could feel how tight my throat was. "What we're about to do frightens you. Please don't let that make you angry or careless."

Alejandro pressed his lips together and looked at me out of the corner of his eye. "I apologize." He shrugged. "I am not angry, but I am afraid."

And why not? He'd spent more of his life here, pretending to be human, than he'd ever spent in the Lands. This was going to be a very strange homecoming, if you could call it that at all.

"We've promised to ask for help," I said. "It's not just your leg." He didn't want to be going back, asking for a personal favor.

I saw he was actually leaning on his sword cane, not just using it as an accessory. "Will I need a weapon?" I said, only half joking. Now that we were about to embark, his warnings of the day before were echoing in my ears.

"Certainly not. Not while I am with you."

What he meant was, for some of the People a human was bad enough; an armed human was just asking for trouble.

I slipped my arm into Alejandro's and we strolled down to the departure concourse, making our way around the people lining up for their trains, heading for the far end and the doors of the Panorama Lounge, where the VIA One passengers waited in comfort.

Alejandro raised his cane as we neared the doors, hugged my arm tight against his side, and I braced myself. We'd come through the crossroads when we first came to Toronto, but this would be my first time through a Portal.

I took a good grip on Alejandro's wrist with my free hand just as a giant fist grabbed me around my middle, crushing the air from my chest, and throwing me toward the door.

The air was sucked out of my lungs until they ached, the world around me blackened, and the blood began to roar in my ears. A great pressure squeezed me like a snowball in the hands of a giant—smaller, smaller, until suddenly the pressure released and I soared free.

The air was cold and crisp, much colder than it should be considering how blue the sky and how bright the sun. And the fact that I could smell flowers. I saw bright flashes of *gra'if* all around me and I heard a "twang" like a harp string and I felt Alejandro's arms go around me as my knees gave out.

Chapter Ten

"PLACE IS DANGEROUS, mate, you don't want to go there."

"Dangerous in what manner?" From what Wolf had seen so far, the humans in Australia—or here in Tasmania for that matter—were unlikely to frighten easily.

The patrons of the bar that seemed also to be the tourist information center, town hall, and doctor's office exchanged glances, but no one seemed inclined to answer his question. Finally, one of the older women who was sitting in the area designated as the doctor's waiting room used her cane to lift herself to her feet and came stumping over to lean on the bar next to him. The others edged away, but with an aura of respectful attention Wolf had not been expecting.

"Whair ye from then, young 'un?"

"Canada," Wolf said without thinking.

The woman nodded. "Don't sound Canadian," she said, and a few of the others laughed. "Must be one of the French ones, then, eh?" She smiled and Wolf noted the unnatural evenness of her teeth. She put out a hand that looked as gnarled and twisted as the head of her cane.

"Becky Upfield," she said.

Wolf was surprised by the heat of her skin. "Edmond Wolfe."

"And what do you want with the mine, Ned?"

"I am looking for something."

Her eyes narrowed, and she looked him up and down. Satisfied with what she saw, she spoke. "Something's what you'll find all right, that's certain. Not sayin' what, mind." More subdued laughter. "Well, Ned, I won't lie. There's some say there's acid poison out there. Some's gone out to look for something as hasn't come back agin—and I don't think it's the acid. Does that worry you?"

Wolf fixed her with his narrowest look.

The woman's smile broadened to the point that her eyes practically disappeared in a nest of wrinkles. "You can't scare me young 'un. Nothing much can now." Again, she seemed satisfied with what she had seen. She looked around the room. "Ben, you take Ned here out to the mine." She looked back at Wolf. "He won't go in with you, Ned. That's more'n I'll ask of anyone."

"I will not require it."

"That's fine, then. Lilly, give the boys a drink before they go. It's parched out there."

"Nice tattoo," Ben began as they got into his vehicle, and then talked nonstop all the way to the mine. Wolf stopped listening after the first few minutes showed that the young man had no idea what was really in the place. This made Wolf wonder whether the old woman, Becky Upfield, knew anything other than rumor. She had certainly seemed as all-knowing as a Singer, and had much the same manner.

Singers. This morning he had caught himself singing as he prepared to leave the apartment. As soon as he noticed, he'd stopped and then couldn't remember the song he'd been singing. But he did remember why he'd felt good enough to sing. The *dra'aj*. From what the girl Valory had told him, all the *dra'aj* he'd taken, over all the time he'd been a Hound, had been released when the High Prince had cured him. Released and returned to the Lands, as the *dra'aj* of any who Faded should be. Reason enough for song.

It could not undo every evil thing he had done, but this knowledge did much to relieve the weight on his spirit. He wished that he knew more, however. What happened to the *dra'aj* carried by a

Hound who was killed, for example? Did it, too, return to the Lands? What of a Hound killed in the Shadowlands—like Stump in Granada—what happened to the *dra'aj* then?

Valory might know, he realized, or she could find out. It might be that the Hunt would have to be returned to the Lands, if the *dra'aj* they carried was not to be lost forever. This was something he could bring to his old Pack mates: not merely a cure, but a restoration. A redemption.

It was something he could bring to the High Prince as well. Would she not wish the *dra'aj* restored, if it could be done? Would that not encourage her to spare the Hunt?

Once they arrived at the mine site, the young human showed no signs of fear or apprehension, merely indicating a dark shadow on the rocky hillside. "There it is," he said. "Gibbings Mine." In keeping with what the old woman had said, he showed no signs of getting out of the jeep himself.

"Thank you," Wolf said as he opened his own door. "I don't know how long I'll be."

"No worries," Ben said. "I'm to take you and bring you back, Becky said." He lowered the seat back, tipped his wide-brimmed hat over his face, and appeared to go to sleep.

Even if Graycloud at Moonrise had not already told him, Wolf would have known to expect a Goblin just from the caution of the townsfolk, and the fact that this was a mine. The entrance showed signs of recent use, but the scents were mixed, old and new, along with a distorted one that oddly overlaid the others. He could not be sure, but it had that same twisted familiarity he was associating with the Hunt. His hand lifted to touch the scarring around his eye and he frowned. Wolf walked far enough into the mine to leave the sunlight behind and waited, letting his eyes adjust to the darkness, before taking a deep breath.

"Vein of Gold," he said. "Graycloud at Moonrise told me where to find you." He opened the collar of his shirt, ready to show the High Prince's mark.

At first there was no answer, but Wolf had learned his lesson in the fountain of Cibeles in Madrid, and waited, listening to the music made by the far-off dripping of water.

Suddenly the smell changed, a crowded city street overlaying a room of old meat. The temperature dropped, and Wolf took a step back, putting his hand on the hilt of his *gra'if* blade.

"Wolf." The voice was low, beyond the hearing of any human. Low and familiar. "Wolf." The voice was stronger, as if the speaker came nearer.

Wolf felt his blood turn to ice.

"Did you bring me a morsel, my love? A precious lick of *dra'aj*?"

"Where is Vein of Gold?" he said.

"Ran away. Ran through the gold that names him, Binds him, flows in his veins. Ran where I can't follow."

A misshapen griffin stepped out from behind an irregularity in the rock wall. Changed to a horse-faced thing with only forefeet. Flickered and changed again. Became a Rider, thin to the point of starvation.

"Don't you know me, my love?" and changed again as soon as the words were finished. But her hippocampus was feathered not scaled, with twisted stumpy feet, not a flashing tail. Changed once more. "I knew you'd come back. I told them all so."

Wolf's lips trembled on the edge of her name. "Swift River Current," he said finally.

"That's right, my dearest, my sunlight." (flicker) And the hand she reached out was a paw. (flicker) A hand. "That's mine, isn't it?" (flicker) She advanced a few inches on tentacles (flicker) on feet. "The bitty bit outside? For me, isn't it? You're not in need." She changed again as soon as she finished speaking and stood, fanged head hanging low, double lidded eyes blinking snik-snik, ribs showing through mottled skin stretched tight, webbed hands, dragging tail.

She could not really want the human, Wolf thought. With his own *dra'aj* glowing like a sunrise, she must be maneuvering to get closer to him. Even if she had fed on Vein of Gold, it would not have made any real difference. She would want more, and more, all that there was. Without her Five nearer to her to make her wait her turn, she would glut herself, absorbing *dra'aj* until the sheer weight of it would rob her of consciousness.

Wolf shifted around to his right, to better stand between the Hound and the shaft that led to the outer world. "That human has not enough *dra'aj* to interest you. Surely you can wait?" Though he knew she could not, would not. Any more than he would have done in her place. "I know where there is *dra'aj* aplenty for you; let me take you."

The thing opened its mouth to speak and flickered once more into the shape of the Rider it had once been.

"What are you saying, Wolf? I can tell you know the use of the human *dra'aj*. How else could you keep your shape so long?"

A cold lump grew in Wolf's belly. Was this how the Hunt was achieving this stability that both Graycloud and Valory had spoken of? In his time, the Hunt had not known of any special virtue in the *dra'aj* of humans, who had barely enough to make it worthwhile to feed from them. How and when had it been discovered?

"You don't need any, I can tell just looking at you. Why would you keep it from me, Pack Leader?" River came closer. "Though now I smell you more closely, there is something different about you."

She took one more step toward him and Wolf pulled his *gra'if* blade free, a sudden blaze of light, almost blinding in the confined space. The Hound changed again, coils of a snakelike body, tails flapping as it wriggled away, throwing its paws (flicker) hands (flicker) claws (flicker) hands up before its eyes.

"How," it croaked.

"I am cured, River. Clean." Wolf lowered his sword, but did not sheathe it. He knew better than to trust her. "I am no longer part of the Hunt."

"Not possible! Who could do such a thing?"

"There is a new High Prince, a Dragonborn. She it was who Healed me, saved me." Wolf swallowed. "She would Heal you also."

The thing that was Swift River Current returned to its sea horse shape, and considered, head to one side, left eye blinking slowly, right eye gummed shut with yellow ichor.

"She would do this?" (flicker) as she regained her Rider shape long enough to speak. "You are sure?"

Wolf hesitated. Could he speak for the High Prince on this matter? Surely she would help the Hunt? She would have saved even the Basilisk, at the end. "I am sure," he said finally.

But it was the hesitation River had heard, and not his final certainty.

"Of course, of course, my dearest, my love. But for now, just for now, you'll let me have that human, won't you? Just this last time. So I'll be nice and pretty and look myself when the High Prince sees me."

Wolf's heart sank. "What good will the human do you?" Let her answer him clearly. Then he would know.

"But that's why I thought you were still one of us—still part of the Hunt, I meant. Because you had your Rider shape, and I will have, too, once I've fed from the man you have outside. We learned that, after we were abandoned here. If we eat enough human *dra'aj*, we can control what we look like, we can be ourselves again. That is why Fox—" She lost her shape.

Wolf raised his weapon once more. "What did you say? Speak on. You would say something of my brother?"

River drew herself up, her back arched, her hands, clenched into fists, hanging strangely in front of her. Her face seemed too long, and yet she was able to speak.

"When you didn't come back, someone had to lead, and who was going to fight him for it? He's your brother, second only to you. Of course he made himself Pack Leader and thinks himself a better one than ever you were. But I know him, just like I know you. He's afraid you're going to come back and take the Pack from him." She smiled, square teeth in her long face. "I wonder, should I tell him you'll never come to challenge him now, or would you still? He says we can stay here; we can feed from the humans. We can control our shapes, and we wouldn't need the People." She swallowed. "We wouldn't need them ever again, if we had the humankind as our nourishment."

Wolf shook his head, unwilling to accept what he was hearing. That she would reject Healing, that she would reject becoming whole again, for this continuation of her perverted existence.

Though a quiet voice inside him said he might have rejected it as well.

"Wolf." She flickered and changed again.

Wolf Moved.

"What was that, mate?" the boy Ben said. "Sounded like a gunshot."

"I heard nothing," Wolf said as he climbed into the jeep. "Let us go. Quickly."

He would have to find Vein of Gold some other way.

I fell to my hands and knees, and began swallowing faster and faster, trying not to gag. To my horror, my stomach lurched, and kept right on lurching. Alejandro put his arm around me.

"No. Don't touch me. Please. Sorry." Slowly, the world steadied and, still swallowing, I managed to look up. "Sorry," I repeated. I took a deep breath and gagged again, retching. I tried to breathe shallowly, and in a minute I was able to raise my head again. *I'll hyperventilate at this rate*, I thought. I would have been mortified, if I'd had any time to spare.

Alejandro without his human guise was almost enough to get my stomach to settle. I would have known him anywhere, of course, even without the familiar dark blue linen suit, and he did bear a resemblance to his human version, but it was as if everything had been buffed and shined, tweaked into perfection, as if even his bones had been more finely drawn. The immediate difference was how much richer his coloring now was, making his human self seem washed out and bland. But what was most striking—and I use that word with care—was how very beautiful he was. Alejandro Martín was a handsome man, but Graycloud at Moonrise could take the breath from your body.

What does Wolf really look like, I wondered, as I realized that what I saw now was what Alejandro's wife had seen, when she'd first found him, hiding, as he thought, in a waterfall in Asturias. She had spoken to him, sung to him, and when he had finally understood that moving water was no refuge from humans, he'd answered. Graycloud had been hiding, not from her (what did he need to fear from the humankind?) but from another Rider, one he had offended, one whom he was not powerful enough to kill. Many times after that first day his enemy looked for him, and always Graycloud stepped into the moving water, and was safe. Safe from the one who came to kill him, but not safe from the spell of the black-haired woman, who came every day to sing. Until finally he came out of the waterfall for the last time and stayed by her side until death made her leave him.

Looking at him now, I could see why that long-ago human woman had taken the chance to sing to him.

"Is it unwell?" A long-fingered hand on my arm and I twisted away, retching, before the tide of images could sweep me away with it and drown me. Another beautiful face, though this one was much harder, and colder, and not just because Alejandro was more familiar. Hair a platinum blond, pulled back into a braid and tied off, eyes a very pale green, like a cat's, skin a sun-darkened ivory. A Starward Rider. Dressed in dark browns and blacks, leather showing wear and tear, and even in one place a patch. He didn't have to dress like this, his *dra'aj* was strong enough to have kept his clothes new looking and bright, but apparently his *fara'ip* had a soul above such things.

He had a collar of some glittery silver around his neck that I realized was *gra'if*, just like Alejandro's sword.

"She is unwell, yes. Perhaps it is the passage through the Portal."

"She is human, then?" He was interested but not in any profound way. He'd never seen a human, but he knew they existed.

"The Songs tell of such passages, of the bringing of humans to the Lands, though they do not tell of this sickness." He was a Singer. He squatted down next to me, and I shied away, entirely a reflex because whatever it was that was making me feel so bad didn't affect my talent, and I knew that the Rider had no intention of touching me. "You'd do well to find a Dragonborn."

"It is the High Prince herself we seek."

At this point, I had to stop paying attention to what they were saying and concentrate on my breathing. Slow breaths, not *too* deep, in and out, in and out. Keeping my body as still and level as I could, to prevent the squirmy feeling in my insides from spiking into full-blown nausea.

"My dear one, we must Move." Alejandro's voice sounded far away.

"Okay." That was the best I could manage, and with that I almost lost it. I tried again. "Let *me* hold *you*," I said. I couldn't bear to be touched, but I knew that I needed his help to stand, and I had to be touching him to Move.

I was barely upright when the SNAP! came and we were standing on a hilltop under a display of stars I would have found amazing if I hadn't been vomiting. Another CRACK! and we seemed to be standing within a circle of stones that made even my nausea-tossed brain think of Stonehenge. Then I got lucky and fainted again.

Now there was a beautiful, warm voice, like chocolate, and soothing hands touching me, spreading comforting warmth through me, and I relaxed into the soothing heat, feeling all the Lands spread around me, seeing all the pockets of territories like a patchwork quilt version of the world tossed onto a field of darkness, all of them the same, all different, and the movement of the *dra'aj*, feel it pulling through my psyche like ribbons of color, the ebb, the flow, the shifting, the swell—HOLD STILL . . .

Scales under my hands, and heat as the ribbons untwisted and became calmer.

And then darkness.

A bitter taste in my mouth. And the darkness again.

"She sleeps." Cassandra joined the Rider Graycloud at Moonrise in the dining area of her pavilion. "I must be honest and say, however, that her sleeping is thanks in great part to the pills you obtained for her."

There were platters of fresh fruits, and others of pastries filled with meat or cheese laid out on the table, along with wine and sparkling water. This last was something Cassandra particularly liked, but which hadn't been available in the Lands until now. It turned out that Water Naturals, giggling, were happy to induce carbonation in their springs for the High Prince. Several were already vying to produce a variety of flavors. Smiling, Cassandra saw that Graycloud had also poured himself a glass, though he seemed uninterested in the food. Outside, the day was a warm one, but here in the pavilion it was as cool and fresh as if the walls had been made of stone.

Cassandra sat down, resisting the urge to rub at her temples. She had found and Healed three more damaged places just this morning, and would have been happy to have left this girl to someone else if that had been possible, and if it had not been Graycloud with her.

"From what Nighthawk had told us, we did not expect to see you here in the Lands, Graycloud, but we welcome you, and your *fara'ip*. I am only sorry that it was an injury that brought you to us."

The Sunward Rider inclined his head to her. "I meant no disrespect, my Prince, and I thank you for your Healing. But it has been long since I was accustomed to hearing my Rider name. Will you call me Alejandro?"

Cassandra smiled when she heard the familiar accents of Spain in his voice. "Then I am Cassandra. I'm sorry Nighthawk is no longer here, but both he and the Prince Guardian are attending to some business of mine elsewhere."

Alejandro inclined his head again. "And Valory? Will she now be well?"

Cassandra leaned forward, resting her elbows on the edge of the darkwood table. "I can make her comfortable," she said. "But I cannot stop the vertigo."

"I have never heard of such a thing." The outer corners of the man's brows were drawn down. "But then, it is long since I have been through a Portal, and never did I bring a human with me."

"I admit my own experience is limited," Cassandra said. "I've asked the Singers who are with us at the moment to consult among themselves, to see if they can Tell us anything from their store of knowledge. But you say she's psychic." Cassandra was glad no one else was here who needed that word explained. She'd found that Max was better at explaining certain human phenomena than she was. She had lived among humans, and that had given her an insight into the world of the Shadowlands, but Max had lived *as* a human, and that gave him an advantage, an understanding, she could never have. "Could that have anything to do with her reaction to the Lands?"

"She became much worse when you touched her." Alejandro's tone was steely, and it made Cassandra smile and raise her hands in conciliation. Alejandro relaxed again, shrugging one shoulder.

"You're absolutely right," she continued. "The girl did become worse when I touched her, skin to skin. Is her ability enhanced with contact?"

"It is." The older Rider was grudging. "But she has touched me frequently, and without difficulties."

"Well, now." Cassandra tilted her head back, unfocused her eyes. "I wonder what would happen if Max touched her." She sat forward again, her elbows on the table. "I'm not an ordinary Rider, I am the High Prince. If Valory is really psychic—and I believe you, Alejandro, that was just a figure of speech—then what she perceives when she touches me might serve to make her reaction to the Lands worse."

"I am afraid I do not follow you, High Prince."

"I'm bound to the Talismans, and through them to the Lands themselves, and the vast network of *dra'aj* that informs everything within them. If the poor girl perceived even a part of that through me, it's a wonder her head didn't explode."

"I must take her back," Alejandro said, standing up.

"You shall, when I am satisfied that the journey itself will not kill her." Cassandra motioned him back to his seat. "In the meantime, we must discuss the impact of the news you bring me. There are two matters of urgency as I see them," she began. "First, this phenomenon of the 'stable' Hounds, as you call them. Second, the existence of the humans who call themselves Outsiders." She paused, continuing only when it was clear that Alejandro had no comment. "I have lived in the Shadowlands myself, and, like you, I had heard something of these people before, though I do not think I have ever met one, nor did I know what caused their condition."

"The stories and rumors of something that feeds on humans, taking their life force from them . . ." Alejandro shrugged. "It is true, we have all heard these stories, and like many of us, I dismissed it as a human phenomenon. It now appears that the Basilisk's Warriors have been bringing the Hunt to the Shadowlands, though infrequently, since shortly after the Exile began. From time to time, the Hunt fed on humans, and it is this which created the Outsiders. According to the one who spoke with us, their numbers have been steadily increasing, exploding in the last few months."

"Of course." Cassandra frowned. "The Hunt couldn't feed on the Riders who brought them. And the rest of you have never been easy to locate." Cassandra leaned back in her chair, lacing her fingers together. "In fact, it's likely they didn't even know that you existed to be fed upon."

"And it seems that since the Basilisk was defeated, the abandoned Hunt has been feeding freely, and almost exclusively, on humans. I have seen news reports myself, and have been told of others, that describe the toll these feedings take. From what I can gather, the areas most affected are Toronto, Rome, and Beijing, with lesser incidents in Granada, Melbourne, and Seattle."

"Places where the Exile lived most recently," Cassandra said. "Or where one of us Wardens was living."

Alejandro inclined his head. "The Outsider with whom I spoke accused us of bringing the Hunt to prey upon humans, and then abandoning them without aid or rescue."

"And they are not entirely wrong." Cassandra clenched her teeth shut, right hand forming a fist. She hadn't expected that her responsibilities to humans would come so soon, and be so complicated. Rider tourism—for want of a better word—had not even started. "I thought I would have more time."

"Pardon?"

Startled, Cassandra realized she had spoken aloud. "More time," she repeated. "Contrary to our expectations, the Cycle does not turn by itself; it is taking all our efforts to restore the Lands and the People to prime condition. The last Cycle did not end in its natural time, but was hastened by the actions and errors of the Basilisk Prince. The damage—" she shook her head, exhaustion sweeping through her in a sudden wave.

"But the Hunt, the Outsiders . . ." Alejandro's lips pressed together and twisted to one side. Clearly, he had not planned to be the advocate of the Outsiders.

"Make the issue of the Shadowlands more urgent, I agree. But not, you must understand, from the perspective of the Lands." Cassandra rubbed at her brows with stiff fingers. She could feel a headache starting behind her eyes. *And who Heals me?* "Here in the Lands, I can find problem areas, even individuals, perhaps even the Hunt, through my bonding with the Talismans. But who will find the Hunt for us in the Shadowlands?" *Stormwolf could*—but she thrust the thought away. How could she ask such a thing?

"They could be anywhere. What we're contemplating, what you're asking, would be to engage in what might very well turn into some kind of guerrilla conflict—"

Alejandro sat forward, as if he would speak, and Cassandra raised her hand. "Even if I decided to begin such an action, I haven't the troops for it, not while I need them here. We *have* taken some steps toward dealing with the Hunt, but you must realize, the Shadowlands are not my first priority. I can't spare anyone for some long, drawn-out campaign, at least not right now."

Alejandro sat back, spreading his hands. "Any help at all would be—"

A Wild Rider appeared in the doorway.

"The sleeper awakes, my Prince."

I could taste something medicinal in the back of my throat, and felt a warm hand on my forehead. I jerked away, wondering what they'd dosed me with *this* time, when I smelt saffron, and opened my eyes to a long oval face, pale as marble, except for storm-gray eyes.

"What did you give me?" And cleared my throat.

"Gravol." Her voice was as warm, as liquid, and as soothing as chocolate. "For the motion sickness and nausea. Alejandro went back through the Portal for it as soon as I knew what ailed you."

I struggled to sit up, and the pale woman sitting on the edge of my bed slipped her arm around my shoulders, moving the pillows to prop me up. The room swayed and then settled down. Not with any feeling of permanence, however. "He went without me?" Strange, but I wasn't getting anything but the minimal buzz from her, as if she wasn't touching me at all.

"Not at all, foolish child, I am here." I turned toward his voice and found him sitting in a cushioned chair to my right, leaning forward with his elbows on his knees and his hands clasped together. I turned to my left and found myself once more looking into a pair of storm-gray eyes in a long oval face.

"I'm Cassandra Kennaby. You are welcome to my home." She smiled, and for the first time I knew what the phrase "unearthly beauty" meant.

"You're the High Prince," I said. It didn't take a psychic to figure it out; I remembered the name. "What's happened to me? Why can't I read you?" I would have thought I'd be happy about that, but I actually found it unsettling.

She held up her hands. They were covered by a pair of silver gloves, with full gauntlets almost to her elbows. They appeared to be made out of scales. Very fine scales.

"Gra'if?"

"You know it, then?"

"I bear a sword," Alejandro said from behind me, and the High Prince glanced at him with a smile. I could see the edge of a *gra'if* mail shirt peeping out from the collar of her red tunic, as well as a torque around her neck. *Gra'if* was made from a Rider's own blood, I remembered Alejandro telling me, and it was unusual for one Rider to have much of it. That was why Alejandro always spoke of "bearing" it, rather than "wearing" it.

"It appears that *gra'if* insulates you against the exercise of your talent. This is contrary to common sense and logic, but then, *gra'if* usually is."

I swallowed three times, quickly. "What happened to me?"

"You appear to have suffered an extreme case of vertigo and motion sickness. Disorientation, dizziness, nausea, and so on, upon passing through the Portal. I was not the nearest Rider with the Healer's talent, but since you were coming here anyway . . ." She shrugged, a gesture made oddly more human by her using it.

"I remember. It was so nice and warm, but then—" I swallowed, and clutched at the side of the bed.

"Hush, now. Relax. When I touched you, at first you began to Heal, but almost immediately your symptoms worsened beyond what they had been before. Can you describe to me what passed?"

I outlined what I remembered of what I had seen and felt. The spinning and the dizziness, the lines of color and the patterns. "Could it be a migraine?" I asked. "I've heard they can cause nausea and light effects." But she was already shaking her head.

"She tapped into your Binding, as you suggested," Alejandro said. "But why should it affect her so? Without doubt, she has Rider blood—it is what accounts for her talent."

"She is definitely Dragonborn or, rather, her ancestor was. That's what your psychic ability really is," Cassandra added, turning to me. "It's a knowing of and recognition of the truth. All who are guided by the Dragon have it, though it manifests in different ways. It's why I can Heal, for example, because I see the truth of the body, and can restore it." A wrinkle formed between her honey-gold brows and disappeared without a trace. "I can also see the truth of the Lands, and, through me, you experienced that truth as well, but unfortunately you are not Rider enough to bear it."

"But the drugs, they are working?" Typical of Alejandro to worry about me. And I had to admit to a mild curiosity myself.

"Certainly, but for how long? Things of human making don't work as effectively, here in the Lands. And that is when they work at all. Valory has been given the whole day's dose of Gravol already, eight tablets, and she is barely able to sit up."

I remembered what the Rider at the Portal had said. "But humans have been brought here before," I pointed out. "At least, there are all those old songs and ballads that say so."

"True," she agreed. "Both pure-blooded humans and children of mixed blood. But psychics? That's something we've never seen before."

"Maybe it's like an allergy," I said. "Maybe repeated, small exposures would give me an immunity." I didn't really need to see the answer in Cassandra's eyes. I already knew it.

"We don't know enough—yet—to solve this problem." Her voice was very gentle. "You have enough Rider blood, and therefore enough *dra'aj*, to sense the Lands, the connection that we all have that allows us to Move, though not enough to Move yourself. It is confusing you rather than helping you."

"So pure-blooded humans would have no difficulties, since they wouldn't be able to sense the Lands at all?" I asked.

"Exactly."

I rubbed at my forehead, feeling the corners of my mouth starting to tremble. My ability, the thing that marked me as part Rider, that might have given me some rights to the Lands, was the very thing that prevented me from staying here. "So what now?"

"Now you will go home, until such a time as we can bring you here without drugs."

That would be never, I guessed, but she was still speaking.

"But first, I would have you both interviewed by Singers. We must give them all the information we can about the new form of the Hunt, and about the Outsiders." As if on cue, another Starward rider, dressed in the same colors as Cassandra, appeared in the doorway. "Would you bring Graycloud at Moonrise to Moon, and ask that a Singer be sent here for Valory?"

I waited until Alejandro had kissed me on the forehead and left with the strange Rider before I asked the question I'd been waiting to ask the Dragonborn High Prince.

"*Are* you?"

She smiled, knowing right away what my question meant. "Your mother? Or many times great-grandmother? No. I bore no children during my time in the Shadowlands." She smiled when she said this, and I thought she might be planning to have children now. It was strange not to be able to read her. Not unpleasant, just strange. "It will have been some other guided by a Dragon, not I, and if your coloring is true, likely a Sunward Rider. As Alejandro will have told you, there was more traffic between our worlds in the time before the Exile."

"But you can do what I do?"

To my surprise, she shook her head. "As I said, I see the truth of the physical essence. I see when that essence is not true, and now that I am bound to the Talismans—to Sword and Spear, to Cauldron and Stone—if I see an untruth in the Lands, or in one of the People, I can repair it, Heal it." She paused, brows drawn down in thought. "I can usually tell when someone is lying to me." She smiled. "But not always, if they are lying to themselves as well. I cannot see the truth of things apart from the person, as you do."

I hadn't thought about it that way, but that did describe what I could do. "Toward the end, when you were touching me, I thought I felt scales—warm, though, not like a snake."

"That was my Guidebeast you felt." She tapped her chest. Her *gra'if* mail gloves had fingernails on them, short, thick, and rounded off at the tips of her fingers, as though they were claws. I was already becoming accustomed to the natural look of Riders, so her fingers didn't seem unnaturally long to me, though her hands were very beautifully shaped. "My Dragon, or rather, the Dragon that is me. It was only through becoming my Guidebeast that I was able to stabilize your condition at all."

I remembered then that she had lived as a human for a long time. And a doctor, Alejandro had said. But she was still speaking.

"I cannot cure the illness that comes upon you here," she was saying. "I cannot stay a Dragon for you. My Healing no longer belongs to me alone."

"You healed Stormwolf," was what I said aloud.

"He is a Rider," she said.

"I haven't told Alejandro," I admitted. "That Wolf, that he . . ." I searched her face and saw she understood. "He's ashamed of it, Wolf, I mean. And now that we know the Hounds can look like Riders, Alejandro would never trust him, no matter what I say." And that was the bleak truth of it, I realized. Alejandro would continue to believe what he believed, no matter what the evidence to the contrary.

Cassandra brushed my hair back out of my face, and just for a second I was a child again, in my bed, and my mother was putting the back of her hand on my forehead to test for fever. Even with the *gra'if* on it, Cassandra's hand was warm and gentle. I wanted to stay in this bed forever.

"I know human addicts, and human addiction. Until I understood what had made the Hunt, I did not believe addiction was possible for the People. But how it functions in Riders?" she shrugged, the gesture looking altogether too human for her, though, like Alejandro, she did it perfectly. "How can I be sure what happens? With human addicts, we could cure the physical cravings, even at times the psychological ones, but we weren't able always to remove the circumstances that led to the addiction in the first place."

"You're afraid this might be true of Wolf as well?" I cleared my throat, swallowed. "You can relax."

"You have no such concerns? You trust him?"

I nodded, finding my mind ready to drift off on the warm tide of her voice.

"Why?"

"Because I *know*."

"You see the future?" I shook my head. "Then you have a very hard road in front of you, Valory Martin. I wish I could be of more help."

You're not asking me why, I thought. Why I wanted to help Wolf. And that was good, because I wasn't sure I knew the answer myself.

We were interrupted at that moment by the Singer, Piper in the Meadow, a Sunward Rider who was guided by a Roc. Cassandra left us, telling me that she would be back when they were ready to Move me, and I should rest as soon as the Singer left me. She gave me more Gravol to take.

"Don't worry about overdosing," she said, smiling her quiet smile, "*that* I can cure."

I told Piper in the Meadow everything I knew about the Outsiders, including everything I could remember of what Nik had said, and what I'd gathered from him the few times I'd touched him. The

Singer hummed while he was speaking to me, but his eyes never left my face, and I knew that he was getting every word. He asked me a couple of questions, thanked me, and left.

I swallowed the tiny pills with the help of the glass of water on the table next to me, tasting the sharpness of the medicine on my tongue washing away under the freshness of the liquid. I had a momentary panic when I thought that maybe I shouldn't be eating or drinking anything here in case it trapped me. Weren't there stories about that kind of thing? But surely Alejandro would have warned me, and Cassandra was doing everything she could to get me home.

I lay back in the bed and tried to relax, surprised to find that after a while there were tears trickling down the sides of my face from under my closed eyelids. Somehow the knowledge that I would soon be back in Toronto, in our house in the Beaches, wasn't very comforting, even though my stomach felt better. With that knowledge came the awareness that this place, the home of at least one of my ancestors, would never be my own.

Chapter Eleven

NIKOS POLIHRONIDIS RAN whistling up the steps of Elaine's double-fronted Victorian. Both the design firm and the architects who occupied the main floor were in, so Nik muted his whistling as much as his mood would allow. For the first time in months he was beginning to feel that they might be getting a handle on things, that everything might yet return to normal—or at least what they'd considered normal for the last century or so.

Arlene and Marg were at their desks when he reached the second-floor landing, but he could see that Elaine's office door was open, so he blew them kisses as he went by. Elaine was dictating into her headset—looked like the Finnegan Brothers were going to settle out of court—and she raised her finger at him. He waited until she finished, and unhooked her earpiece.

"How are you feeling?" he said as he threw himself into the more comfortable of her client chairs.

"I believe the expression is dazed and confused." Elaine leaned back in her own chair and sighed. "Nikki, I take back every time I ever felt impatient with you, and every time I got pissed when you took off, leaving me to deal with clients while you ran off to help someone. I had no idea." She pressed her lips together and shook her head, her eyes glinting. "How long have you . . ." She rotated her hand in a "keep going" gesture. "Tell me it gets easier."

"Obviously it does. Look at me. You've known me how long?" Nik used his most matter-of-fact tone. Elaine was scared, but an attitude of business as usual would be the thing to steady her. There were still things he needed to tell her—thank god she'd never shown much interest in having children—but he'd save that till later. When she was stronger.

"What happens now?" Elaine's eyes flicked to the light blinking on her phone until it stopped.

"You have to be careful the first month or so, but Marg and Arlene already know what to look for, so we've nothing to worry about." *Except where I'm going to get you your next shot of* dra'aj. Nik was careful to keep smiling.

"I didn't say anything to the ladies." Elaine lifted her head toward the outer office, where their assistants sat.

"Good." It was one thing for Elaine to know—lots of Outsiders had a normal person they confided at least part of the truth to—but experience had shown them it was better their condition didn't become general knowledge.

Elaine's eyes shifted to look over his shoulder and Nik turned around. The smile faded from his face when he saw the short man with the dark blond hair and Slavic features who stood in the doorway, Arlene hovering behind him.

Nik forced himself to look welcoming and got to his feet. "It's okay, Arlene. This is an old colleague of mine from Kitchener." Poco helped him out by giving him the handshake, shoulder-hug, kiss-on-both-cheeks greeting of the Mediterranean intimate. "Elaine, I don't think you've ever met—"

"Your cousin from out of town?" Elaine put out her hand and seemed pleased when Poco kissed it.

The small man's blue eyes twinkled as they shifted from Nik to Elaine and back again. He slapped Nik on the arm with the back of his hand. "Dude." He turned back to Elaine. "My friends call me

Poco, and now you can do the same." He looked around at Nik. "Just now I've got something I need Nikki for, so if you don't mind . . . ?"

"We can go to my office." Nik picked up his cue.

"I hope to see a lot more of you from now on," Elaine said, as she sat back down and picked up a folder.

"Nuthin' more likely, darlin'."

As he led Poco to his own office—a corner office, just like Valory Martin had said—Nik braced himself for the blast he knew was coming. Poco waited until the door was closed behind them.

"Are you out of your mind? What were you thinking?" At least Poco was keeping his voice down.

Nik bit down on the angry retort trying to force its way past his lips. What was he going to say? But this is Elaine? Exceptions should be made for her? He tried to dial down on the emotion. "You don't tell me what to do, none of you. I don't answer to any of you. I'm senior—"

"And what? That means you don't have to follow the rules the rest of us follow? My god, Nikki, you know better than anyone—" the little man squeezed his eyes shut and took a breath before continuing. "These are *your* rules, Nikki. You're the one who came up with them. Do I have to remind you what happened with the 'Spanish Influenza'?" Poco made quotation marks in the air with his fingers.

Nik's temper flared again. No, he didn't have to be reminded of the last time a group of Outsiders had decided access to *dra'aj* didn't need to be regulated. Just because spreading around a deadly virus wasn't directly killing people didn't make it okay.

"We agreed, Nikki. When we saw how things were going, we agreed no new ones would get fixed." Poco's control just made his anger all the more apparent. "I know she's your friend, I know you went to law school with her, but—dammit—we all have someone."

He couldn't. He absolutely could *not* explain why Elaine was different, not just someone he'd known for years, but *family*. Terribly remote, ten generations away—but still his sister's child to him. No other Outsider of his age had any living relatives—even someone like Poco, who for all his anger really did understand, wouldn't have let him make an exception for her.

"I've spoken to the Rider," was what he did say.

Poco squeezed his eyes shut, his hands were fists. "And?"

"And he's going to help us. They. They're going to help us."

Poco pumped his fist into the air. "Dude, you should have led with that."

Nik raised an eyebrow, but refrained from pointing out that Poco hadn't given him a chance to lead with anything. "I was waiting until I had something concrete in place. We're still talking over the details."

"Okay. Okay. But this could change everything."

Nik hoped that was true. He hoped it wasn't going to be just Alejandro Martín helping them.

Poco stopped nodding and smiling and looked at him once more with hard eyes. "This is still all going to take time, though, isn't it? And in the meantime, when will Elaine need a fresh fix? Couple of days?"

Nik looked away. "About that."

"What are you going to do?"

Nik took a deep breath. "She can take mine."

"Dude! You *have* lost your mind! How's that going to help anyone?"

"I've gone on short rations before. Elaine can't, not at this stage."

The short man shook his head. "You let us know. Call me, or Eva or someone. Don't do this alone."

"It'll be okay. I can wait."

The short man shook his head. "You better hope you're right." Halfway to the door, Nik stopped him with a question.

"Wait a second, how did you know?"

Poco turned back, fixing Nik with his sharp blue eyes. "How did I know? How do you think? Eva told me." He came back into the room until he was standing close enough to put his hand on Nik's shoulder. "You think we don't keep an eye on you? Where would the rest of us be without you?"

"But if they are now feeding from humans, can we even use one of the People as bait?"

Nighthawk glanced at Twilight Falls Softly. The Singer was a

Starward Rider. She was shorter now than her natural height, but they had made very little change to her coloring, and her alabaster skin and blue-green eyes attracted a fair amount of attention among the Spaniards in the subway car. As for himself, Hawk kept much of the natural Sunward ruddiness, though his hair now looked more copper than auburn, and he'd given himself a few freckles. He'd had plenty of practice looking human after all the time he'd spent as Warden of the Exile.

"I believe we can," Hawk said in answer to the Singer's question. "I believe any of us might make a successful bait. These are addicts. Because they have a source for the substance they need, that means nothing. They will be unable to resist taking more as they find it, and still more."

Twilight nodded, peering around at the subway car with intense interest. She'd heard much from the two Princes about the Shadowlands, but Hawk knew that tales, even for a Singer, did little to prepare you for the place.

She leaned toward him. "I was not aware I would actually feel that we are still in the same area, the same place."

Hawk nodded. "It is strange at first, particularly if you don't know what causes the feeling. You can walk for months—I have done it—and never leave the one, solid place that is the Shadowlands. In the Lands, 'here' has, for Riders at least, a specific and singular meaning; in the Shadowlands 'here' is relative.

"The question in my mind," Hawk continued when he could see the Singer had finished storing away his words, "is how the Basilisk Prince kept the Hunt from feeding on his followers in the first place."

"That would be the Horn," Twilight said. "You've forgotten," she leaned in toward him to speak over the noise of the subway as it passed around a curve. "The Basilisk had the Horn, and the Horn controls the Hunt. Apparently in more ways than simply calling them."

The train pulled into a station and Hawk shifted Twilight over to allow a group of humans access to the doors. The Singer coughed and Hawk covered a smile by turning his head. Nothing could prepare one of the People for what the Shadowlands smelled like, the sweat of the bodies, the fumes of the automobiles—or the food cooking for that matter.

"Is this a common method of travel?" Twilight cleared her throat. "I am sure I have heard both the Princes speak of horses."

"Many human cities have subways," Hawk said. "And the High Prince instructed me to use human transportation where time allowed. As for horses . . ." Knowing the needs of Singers, Nighthawk launched into an explanation, beginning early in the history of humankind, though not quite so far back as the actual domestication of the beasts.

Twilight paid close attention, not faltering once through the elements of human history, technological development, population pressures, and the like. It had been many years since Hawk had dealt with a Singer, but he remembered that they preferred to be told everything one knew on any subject. Twilight held up a finger, as Hawk uttered a particular phrase.

"Did you say 'air planes'?" she asked. "Are you saying that humans can fly?" Her interest was understandable, only Riders with the right kind of Guidebeasts—dragons, say, or griffins or rocs—could fly.

"It is not the humans who fly, exactly," Hawk began again, and was soon deep into questions of cross-sections of wings, lift, and aerodynamics.

"Fascinating," Twilight said. "Though truly I can see that it would be difficult to put such knowledge into a Song." She looked around once more. "This is not a plane, unfortunately, but traveling through the earth like a Troll has its interest as well." She leaned in again, lowering her voice even further. "Not the least of which is being able to closely observe humans themselves. I was unprepared to see so many different Wards."

Hawk shook his head. "Human coloration has nothing to do with Wards, humans are grouped in other ways. You can see for yourself that human coloring is highly mixed. Not only can you find in a single human the red hair of Sunwards, the pale complexion of Moonwards, and the blue eyes of Starwards, but there are also some with complexions of brown and yellow—in all manner of shades—that do not exist among Riders."

"It is true that this close to them, humans seem very different from one another. Except for the smell."

Hawk smiled again. "I assure you that after a few days you simply stop noticing it." He took her lightly by the elbow and steered her closer to the exit. "Come. Let us return to the task at hand. We must not forget that any Rider we meet with, with the exception of Alejandro and Wolf, must be treated with caution, as possibly a follower of the Basilisk."

"Or a Hound," Twilight pointed out.

"Or a Hound," Hawk agreed. "As inconceivable as that seems."

Twilight frowned, the corners of her mouth showing how troubled she was by the idea. "Surely, any Rider who avoids us will be a follower of the Basilisk," she suggested.

"Not necessarily." As the train entered the "Banco de España" station, Hawk positioned them in front of the doors. "Any who has lived here hidden might also, if they do not know us."

"Your task is more complicated than I thought." Twilight followed as Hawk led her up a series of staircases, slowing to examine the escalators more closely. "It seems obvious that the same traps or lures could not be used for both the Hunt and the Basilisk Warriors," she said when her examination was complete. "Unless, of course, the two have allied once again. What is this rock?" she added, touching the pavement as they came up the stairs.

"Concrete," Hawk said. "It is manufactured. 'Man-made' they call such things here."

"Truthsheart says they have no magic." Twilight's fingers lingered on the pavement. She ignored the muttering of people who had to move to get around her.

"But as I have been explaining, they have something else, called technology, and engineering. With these, they accomplish many of the same results that we do using magic."

"Then how do you know it is *not* magic, just one that we cannot understand?" Twilight grinned to show that she jested.

"Because there is no *dra'aj* involved, just ingenuity."

They had reached street level, and though it was still only June, heat rose up from the pavement, as hot and dry as though they were in a desert place. They were now on the south side of the Plaza de Cibeles, and the Singer stood still, looking around her, recording everything she saw and heard, humming under her breath the tune that would from now on accompany the telling of this tale. The flood of pedestrians broke around them, some smiling amiably, and some glancing at them with irritation until they saw the look on

Hawk's face, whereupon they went about their business. Hawk's sword was disguised as an umbrella, but he'd had centuries to learn how to look armed and dangerous in any circumstances.

"There is the fountain of Shower of Stars." Hawk pointed to the center of the traffic circle, where crowned Cibeles sat in her chariot drawn by lions. "An example of what we've been discussing. The water's movement is caused by pumps and valves, not by magic."

"And yet it conceals what lies within it from our eyes," Twilight said. "So the nature of the water, and its function, is not affected by this 'engineering.'"

"But the moving water will not hide us from humans," Hawk said. "So we cannot be long. What is it?" The Singer had been frowning, but was now smiling again.

"I was wondering how it was that the fountain did appear to hide Shower of Stars from humans." Twilight gestured at the people around them. Many were taking photographs, it was true, but it was obvious that they saw nothing untoward in the fountain. "But of course she is a Water Natural, and has the same nature as the water itself, and while in it, can take any form she chooses, seen or unseen." The Singer hooked her arm through Hawk's. "She also is unaffected by the engineering."

"Are we ready, then?" Hawk said. Twilight nodded, and they Moved, finding themselves standing in a cool green room with iridescent walls, sparkling in spots with a diamond luster.

Hawk cleared his throat. "Stars? Shower of Stars, it is Diego Rascón. It is Nighthawk come to see you, with a friend from the Lands."

Nothing. Just the sound of water all around them. Twilight put her hand on Hawk's arm. "Let me try," she said. "Shower of Stars, I am Twilight Falls Softly, and the Hydra guides me. I am *fara'ip* of the Water Sprite, Tear of the Dragon. I am here to help you return to the Lands."

Still nothing. Twilight pursed her lips. She gestured and Hawk drew back. She took several deep breaths and began to Sing, strong, heavy notes that became deeper as her throat lengthened and grew. Hawk raised a trembling hand to his mouth. Twilight was becoming her Guidebeast. It had been longer than anyone now alive could remember since such a thing was commonplace, and Hawk watched in awed fascination as Twilight became an ivory-colored water snake, spiky-finned, and with three heads. Hydra. One head turned its blue-green eyes on Hawk, while the other two began tasting the waters around them with their tongues.

It might almost be easier, Hawk reflected, to make the transformation yourself, than to watch as someone else did it. He hoped he would soon have the chance to find out.

When Twilight returned to her Rider shape, it was with a frown on her face.

"This water is empty," she said. "The Natural is gone." She looked around her, lips parted, fear in her eyes. "A part of her *dra'aj* is bound to the place, and remains, but this heart of the fountain will collapse as soon as the memory of her Fades." Twilight turned to Hawk. "We must Move, or be revealed."

"And I know where we must go." Hawk reached for her hand. "Quickly, we must find the Troll."

"Hold! Identify yourself!"

This made the fourth time Wolf had been asked to give his name and Guidebeast since coming through the Portal in Beijing. The first three times it had been Wild Riders who had stopped him, but these two, stepping out from the Trees that formed the perimeter of the High Prince's camp, were wearing the red, black, and silver that were her colors.

Though there could be no more than two or three score People in this clearing among the Trees, the place had the bustling air of an armed encampment of hundreds. There were Wild Riders eschewing tents to sit by fires burning in the open air; there were two lesser pavilions, one in the green and gold of Honor of Souls; there was also a Troll and, closer to the horse lines, an Ogre. All were armed, many of the Riders with visible *gra'if*.

Wolf found himself looking for familiar faces. Any familiar face would do, but Walks Under the Moon, the High Prince's sister—*she* he could approach and be sure of his welcome. Several Wild Riders nodded to him, and Wolf nodded back, but he did not know any of them well enough even to put a name to them.

He snorted, the impatience that lay under all his thoughts rising for a moment to the surface. However hard it was to be alone, he could not easily change his circumstances. Best he remember that, and keep his mind on his task.

He forced his pace to slow as he neared the High Prince's pavilion, its silver roof, red walls, and black banners gleaming like dragon scales in the bright sun. Part of him wanted to rush forward, brushing aside anyone who would stand in his way, and throw himself at the feet of his Prince. It had been simple when she was just Truthsheart, and she had taken him in her arms and Healed him. Now that she was High Prince, he shared her with everyone who made up her *fara'ip*, and somehow this made him feel more distanced from her.

"You have some purpose here?" This was a Starward Rider, dressed in blue and purple, who wore his ash-blond hair hanging loose down his back. He had a sword at his right hip, and an archer's arm guard on his right arm, but bore no *gra'if*.

"I would speak with the High Prince."

"You would?" The Rider looked Wolf up and down, clearly unimpressed with the dusty boots, wide-brimmed hat, khaki trousers, and cotton shirt suitable for travel in the Tasmanian winter. Wolf stifled the urge to brush himself off.

"Many wish to approach the High Prince. Indeed, who would not?" But the Starward Rider did not step aside. Nor did he ask Wolf for his name.

Wolf was debating whether to turn away—was what he had learned from Swift River Current really as significant as he thought?—or to insist on his rights, when a Wild Rider in battered leathers with *gra'if* showing at his throat, came out of the entrance, and greeted him before he could speak.

"Stormwolf. Have you been here long?" The sideways glance Wings of Cloud gave the Starward Rider almost made Wolf smile. "This Rider was with us on *Ma'at*, the Stone of Virtue, and fought by the side of the Guardian," Wings said, addressing the Starward guard. "He is always welcome to the Princes."

The Starward Rider's inclined head was almost a bow, considerably more courteous than his behavior thus far, but he still did not offer his own name and Guidebeast. Wolf lifted his brows and barely nodded in return. He should not let such things annoy him, he thought, as he allowed Wings of Cloud to draw him into the pavilion.

"Supercilious ass," the Moonward Rider said as soon as they were out of earshot of the man at the entrance. "One of those who overvalue ceremony, and thinks himself favored because he is a Starward, like the High Prince. Making him stupid as well as pompous." The corridor they entered seemed somehow to be walled in darkwood paneling.

"Friends have turned to enemies for smaller things before. I know a Song—" Wolf frowned. Where had that thought come from? "But what of you? Are you well?" It struck him suddenly that Wings had lost a brother at the battle on the Stone, a twin. That was hard, very hard. A brother's loss was something that Wolf understood very well, though caution held him back from sharing this with Wings.

"I survive." The Moonward's voice flattened slightly. "Some days are harder than others, but the High Prince keeps me too busy to brood." He turned to Wolf, but his ready smile did not quite reach his eyes. "Do you think she does this on purpose?"

"She is a great Healer." The Wild Rider was not the only one the High Prince was keeping busy, Wolf realized. Could she be treating him with the same prescription of hard work that she was using on Wings of Cloud? For the life of him, Wolf could not remember whether Wings knew his own history, knew he had once been a Hound. He told himself it was not cowardice, but caution that kept him from referring to it. "I think we must assume that whatever she does, she does with purpose."

Wings stopped suddenly, his brow furrowed, bringing Wolf to a stop with him. "Wait, you will not have heard," he said. "The Griffin Lord has Faded."

Wolf stood blinking for a long moment. Lightborn? Lightborn *Faded*? "Was it the Hunt?" he said, his voice sounding far away.

"The Hunt? Why would you think of such things? As if the reality was not difficult enough?"

Wolf shook his head, momentarily at a loss for words. "It is just—so suddenly? What could have happened?"

Wings put his hand on Wolf's arm. "Some of the Basilisk's Warriors cannot surrender."

"There are always fools, in every conflict, but—"

"No, you misunderstand. Not they *will* not surrender, they *cannot*. The High Prince says it is a Chant, similar to the Chant of Binding. Lightborn," Wings of Cloud exhaled sharply. "Lightborn thought the Rider merely frightened of capture, and did not expect the blow that killed him."

Wolf looked down the corridor toward the entrance, then back, in the direction they were headed. This news changed things; there was something else he needed to do now.

"The Lady Moon," he said. "Do you know where she might be found?"

Wings studied his face before finally nodding. "You are in luck, my friend. She is here, in this very pavilion, but this way." The Wild Rider drew Wolf back to a cross corridor lined in orange silk that they had earlier passed by.

"You will deal carefully?" Wings said, as they came to a door made of a sliding screen painted with Manticores. "The loss has been greatest for her."

"She loved him." Wolf glanced at the door and back to the Wild Rider. "I know."

Wings of Cloud rested his hand on Wolf's shoulder, squeezed lightly before letting him go. "I like you, my friend. You are quiet, as though you bring some of the stillness of *Ma'at* with you. I'd rather see more of such as you, and less of those like our friend at the entrance. Have you ever given thought to becoming a Wild Rider?"

An unfamiliar tightening in his chest stopped any quick answer he might have made. This was tantamount to an invitation to join the *fara'ip* of the Wild Riders, which meant that others among them must feel the same way, must have spoken of him among themselves. It was the first such gesture of friendship he had received since his Healing.

No. He was wrong. This was the first such gesture from another Rider. The human girl, Valory. *She* had offered to be his friend. Wolf shrugged away the image of her warm golden eyes. Like the High Prince, Valory knew and accepted him for what he was, but she was human. He could not expect that many others of his own kind would feel the same.

"I value your welcome, more than I can say," he told Wings. "But for now I must think of my duty to the High Prince." He would have to tell them. He could not become part of a *fara'ip* unless the truth was known to all. Even if it meant the welcome would be withdrawn. "Perhaps, when my task is discharged . . ."

"Of course. We will not forget." Wings gestured at the door. "When you are ready to see the Prince, Moon will call me."

The sliding darkwood-and-silk panel opened into a room full of sunlight, and the smell of rainfall on summer grass. There were several people already in the room, but before he could announce himself, he found his arms full of a Starward Rider dressed in the colors of the High Prince.

"Wolf, what brings you—" Moon released him and stepped back far enough to see his face. "Oh. The same thing that brings everyone." It was hard to be certain in this light, but it seemed that Moon's almond skin had paled to alabaster. Certainly her gray eyes, so like those of her sister, seemed to carry an extra shadow.

"You smell differently," he said.

Now her eyes lightened, and her smile broadened. "That would be the child." She put her hand on her belly, though so far as Wolf could see, there was yet no swelling there. "I carry a small grifflet, though whether lord or lady, my sister will not say."

"But then you . . ." Wolf let the words trail away as he studied Moon more closely. The slight giddiness in her speech, the way her heart beat faster. "You have more *dra'aj*," he said, and his heart grew cold. *How is this possible?*

"No, not I." Moon patted her stomach. "Again, it is the child, and the *dra'aj* is his." Lightborn's she meant, though how that was possible Wolf could not imagine. "But come, we need not be standing here." She drew him farther into the room. The other two Riders, after being introduced as Singers helping Moon with a search, excused themselves with sympathetic smiles. Moon pulled him down next to her in the wide window seat.

"Moon, I am more sorry than I can say."

Her faced hardened to a mask so quickly that Wolf cursed himself for speaking. But then she softened again, her eyes half-hooded, and slipped her hand into his.

"I wished you with me, when the news came." Her voice was barely more than a whisper, as if she could keep the grief away if she were quiet. "You are the only one who has known my heart from the first." She looked at him, silvery tears welling in her eyes. "At times, it is more than I can bear."

"It becomes less sharp," he told her, covering her hand with his own. "There will come moments, more and more, when you do not think of it. But it will never go completely. You will never lose him completely."

She squeezed his hand and drew hers back. Her eyes glittered again as she turned away.

"Did you come first to me?" she said. "I was not expecting you back so soon."

Unsure how much to tell her, Wolf looked down at his clasped hands, then let his eyes wander to examine the room itself. It was a strange hybrid. The walls by the sliding door were the taut silks of the Princes' pavilion, here flame colored, while the window wall where they sat was paneled, a layer of darkwood covering a wide thickness of stone. As if to emphasize its difference, the window looked out onto a rocky coast, where the tide was only beginning to turn. He glanced sideways at Moon, and the drifting melancholy of her face brought him to a decision. Telling her would be good practice for speaking to the High Prince, and it would serve to distract her as well.

"I found someone I was not, exactly, looking for." When Moon turned to lift an eyebrow at him, Wolf began by telling her of finding Nighthawk, and Graycloud at Moonrise.

"Graycloud has been here himself, with his foster daughter. I spoke with him, though not with her."

Wolf drew in his breath. Valory had been here; she had spoken with the High Prince. *Did they talk about me?* "He came, then? He had hoped that his injury would not worsen."

"They came with other news, they spoke of the human Outsiders, and of what they called stable Hounds. I was just now consulting with the Singers, asking them to search for any Song that might tell us of such things."

"Then I have something to add to your knowledge. When I was with Graycloud and Valory Martin, we did not know how the Hunt were keeping their Rider shapes." As he told Moon about his encounter with Swift River Current, she left the window seat, going to pour two cups of wine from a dark clay bottle sitting on a table against the silk wall.

He took a cup from her gratefully, and only just stopped himself from draining it at once, forcing himself to savor the taste. He waited until Moon had seated herself again to continue.

"She did not at first realize that I was no longer . . . that I was not—"

"That you had been Healed."

Wolf nodded. "She thought that I kept my Rider shape because I had fed on humans. She claimed that feeding on human *dra'aj* could stabilize us—them—somehow, enabling them to control the changes."

"Interesting." Moon clasped her hands in her lap and tapped her thumbs together. "A valuable addition to our knowledge. Is there something more you can tell us from your unique perspective?"

Wolf gritted his teeth. There it was. Even Moon, who was like a sister to him, knew that it was his "unique perspective" that the High Prince valued. He steeled himself, and continued. "We all fed on humans from time to time, but very seldom, and only in the absence of other *dra'aj*. Theirs is," he shrugged, "unsatisfactory." He lifted his cup, swirled the ruby-colored liquid. "As if this wine were watered away to nothing." He lowered the wine again without tasting it.

"Not many in his court knew it, perhaps even you did not, but the Basilisk would give us Solitaries to feed from, and Naturals, those who displeased or disobeyed him. Even, on occasion, Riders. Only when we were taken to the Shadowlands would we feed from humans. We did not feed on our escorts, the Riders who took us." Wolf wiped the grin off his face as soon as he felt it forming. "Though we thought of it, of course."

"Were there many of you? The Songs speak of single Hounds, though you are called the Hunt." Moon's voice was firmer now, more its liquid self. As Wolf had suspected, this distraction was doing her good.

He considered her question. "We *are* a Pack, this is true. Until we were taken to find the Exile, there were not many of us taken to the Shadowlands, never more than one or two Fives at a time."

Moon shifted to look at him more directly. "Fives?"

"It is how we are counted. In Fives. When the period of Exile was ending, we were six Fives—"

"So there are *thirty* Hounds in the Shadowlands?" Moon seemed to be doing some mental calculation of her own.

Wolf shook his head; this was what he'd been trying to work out himself, with limited success. "No. Some returned with me, and were killed here. Some remained in the Shadowlands, and were killed there . . ." He stopped, and risked a glance at her.

"How do you know this?" Again that quiet, gentle tone.

Wolf watched Moon's face. This was something he had not told her—not the only thing, but still something she might find difficult to forgive. "I was Pack Leader." Wolf waited.

"*You* were?" Moon shut her eyes and Wolf thought he had lost her. Then the corners of her mouth turned down, and she leaned against him, resting her head on his shoulder. "Are we not a wonderful pair, you and I? Tools of the Basilisk. At least you were compelled, while I—"

"Were compelled in your own way. As was Lightborn, also, in his own way." It was part of what drew them together, Wolf knew. "But we are not his tools now, and we act to save those who were." He stood and put his wine cup down where he had been sitting. He and Moon had gone down this path many times, and he saw no profit in treading it again.

Moon tilted her head back, staring up at him, her gray eyes speculative. "That is what you were doing now, in the Shadowlands, isn't it? Not just your mission, but trying to save them. Your old Pack."

He shrugged, unwilling to put it into words, but equally unwilling to lie to his only friend, especially in the face of her loss. Her smile was a small thing, but a true one.

He smiled back. "I must go to the High Prince now and give her my news."

Moon shot to her feet, gripping his arm in both hands.

"Wait? You *did* come to me first? Then tell me, do you wish to return to the Shadowlands? To help your old Pack mates? Then you must *not* go to her!"

"What do you mean?" Wolf felt as if he had been turned to stone. Would the Prince take his task from him, withdraw her favor? It burned him like acid that he could only serve the High Prince with what remained to him of his Hound self, but to not have even those skills of value to her—he now found that much worse. He had done everything she asked. He did not deserve to be turned away, useless and alone.

What would become of his brother if this task was given to another? He could not fail Fox again. The pressure of Moon's hands on his arm brought him back.

"Wolf, when she sent you to the Shadowlands, my sister did not know the Hunt was there, that she would be putting you in the path of your old Pack." Moon shook him. "Do you not see? She thinks it too much to ask of you, too difficult for you to bear."

"What of the missing People?" He heard his voice as though it came from far away.

"She plans to ask Graycloud if he will undertake the task. Nighthawk can assist him. Both have a great knowledge of the Shadowlands. And both bear *gra'if*," she added.

"You say 'plans,' so she is already resolved?" Fear gave Wolf a strange courage, and he found he was shaking his head. "Graycloud at Moonrise can find only the People he already knows of," he said. "What of those in hiding even from him? He will not be able to track down these unknowns. And what, then, of the Hunt?"

"Surely even this one encounter has shown you that it is too difficult for you—oh!" Moon released his arm, and sank slowly into the window seat. "It was there before me and I did not see it. 'Some remained in the Shadowlands,' you said. *She* did not know, my sister did not know, but *you* did. Even before you went, you knew the Hunt was there."

"Moon, listen to me." Wolf flung himself down before her, his hands on her knees. "Do you not see? I did not fear to meet with them, I *hoped* that I would. I hope that when they see me, they will see what their own futures might hold—futures they could never have imagined possible. If others are sent, the Hunt will only be killed." He rested his head in his hands. "And the *dra'aj* they carry would be lost forever." He looked up again. Moon's gray eyes were worried in her Starward-pale face. "Valory Martin told me that the *dra'aj* I took was restored to the Lands when your sister

Healed me. The same would be true of others. Is this not worth the risk?"

"You believe that others would come to be cured?"

"I believe they must be given the chance," he said. "I am proof that a cure is possible."

"A way to undo the evil you have done." It was not a question, but Wolf nodded just the same. He knew Moon would understand. She was nodding, and her mouth became firm as she gave a final, decisive nod.

"Then you must *not* go to my sister." Moon stood and began pacing, as if activity somehow lent weight to her words. "She would forbid you to return."

Wolf got to his feet. "Wings of Cloud has seen me." He remembered the supercilious Starward Rider at the entrance to the pavilion. "And others."

Moon waved this away. "I will account for it, so leave it to me. But go, now, before someone mentions to the High Prince that you are here."

"Wolf?" The note of worry in her voice stopped him at the door. "What if they will not accept the chance, the hope that you will offer them?"

Wolf knew what she was really asking him. Which was his true Pack? The Hunt, that he had been a part of for so long? Or the Riders? He remembered the chase, and the glorious hot rush of stolen *dra'aj* as it filled him until he thought he would burst. But he also remembered the hollowness, the starvation, when there was no more *dra'aj* to be had. The constant awareness of the void, of the itch that the *flickering* could not scratch, of the cold and of how alone he was, always, even in the middle of the Pack, in the midst of his brothers who at any moment could become his killers, if the temptation of his *dra'aj* became too much for them.

Here, now, he was part of the Lands once more, aware of all its spaces and places. A Rider, relieved of the terrible hunger. And more, part of a *fara'ip*, not a Pack. Even if he was still asked to chase, to Hunt, it was without that terrible hunger, that need to feed.

He raised his eyes to Moon's.

"You did not choose to free yourself of the Hunt, Wolf," Moon said. "My sister forced that freedom on you." *I cannot lose you, too,* were the unspoken words that lay under her questions.

"But I am grateful for it." If ever he had doubted, Wolf knew now that this was true. "I would not have it undone, not for anything."

"And if the others do not choose what you now embrace?"

Wolf considered. River had turned away from him, would the others do the same?

And if they did?

"I would give them the chance, but they are the Hunt," he said at last, surprised at how steady his voice was. "If they will not be cured, they must be dealt with as we deal with Those Who Hunt."

Moon took a deep breath, and her throat moved as she swallowed. She came to him, and held him firmly by the shoulders, a wrinkle of concern between her flaxen brows.

"If they must be killed, you do not need to be the one. Let my sister send others to do it. Only take care. I would not lose you." Her voice trembled as she said the words aloud.

"You will not."

Moon's smile twisted a bit as she stroked his cheek, but it was genuine. Her expression changed as she glanced at the door, and she retained her hold on his arm. "You have already been seen by so many . . ." She smiled again, and this time it was an unalloyed expression of delight. "The window," she said, turning toward it. "Go through it, and Move from there."

Wolf stood for a moment in the surf, letting the cold water soak the cuffs of his trousers. He thought about Moon's concern, and her championing of him. Then he thought of the offer Wings of Cloud had made him, and realized that he would have to reject it. If he could not even tell Moon about his brother, and the debt that he owed him, how could he dream of one day telling others exactly what he had been?

He scrubbed at his face with his hands. He could still feel the comfort of Moon's presence, the warmth of her affection—and the proof of it she had given him by warning him of the High Prince's intentions. How much stronger those would have been, if she had known that the new Pack Leader of the Hunt was Wolf's own brother. If Truthsheart already questioned whether he could survive an encounter with the Hunt, she would be sure a meeting with his brother would be too much for him.

Wolf could only hope she was not right.

Max Ravenhill Moved into the clearing that *Trere'if* left free just outside the pavilions and tents of the High Prince's court. He didn't Move directly into the pavilion itself, precisely because it *was* her court. It might be his home as well, but protocol was protocol.

Trere'if filled the whole Vale where the Basilisk Prince had created his citadel and capital. The Tree Natural's restoration to his own place had been Cassandra's very first action as High Prince. If anyone, including *Trere'if*, had asked him where he was coming from, he'd have said the Jade Ring, though that wasn't exactly true. He was Guardian of the Talismans. The Sword, the Spear, the Cauldron and the Stone, symbols of the Lands, and the *dra'aj* that formed it. There were very few people who knew that the Guardian Prince was the only person who could Move to *Ma'at*, the Stone of Virtue, that it was impossible for anyone else, even if they had visited there, to hold the place firmly enough in their minds to Move. Cassandra, as High Prince, could fly there, in her Dragonform, but not even she could simply Move there.

Max walked through the camp quickly, nodding at some, raising his hand to others. The Wild Riders were gone, he noticed, every Rider in the clearing was wearing someone's colors—most of them Cassandra's own, of course.

He didn't stop until he heard voices through the drape of tent that was the door of her private sitting room, and didn't go in until he recognized the second voice as Moon's.

"What's this you're saying about Stormwolf?"

Cassandra looked at him and smiled. "Do you know I can't feel your *dra'aj* when you're on *Ma'at*? Did you find the Horn?"

Max threw himself onto the padded stool nearest her and took her hand. "I regret to say I did not."

"Destroyed, do you think?"

"If the Basilisk was wearing it—and I'm sure he was, just as Moon thought—" he gave the younger Rider a nod. "Then it must have been destroyed when he was." He kissed her hand and got to his feet, heading for the table and the carafe of cool water that sat on it.

Cassandra stood, stretching her arms above her head, and came to join him. "So there's no chance of controlling the Hunt that way."

"Maybe it's for the best." Max handed her a glass of sparkling water. "I've got little stomach for simply summoning them and putting them to the sword."

Cassandra smiled at him over the rim of her glass, and her gray eyes glinted. "You were always more sentimental than I."

"Goblins are more sentimental than you."

She smiled again, putting her free hand flat on his chest. Max took her hand in his and kissed her palm. "What were you two arguing about when I came in? What's happened?"

Cassandra arched her golden eyebrows. "We were not arguing."

Max started to grin, but stopped when he saw that Moon was genuinely distressed. "What were you discussing, then?"

"Moon tells me that Wolf came to see her."

Cassandra had turned until he had her in profile. It was like looking at an old Roman coin. Moon looked down at her feet in a way he hadn't seen since the Basilisk had still been alive. "Nothing unusual in that, surely? He would have come as soon as he'd heard about Lightborn."

"Except that he did not know until he arrived, and Wings of Cloud told him," Cass said quietly, glancing at her sister.

"Then that wasn't the reason he came."

Cassandra turned toward him, the corner of her mouth lifting for a moment. "Apparently there is some quality in human *dra'aj* that allows the Hunt to remain in one shape for a long—or at least a long*er* period of time." She looked up at him. "They can look like their original selves, like Riders."

Max suddenly wished he was sitting down. More, that he was still the Exile, and that he and Cassandra were sitting in a sidewalk café in some Mediterranean seaside town, with none of this to worry them.

"Can they do anything else like Riders?" he asked. *My god, if they could Move.* "My sentimentality aside, is there really any doubt about what we should do?"

Cassandra stepped away from him, picking up a pawn from the Guidebeast game. "Moon told me none of this until he had returned to the Shadowlands, where he plans to continue in his task." She looked up from the small silver dragon with ruby eyes she was turning around in her fingers. "He also plans to track the Hunt."

"He *what*?" Max couldn't stop himself from turning on Moon, but he managed not to say anything else. Particularly not: "Are you insane?" She'd had a catastrophic loss, and he wouldn't want to do that to her.

"It's not what I wanted, certainly not what I would have allowed to happen, had I been consulted." This last was definitely aimed at Moon, who only pressed her lips tighter together. Since the death of the Basilisk, Moon had been very meek, very docile—if anything, Max would have said she was too conscious of her own guilt. He knew he should be happy that she was finally able to disagree with her sister. *But did it have to be over this?*

"However," Cassandra was still speaking. "He *is* the only one I have with tracking abilities that come close to what the Hunt can do. He *would* be the only one who could find them, when they do not wish to be found. He also wishes to offer them the chance to be cured."

"You'd do this?"

"They are of the People, they are ours. From the moment I first understood that they were Riders who have somehow become addicted to *dra'aj*, they became part of our responsibility."

Max pulled up a chair and stood by it pointedly until Moon sat down. He turned to his wife, but she was already seating herself. He positioned his own seat where he could see them both easily. "Who else knows about this?" Cassandra's eyes moved to Moon's face.

"No one from me," the younger Rider said. "When I think of what I said before—" She waved one hand in the air. "All the People who have never been to the Shadowlands . . . they will say we should close the Portals, and let the Hunt have the humans."

Max whistled silently through his teeth. "So we're keeping this all to ourselves for the moment?"

"Are we not stretched as it is, between the strange Binding of the Basilisk Warriors, and the restoration of the Lands?" Cassandra looked down at the pawn she still held in her hand and frowned.

"There is something else, a smaller thing, I hope." Moon's voice was certainly small enough.

"Honey, pretty well anything would be smaller than this." Max was rewarded with a smile from each woman. Small, but smiles.

"There was something else Wolf wanted to tell me, but he could not bring himself to speak of it."

Max watched Moon's bent head for a moment, then turned to find Cassandra looking at him. He narrowed his eyes, and reminded himself that Cassandra was *not* sentimental. "I have a bad feeling about this."

"Then there is something we can all agree on."

Chapter Twelve

WE HAD SOME TROUBLE with the Portal at Union Station, and I'm not sure exactly what Alejandro had to do, but we were back in our own living room practically before I realized there was anything wrong. At first I couldn't wrap my head around the idea that it was only the late afternoon of the same day we'd left. Somehow I expected to find that more time had passed while we were in the Lands, but Alejandro explained that it didn't always work that way.

"Time does run differently," he said, as he fussed around the kitchen throwing together a salad Nicoise. Now that my motion sickness had disappeared, I was starving. "But the how and the why of it depends on many things. With whom you pass through a Portal, for example, and your own level of *dra'aj*—to say nothing of where, precisely, you stay while in the Lands. There are places, for example, where time does not pass, where it is always midnight, or always a spring morning. So you are as likely to return to an hour very close to the one you left as to find it much later."

"That's not what the stories say," I pointed out. I'd expected to have a headache, or at least to feel run down, as I had every other time I'd been sick. But there was nothing, no aftermath at all. As if we'd never left this world. Even the High Prince was starting to feel like a dream. I kind of wished I was alone, so I could figure out how I felt about that. "Usually the human feels like he's been gone a few hours, and when he comes home, years have passed and everyone he knows is long dead."

Alejandro looked up from arranging tuna on the bed of greens. "But I have told you, *querida*, the stories humans tell about the People are not so very accurate." He put down the fork and set the empty tin into the sink. "And many of those stories, you will remember, involve Solitaries. Trolls, Dwarves, Goblins, and the like. Solitaries and Naturals themselves live a different order of time from the rest of us."

He popped the hardboiled eggs through the slicer and arranged them around the tuna. I placed two glasses of water, two wineglasses, and the cutlery on a tray and followed Alejandro outside onto the deck. Whatever explanation accounted for it, the sun still felt as if it was in the wrong part of the sky. I shivered.

"*¿Te traigo un jersey?*" Alejandro switched to Spanish, just in case any of our neighbors were at home. Even if you weren't listening deliberately, you could hardly help but overhear what was being said in the next yard.

"*¿Como lo explicaré?*" I said. "*Hace casi treinta grados.*" I could just see trying to explain to either Barb or Shari why I was wearing a sweater when it was almost thirty degrees. That was one of the easy things about coming to Canada from Spain, temperatures, weights, and distances were metric—even if Canadians had a habit of measuring distances by traveling time rather than actual kilometers. *How did they measure distances in the Lands?* I wondered. It looked like I would never need to find out.

We were just getting settled at the table, and Alejandro had that look on his face that meant he had something serious to discuss when the phone rang and he went in to answer it. I glanced through the window. I'd noticed that the younger you were, the more likely it was that you would check the caller ID before answering and then letting the call go to voice mail once you'd checked. It was something I had taught myself to do, to fit in.

Alejandro, true to his own apparent age, had answered the phone and was speaking. I saw him glance at me, notice me watching him, and hold up his hand to keep me in my seat. The previous owners' *Vogue* magazines were still coming to the house, and the latest one had been left out on the table, the cover and pages curled from the day's humidity. I snagged it by one corner and pulled it closer. Maybe checking out the photos of what Alejandro called "*las flacas*," the skinnies, would distract me. My whole life I'd been dressed by someone else, and Alejandro was doing his best to teach me about clothing and fashion, and how to use clothes to give the impression I wanted to give—age, economic status, that kind of thing. He'd laugh at the models in the magazines and on the runways, but not as though he found them very funny.

"They are like sticks," he'd say, warning me not to fall victim to the idiocy. "Chosen for the purpose of focusing all attention on the clothing, of showing it to the best advantage. Believe me," he'd say, shaking his finger at me. "Women are not meant to be clothes hangers! It is entirely the contrary. It is the purpose of clothing to make women look beautiful. When a woman enters a room, one should say, 'How wonderful she looks,' not 'What a nice dress.'" Then he would make that Spanish face, and shrug that Spanish shrug.

Not even knowing what he would say about the models I was looking at could make me smile just then. I found myself wishing that I *was* still feeling sick. Then I could pretend it was the flu, and not the Lands themselves that had affected me so drastically.

Come on, I told myself, squeezing my eyes tight. *Stop whining*. A little over two years ago my world had consisted of a handful of rooms—sometimes without windows. The inside of a closed car. Books and movies that had been chosen for me. And the snippets I'd been able to gather from the psyches of the very few people I was allowed to meet and touch.

What had I seen since? A couple of cities? A house in the countryside? Maybe a few hundred square kilometers of this world? Certainly no more. I hadn't even begun to explore all there was *here*. Was I really going to waste time feeling sorry for myself because there was another world I wasn't going to visit again? Surely I couldn't be that shallow?

Well, maybe a little. It was hard to be grown up when you'd never had a childhood. When someone tells you that you can't miss what you've never had, you know you're talking to someone with no imagination.

Alejandro's shadow passed over me. "*Fue tu amigo,*" he said. "Nik."

I pushed the magazine away and picked up my fork. I didn't have time to feel sorry for myself, no matter how much I wanted to. There were people with real problems out there.

Walks Under the Moon and her three principal Singers had put in a good morning's work reviewing the lore of the Horn when the arrival of the Warden Nighthawk was announced.

"Nighthawk?" Moon tried to keep a welcoming look on her face. What could the old Warden want with her? She'd Moved herself and the Singers who helped her with her researches to Lightstead, the home she had shared with her sister and their parents before the time of the Exile. An icy hand clutched at Moon's heart, and her hand went automatically to where her child lay growing. Nighthawk had been sent to the Shadowlands. Did he bring news of Wolf?

"Bid him enter, please."

Jade Enchanter, the young Rider who brought her the news, eyes shining with excitement, hovered while she asked her Singers to excuse her, barely waiting for the older Riders to clear the door before he burst out.

"He has brought a Troll with him from the Shadowlands." He was practically dancing. "I have never seen a Troll, Lady Moon, may I stay?"

"We shall see." So used was she to her sister's court, Moon had to remind herself that many of the younger Riders had never encountered Solitaries. That Jade Enchanter wished to was a good sign that her sister's policy of complete inclusion for all People was finding some fertile ground, if only that of curiosity.

But when Nighthawk reached her study, supporting the Troll with obvious difficulty, Jade Enchanter at first shrank back to her side in fear, before venturing out again, concern in the angle of his shoulders.

The creature who stood panting painfully just inside the doorway looked as though he had stopped halfway in a change from Troll to a human disguise. He was tall enough to need to stoop, though her ceilings were high, thicker through the shoulders than even some of the Tree Naturals she had met. His left arm was huge, dragging on the ground, his right more human-sized. He was gray all over, even the inside of his mouth.

She searched the Rider for injury, but Hawk's human clothes showed no marks.

"Older Brother, you are injured." Moon stepped forward, her hands outstretched. The Troll backed away before she could touch him, but not before she felt the heat rising from his skin. Moon glanced at Hawk. "Why have you not taken him directly to the High Prince?"

"I will if you have no Healer here," the Sunward Rider said. "But if we can, I think we should keep this to ourselves for the moment. Wait," he held up his hand as Moon started to protest. "Hear his story first."

"Jade Enchanter." Moon turned to the boy still behind her. "Go and fetch Mist in the Trees." The boy scampered out of the room, looking back over his shoulder as he went. As soon as he had cleared the door, Moon turned to Hawk. "Tell me, quickly, what has occurred?"

"I took Twilight Falls Softly to Madrid, and found the fountain of Cibeles deserted, and the Water Sprite gone. I sent the Singer back to the High Prince to report, and went myself immediately to check on Mountain Crag." He indicated the Troll with a tilt of his head.

"And you, Older Brother, what attacked you?"

"A dog that was not a dog, the beggar. I drove it off with my sledges, my hammers." The Troll grinned, and Moon had to force herself not to look away at the sight of his teeth. This was one of her sister's People. One of her own people, if it came to that: sick, injured, and come to her for help. This was not the time to remember old tales, and let the word "Solitary" cold-foot it up her spine.

"A Hound?" Moon came closer and helped Hawk support the Troll until it could sit on Moon's worktable. The darkwood—from an ordinary tree, not a Tree Natural—groaned, but it was thick and the table well made. "Did it bite you?"

"Barely a nip, scarce a scratch, it is." The Troll swallowed, and Moon could hear the roughness in his throat as he did so.

"You burn with fever." Moon reached out toward his face, in

vague recollection of something her mother, and then her sister, had done. Where was that fool Healer? "Do not fear, the Healer will be with us soon. You are still conscious, and with her help, you will not die."

"Won't be coddled." The Solitary shifted, and the table creaked again. "Think I'm a child?"

"Come, only a Troll could have lasted as long as you have with a Hound bite sucking the very *dra'aj* from you. Any other of the People would have succumbed."

Moon caught the direction of Hawk's thoughts: pride could be a tool to keep the Solitary alive. "Truly, only a Troll, and not many of them. Songs will be sung of this." She reached out again and this time Mountain Crag let her take a grip around his wrist. Luckily, she was on the side of the human-sized arm, or she would have needed both hands.

"That's right, Songs." He stamped the floor with one foot and it seemed that the whole building shook.

A bustle in the doorway heralded the arrival of Mist in the Trees, Jade Enchanter on her heels. Like many of Moon's staff, this Rider had originally come from the service of Honor of Souls, Lightborn's mother. There were a few of her own people left from the time when her father had been alive, but not many.

"Off you go then, my lady and lord. I work the better with privacy. Young Jaden's Dragonborn, and can help me." Jade Enchanter grinned as the older Rider actually made shooing motions with her hands, and even Hawk made no protest as Moon led him away to her private sitting room.

"If Mountain Crag was visited by a Hound, I thought the same might be true of the Fountain Sprite." Hawk sank into the cushioned chair Moon indicated and nodded when she pushed a decanter of pear brandy closer to his hand. "And perhaps she was not able to fight the beast off."

"It is one explanation, certainly—" Moon began.

Nighthawk rapped the tabletop sharply with his knuckles. "But why is this happening now? There's no logic, no cause and effect—but perhaps logic's the wrong word when speaking of the Hunt." He poured himself a glass of the brandy. "The Hunt has been in and out of the Shadowlands many times since the Basilisk brought them under his control. How is it that they are only now preying on these hidden ones?"

Moon sat down in the nearest chair, accepted with a nod the glass Hawk poured for her. "These are all excellent questions," she said. "But I'm still unsure why you have brought them to me."

Hawk sat staring at the surface of his brandy a moment before he took a deep breath and looked up. "I have known your sister a long time. It is I who trained her, during the period of the Exile, to use the weapons and the *gra'if* she bears. I know how being a Healer gives her a particular view of the world, and I know of her great loyalty." He took a mouthful of his brandy, and Moon was reminded to do the same.

"Now she is High Prince, and beset with problems and worries the like of which I can barely grasp." He put his glass down. "Before I add to these travails, I would like to be sure that what I have is more than a suspicion. And so I come to you, as someone who might have answers. Though you are not yourself a Singer, you have gathered the Singer's lore."

Moon sat up straight, bringing her knees and ankles together. When she noticed what she had done, she smiled. She had sat this way when she was a child, and her sister had been teaching her. "If I do not know the answer myself, I would very likely know where to find it."

"First, is it true that the Hunt will follow the trail they are set on, to the exclusion of all others?"

"So much the Songs tell, yes." She had encountered that fact among many Songs, old and new—and she'd found that the more often a piece of lore was repeated from Song to Song, the more dependable it was.

Hawk leaned to replenish her glass. "Do they tell *how* a Hound is set upon its trail?"

Moon hesitated. "That is not so clear," she began. "Of necessity, these Songs tell the tales of those who were being tracked. No Song tells the point of view of the Hound. Mentions of the Horn I have already spoken of, but as for whether they can be set on a trail without its use? That I cannot say."

"Without the Horn, do they govern themselves?" Hawk leaned forward, amber eyes narrowing.

"We cannot even be sure of the function of the Horn, from the Hunt's perspective," warned Moon. It was so difficult, sometimes to make people see the logic of things. "Did the Basilisk control them completely with the Horn? Or was he also offering other incentives? Does the Horn merely summon? Or does it command? These are among the questions I am seeking to answer now."

"We know of someone who was set on the trail of People in the Shadowlands." Hawk pursed his lips and took a deep breath in through his nose before continuing. "One who has visited both Shower of Stars and Mountain Crag. If the Sprite is Faded, it must be at the hands of someone who knew she was in the moving water of the fountain. Someone to whom she would allow entry."

Moon felt the temperature in the room drop. The older Rider's bronze face was grim.

"If you speak of Stormwolf," she said slowly, "did you, Nighthawk, not tell us that he helped you kill the Hound that had been following you in Granada?"

Hawk lowered his eyes and nodded. "But would it be unheard of, or even unusual, for one member of the Hunt to turn on another?"

Moon sat up straighter. "You think his helping you was a ruse? But Wolf is not a member of the Hunt. He was cured of his affliction by the High Prince herself."

Hawk turned his free hand palm up. "Truthsheart was not yet High Prince when she cured Stormwolf. Even so, I do not suggest that the fault lies in her, but in him."

"This is the trouble you do not wish to bring her."

"Can we bring this to Truthsheart without further proof? *Should* we?" Hawk lifted his shoulder slightly and tilted his head to one side. His amber eyes were rounded with concern. "What would be the reaction, even among the most open-minded of the People, if they should learn Truthsheart has tamed one of the Hunt, and he has proven to be not so tame after all?"

Moon stood up. She felt like shaking him. "You speak as though you were still the Senior Warden of the Exile, and my sister was still a novice under your supervision. You forget yourself, Nighthawk. She is High Prince. Do you doubt her Healing? I cannot, that is certain. I have been Healed by her myself, Healed of a sickness of the soul as great as any Hound's. Before or after the Stone acclaimed her, what does it matter? She was acclaimed because of what she was already."

Hawk bowed his head, placing his hand over his heart. "Your pardon, Walks Under the Moon. You are right. It is too easy for me to slip into my old role. I assure you, I do trust your sister's Healing." Hawk raised his head. "Before *and* after she became High Prince." He shrugged, and grinned at her. "If I am being honest, I liked Wolf immediately, and I do not like to think that my judgment should be so poor. But I also know that a person can be led astray by clinging to old loyalties, and that even the best intentions can lead to tragedy and disaster. The humans have a saying, 'Measure twice, cut once.' "

Moon flushed. Impossible that what Hawk suggested should be true, but . . . Wolf *was* concerned with his old loyalties, even if not in the way Hawk suggested. "You are wrong about Stormwolf." Moon could hear the tremor in her voice and cleared her throat. "You may ask Lightborn's mother, Honor of Souls, if you doubt it. After the turning of the Cycle, she fostered us both. There is nothing wrong with Stormwolf. I swear it."

"If it is only circumstances which are against him, all the better." Hawk held her eyes with his until she acknowledged his statement with a grudging nod. He leaned back in his chair, fingers tapping out a rhythm on the arms. "Perhaps he is being used—followed, tracked without his knowledge. But if so, we must know."

Moon felt herself growing colder, though the fire in the hearth burned true, the work of a Fire Sprite as were all the fires in her home. She knew Wolf was innocent of wrongdoing—or of this evil, certainly. But Hawk's suggestion that Wolf was being used as a stalking horse was a legitimate possibility. Righteous indignation would not resolve this.

She had lived with Wolf in the same home after the Cycle had turned. Eaten with him, walked with him, Ridden with him. He was no Hound, that she felt was a truth beyond doubt. But not everyone would feel the same way, not everyone would be persuaded by her words alone.

"We must have proof," she said finally. "In that, I agree. But I am not so sure we do right in not telling my sister."

Hawk leaned forward, his face creased in concentration, the ruddiness of his Sunward coloring somehow rough, as if he carried with him the years he had spent in the Shadowlands. "You have said it. One way or another, we must have proof before we speak. If we can answer this question ourselves . . ."

Moon pressed her lips together, refraining from pointing out that she, at least, did not need the question answered. "The last time I made plans without my sister's knowledge, it did not go well." But to go to her now, with this news, so soon after letting Wolf return to the Shadowlands without permission? "If you find even one more person who has been visited by the Hunt, or who is missing after Wolf has visited them, then we must tell her of your fears. It is her responsibility, not ours."

Hawk drained his glass of brandy and stood. "You are right, Moon. She is High Prince; I will not act further without her knowledge." His voice was steady, but Moon thought he looked troubled.

"In the meantime," Moon smiled, "I may have news of my own to report to my sister. I believe I have found the first thread that will lead me to the Horn." She took a deep breath, heat rising in her cheeks as the older Rider gave her a deep bow.

"Possession of the Horn would certainly do much to solve the problem of the Hunt. While you pursue these efforts, I will return to the Shadowlands and see if there is more evidence to be found." Hawk looked down at his hands and back at Moon, a slight frown on his face. "I am certain we will find Stormwolf innocent in this." His tone was firm, but the look on his face spoke more of hope than certainty.

"I have already pledged myself to help these people. That is enough! Why must *you* put yourself in any further danger? You have only just met them." Alejandro was checking the pockets of his suit jacket for mobile, billfold, and keys.

I blinked. I *had* only just met them, I realized. All the time we'd spent in the Lands had only been hours here. It was only, what? Days since I'd met Nik, gone with him to take Elaine to the palliative care ward? I scrubbed at my face with my hands. It felt like weeks. And here was Alejandro, like a parent telling me to stay away from the bad boys.

"*You* didn't know *me*." My headache was coming back.

For a second he stood completely still, eyes wide, mouth open. "That is different! Vastly different."

I let my hands drop. "Right, because you're *so* old, and you've been around *so* long, and you have *so* much more experience than poor little human me." He was being so unfair, and on top of all the other unfairness I'd had piled on me just recently, it was too much. A volcano erupted inside me, and the words came pouring out like lava. "You have no idea what I've experienced, no idea at all." I was on my feet jabbing at him with a stiff index finger. "Dozens of lives, maybe hundreds—so many people I can't even remember them all. And people, *human* people. Like I'm human, like Elaine's human, and Nik. Like—" I stopped before the words came out, but it wouldn't take a psychic to know what I had almost said. Like Alejandro *wasn't* human. It would have been unforgiveable to say it, and some knowledge of that stopped me from speaking the words aloud. But they hovered in the air between us, no less real because unsaid.

"You are my *fara'ip*," was what Alejandro finally said. But not at all like he was reminding me, more like he was reminding himself. I felt a little chill.

But then I knew what he was saying, and it made my breath come a little easier, and my heart slow down a bit. We were the same *fara'ip*. That couldn't be changed by anything that either of us said, or even anything we did. It couldn't be taken back, but that made it a double-edged sword. It meant there were things you couldn't say, maybe things you couldn't do, because you *were* in the same *fara'ip*. It was what had stopped me, I suddenly realized, from saying that Alejandro wasn't human, and that because of that, he wasn't really on the same side as me.

So he was reminding both of us, really, that we were always on the same side, no matter what.

So I did something I'd never done before. Something that startled me almost as much as it did Alejandro. I burst into tears. Suddenly it was all too much for me. I had to face that in trying to help both Nik and Wolf, I might not be doing the best I could by either of them. I had to face that after years of isolation, I was attracted to both of them, but only one of them was mostly human. I had to face that I still hadn't found my other family, or the place I belonged—

and that there was one home, at least, I'd never be able to go back to.

I was dimly aware that Alejandro had his arms around me. Was I ever going to know anyone else well enough to stand like this with them? Well enough that all I would get was their immediate emotional state? Touching Alejandro, I could feel the Healing that Cassandra, the High Prince, had given him. I could read the shift in his *dra'aj that* acknowledged his visit to the Lands. He didn't feel younger, exactly, just refreshed, like he'd gone to a spa. I hadn't known that just living so long in the Shadowlands would have affected his *dra'aj* in this way. He was older even than I had believed.

I was just framing a question arising out of that thought when the phone rang, and Alejandro released me. He didn't answer it, however, just stood looking at it with his brow wrinkled, so I went over to see for myself what the call display said. "Unknown caller."

I touched the phone with the tip of my finger. "Nighthawk." I frowned, concentrating. "I think he's alone."

I left Alejandro to his call, reminded by it that I should check my own messages. Unlike most humans my age—and unlike Alejandro who was neither human nor my age—I didn't have a bunch of girlfriends from high school or university to text me, friend me on Facebook, or follow me on Twitter. Unlike most humans my age, mobiles, tablets, e-readers, even computers, were something I'd only learned about in the few years since Alejandro had rescued me from the Collector. So checking my phone or computer for messages or emails still wasn't second nature to me.

All I had was a text from Nik. MT ME? *He wants to see me.* My lips curled into a smile. Had he left that text before or after he'd spoken with Alejandro? Here I'd just been wondering whether I'd ever know anyone as well as I knew Alejandro. Could Nik be a possibility?

Alejandro was off the phone. "Hawk has returned from the Lands. He has asked for the whereabouts of Stormwolf."

I took a deep breath and let it out slowly. Suddenly, the idea of another Rider was more than I wanted to deal with. If my trip to the Lands had taught me anything, it was that my connections with any of them were going to be limited.

"So it's off to Australia for Nighthawk?" I did the best I could to keep the resignation I felt out of my voice.

Alejandro nodded, but his eyes were on my mobile. I hadn't put it away, and I could tell that since he'd told me about his call, he expected the same courtesy in return.

"Nik," I said. "Just to say everything's okay, I guess."

Alejandro's face clouded over. Here we go again. This, I thought, is really how teenagers must feel. "Just tell me what you're thinking," I said. "Keeping in mind that I don't need your permission to talk to anyone."

He waved this away. "It is only that I wish you to take care. It is one thing to know these people are no danger to you in themselves, that they mean you no harm. It is another thing entirely to put yourself in peril in order to help them. They have all been touched by the Hunt."

"It isn't just that they mean me no harm." I spun my mobile on the table, stopped it, and set it spinning again in the other direction, wondering how to say what I needed to say. "These are all good people." I remembered the look on Nik's face as he showed us the news clips. "Aren't these the kind of people I should want to help? The kind of people who would make good friends? You didn't turn me away, when I needed *your* help."

Alejandro's smile was crooked, his old familiar grin that made me feel warm all over. "I see." He nodded. "So this is my fault, then, *querida*?"

I grinned back. "Sure. I'm just following the example you set me." My tone dropped into seriousness without my really intending it to. "You wouldn't want me to do anything else."

"I would, though I am ashamed to say so. But I am proud that you will not listen to me. Afraid, but proud."

"Then we're okay."

Fox flipped the cell phone shut and sat looking at it, watching as the numbers that told the time faded.

"River on her way?" Badger sat across the table from him. Fox hadn't noticed before that she was a Starward Rider. He couldn't tell whether she looked paler than usual in the dim light at the back of the Hair of the Dog.

"No reason for us to be scattered now," he reminded her. "We're not looking for the Exile anymore."

Badger shook her head. "I'm sorry about Stump." Fox lifted one shoulder and let it fall. Encouraged, Badger continued. "I don't know what possessed him, though he was always impulsive. He just didn't get it that it's still dangerous here." She looked away and when she looked back, her eyes had changed color. "It's better now we're all together."

"You can have Longshadow to replace Stump." Fox picked up the glass on the table in front of him and put it back down without drinking from it. "Once the others are here, we'll see how many more we need."

Now Badger was grinning, her teeth too many and too long. Fox tapped his own mouth and she quickly covered hers with her hand. When she lowered it, she looked normal again. Evidently, Stump wasn't the only one who could get careless.

"So there's more of them? More like Longshadow?"

"Looks like it." Fox smiled as he picked up the cell phone. It was strange to be thinking about Riders as more than just a source of *dra'aj*.

The booth where he'd established them was tucked into the corner farthest from the bar, and secluded enough that the casual observer could easily overlook it. Even the bar staff, busy at this time of day, would approach it only if waved down. Fox was finding it difficult to judge the passage of time here in the Shadowlands. He'd been expecting daylight when he left the den in the empty sports arena, but it was evening again, twilight heading into dark. He'd thought they'd broken the whole nocturnal predator habit, but it looked now like that had just been part of the compulsion of the Horn.

"We really don't need to be so careful, do we, Fox? Now that there's no Horn?"

"Really?" Fox pulled back his upper lip and Badger dropped her eyes. He was Pack Leader now, not just a Five leader like her. She should remember that. "You mean like Stump could stop being careful? Just because the humans aren't any danger to us, doesn't mean there's no danger out there." He pointed at her. "We don't know enough. We're still outnumbered, and we're split. What's happening to the ones left in the Lands? What's happened to the Horn? Just because it isn't compelling us right now doesn't mean it doesn't exist. No. There are still too many questions for us to get fat and happy." Should he tell her about his plan, or should he wait until all of them had arrived?

The door to the place opened, bringing a familiar scent with a waft of warm air. Two scents. Fox's heart beat faster, and saliva formed in his mouth. Snowfang appeared at his elbow, but it was the Moonward Rider standing next to him who activated Fox's thirst. He forced himself to ignore the Rider—and his *dra'aj*—and looked at Snowfang.

"You weren't at your den, Pack Leader," he said.

"I'm here."

Snowfang was agitated, his eyes flicking toward the glass of water on the table and back up at Fox's face. Fox nodded. Looked like he wasn't the only one affected by the Rider's *dra'aj*. The hand Snowfang put out for the glass of water on the table (flicker) became a twisted mess of claws and talons before re-forming in time to grasp the glass.

"Watch out," Fox warned. "Don't drop it."

Snowfang took several deep swallows, lowering the glass with a sigh. "What do we care? These are sheep, and we're wolves."

Fox had the other Hound by the throat almost before the words had finished exiting from his mouth. *Another one.* He held fast, watching Showfang's face redden. One of the wait staff, coming toward them, turned around and went back to the bar. "We care because I say we care, and I'm Pack Leader." He waited, still holding fast, until the other lowered his eyes, turned his hands palm up, the closest he could come in this place to rolling over and showing his belly.

When Fox released him, Snowfang swallowed and rubbed at his throat before gesturing toward the Moonward Rider. "This guy came looking for you, Pack Leader."

Now Fox turned to look the Rider up and down. He had the usual Moonward pallor, with raven-black hair and jadestone eyes. The eyes narrowed, but he didn't look away. Something about his scent was familiar, though not enough for Fox to be sure he'd seen the Rider before.

"So he's found me." Fox looked up at Snowfang. "Why are you still here?"

"Pack Leader, we've got a scentless one for you, like you wanted. It's in your den."

"Go." He flicked a glance at where Badger still sat across the table. "Both of you. I've got business here."

The Rider had stayed silent and watchful during the whole of Fox's exchange with Snowfang; unusually patient for a follower of the Basilisk Prince.

"Who are you?" Fox indicated the now empty seat across the table.

The Rider smiled as he sat down. "I expected to see Wolf."

A fist clenched in Fox's chest. "You know where he is?"

The Rider shook his head, his eyes never leaving Fox's. Brave, or foolhardy? It was difficult to know. "I last saw him with the Basilisk Prince." He shrugged. "Haven't seen either of them since."

Fox nodded. "So I'm Pack Leader now." He leaned back at the approach of the waiter. Another brave one. "Beer," he told the human, and waited until he returned with two pint glasses.

"I hear your Pack increases." The Rider picked up his glass of beer and took a sip, pulling a napkin out of the dispenser to wipe off his upper lip.

"And yours decreases, unless you've got a new Pack Leader as well? Someone who's planning to take over for the Basilisk?"

The Rider shrugged again, this time smiling. "Things have changed. There is a real High Prince, not a pretender. A new Cycle."

"Something tells me if you were going to join up with her, you wouldn't be here." Fox smiled, letting his teeth show.

The Rider wrinkled his nose, took another sip of his beer.

"Some will. Those who can, once they've come to their senses and stopped believing that they can continue preying—if you'll pardon the use of the word—on the small and unimportant. Some will not. Some do not wish to serve the High Prince. Frankly, some of us would rather serve ourselves. And have others serve us."

Fox found himself smiling. "You mean *you* would. I don't see much 'us' about you, buddy. You'd like to be Pack Leader?"

Now the Rider was nodding. Short, shallow nods. "But not of your Pack, and not in the Lands. The High Prince is Riding us down, and she cannot stop. In the Shadowlands, however, that might be different."

"So why come to me?" Though again, Fox thought he could guess the answer.

The Moonward Rider's face hardened, and his lips thinned, but he waited to answer until the tension had left his shoulders.

"From what I understand now, we needn't be enemies. Our needs are not in conflict. On the contrary, we may be able to help one another."

"How so?"

"Your numbers are few. You would not need to increase them—and therefore decrease your supply—if you had allies you could count upon. And who can count upon you to leave them *dra'aj*-whole."

Fox picked up his own glass and took a careful swallow. He'd been thinking along these same lines himself. There might be a few more Riders, maybe even some of this one's followers, who were far enough down the path Fox had followed so long ago to become Hounds, but once the Fives were complete, were any more actually needed? Sure, there was plenty of *dra'aj* here, but why share it if it wasn't *absolutely* necessary?

"I think we can come to terms, Rider." Fox stood, picked up the used napkins on the table and gave them the appearance of human money. "Let's not waste any more time."

Chapter Thirteen

I ENDED UP NOT CALLING NIK BACK. It seemed like a small enough thing to do for Alejandro, especially after he'd agreed that I could tag along to the meeting he'd already arranged.

Now that the time had come, I found the idea of speaking to Nik made me feel a bit shy. It was nice to know that he liked me, and wanted to see me, *that* made me feel warm all over—but it didn't help me to know what I wanted to say to him, let alone what I wanted to do.

As usual, Alejandro wore one of his summer-weight suits, a beautiful deep blue with a crisp white windowpane shirt and a silk tie, but I decided to go a bit more casual—though not quite as far as the khakis and hoodie Nik had last seen me in. I decided on a taupe linen shift, square-necked, with a dull turquoise trim, along with some high-heeled espadrilles of the same blue-green shade. My shoulder bag should have been straw, or even a natural leather instead of black, but I hadn't yet reached the point where I could have matching accessories for every outfit. A clutch that matched the shoes was tucked into my bag.

The lady I'd previously seen in a print dress met us at the top of the stairs and introduced herself as Arlene before ushering us into Elaine's office. Elaine was sitting behind her desk, but rose as we came in. She looked spectacular, at least in comparison to the last time I'd seen her. Her makeup was impeccable and her dark blonde hair and rosy fingernails looked as though she had just come from the salon. She was wearing a sleeveless green silk-knit top with the skirt of a dark gray pin-striped suit; the jacket was hung casually over the back of her chair. The pleated detail on the skirt was repeated on the pockets of the jacket. Her open-toed, sling-back shoes were the same ruby color as her earrings and necklace. Seeing this change in her was like watching one of those makeover shows.

There was a television on a side table, tuned to a news channel, and I could also see news feeds on two of the computers on Elaine's desk. Some of the talking heads were familiar—one of them was the spokesperson for the Ministry of Health. Elaine muted the sound on all three devices as she came out from behind her desk.

"No one's actually saying the word 'epidemic,'" she said, gesturing at the screens, "but you can tell they want to. They're reporting new cases all the time, and people are being asked to stay at home, since the hospitals are already crowded." She shrugged. "At least we'll have a good idea where everyone is, if we ever get a chance to help them."

She put out her hand as she came toward us, drew it back as if she'd changed her mind about shaking, and then, shrugging, extended her hand again. Alejandro gave her the kind of bow that Spanish grandees must have given people in the sixteenth century, and I could see that she was genuinely impressed.

"So you're the Rider," she said to him. "I'm not sure I can see anything different about your *dra'aj*—" she pronounced it as though it had only one syllable "— but Nik says that will come." She turned to me. "And you're Valory Martin." She put out her hand with less hesitation this time, glancing between us as she added, "The two of you live together?"

Alejandro smiled. "We do not 'live' together, not in the complete connotation of that word. We are *fara'ip*. Like family."

As she nodded and released my hand, I flashed on images [a cream-colored cocktail-length wedding dress; sorrow mixed with joy] that seemed to say something about her future. [She wouldn't have children; none of them could; that was the sorrow.] Her fragments were tight together, but layered somehow, and I realized she'd had another infusion of *dra'aj* since I'd seen her last. I gave her what I hoped was a normal smile.

"There *is* something different about you," she said, smiling at me with her head on one side. "Not an Outsider, different in another way." She shook her head. "Is it because you're psychic?

My stomach dropped a couple of inches. It never occurred to me that Nik would have just told Elaine what I was. Who else had he mentioned it to? How many people could know about me before my secret wasn't safe anymore? How long until one of them innocently told someone like—well, it didn't have to be someone like the Collector, did it? I knew enough to be sure that there were business people out there—and governments for that matter—who would see me as a valuable asset to be kept for, say, national security.

What I'd told Alejandro was true, Nik and Elaine were both good people, but that didn't mean they didn't also have their own agendas.

Elaine gestured to where a couch and a couple of client chairs were arranged around a low coffee table holding an insulated coffeepot with a brushed steel sugar bowl. She had mugs instead of cups with saucers, but the mugs were obviously high-end china. Cream, in a pitcher that matched the sugar bowl, was taken out of a small refrigerator hidden in a sideboard.

"Nik's just finishing up," she said. "It seems silly to be carrying on, business as usual, but once we resolve all of this, I'd like to have a business to come back to."

I had to admit, I knew exactly how she felt.

"I've been coordinating information I think we're going to need," she continued. "Sightings of the Hunt, and . . ." she hesitated.

"And some Riders." Nik came in as we turned toward the door. He was wearing the slacks of a tan suit, though he must have left his jacket behind in his office. The sleeves of his ivory shirt were rolled up, and he was loosening his tie as he came. His skin and hair looked very dark against the shirt. "So you're not bringing good news, are you? Not if there are Riders with the Hunt."

"These would be the same Riders who have been with the Hunt all along, the ones who brought them here," Alejandro pointed out.

"Why should I believe you?" Nik stood looking down at Alejandro, his brows pulled down in a frown.

"These Riders were followers of the Basilisk Prince. They are our enemies as well."

"So the enemy of my enemy is my friend, that's what you're saying?" Nik grabbed one of the other chairs by the arm and dragged it over to the table, situating himself at one end, so he had Alejandro on his right, and me and Elaine on his left. He helped himself to a black coffee, took a sip, and settled back into the chair, propping his left ankle on his right knee.. He should have seemed relaxed, but all his movements were sharp with tension.

And he hadn't looked at me yet.

"Unfortunately," Alejandro said, "the news is worse than this. We can expect no help from the High Prince at this time. The very troops who would be best able to help us are the ones the High Prince most needs herself to deal with the Hunt and the Basilisk Warriors still in the Lands. Until the threat there is dealt with, none can be spared."

Nik's eyes shut tight and his exhale was more than half snort. "That's just great! So we're back to where we started." Nik clenched his teeth so tightly a muscle jumped in his jaw.

"No, you aren't," I said. "You have Alejandro, and you have me."

Nik transferred his glare to me, but his face almost immediately softened. "Sorry." The grim line of his mouth relaxed to something very close to a smile, and I felt my heart skip a beat at the warmth in his eyes. I hoped I wasn't actually blushing. I cleared my throat.

"And there are others like Alejandro—Riders or what have you—who are already living here. They've got a vested interested in seeing the Hunt dealt with, since they'd be at risk as well." I pointed out.

Nik was nodding now. "Okay. Good. How many?"

Alejandro set his mug down on the table, frowning. "I cannot say for certain. Most of the People here are Riders, but as for how many bear *gra'if* . . ." He shrugged.

Wolf bore *gra'if*. The thought sent a shiver up my spine. Would he, *could* he, track down and kill his old Pack mates? Something told me this might not be the best way for him to deal with his own conflicts. I couldn't go to him for this, not, at least, until I'd exhausted other possibilities. Maybe I should wait and see if Cassandra's people found the Horn?

Elaine was sitting very still, very straight and quiet, and when I looked at her now, I saw that she was doing her best to watch Alejandro without actually staring at him. He looked human, of course, but even without looking like a Rider, he was still a very handsome man.

I thought about my own reaction to Alejandro, the first time I'd shaken his hand, and known him for what he was. Not just a gifted human like me, and the others who'd been "collected," but another type of being entirely. Looking back on it, I think I'd been so overcome at finally finding someone who would help me that I simply hadn't been fazed by the fact that he wasn't human. Sure, I'd been surprised, but my ability means that I never have to wonder whether something is true. I realized that I was only now having to deal with the ramifications of what humans have always called Faerie—and that surprised me more than it should have. Alejandro and I had come to Toronto to look for my family, not to get involved with Outsiders, Riders, and the Hunt. Whatever it meant to the rest of the People, it looked like the turning of the Cycle was only complicating things for me.

"And there is still the Horn," Alejandro was now saying, echoing my own thought of a moment before. "The High Prince has her people looking for it even now. And if it is found, it can be used to control the Hunt."

"That's our best chance," I said. "Right now they're scattered, so even if we had more help, we'd still have to chase them down, maybe one by one. With the Horn, the idea is that we could get them all together. But it's not a sure thing, so in the meantime, Alejandro's going to find the other Riders who will help us."

Alejandro glanced at his watch, and got to his feet. "I am meeting someone this very afternoon," he said. "And I will report my progress as soon as I have any."

Nik walked us down the stairs to the front door. He even shook Alejandro's hand, apparently over his distrust for the moment. When he turned to me with his hand extended, I couldn't not take it, though I meant to keep the touch down to a minimum [left-handed; owned a pair of dueling pistols that had belonged to Lord Byron], but Nik had other ideas.

"I was glad to hear you say 'us,'" he said, looking directly into my eyes. "To know that you're on our side." He was still holding my hand, so I can't say I was entirely surprised when he kissed my cheek.

Wai-kwong sat with his hands tucked under his thighs, just in case they might shake. He was perfectly justified in being afraid—hell, he was justified in being terrified, these were *Hounds*—but no need to let them know it. If he kept his head, he'd get out of this. And if he kept telling himself that, his stomach might actually start to believe it. Still, the Hunt rarely bothered to kill their human prey, and as for the worst they could do, well they'd done that to him already, hadn't they? He'd lived through it once, he could do it again.

Or so he kept telling himself.

If he kept his head, he might even learn something. He'd never heard that an Outsider like himself had been taken by the Hunt, usually they fed and passed on, showing no interest in their prey once the *dra'aj* had been taken. He wiggled his feet in their dirty red Converse running shoes. They hadn't bothered tying him to the chair, knowing he couldn't move fast enough to escape. Would he be the first person who had an actual conversation with one of the Hounds? Not that any of these had been inclined to talk to him so far. He tried not to look at the one in the corner who occasionally flickered into something else, mostly a dog, but sometimes a misshapen thing sort of like a snake with hooves that made Wai's stomach lurch.

He tried to take a deep, slow breath without making it too obvious. Thank god it wasn't long since he'd been topped up. Wai didn't want to think about how much harder this would all be if he was brittle with emptiness.

The three Hounds in the room with him all turned toward the door, though Wai hadn't heard anything. He knew where they were, which was more than the Hounds did, he thought. This building was Maple Leaf Gardens—or had been. The hockey team played in the Air Canada Centre now, like the Raptors and the musical acts that weren't big enough for the Sky Dome—he meant the Rogers Centre, it wasn't called the Sky Dome anymore.

Is it still called babbling if I only do it in my head? he wondered.

Two guys came through the door. The first guy looked like a young Ian McShane, only taller, like he'd been stretched, and Wai-kwong figured the actor never had quite that look on his face, even though he'd played some pretty bad guys. He looked normal enough for someone Wai knew wasn't human, but he'd already seen the guy in the corner morphing, so there was no doubt in his mind that this was another one of the Hunt. And an important one, judging from the way the others circled around him like dogs around the alpha.

The second guy had a different look entirely, for all that he had a similar coloring, dark, almost blue-black hair, skin like old parchment. He looked younger than the first guy. He stood back, his arms folded, looking carefully around him like he'd never been here before. *Not a Hound*, Wai realized. Didn't have the distinctive layered feeling to the *dra'aj*.

The first guy, the Hound, walked straight up to him, grabbed the hair on the top of his head and yanked back, as if he was searching for something in Wai's face. He squeezed his eyes shut as the Hound's nostrils spread wide.

"Don't drain me," he said. "Please don't drain me, I'll tell you whatever you want." The hand released his hair and Wai let his head fall forward, forcing himself not to look, not to check if his performance had worked. If they thought he was most afraid of being drained—maybe they wouldn't bother to kill him.

"We'll do whatever we want," the Hound said. "And so will you. You're one of the scentless ones." Wai's face must have shown confusion, because the Hound continued. "You've fed one of us already." It wasn't a question, but now that he understood what was meant, Wai nodded all the same. Let them think he was cowed.

"So how come you've got *dra'aj* now?"

"I don't know." Wai had lifted his hands to block the blow, but nowhere near fast enough. He spit blood out on the floor. He'd lost feeling in his cheek, and his teeth felt loose, but nothing worse yet. He smiled, but only on the inside. His plan was working.

"Only the older ones know, okay?" he said. "They arrange it. There's some kind of free-floating *dra'aj*—I don't know how they detect it, honest. They use it to keep the rest of us in line." Wai was pretty proud of the lie, considering he'd just come up with it on the spur of the moment. The resentment he'd tried to put into his voice must have worked as well. He saw two of the lesser Hounds exchange glances behind the back of what he figured must be the Pack

Leader. The idea of having and withholding rewards and favors must seem natural to them. He licked his lips, tasting blood, and hoped his luck would hold.

"Tell me what you know about the Riders."

Wai shot a look at the other guy, now standing off to one side, still with his arms folded across his chest. Wai was on safer ground now. He didn't have to pretend to feel what all Outsiders felt about Riders. "We don't give a crap about them," he said, his voice as tough as he could make it. "Like they don't give a crap about us."

The Pack Leader raised his hand as if to brush the hair from Wai's forehead and he flinched away. "Remember what I can do to you if you lie," the thing said. "Your kind has been seen talking to them."

Now Wai was worried. When had they been seen? The only Rider he knew was that Alejandro—there was that other one, the dark one, but he'd only seen *him* that time with the girl Valory. If they knew about the Riders, did they know about the girl? Wai felt instinctively he shouldn't say anything about her, but how could he avoid it if he was asked? Bottom line, he needed to get away from these things in one piece. Valory was friends with the Riders—she lived with one, for crap's sake—and maybe they wouldn't help at all if something happened to her.

Wai also knew that Nik would want him to get out of this alive. No matter what he had to do. "There's more Riders around," he said, trying to buy some time. "New ones. One of them has a human girl living with him. We were hoping he might listen to us, get us some help."

"Help from the Riders, help against us?" This was one of the other Hounds, stepping forward to the leader's side. Without even straightening, the leader snapped out his hand. The limb elongated, grew an extra joint, and the other Hound went flying, crashing into the bare brick of the far wall, changing into a thick-scaled snake with three heads, two heads, becoming a shaggy white dog with liver-colored spots, as big as a mastiff, with the claws of a hawk, that slouched away—awkwardly—whimpering.

The Pack Leader's arm returned to its human shape. Wai-kwong shuddered.

"The girl, that's the strange one, the one who has an unusual level of *dra'aj*?"

Wai had only just been told what was unusual about Valory. Would a psychic be something the Hunt could use? Could he avoid telling? "That's not so strange," he said. "Lots of humans have more *dra'aj* than others. Like, artists, or scientists, or something." He could only hope he wasn't giving them something they didn't already know. "Please don't drain me," he pleaded, frightened to hear a whimper in his voice, telling himself he'd done it on purpose. "Kill me if you have to, but please don't drain me." He shoved his hands between his knees. His shoulders hitched up toward his ears.

"Don't want us to bite you, that it?" The leader squatted down in front of him, and Wai looked away without turning his head. Its breath smelled of old meat, like a butcher shop that had seen better days. "Tell us everything you know about the girl."

Don't tell, he thought, no longer sure why. *Don't tell.* But his lips were parting all by themselves.

"Something happens when she touches you," Wai squeezed out between his clenched teeth. It was all too easy to let the tears come. His stomach crawled at the idea that he might be giving up the girl. *Nik wants me to live through this.* Somehow that thought wasn't as reassuring as he wanted it to be. "I don't know what it is, I swear. It doesn't work if you touch her," he added, hoping to buy the girl some safety that way. "Only if she touches you. Something good happens. That's all I know."

"I believe you," the lead Hound said. It bent toward him, was reaching out when—

CRACK!

Wai-kwong's ears popped and a woman appeared, her laugh high-pitched enough to stab.

"I knew it! I knew we could do it. Fox, my heart, my love—we can *MOVE.*" The woman, oh so beautiful despite being thin like an anorexic, ran to the Pack Leader still squatting in front of Wai, holding out her hands like someone offering to dance.

One second the leader was squatting next to Wai, the next he was on his feet and the woman was lying on the floor, her hand cupping her face. Wai hadn't seen anyone move. The leader put his foot on the lady Hound's throat and she whined.

"Did I say you could?" the leader growled. The thing on the ground changed and Wai shut his eyes. It must have replied wordlessly in the negative because the leader said, "And you won't try it again unless I say so, will you?" The response must have been the right one, and Wai cracked open one eye.

"Now, what news was so important that you defy me to bring it?"

"Your brother, Pack Leader." The woman was a woman again, but didn't call the leader "Fox" this time. "I've seen him, spoken with him." She looked up, but remained on the floor.

"Does he return to us?" There was an odd tone to the leader's voice, Wai thought. Both like he wanted it, and like he didn't, at the same time. This was starting to get interesting.

"Pack Leader, Pack Leader, please."

Uh-oh, thought Wai, the answer wasn't going to be a good one.

"Wolf can't return to us. He's a *Rider* now, Pack Leader. He's no longer one of the Hunt."

The woman cringed again, covering her head with her hands, but all the Pack Leader did was step away. He turned his attention back to Wai, and drew the palm of his hand down along Wai's face. Cold. Cold enough to suck the warmth from where it touched, from everywhere. What colors there were in the room seemed to fade. Wai put his own hands to his face and moaned, falling out of the chair to his knees. He felt the hands under his arms, dragging him to the door, as if it was happening to someone else. The warmth of the summer night outside barely touched him as they shoved him out onto the sidewalk.

"Tell your leader I want to talk to him."

After a few minutes Wai managed to convince himself to stand, and staggered to his feet, stumbling into the path of two people who swerved to avoid him. He needed to act quickly, before the deadly lethargy, the deadly indifference, could set in completely. Oh, lord, he'd forgotten just how bad this was. Maybe he'd been too confident of his own abilities; surely there was no way he'd be able to last this out. He pushed the thought aside, but it kept circling back. Wai searched his pockets, gritting his teeth when he found his phone missing. He looked around, checking his bearings. He was on Church Street. That was the corner of Wood, right over there, and kitty-corner across the intersection was the Hair of the Dog. He'd eaten there once with a girlfriend. *Cross at the lights*, he reminded himself. *Don't take stupid chances.* He crossed Wood, holding himself upright, resisting the urge to wrap his arms around himself. The doors, heavy wood and glass, were almost too much for him.

"Is there a phone I can use? I've had a dizzy spell," he said to the young man behind the bar. The bartender frowned, and put down the glass he was polishing.

"Here, Corey, I've got it." A short-haired older man, sitting nearby with a lady dressed in black, stood up, pulling a thick cell phone out of his pocket as he rose.

"You want 911?" he asked, flipping the phone open.

Wai shook his head. "My friend," he said. For a second the man looked as though he might argue with him, but ended by handing Wai his phone. He dialed the number all of them knew by heart.

"Nik? It's Wai-kwong. It's happened again. Yes. Please come get me."

He gave directions, closed the phone, and handed it back to the short-haired man. "Sit down here," the man said. His wife shifted over on the bench to make room. "Do you want something to eat or drink while you're waiting?"

"No, thanks," Wai said. "I'll be fine, as soon as my friend gets here." He thought about what he'd done, what he'd said, and about his escape. He found the smile he gave the man and his wife was a genuine one.

Cassandra turned away from the vista of the sea that she was not looking at to confront the Sunward Rider standing on the beach behind her.

"You are certain of this?"

"As certain as I can be, High Prince," Nighthawk said. "It is that there are three incidents. There is virtue in the number, as you know."

Of course there was. But to suspect *Wolf*. She looked at Max, leaning against a boulder where the spray from the waves could not reach him. A short way down the beach a group of eight Wild Riders waited for her to rejoin them.

"You know what they say," Max told her in answer to her look. "Once is accident, twice coincidence, third time . . ."

"Conspiracy," she said. She turned back to Nighthawk. "But what of this Goblin? You say *he* was not harmed?"

"But only because his gold warned him, and he was able to escape. I'm afraid there is no doubt, in that particular case, that Wolf was there at the same time as a Hound."

"Many of us have been in the same place at the same time as a Hound." This was Max, and while Cassandra wanted very much to cling to what he'd suggested, wasn't this exactly what she feared would happen? That meeting with the Hunt might prove to be too great a temptation for Wolf?

"It is possible that Stormwolf is not directly at fault." Hawk seemed to think this idea a conciliatory one. "It is possible that he is unwittingly leading others to their prey."

"At the very least, Stormwolf must be found and recalled." Cassandra took a deep breath and let it out. She could not believe she'd made such a mistake; she'd hoped that such a thing was impossible, now that she was High Prince.

"Go. Find him. Tell him I have asked him to submit to your authority and return."

"And if he does not?" Hawk asked.

"Then we will know for certain whether he is innocent."

"Those who guard the Portals must know, at the least, that Stormwolf is wanted," Hawk said. "They must detain him should he return to the Lands unknown to us."

"Tell them to detain everyone," Max suggested, coming closer. "After all, anyone returning from the Shadowlands might be a follower of the Basilisk. If everyone returning is required to report to you, Stormwolf won't be singled out." When Cassandra hesitated, Max added, "Most of the Portal guards are Wild Riders. They're well-disposed toward Wolf; they'll make sure he's well-treated."

"I am well-disposed toward him myself," Cassandra reminded them. She stood and pulled on her *gra'if* gauntlets. "He, and all that he has done, whatever that may be, are my responsibility."

"I will bring him to you, Truthsheart, rest easy."

The Rider sitting on the back deck when we got home was a Sunward, like Alejandro, and reminded me of Sean Connery. His auburn hair, not as dark as mine, looked as trim as if he'd just come from the barber, and his goatee came to a precise point. His eyes were dark amber, his skin ruddy, but not as though he'd been out in the sun too long without sunscreen. More a healthy red-gold glow.

Alejandro greeted him with the double kiss and much slapping of shoulders before finally turning to smile at me. "This is my *fara'ip*, Valory Martin."

The Sunward Rider stepped forward and, like Alejandro, he smiled. "I am Nighthawk," he said. His voice had the same kind of faint accent that Alejandro's did, and I realized that this was the Rider who had been living in Granada, the one who had been a Warden of the Exile. "My mother was Flyer in the Dusk, and the Dragon guides me." He didn't seem surprised when I didn't offer my hand, just bowed deeply to me, like a *hidalgo*.

He knows, I thought. Alejandro must have told him.

"I'm honored to meet you." I inclined my head in a shallow bow, and saw Alejandro's faint smile of approval.

They let me precede them into the house—just like well-brought up Spaniards—but left me in the sunroom to take off my shoes, going straight into the kitchen, just as if they were human. I could hear them speaking some form of what they thought was English. I still don't completely understand how the language thing works with the People. Alejandro says that there's really only one language, and that we're all speaking a variation of it, and that if my ears were attuned in the right way, I would understand what he meant. I know that what he says is true; after all, I can read people whether we speak the same language or not, but I also know that there's more to it than even Alejandro realizes.

I sat with one shoe off and one shoe on, debating letting Alejandro deal with Nighthawk by himself. I was still buzzing from talking to Nik and Elaine—and a little from the kiss I could still feel on my cheek, since I knew *exactly* what Nik had meant by it—and I wasn't entirely sure whether what I felt was excitement, or fear. Both emotions made the same kind of fluttery feelings in the belly. I knew what Nik felt, but I wasn't so sure about myself. Whenever I found myself smiling about Nik, I'd think about Wolf, and the heat I'd seen in his gray eyes.

I'd told Alejandro that I'd wanted to help Nik and Elaine, and I'd meant it, but uncomfortable didn't begin to describe how I felt at the idea that they, and who knows how many other Outsiders, knew my secret. What kind of long-term relationship could I have with anyone who could be so careless with my life?

With a sigh, I pulled off the second shoe and continued toward the kitchen. We had a guest. Alejandro says that a guest is a jewel on the cushion of hospitality. I'd never hear the end of it if I didn't join them.

Alejandro glanced at me as I leaned against the counter, and he turned back to the chorizo he was slicing.

"When were you planning to tell me?" His voice was as hard and as sharp as the knife in his hand. My mouth was suddenly dry. I glanced at Nighthawk and surprised a look of sympathy on his face. I didn't have to ask what Alejandro was talking about. When I didn't answer, Alejandro turned around to face me.

"You cannot say that you did not know," he said. "When were you going to tell me that Stormwolf was once a Hound?"

At least he wasn't saying that Wolf was still a Hound. I straightened my spine and decided to go on the offensive.

"Gee, I don't know. When would have been the right time?" I didn't wait for him to answer. "Before or after you admitted you weren't listening to me? That you weren't respecting what I learned? Maybe I just didn't want to have that discussion all over again."

"Well, what we have been 'discussing' is the disappearance of the Water Sprite, Shower of Stars, who you no doubt remember, and it appears there has also been an attack by a Hound on the Troll, Mountain Crag, requiring a Healer's intervention."

There was a gentle, almost apologetic cough. "There is also the matter of the Goblin, Vein of Gold, who was also visited by Hounds, though he was able to escape." Hawk's voice was deeper, darker than Alejandro's.

Alejandro arranged the chorizo on a plate with sharp, precise movements but instead of passing it to me, walked it around himself and placed in on the table where it joined wine, bread, and manchego-filled dates. He might be angry, but by god, food still had to be eaten.

His eyes held mine. "Hawk has been sent here looking for Stormwolf, to see if he can shed any light on these incidents."

Hawk followed Alejandro into the dining room, taking a seat along the side opposite the pass-through. I stood with my hand on the back of my usual chair, closest to the kitchen doorway.

As Alejandro poured wine, I thought back to my three encounters with Wolf—*one* of which, I had to remember, Alejandro didn't know about. I couldn't recall reading anything about Shower of Stars from him, and all I was getting about the Troll was an image of the aqueduct in Segovia, whatever that meant.

"If you think Wolf had anything to do with these disappearances, you're wrong." I pulled out my chair with maybe just a touch of unnecessary force and sat down. "And I can prove it. That is, if you're going to believe me." I looked at Alejandro, my eyebrows raised as far as they would go. This was his chance to prove that what he'd said the day we'd had our fight was true.

He lifted his wine, and put it down again without drinking. "You should have told me," he said. "Trust must work both ways."

I loosened the muscles of my jaw. "Okay," I said. "But I saw this as someone else's secret, not my own. I made a judgment call, and I'm sorry you got caught in the middle." Well, maybe not *strictly* the *whole* truth, but close enough to save the moment. "It's going to happen that there are things I can't share with you." His face began to cloud over again. "Even if this wasn't one of those things," I added quickly. "Nothing's changed. Wolf is still the person we know, whatever he might have been in the past."

Hawk cleared his throat, and I was happy to turn away from Alejandro's still suspicious face. "But you will acknowledge, that having been what he has been, we must question him," Hawk said. "You said you could prove your assertions?"

"I can." I looked over my shoulder at Alejandro. He'd gone back into the kitchen for a bowl of olives and was just placing it on the ledge of the pass-through. "Do you have something from any of these People, a possession or piece of clothing that I could get a reading from? What about the Troll? You said he was still alive, could I touch him? Or what about something from his apartment?"

Hawk turned his dark amber eyes to Alejandro. "She is a Truth-reader?" he asked. I was just getting offended that he hadn't asked me directly when he looked back at me and smiled. You would have thought it was Christmas day and he was a kid with a new toy.

I felt Alejandro looking at me. His face was still stiff, but he gave me the tiniest of nods, telling me he was going to let me handle it. I breathed a little easier. He was going to forgive me.

"I can give you a demonstration if you'd like," I said, though from the look of delight still on his face he wasn't going to need it. I was just about to ask him to let me have his watch when he spoke.

"I have an excellent idea," he said, his voice rumbling with eagerness. "Would you be willing to come to the Lands to gather truth from Mountain Crag?"

Ooh. That was the question, wasn't it? Even the thought of having to go to the Lands made me shiver, and swallow carefully.

"Has he been Healed?" Alejandro cut in before I could answer. "If the Troll has been Healed, then the traces of the Hound would be gone from him, as they are from me, and Valory might very well read nothing from him."

I saw right away where he was going. "But if his apartment hasn't been cleaned—or even if it has—I'll be able to get a reading there. Whatever or whoever attacked him will at least have brushed up against something in the struggle."

"Then it is back to Segovia," Hawk said, "and Jenaro's apartment." I noticed that when he spoke of the Troll's human life, he used his human name. "I can take us there directly from the crossroads." He looked at the table. "Once we have eaten."

"Whenever you're ready," I said.

"It is very good of Valory to agree to help with this," Alejandro said, his eyes fixed on his own plate. That was as close to an olive branch as I was going to get at the moment.

"Happy to help," I said.

"I will be happy to learn that Wolf is innocent."

I looked at Hawk. "He is."

Chapter Fourteen

THE *CRACK!* OF DISPLACED AIR was muffled by thick carpets and heavy curtains. Wolf breathed in the faint saffron scent that lingered in the High Prince's Royal York apartment. Eyes closed, he listened, letting ears and nose tell him that he was alone, the apartment empty. He went into the tiny kitchen and opened the refrigerator. This was the closest thing in the whole of the Shadowlands to the type of magic one found in the Lands. Here, food appeared, fresh and tasty, whenever he opened the door. Of course the scents told him that it was brought by humans, replenished on a regular basis, and did not appear out of some quality of the refrigerator itself. Today there was fresh fruit, new cheeses—one with a pleasant blue marbling—and a tub of an almost liquid creamy substance with a pleasingly sharp taste. The dried and cured meats were the same that had been there before he'd left, but better wrapped than he had left them. There was also a brown paper bag with small dark seeds in it that smelled profoundly of ganje.

He had found and informed two more of the People Alejandro

told him about. Both Riders, they had been living in a place called Mumbai. One had received his news with joy, and had set out immediately for the nearest Portal. The other was even more uninterested than the Troll Jenaro had been.

"Nothing for me there," he'd said dismissively. "Minor son of minor family, neither Singer, Warrior, nor Healer. What's there for me but service to someone stronger, more important? Better I stay here, where I am of consequence and have a place, family, children."

Wolf had left him to his Internet empire.

Wolf pulled a bottle of beer out of the refrigerator and twisted off the cap. Not quite as good as it would have been coming out of a barrel, he thought, but still an elegant compromise for a people whose barrels had no magic. He went into the sitting room and stared out of the window at the train station across the street. He went into the bedroom, where the bed had been made up and the curtains opened. He returned to the sitting room and stared at the bookshelves before returning once more to the kitchen. He opened the refrigerator and stood contemplating the contents. He wasn't hungry, he decided, and let the door swing shut.

He leaned back against the granite-topped counter, bracing his hands wide. He'd been focusing hard on his task, hard enough that he'd managed to avoid thinking about his meeting with Moon—about what he had and hadn't told her—but he could not do this forever. She'd agreed with him that he should try to rescue as many of his old Pack mates as he could. Would she have agreed so readily if she had known one of them was his brother?

While traveling he had found several other faint trails, old scents that would eventually lead him to one of the People, and one or two of the newer, strange scents that were most likely those of stable Hounds. But he had chosen not to follow those trails. He was certain none of them was Fox's, and surely it would be best to approach Fox first? The Pack would follow its Leader, and if he could persuade his brother . . . Wolf swallowed as the beer in his stomach roiled.

Persuading his brother. That had been where this difficulty began. Fox would not even be a Hound if Wolf had not—No. He pushed himself away from the counter, pushing the thought away with the same action. He would not think of *that.*

Wolf sank into one of the soft chairs next to the fireplace and shut his eyes.

"L'as tu vu?" Nik scanned the expanse of the Royal York's lobby as if he could spot the Rider himself.

"Même pas son omber," Yves Crepeau said. "Not since I arrived, in any case." He was sitting with an e-reader in a wing-backed chair that gave him a good view of the main doors, the circular staircase, and the elevators.

Nik took out his cell phone, stared down at it, and then thrust it back into his jacket pocket when he realized he hadn't even registered the display. Calls to both Valory and Alejandro were going straight to voice mail, so either their phones were off, or they were somehow out of range. He eyed the bank of brass-decorated elevators. Alejandro did say he was going to talk to other Riders. And this guy was another Rider.

"I'm going up."

"I'll come with you."

Nik stopped in his tracks. "Not a good idea to risk both of us, Yves."

"Not a good idea to risk yourself. Poco said—"

Nik looked away, sighed, and looked back. "Look, I don't know what Poco's told you, but you can see for yourself that I'm fine. I've had more experience than most of you put together, so—"

"So that is precisely why we are concerned."

Nik's mouth snapped shut. It wasn't everyone who would interrupt him like that.

"You are like the captain of the ship," Yves said, his quiet voice steady and matter-of-fact enough that Nik couldn't take offense. "Yes, you give us orders, and we obey you. But if we see you putting yourself in danger?" Yves raised his index finger, started to point and then, as if noticing what he was doing, lowered his hand again. "The captain does not leave the ship, Nikos—how many times does television get this wrong?—the captain sends others."

Nik looked away again, but when he looked back, Yves was still scrutinizing him, head to one side. The man was right, and Nik knew it. But. "Don't push that analogy too far, Yves. Sometimes, the captain sends the crew to safety, and then he goes down with the ship."

"Not on my watch." Yves grinned at him. "Sir."

Nik shook his head. "Okay. Fine. But this time, as a special favor to me, you'll wait down here. Got it?"

Yves' eyes twinkled. "*Oui, mon capitain.*"

He slapped his friend on the shoulder and turned toward the elevators.

The knock on the door startled him, and Wolf almost Moved without thinking. But this could be someone looking for the High Prince, or at least her human persona. Even if it were one of the servants in the hotel, he should probably answer.

There was a glass lens set into the door, which revealed and magnified the outer corridor. Wolf would have preferred to rely on his own senses, but the person standing on the other side of the door had that same scent/not scent that he had noticed before. An Outsider?

The lens distorted size, but not coloring. The Outsider was much shorter than Wolf, but with a distinct Moonward look to him. Curly black hair, cropped close to his skull. Skin like ivory with an undertone of olive. The only non-Rider feature was his very dark eyes. And his rather prominent nose. What would bring him here? Wolf opened the door.

The man nodded at him. "You're the Rider? Stormwolf? The one who took Valory that day? I'm Nikos Polihronidis." The human stuck out his hand. "Call me Nik."

At the mention of Valory, Wolf had a sudden image of her dark red hair, her pale skin, and her golden-caramel eyes. Her smile had been warm, and her eyes understanding, carrying concern without pity.

"Does Valory send you?"

"Not exactly. Can I come in?"

Wolf backed away from the door and the Outsider entered, looking around him with a small smile, as if pleased by what he saw.

"My business partner would love this place," he said, his smile fading as he turned back to where Wolf leaned against the closed door.

"If Valory Martin did not send you . . . ?"

"I was hoping I'd find her here, or maybe you know where she's gone? Or Alejandro Martín?"

Wolf moved his head from right to left in slow arcs. "I have seen neither Valory Martin nor Graycloud at Moonrise since the day we were all in the square." Since that night, was more accurate, but the human did not need to know this.

"Graycloud? Okay." The man took a deep breath. "I represent a group of people who've been injured by the Hunt," he continued. "Has 'Graycloud' mentioned this to you?"

Wolf studied the man, head to one side. "You represent? You are their . . . leader?" He had almost said Pack Leader, but if these were the Outsiders, he did not wish to reveal his own connection to the Hunt.

"In a manner of speaking, yes. I'm the Senior—"

"The Senior?" Wolf gestured, and the Outsider preceded him into the sitting room. "You have lived *very* long?" If this was one of the Hunt's early victims, it was possible he had insights Wolf would find useful. He pulled a chair out from the dining table, waited until the Outsider accepted it, and then sat down himself.

The man studied him a while, head tilted to one side, before responding. "I'm not the first, if that's what you mean, but I might very well be the first to live."

Wolf blinked. "The same might be said of myself."

"You survived the Hunt?"

"In a manner of speaking, yes. Do you mind if I ask you how . . ." Wolf didn't know how to continue.

"I was found by monks, wandering on the side of the road, where the Hound had left me. They thought I was witless and took me in." His eyes grew darker as he looked back through his memories. "They didn't let me kill myself, not even through neglect. They thought it was a sin. It still is, of course, the sin of despair, to be exact." Nik looked at him sideways, the corner of his mouth twisted up in a grin. Then his eyes narrowed. "But you know about that, don't you? Despair, I mean."

Wolf wondered what could be showing on his face. "Are you a Truthreader also?"

"Nope. Just been around a long time, like I'm saying. It's interesting that the—" he gestured at his face. "The facial expressions, that kind of thing, seem to be the same for all of us."

Wolf resisted the urge to wipe his hands over his face in an attempt to wipe away what was apparently written there. "How did you live?"

Nik leaned back in his chair, more relaxed now, as if he was gaining in confidence. "They put me to work, caring for the sick and dying. And one day, I was there at just the right moment, and the *dra'aj* that was leaving a dying woman—not that I knew what it was then, you understand—her *dra'aj* entered me, and I was well again." Once more he smiled that twisted grin. "A miracle." He shrugged. "So I looked for others like me, through the hospitals and hospices, and eventually we found out what was really happening to us, and now, here we are." He spread his hands again.

"You worked to save them, the others of your kind." Wolf felt a kinship with this man, this human Outsider, that was most unexpected.

"We all do, together. We still do. What's happening now . . ." Nik rubbed his hand over his hair. "This concentration of the Hunt, well, it's the worst thing we've ever faced. Alejandro's recruiting Riders to help him against them—"

"Against the Hunt? When did this happen?" Moon had said that the High Prince would ask Graycloud and Nighthawk to find the hidden People, but to attack the Hunt?

"Since that day," the man was saying. "They're feeding all the time now and—"

Wolf cut him off with an abrupt chop of his hand. "I know this."

The man's face hardened. "Well, we'd like it to stop, and Alejandro—Graycloud—is helping us. He said your High Prince would help us, too, as soon as she could."

"I need to speak with Graycloud," he said. And with Valory. This man Nik was not a Truthreader, but Valory Martin was. She would know exactly what was going on. She would help him. She knew his secret and was still his friend. Perhaps, in Valory's company, the spinning of his thoughts would come to a rest, and he could see clearly what he should do next.

"That's what I've been trying to do, but all I get is voice mail—"

"Come." Wolf took the human by the arm and . . . Moved.

"What—"

Wolf became aware that Nik was squirming and let go of his arm.

"What do you think you're doing?" The man backed away from

him, rubbing his arm and looking around him. But his face showed confusion, defiance, and perhaps a little awe. Not fear.

Wolf blinked and shook his head. "I am sorry," he said. "You agreed that we should speak to Graycloud, and so I Moved us."

"Well do me a favor, don't do it again." Nik swallowed. "At least, not without warning. I gotta make a call." He pulled one of the ubiquitous cell phones out of the inside pocket of his jacket.

An orange-and-white cat observed them, its head popping up from the over the back of the chair it had been sleeping in. It hopped to the floor and approached, placed its forefeet on his knee, and stretched.

"Ow!" Wolf jumped backward as the claws dug in. The cat sat down, wrapping its tail around its front paws, and watched him. It blinked.

"It's okay, Yves, I'm still with the Rider. Right. Later." Nik returned the phone to his pocket, and stuck his head into the kitchen. "Hello?"

"There is no one here, only the cat." Wolf squatted and held out his fingers. The cat looked at him but came no closer. Wolf raised his head and sniffed. Another had been here, however, someone he knew. Nighthawk. So, it was possible that the two Riders had gone looking for others. But, in that case, where was Valory?

Wolf eyed the Outsider, who was looking at a pad of paper on the kitchen counter. He turned back to the cat.

"How long have they been gone?" he asked. "When will they be back?" The cat got to its feet and walked through the doorway into the kitchen.

"Um, the cat doesn't speak." From the tone of his voice, the human wasn't as sure of this as his words made him sound.

Wolf nodded. "So I see."

Wolf picked up the pen that sat on the pad of paper, frowned, and put it down again.

"Did you want to leave a message?"

Wolf looked from the human to the pen and paper and back again. "A message?"

"Yeah, you're right. Probably not a good idea to let them know we were in the house." Nik looked at him. "This thing you do, can all of you do it? Moving me around, I mean."

"Any Rider can, yes."

"Cool. Listen, I'd like you to meet my friend Elaine."

Walks Under the Moon massaged the muscles around her eyes, moving her fingers slowly, trying to ease away the feeling of exhaustion that claimed her.

"Enough," she said to the Singers sitting around the table in her workroom. "I believe we have sifted every Song, every partial lyric, pieced together every lost fragment—you must be at least as tired as I, and with nothing more to show for it but the same new thread." She let her hands drop.

"Ah, but at least this time the thread refers to a place, the mountains of Ice Tor," the Sunward Singer, Cloud of Witness, said. "If, as we believe, the Moonward hero of one of my Song fragments is indeed the same person as the Moonward Rider mentioned in Piper's fragment."

"But I think it is clear," Piper in the Meadow added, "that that person definitely had possession of the Horn at one point in her career, and it is at least possible that she came from Ice Tor."

The third Singer, Owl at Midday, poured himself another cup of ganje and said nothing.

"I know this appears nothing more than a web of 'maybes' and 'what ifs'? But it was with just such a slender thread that I once found the Tarn of Souls, and the Chant of Binding," Moon pointed out. "The mountains of Ice Tor undoubtedly still exist. We must find the Song that tells us where."

Owl cleared his throat. He was the senior Singer in the group, and the others were inclined to defer to him. "I think, Lady Moon, you have overlooked a resource that has nothing to do with the Songs."

This was such a radical suggestion to come from a Singer that Moon was momentarily dumbstruck. The Songs were the history of the People, the idea that there might be old knowledge found elsewhere was startling.

"I refer, of course, to your sister, the High Prince."

Moon realized her mouth was open and closed it. Owl, seeing that she had his point, remained respectfully silent, though Moon was sure his eyes were twinkling as he examined the surface of his ganje.

Her sister. Of course. Was not the High Prince bound to the whole of the Lands? Surely, Cassandra would know where in those Lands the mountains of Ice Tor might lie? And even if she did not, at the least Truthsheart could heal Moon's headache.

"Brilliant," she said, getting to her feet. "I thank you for the work you have done, and the suggestion you have made. If you will now excuse me."

Her heart already lighter, Moon composed her mind, subtracting the details of her workroom and substituting the rocks, mosses, and trees of the clearing just to the south of the High Prince's camp, where it was permissible to Move. She stumbled; in her eagerness she had miscalculated the height of the ground in this precise spot, but a nearby Tree put out a branch for her to steady herself on.

"My thanks, *Glinde'in*," she said. "That was kind of you." The Tree shivered, exactly as if it were a young child giggling. In a way, Moon thought, that was exactly what *Glinde'in* was. With a final caress the branch withdrew and Moon made her way into the camp proper, finding her footsteps inexplicably slowing as she went. Or perhaps not so inexplicably. Cassandra might still be angry with her for the steps she had taken over Wolf—not that she had shown her anger. Like everyone else, her sister was treating her with great delicacy.

Moon chewed on her lower lip, stopping completely as a Sunward Rider in a yellow tunic led a Cloud Horse across her path. Riders were coming and going from the horse line, exchanging tired mounts for fresh, it seemed to Moon. One or two of the Cloud Horses looked her way and whinnied, as if they meant to greet her. In case it was so, in case they were Lightborn's, Moon raised her hand in salute. The whirl of activity had, as she suspected, her sister at its center. Moon lifted her flaxen eyebrows. Perhaps she should slip away. There must be some other way to find Ice Tor.

But before she could act on her thought, Cassandra's head lifted, swung around, and her eyes met Moon's. There was nothing to do now but match her sister's smile, and go to her.

"I come at a bad time," Moon said. Her sister's kiss, her sister's arms, made a sudden sob catch in her throat, and for a moment Moon clung to Cassandra as she had when a child.

"Of course not," Cassandra stroked Moon's face as though pushing back a loose curl. Moon felt her headache melt away as the warmth of Cassandra's presence enveloped and relaxed her. "You are always welcome to me."

Moon swallowed, her throat suddenly thick. She had been without family for all the time that her sister was Warden to the Exile, had almost lost her chance of regaining it. She had never thought to feel that loneliness again. She had her sister now, and Max, and Stormwolf; she was not alone. How was it, then, that at these moments, with her sister's arms around her, she felt Lightborn's absence the heaviest?

"Moon, my dear one, is there something specific you need of me?"

Faced with a direct question, Moon found her voice. "Do you know of a place called Ice Tor?" As her sister's eyebrows drew down in a vee, Moon explained her line of thought, gaining strength as she spoke.

"Sound reasoning." Cassandra shifted as if her *gra'if* mail shirt had suddenly become uncomfortable. "I'm sure I do know the place, but not by that name. I know and feel the very essence of the Lands, but I do not necessarily know what name has been given, or might have been given in the past. Without a description, I can only point to general areas."

"High Prince, we are ready." The Starward Rider who spoke was someone unknown to Moon.

"One moment." Cassandra turned back to Moon. "Is this for the Horn?" Moon nodded. "Perhaps there is some Natural or Solitary you might ask."

Moon shook her head. "Possibly, but by custom they share their lore with our Singers, and I have spoken to every Singer who has knowledge of the Horn."

"Still, you might ask *Trere'if*. He's eldest of the Tree Naturals, and may know of some clue now lost to the others." Cassandra turned away again, this time to mount the Cloud Horse that was being held for her.

"A lost Song? But if it's lost . . ." Moon let her voice die away as another idea occurred to her. There was someone else, someone she'd not been thinking of as a Singer. "It's worth a try, certainly," was what she said aloud.

"Shall I send someone with you? One of the Wild Riders who

knows the Naturals well?" Cassandra's honey-blonde eyebrows drew down.

Moon drew herself up, squaring her shoulders. "I think I can manage to speak with even so formidable a Natural as *Trere'if* by myself," she said, finding that her tone was stiffer than she had intended. Let Cassandra think her offended, so long as she was allowed to leave alone.

Cassandra leaned down to stroke Moon's cheek. "I'm sorry. It is only that I have developed the habit of worrying."

And then she was gone, and Moon could not tell her what she planned to do, no matter how guilty she felt. Moon walked as quickly as she could to the clearing where she could Move. She had always understood when Wolf refused to speak of what it was like to be a Hound—indeed, all things considered, Moon had thanked her Guide the Manticore for it. But she also knew that occasionally there came to him, from time to time and in flashes, memories of *before* he was a Hound. Moon remembered the way he listened to the Singers at Honor of Souls' fortress, the look on his face, the way his body moved unconsciously to the music, making her almost certain Wolf had been a Singer once upon a time. Moon also knew of Cassandra's theory that Wolf's time was long before the present, perhaps even more than one Cycle ago. Moon shivered. Did the Hunt live through more than one Cycle? What a horrible thought.

Cassandra might let Moon go to *Trere'if* alone, but she was not likely to want Moon in the Shadowlands unescorted. Moon looked down at her clothes. She was sure she knew enough from the books Max had given her to be able to pass as human.

I could not tell her, Cassandra thought as she and her troop neared the Quartz Ring. The news that Wolf might be a tool of the Hunt would be too much for Moon to bear so soon after the loss of Lightborn.

She would have felt easier about her decision, if she hadn't been sure that Moon also was keeping something back.

"You look concerned, my Prince."

"I was just thinking how much simpler things might be if I had a Truthreader among my people," she said, smiling to show she was not serious. *Too bad it would kill Valory Martin to live here.*

Alejandro, Nighthawk, and I were standing in a dimly lit front hallway. I'd seen enough of them in the time I'd lived in Spain that it felt familiar. A wide wooden door behind me, made up of many layers and sections of thick oak, an elaborate locking mechanism two thirds of the way up on the left-hand side, a massive pommel in the center of the door to serve as handle, and a tiny metal slot at eye level—for someone in the 1400's—that covered the grated peephole. We were standing on a floor that looked to be tiled in slate. The tiles on the wall picked up the blue-gray color, and along with some greens and some whites, made a complicated pattern up to about shoulder height—again, for someone in the 1400's. The wrought iron base of a half-moon hall table lay on its side, its glass top shattered over the floor. There had been a vase of flowers on the table, but they were now so dry they didn't even smell.

There was also a spatter of blood on the walls and floor that wasn't dry at all.

Hawk held his arm out in front of me, barring my way. I stopped as quickly as I could, but not before I brushed against him. [His clothes were made by a tailor in Madrid.] "I am not so very sure it is safe to touch it."

"*Now* you tell me." I squatted to get closer to the blood. It had to be the Hound's own, and it looked as though it had only just hit the surface of the tiles. One large glob even dripped off the leg of the hall table, though nothing hit the floor under it. I reached out a finger and caught the next drop as it fell.

[Agony. Thirst. Craving. Dark and cold. Blows. (flicker) space too small. (flicker) Phoenix. The smell of *dra'aj* filling everything (flicker) Pain. Cold. SNAP!]

"Valory!"

A sharp pain on my cheek, and I held up my arm to ward off the next blow. "Okay, okay. Sheesh." I put a hand up to my face. "I hope that isn't going to leave a mark." I seemed to be sitting down. I looked around and saw that we'd moved out of the hall into a small sitting room. I'd been seated in the only upholstered chair, a massive thing with sagging springs. Alejandro was crouched on his heels in front of me, and Hawk was rummaging in a low cupboard against the wall to our right, finally lifting out a bottle of brandy with a smile.

"You were taking a very long time." Alejandro's voice sounded tight. Hawk handed me a glass of dark-gold liquor. Alejandro sat on the arm of my chair.

"Just making sure I got everything I could." I shivered, and took a sip of the brandy, coughing as I remembered the feeling of the flickers and the pain/not pain of the blows the Hound had felt. "It was definitely a Hound," I said. "She got out of here pretty fast. Didn't go far immediately, bounced around a bit . . ." I concentrated. "She ended up in North America, though I don't know why she went there."

The two Riders looked at each other.

"Not Australia?" Alejandro said. "She did not go to the Goblin, Vein of Gold? That is where I sent Stormwolf." He turned to me. "It did not follow him?"

Frowning hurt my head. "They weren't *here* at the same time, I can tell you that, she definitely came after him." I hesitated. "Wait. She knew he'd been here, but it was . . ." I sat up straighter. "She *was* following a Rider's trail; she just didn't know it was Wolf's. And like I said, she didn't go far, although there were a lot of changes. I'm sure she's in North America now." Hawk glanced at Alejandro, clearly wondering how I could know so much. "That's her blood dripping out there," I pointed out. "It's still wet, as if she were just now injured. For the blood, it's as if no time has passed at all, as if it was still part of her." I shivered again. "It's like touching her."

"How is she moving so quickly?" Hawk said. "I cannot see a Hound booking a flight, nor can I imagine it waiting to go through customs."

"But if they're stable," I said, "If they look normal? What would stop them?"

"How stable are they?" Alejandro said. "How long can they hold their shapes? The Atlantic flight is seven hours at the least."

"Another Rider *has* been here," I said, slowly, still trying to sort through the images from the front hall. "Not Wolf, and not either of you."

"One of the Basilisk Warriors?"

I shook my head, that wasn't what I was getting. "Can a Rider

Move a Hound?" Suddenly I remembered the SNAP! I'd felt when the blood touched me. It had been that, and not the slap Alejandro had given me that had focused my attention and woken me up.

"Is there any way for the Hunt to Move themselves?" I asked.

Both of them were shaking their heads even as I asked the question, but Hawk stopped shaking his first, and seemed to be thinking something over. I waited.

"You speak of 'she' and 'her,'" he said. "It is female?" When I nodded, he continued his thought. "I have never thought of them as having gender; I suppose more is known about them now, since we learned about the Basilisk."

"She isn't a Basilisk, she's a Phoenix." Now they were both looking at me again, and again Hawk's face was tight.

"It has a Guidebeast?" The incredulity was clear in Alejandro's tone. Incredulity and a kind of horror.

"Well, not exactly. Not the same way any of you do." *Or Wolf does*, I said to myself. I'd just as soon not remind them of him, however, now that it seemed he wasn't involved.

"But it would have one, in some broken, twisted way; it would indeed have a Guidebeast." Hawk seemed to be thinking aloud. "It may not yet be generally known," he added, his gaze returning from wherever it was his mental abstraction had taken him. "But the Hunt were once Riders. The High Prince herself made the discovery, when she was the prisoner of the Basilisk. They eat *dra'aj*, they crave it, they must have it, more and more of it, and it is this craving, this addiction, that makes them the Hunt." He looked at Alejandro. "But once, who knows how long ago, they were Riders."

"But the shifting of shape?"

That did it; a piece of the puzzle had finally fallen into place for me. "They *have* to keep changing," I said. "Don't you see? They've absorbed the *dra'aj* of all these other People, and therefore their Guidebeasts as well, that's why they keep changing, and why they can't maintain one shape, not even that of their own Guide."

"Even though they must have more than enough *dra'aj* to manifest, they cannot keep to one form, but must play, over and over, the forms they have stolen." Now there was pity along with the horror, in Alejandro's voice.

"And that's why human *dra'aj* stabilizes them," I concluded in triumph. "Because humans have no Guidebeasts."

"So they are looking now for human *dra'aj*?" Hawk was not as convinced as I was. "Why, then, the attacks on Shower of Stars? On Jenaro the Troll? And on the Goblin?"

It should have been funny to see them both looking at me for answers, considering by how much I was the youngest in the room. Then it hit me, and my stomach dropped. They thought of the Hunt as an alien thing, apart from the People. And they thought of me the same way, even Alejandro—though to be fair about it, Alejandro at least knew in his bones that I had ways of knowing things I shouldn't otherwise know. To Hawk, it just made sense that, as a non-Rider, I would have insight into how non-Riders thought. I didn't know whether to be pleased or insulted.

"Okay." I nodded. I thought we could approach things like a cop or a detective would—at least, the way they do in mystery novels, though I didn't tell the Riders that was what I was doing. "We know the Hunt are feeding off humans more than they did before because of the increase in the numbers of Outsiders. So, I think we can agree that they're doing it on purpose, that they're actively seeking out stability, not just finding *dra'aj* where they can."

"This is logic," Alejandro said, nodding.

"So, if they're also trying to take the *dra'aj* of, shall we say, their more traditional prey, either the human *dra'aj* is not enough for them after all—"

"In which case they are still a danger to the People," Hawk said.

I saw the implications of that, but I went on building my logical case. "Or they're eliminating potential enemies—"

"In which case, their danger is limited to those of the People who are still in the Shadowlands. If we all return to the Lands, the Hunt here will present no further problem to us."

I felt Alejandro stiffen at my side. Was it just that he wouldn't want to abandon me, his *fara'ip*, and the place that still, for him, held traces of his true love? Or did he remember that the Hunt was feeding on real people, innocent people, even if they weren't *People*? Did he remember his promise to help them?

"It may be more simple," he said. "They are addicts, and as such cannot forgo feeding on *dra'aj* when an opportunity presents itself."

"We were going to ask you about helping the Outsiders," I said. "The human victims of the Hunt? Are you just going to let the Hunt go on making more of them? If they used to be Riders, as you say, then Nik and the others are right in saying that you have some kind of responsibility for their existence, for dealing with them."

"I am not unsympathetic," Hawk said. "But you must realize that for those still in the Lands, the first concern will be the safety of the People." I made sure not to look at Alejandro. This attitude fit too closely with what he'd warned me about. "If we take this report back to the High Prince, there will be many who will say that once our People return, and we are in no further danger from the Hunt or the followers of the Basilisk, nothing more need be done."

"I wouldn't be too sure about that." There was a hot, angry spot growing in my chest. I wasn't sure about what I was going to say next, and I didn't want to examine too closely my motives in suggesting it, but the idea that Riders would just turn their backs on humans was making me boil.

"I know what Moving feels like from the inside," I began. "I knew that Alejandro could Move the very first time I shook his hand, and I could tell that about you, and about Wolf. That time I met her, I knew that Shower of Stars couldn't Move, at least not the way you guys do."

"Is there a point, my dear one?"

I pointed past Hawk to the front hallway. "That Hound Moved—not far, I grant you, and maybe she wasn't even aware of it herself—but I felt the actual Move when I touched the blood, the same way I can feel the ability."

"This is not possible." Hawk's voice was a strained whisper.

"Why not? Maybe they can't keep a Rider's form long enough to spend hours on a plane, but it doesn't take hours to Move. In a way, it doesn't take any time at all. And who knows, the more human *dra'aj* they get, the more stable they become. Maybe one day they won't change at all. But they'll still be the Hunt, won't they?" I looked up at Alejandro. "It's not like they'll have gone through rehab. They won't be cured, like Wolf is."

"If they can Move, they will be able to use the Portals." Hawk's voice was icy cold.

Part of me felt triumphant, but not in a good way.

Fox rolled out of bed and padded away to the window in his bare feet. Swift River Current gave a satisfied groan and stretched, her hands high above her head.

"I'd want to keep these forms just for this," she said, rolling onto her side to face him. "When was the last time we indulged without hurting ourselves?"

"I can't remember," he said, turning back to her. He reached out for the clothing he'd tossed on a nearby chair, saw his hand tremble, felt the sweat that broke out on his forehead. He glanced at River, but she hadn't noticed. They were both sweaty anyway, they'd had quite a workout, but Fox knew there was more to it than that. He needed *dra'aj* and soon. Just for a moment he eyed River, wondering what would happen if he took hers. She'd fed on humans exclusively since returning from the mine where she'd spoken to Stormwolf, but would *dra'aj* taken from her still have the properties of human *dra'aj*? Or would filtering through a Person change it?

An interesting question, he thought, but not one he needed to answer this minute. Instead, he sat down and began to pull on his clothes. River watched him from the bed.

"What'll we do about these scentless ones?" she said. "What's your plan?"

Fox'd heard that tone before, many times. Let her use it, if she felt like it. One day he'd remind her again that he was Pack Leader now. "Why? What should be done?"

River shrugged. "They're useless," she pointed out. "They're just using up the resources our prey needs." She looked up at him. "Except that one you fed on, the young one, he got his *dra'aj* back somehow." There was a hunger now in her tone that spoke to the emptiness growing in him.

"Not all of them get more *dra'aj*. It looks like it's a reward, doled out to those who obey. Which means the scentless ones are organized, there's a Pack Leader." Fox pulled the T-shirt on over his head. He smoothed his hands over the material, removing the wrinkles. Most of the humans he'd seen had unwrinkled clothing. He'd be interested to learn how they managed it, since there was no *dra'aj* in the materials themselves.

"So should we find these leaders, then? Could there be any benefit for us?" River rolled to a sitting position, pulled her knees up to her chest.

"Sure, if they'd tell us where they got their new *dra'aj*. But once we know that, we wouldn't need them anymore."

"Could there be more than one source? The *dra'aj* you took from the young one was as human as any. They're not pulling *dra'aj* from any of the People, or from the Lands." She paused, thinking. "Though they might try."

Fox slipped on his shoes. "It doesn't matter *where* they got it, or how they restore it. What's important is that what they take is *ours*." He stood, realizing that his thoughts had clarified. "We'll eliminate them. Don't let new ones live. Kill the ones who already exist."

"What if they ally with the Riders?"

Fox waved this away, wrinkling his nose at the very idea. "Riders aren't going to ally themselves with humans. They're lesser beings."

He paused in the doorway to look back at River. She'd stretched out once more on the bed, reveling in her restored form. The painful thinness was gone, now that she had plenty of the human *dra'aj*. She was Phoenix-guided, and that explained her fieriness. She thought she was guiding him with her advice, controlling him, even; thought she was the Pack Leader's mate. Again, Fox wondered what her *dra'aj* would taste like. But she was useful. Her questions and proddings helped him sort out his thoughts. He'd let her live while her usefulness continued.

After all, her *dra'aj* would always be there.

"We've found her, Pack Leader, the Rider's human pet."

Fox looked across the table at Badger. There weren't many patrons in the Hair of the Dog today, in the middle of the afternoon, and most of them were sitting at the outside tables. Fox'd taken the *dra'aj* out of a young woman seated by herself as he came into the bar. He'd have fed from the bartender, or one of the wait staff, but he'd noticed that it affected the quality of the service. That was something he needed to think about. If the Pack didn't grow, they might want to keep some humans whole, as servants. Maybe some scentless ones, he thought, considering the one he'd interrogated. They could be kept in line with the knowledge of what could happen to them.

He gestured, and Badger sat down across from him, setting down a yellow book with soft pages on the table between them. Badger opened the book and pushed it closer, pointing to the right-hand page. Fox'd seen these drawings before; maps the humans called them, a way to show location. Cold, scentless things, but useful and informative in their way. So far, only some of the Pack were able to make the mental leap that allowed the symbols and drawings to make sense. Their Rider allies had no problems with it, however, and Fox was certain that soon, when all the Hunt had permanent, stable forms, the ability would spread.

"These are the three places her scent's strongest," Badger was saying. She tapped on the page. "Here she's been fairly recently, with her Rider. It's the lair of a scentless one, and others of the same kind've been coming and going as well."

Fox nodded, making note of the place. If it was some kind of a center for the scentless ones, he might find the leaders there.

"This's actually where we caught the guy you fed from." Badger's voice trembled at the thought of feeding, but she very quickly got it under control. Fox ignored it, waiting as she turned to a different page and tapped at another spot. "Her scent's strongest here, as well as the scent of Riders, mostly a Hippogriff, old but still powerful, and the scent of *gra'if*." A whine entered Badger's voice. She cleared her throat and turned to yet another page. "Here, the girl's only been once, but she lingered some time. There's also the scent of a different Rider. He's the one we told you about, the one whose scent is familiar somehow, and somehow not."

Fox grew still. Was that Wolf's lair? So far, only River had recognized their former Pack Leader.

Fox took the book and flipped the pages to the second location. "This spot, where her scent's the strongest? Hold back from it for now. Just keep a watch on the girl's movements. If she ever leaves the place alone, I need to know."

Badger nodded. "From the scents, there seems to be a lot of movement. Riders. In and out."

"Then you'll be careful." Fox turned to the first page. "Here, where the scentless ones gather. Go in, and see what's there."

Badger hesitated, but finally gathered herself to speak. "There's not that many of us, Pack Leader."

Fox looked up, and waited until Badger lowered her eyes. "Then maybe we'll ask our allies to go in for us."

"And this last place, Pack Leader?"

Fox turned the page back to the final spot Badger had shown him. He stared, placing his finger on the spot as if somehow that could link him to Wolf. "Leave that place for now," he said. "Go, give the Pack my orders."

"At once, Pack Leader."

Chapter Fifteen

IT SEEMED LIKE HOURS LATER that Alejandro and Nighthawk were still debating, pushing ideas back and forth, revisiting the same suggestions over and over. They should have been talking strategy, and they *had* started out making a new list of others who might help us against the Hunt, but between Naturals and Riders without *gra'if*, the list wasn't getting any longer. And they were still talking.

Nighthawk seemed to have gotten over his suspicion of Wolf. At least, that's what I thought.

After the horror of the Troll's house, I'd been half hoping we'd go to our old apartment in Madrid, but the one thing both Riders agreed on was that we needed to be back in Toronto, where the Hunt was concentrating, and where Wolf had been instructed to make his headquarters. So here they were once more sitting at the dining room table. I was still too wired to sit still for very long, so I was washing the dishes that couldn't be put in the dishwasher. As the only one in the place who could get drunk, I was also the only one drinking soda water.

"It is clear—and significant—that the Hunt is aware of Stormwolf," Hawk said at one point. "But it seems from what Valory has said that they are only aware of him as a Rider. Once his presence has alerted them, they become aware of the presence of others." He shrugged. "Still, I must ask myself, how far is *he* aware of *them*? After the encounter in which he helped me, he knew about the Hunt, is it conceivable that he would not know he was being followed? Even if he was not leading them deliberately—"

"Which he wasn't." I put down the glass I was drying and leaned into the pass-through. "How many times are you going to go over this?" Though that was unfair to Alejandro; it was Hawk who kept on circling back to this point. Still, I was starting to lose my patience.

"What is it you have against him?" I asked the Sunward Rider outright. "Why are you so sure one minute that he's a good guy, and so sure the next that he can't be?" Alejandro inhaled sharply, lifting his hands a few inches from the table. "What?" I said. "I was a good girl and helped out, and it's too much for me to get some answers?"

Hawk held up his hand, shaking his head from side to side. "You are sure, in yourself." He tapped himself on the chest with his index finger. "I wish I could be as sure. I have seen the Hunt, many years ago, when I was young. It was then I learned to fight them, to strike and keep striking no matter what form they took; never to look them in the eye. As for Stormwolf . . ." Here Hawk shook his head again. "He helped me; he brought me news that gladdened my heart. What if that blinded me? What if he was playing a double game, and I did not see it?"

I came around into the dining room and sat down next to Hawk. If I'd known him better, I'd have given him a hug. "It isn't Wolf you distrust," I said. "It's yourself. You're afraid that all these years among humans have damaged your judgment."

"Enough, *querida*," Alejandro said. "Come, Nighthawk, the High Prince herself has passed Stormwolf as trustworthy."

I looked around at him. "And so do I."

Hawk sat still, his hands on his knees, for what felt like a long time. Finally, he stopped chewing on his lower lip and looked up. I was relieved to see the twinkle back in his eyes. "And your opinion is worth something to me." Hawk turned to face Alejandro. "She is a Truthreader. I had forgotten that I cannot pick and choose what I would believe of what she says. It is all truth." He took a deep breath and released it. "I am satisfied that Stormwolf is innocent of wrongdoing. The question before me is whether I return him to the High Prince, as she has asked me to do."

"Wolf should be here," I said, the words out of my mouth before I had time to think. Both Riders were looking at me with identical expressions on their Sunward faces. "It's just, what we're talking about, what's happening in the Shadowlands with the Hunt and the other People—about Wolf *himself*—this is all his business." Both pairs of amber eyes narrowed in thought. At least they weren't arguing. "Doesn't he get a vote? What if he doesn't want to go back? He needs to know what's going on."

Hawk was shaking his head. "The High Prince has given me this task."

"She hasn't given it to us," I pointed out. "Alejandro and I aren't obligated to turn him over."

"He may very well decide for himself to obey the High Prince's command," Alejandro said. "Valory is right. You cannot take that choice from him."

Hawk drummed the table with his fingers. "He would have to be told, in any case." Nodding, he started getting to his feet.

"Hang on," I said, motioning him to sit down again. "If we all go, won't he feel we're ganging up on him?" As I spoke, Alejandro looked at me, his eyes narrowed in speculation, and I felt heat in my face. I could only hope Hawk wouldn't notice. "I just mean that if I go, it's more neutral. I can explain and then call you guys." Or give him a chance to run, if that's what he decided to do.

"And if he is not there?" Alejandro knew I meant to go to the Royal York.

I shrugged. "I'll figure out some way to leave him a message."

"Take your mobile."

I grabbed my bag and headed out the door before either of them could think of more to discuss. I was letting myself out the back gate when Alejandro appeared next to me. Before I could say yes or no, there was a CRACK!, a moment of vertigo, and we were in a deserted back corridor of Union Station.

"You are flushed, and your pulse is rapid. Are you well?" Without actually touching me, Alejandro tucked away a lock of hair that had escaped from my ponytail.

He was right. I made myself slow down and take a couple of deep breaths. What was I so excited about? I was looking forward to seeing Wolf—and I admit that realization sobered me. Sure, I knew more about him than a regular girl in my situation would have known about a regular guy—but neither of us were exactly regular people.

"*Querida.*" Alejandro kissed me on the forehead. "Be most careful. No one knows better than I the allure that can arise between human and Rider. But you are neither of you merely those things. And this is a very difficult time for us all."

"So *you're* psychic now?" I don't know how successful my smile was.

"No. But neither am I blind."

We'd reached the exit doors, and I turned to face him fully. "Alejandro." I hugged him. "Thanks. Thanks for letting me do this my way."

"We are *fara'ip*."

I watched him walk back into the shadows and went on with a lighter heart.

I decided to go up to the street rather than through the underground mall to the hotel. For one thing, it was a brilliant summer day, not the dead of winter. And it wasn't hot enough yet to need the air-conditioning of the lower levels of the city.

As usual, Front Street was busy with taxis stopping and picking up passengers from the train station, so I walked down to the lights at the corner. I could cross more safely there, and it would also put me closer to the hotel entrance I wanted. I was dressed okay, a little wrinkled maybe, but as Alejandro always said, "My dear one, that is how you know it is linen."

As I stepped off the curb, the old man next to me stumbled, and without thinking I caught him by the forearm. [The hunger, the need; the prey; a beast, single-horned and cloven-hooved, acid dripping from the tip of a horn that melted away and renewed itself over and over; patchy skin, scaly hooves; a Hippogriff that caught at my heart, making me think of Alejandro; the prey; a snake with wings; a thin Asian boy, eyes wide open, pupils pinpoints; a Chimera; my brother; three more, lesser than he, all three watching; the chase, this world; one following; where's Wolf? The girl's touch should be doing something, what? Where's my brother? The prey, the chase, the hunt. Our world. The *Hunt.*]

It felt like my heart stopped beating, though I don't think my expression changed. My early training saw to that. Or maybe this Hound didn't know enough about human expression to read it. There were a couple of other people around us by then, all reaching out to help, so I was able to turn and walk away, face front, just as quickly as my high-heeled shoes would let me. Still not looking behind me, I reached the other side of the street and went directly under the portico, avoiding a black stretch limo with a chauffeur waiting by the passenger door, and walking through the doors into the Royal York.

I walked stiff-legged across the short lobby up the wide brass-edged steps, gripped the brass handrails with numb fingers. When I reached the top, I shied away from a white alabaster Chinese lion, sitting on top of a beautiful display table with a top made of green marble three inches thick. For a moment the lion had looked like one of the shapes I had seen when the Hound touched me.

And that made me stop, put my hand down on the cold marble of the tabletop, and lean on it, waiting for my lungs to stop shuddering as I drew in a breath, and my knees to bend without dumping me to the ground. The floor was made up of intricate tiles, laid to look like a black-and-white lattice on a soft orange background. Beautiful. Maybe granite, maybe marble, it was hard to tell when they kept moving back and forth, approaching and receding.

I reached into my bag and took out my mobile. Still leaning on the table, I waited while Alejandro's number rang, willing him to pick up. This wasn't something I wanted to leave on voice mail. Finally I heard the sound of the connection, and his voice, a little anxious, "Yes?"

"*Un perro de caza,*" I whispered. "*Delante del hotel.*" I took a deep breath, but my heart was still pounding. "It was looking for me," I continued, still in Spanish. "Waiting for *me*."

"Bah! I knew I should not have left you. Are you injured?" I could imagine Alejandro waving his free hand to shush Hawk. Just hearing his voice made the vise around my chest loosen.

"No. I touched it, but it seemed very careful *not* to—to feed." Something for which I was thoroughly grateful. "Something about a young Outsider, something he said to it. They left him, drained but alive." A few more seconds and I might even have been able to say where, and what had happened to him, but the contact had been broken. I was grateful for that as well. I didn't want to know if I was strong enough to go on touching that thing, even if it meant I could help someone else. I didn't want to find out that I wasn't that brave.

"Where are you now?"

I told him, and answered the question he was about to ask. "So far as I know, the Hound's still outside."

"Do not come home alone. Stay there until I can come for you."

As if I needed to be told that.

As I put my mobile away, I became aware that a woman was looking at me with concern on her face, and I straightened up and smiled at her.

"Warmer than I thought," I said. The last thing I needed was for anyone else to touch me just now. Relieved that I seemed to be okay, the woman nodded and descended the staircase behind me, heading for the door and the street. The sweat on my forehead had dried, the trembling had stopped, and the latticed tiles had stopped moving. I tucked my bag more firmly under my arm and turned toward the broad alcove, twelve feet away, where I could see the brass doors of the three elevators. *Whoever designed this hotel really liked brass,* was the useless thought that floated through my mind. *Must be a bugger to keep polished.*

There was another woman standing in front of the bank of elevators. She was taller than me, and much slimmer, but without being one of *las flacas*. She had very fair coloring. She was wearing a pair of narrow black slacks, strappy silver sandals, and a tapered blood-red blouse with cap sleeves. I was intrigued because I couldn't actually tell what the materials were. I began to have a bad feeling.

She shot me a glance and looked forward again so abruptly that I actually looked behind me to see what had unnerved her. The corridor that stretched out from this side of the elevator lobby was empty. Then I saw that her eyes were flicking from corner to corner, as if she were trying to see everywhere at once. *Agoraphobic?* I wondered. Or just paranoid? It was then I noticed she hadn't pushed the button for the elevator, so I leaned forward and did it myself, careful not to get any closer to her. I could smell the scent she was wearing, something floral but very light and airy. She looked from me to the button and back again.

"This operates the mechanism," she said, as though it were a statement and not a question.

I nodded, as if this was the kind of thing adults in the twenty-first century said in front of elevators all the time. That vise was starting to squeeze my chest again. She was tall, beautiful, with impossibly flawless skin and coloring, and dressed in materials I'd never seen before. There was one fairly obvious conclusion, but I thought a supermodel would likely know an elevator when she saw one.

I figured I didn't have to touch the woman to know she wasn't one—a woman that is. The real question was, Rider or Hound? And if Rider, good guy or bad? Either way, we were probably headed for the same place. And that meant I had to know.

I gritted my teeth and brushed her with my fingertips on the bare arm, just above her elbow, bracing myself for the expected wave of images. [Manticore; three Riders Singing, one from each Ward; gray-eyed Dragon with honey-gold hair; a Moonward Phoenix; a man in a window seat, staring at the clouds; a room that disappeared; a terrible loss, a Griffin, gone and took her heart with it; a child, growing inside her, wrapped with a ribbon of *dra'aj*; *Manticore*.] Oh. [She had once horribly betrayed her sister, and been forgiven; she was very curious about books and reading, since Riders had neither; she'd had a dog named Hilt when she was a child.] She was excited about being in the Shadowlands, and she was looking for the Horn [a tiny flute, made of bone, Dragon or maybe Griffin] this was her chance to really show what she could do [she had a jeweled pin someone named Lightborn had given her tucked on the inside of her collar] She preferred her sister's colors to those of the Basilisk Prince.

She was no danger to Wolf; she just needed to tell him something the three Singers had told her. I could feel my pulse slowing down again.

I pointed at the buttons. "This one if you want to go up," I said, indicating the one I'd pushed. "And the other if you want to go down." I kept my tone as neutral as my still tight throat would let me.

"So, not the direction the mechanism needs to travel to reach me?"

"Well, no." I hadn't even thought of that. "You're not likely to be sure where the, uh, the elevator is."

The elevator came at that moment, and I entered the car to show her how it was done. She came in after me, looking around her now with curiosity more than anything else. I touched the floor button and looked up at her. "Which floor?"

She had been watching me, and had seen how the button I'd touched had lit up. She reached out and touched the "8," pulling her hand back sharply when it, too, lit up. That seemed to disprove my theory.

"You wanted the eighth floor?"

"No," she said. "I wished to see whether the light would appear for me or only for . . ." she licked her lips and fell silent.

"Only for humans," I finished for her.

This time she looked at me closely, studying my face. Again, there was no fear, no worry in her eyes, just curiosity. I was reminded of a friend Alejandro used to play chess with in the Plaza Mayor in Madrid, on summer evenings. Alberto would study the chessboard, calculating the possible moves, in just the dispassionate way the Rider was studying me.

"I'm Valory Martin," I said. "I'm the *fara'ip* of Graycloud at Moonrise. The High Prince of the People has named me a friend."

A light went on in her face as she smiled. "You know my sister? She has mentioned you to me, a Truthreader. I am Walks Under the Moon, my mother was Clear of Light, and the Manticore guides me."

Now that I knew, I thought I could see a resemblance. Walks Under the Moon's face was a little less oval than her sister's, more heart-shaped, and her coloring was a different shade, though she was still clearly Starward. Their eyes, though, were identically gray.

"You're looking for Stormwolf?"

"You also?" She gave me a look then that it took me a minute to recognize. She was smiling, and looked me up and down as though she'd known me my whole life. My eyebrows shot up when I realized what she was doing. She thought I was interested in Wolf, and was checking me out—not like his wife or girlfriend would, more like a sister. I wondered what my sudden blush was telling her.

"You may call me Moon," she finally said. Evidently I had passed some test. "Wolf is my *fara'ip*."

The elevator finally came to a halt on the top floor, and I gestured for her to leave first. "The person nearest the door should get out first, though you'll find some older men will let you precede them, even though they're closer." It seemed strange to be passing along the same bits of instruction Alejandro had been giving to me not so long before.

Moon went directly to Wolf's door and placed her hand on it. "He is within," she said, and used the dragon-shaped knocker while I had my hand half outstretched to stop her. Suddenly I wasn't as sure I wanted to speak to him as I had been back in my dining room. Was it the encounter with the Hound that had me second-guessing, or was it the presence of his *fara'ip*?

For half a minute I thought Moon must be wrong, but then the door opened. Wolf looked straight at me, as if there was no one else there, and I swallowed, feeling a sudden warmth blossoming in my chest. But it was very quickly followed by a chill, as something I'd read from the Hound on the street fell into place. I immediately pushed past him into the suite, without waiting to see how he and Moon would greet each other. I went all the way into the sitting room, and to the far wall, but then found I was too nervous to stand by the windows. I crossed my arms, hugging myself, and came back far enough to stand with my back to the fireplace. Cold now, but somehow comforting in its solidity.

At least, it was comforting until I thought about what could come down the chimney. I sidled away. I looked up to find both Wolf and Moon watching me, the identical quizzical expression on their faces. If it wasn't for the differences in coloring, they might at that moment have been real siblings.

"Did you get my message?" Wolf asked. He held his hand up to his face as if he was holding a phone. "We left you one, Nik Polihronidis and I. He is a very brave man."

Nik and Wolf together? I started to reach into my bag, but stopped. Not much point in checking messages now.

"Your brother is looking for you," I said before I could consider whether or not I should.

Wolf was naturally pale, like any Moonward Rider I would guess, but now his almond skin went so white the faint scars around his eye stood out. Moon took a step to one side and looked at him, brows drawn together, mouth twisted in a frown. Clearly this was news to her, and I wondered whether I should have kept quiet. The shock of the realization had just been too much. Not only had Wolf been a Hound himself, but his brother had been part of his Pack—was *still* part of it.

"Where did you encounter him?"

"Outside." I gestured at the window with a hand that had, maybe, started to shake again. "He doesn't know you're in here, which I guess is lucky, huh? Only that you've been seen here."

Wolf lowered himself onto the front edge of a wing-backed chair. "If you touch me," he said, looking up at me, and holding out his hand, "it will save me from having to explain." Part of me realized that no one else beside Alejandro ever knowingly volunteered to be touched by my talent, and the implication of absolute trust would probably have frightened me a little, if another part of me hadn't been so pissed off.

"But it won't save *me*." I could hear the harshness in my voice and cleared my throat. "*I'd* still have to explain it to Moon, here, wouldn't I? So why don't *you* go ahead? Cut out the middle man?" Why should I make it easier for him?

Moon looked at me with narrowed eyes, and then she transferred the look to Wolf without change. She didn't know what was going on, and she was reserving judgment until she did.

Wolf sat a few minutes longer with his head in his hands. Long enough that I wondered if I would have to touch him after all. Finally, he raised his head.

"As Valory says, I have a brother. And, as she knows but does not say, he is among the Hunt." Moon made a strange noise and Wolf cleared his throat, sat up straighter, and rubbed his hands along his thighs. "He may be Pack Leader now. Now that I am no longer there."

"Your brother. You have a brother." Moon's voice was as thin as Wolf's had been. Apparently, this news wasn't sitting well with any of us.

"Why have you not spoken of this? Does the High Prince know?"

"Which of us can say what the High Prince knows and does not know."

I wrinkled my nose. "By which *he* means no, at least, he never told her." I rolled my eyes and sat down on the edge of the hearth, realized what I'd done, and moved to the other chair. Moon came and sat on the arm of it. The easy intimacy of that didn't strike me until later. At the time, all I felt was that she and I were on the same side.

"It is not quite as simple as that." Wolf's tone had hardened, his eyes flicking back and forth between us. He wasn't defensive, he wasn't pleading.

"It never is," I said to Moon, out of the side of my mouth. I regretted it almost immediately. After all, I was the one who was making him tell the tale, and snarkiness was uncalled for, not matter how irritated I was. "Sorry," I said. "I know this isn't easy for you, but honestly, it's not easy for any of us."

He inclined his head once, in a sort of bow. "It is not so much that I wished to hide the facts of my life with the Hunt, as it is that I wished to forget them. I did all that I could to put them from me. But memories are not old shoes, to be cast away when desired . . ." He spread his hands out as if he wanted to grasp something. "When we were with Honor of Souls," he said, speaking directly to Moon, "the Hunt no longer seemed part of my life. I remembered being a Hound but not the way I remembered the fight on the Stone of Virtue, the transformation of the High Prince, and my fostering with you, Moon."

"You seemed then to be someone awakening from a dream." From her tone, Moon was thinking back.

"A nightmare, more like. It is more as though my life in the Hunt had happened to someone else." He gestured at the window, in the direction of Union Station. "All this world is familiar to me. I have been here as a Hound, Hunting the Prince Guardian when he was in Exile. But I feel rather as though I know it from a Song I once knew well."

"So you felt that you no longer had a brother?" I could tell Moon was trying not to judge, and maybe finding it harder than she hoped. Something lay behind that, I thought. She had a sister herself, whom it was obvious she loved very much. Was it as simple as that? She couldn't understand how Wolf could set aside thoughts and memories of his brother.

With a shock that made me blink, I realized that I could have a brother, too, or a sister, and not even know it.

Wolf was shaking his head. "No. I remembered Foxblood. But I could not remember whether he had returned to the Lands with me. When the High Prince set me this task, I was looking for him . . ." His voiced died away.

"While you were looking for everyone else," I said.

Without raising his head, Wolf looked from me to Moon and back again. She was close enough to me that I could smell her floral scent, feel the warmth from her body. If I moved a fraction of an inch, I could touch her.

"I did not shirk my task," he said, and I believed him. "But I did hope to find my brother. To undo what I did to him."

"You made him a Hound." The words were out of my mouth before I could stop them. Moon leaned away from me, but only to see me better without moving from the arm of the chair. "When I touched Foxblood just now," I said. "Out on the street. That's part of what I saw, what I read from him. He follows you. He's always followed you." I pressed my hands together, palm to palm, lifted them to tap my fingers against my lips. "He thought you were stuck on the other side of the Portal. Now that he knows differently—is there someone named Running River? River Current?—now he's trying to find you."

Wolf shuddered and buried his face in his hands. Moon looked at me, and I nodded. She rose and, kneeling beside him, took him into her arms. He allowed it, I saw, but he didn't relax into her. No way was he letting himself off the hook.

Moon swung her head to look at me. "Would you do what you require? Would you touch him to see if he has kept anything more from us?"

"That's a tall order," I said. "There might be all kinds of things about himself he hasn't told us. Perfectly innocent things." But a change of direction often helps to put things in perspective, I thought and, mindful of what I was doing there in the first place, I thought I had the perfect distraction. "I'm not here by chance. Three of the People you've found here were also visited by Hounds. Nighthawk thought you might be involved somehow, if only by accident. The High Prince asked him to bring you back to her."

"He said he would not." Moon was on her feet. "He said he would . . . *three* People?" She looked as though she needed to sit down.

"He was looking for more evidence?" I nodded. "And he thought he found some, that's why he told her. He knows better now, but—"

"She asked for this? She believed I led the Hunt to her People?"

Moon and I looked at each other, and I can only think that my face must have shown the same distress that hers did, maybe more, since I knew just how deep the despair we'd heard in his voice ran. And there was just the touch, just a vibration of anger. After all he'd done for her—that's what he must have been thinking.

"She wanted you to be safe," I said. "She did think it was possible that the Hunt has just been following you without your being aware of it," I added.

"Impossible," he said, with an abrupt stroke of his hand. "I would have scented them. Hounds are always . . ." His voice faded away.

"But you're no longer a Hound." Moon's voice was gentle. "You're a Rider now, and they could not prey upon us, if they were not able to pursue us."

Wolf was nodding, but almost as if he didn't want to believe it.

I thought it was time to interrupt again. "The point is, Hawk still thinks you should go back, and I thought . . ." I swallowed. "I thought you might have other ideas."

"You could return with *me*," Moon suggested. "We could go directly to my sister."

"Is this why you came? To arrest me more sweetly than Nighthawk could do?"

Moon got to her feet, leaving Wolf alone in his chair, and crossed to the far side of the fireplace. Her lips were pressed tight, and her hand was touching the pin she had in her collar. I rolled my eyes. Typical. Here we were trying to help him and, somehow, all this was our fault.

"I came to ask if you could remember anything about the Horn." The tightness of Moon's voice showed that her thinking had been much the same as mine. "The High Prince has tasked me with finding it, or making a new one."

Wolf sat up straighter, drawing his sloe-black eyebrows together. "The Horn? She would use it? Then I will not be able to help them, to offer them the chance of the cure I was given."

Had forced on him was a more accurate description, I thought, but he was happy about it now, so maybe that wasn't as big a distinction as I thought.

"But do you not see how having the Horn would help you in *your* plan?" Moon's gray eyes sparkled. They were on the same side again. "I have researched the Songs that speak of the artifact, and have only one clue that may be useful. A fragment of Song. It is a mountain I search for, or a range of mountains. 'Born of Ice Tor, the caller of the Hunt' is how one fragment has it. I wondered," here, her voice softened, "I wondered whether you might know, might remember, some Song from before the time you were a Hound, that might give me some further clue."

Wolf was shaking his head. "I believe I might have been a Singer, that is true. But of what I Sang . . ." he shook his head.

"Just a minute." I got to my feet. "You want to know where Ice Tor is, is that it? And you think Wolf might have known, once upon a time?" Moon nodded, watching me. As soon as I was close enough, I took a firm grip on his forearm, just below his rolled sleeve. His skin was wonderfully warm. [A lyre made from living Wood and *gra'if* and the hair of a Water Sprite; a Starward Rider, impossibly old, listening to him Sing; a new tune, but an old Song.]

"From the Quartz Ring," I said. "Across the Moor of Ravens, beyond the Sea of *Ma'arban*." I hoped I was pronouncing it right. "That is where Ice Tor dwells."

"Dwells?"

I'd taken my hand way. "That's what I read. I'm afraid I can't interpret it any further without more context, but it could be a metaphor, right? You know, if it's a song lyric?"

Both of them nodded, Moon with a pleased smile on her face, Wolf still frowning. I wondered if he now remembered something about the mountain range, or the Song he'd once known.

"So what now?" I asked.

"Now I will go to the Quartz Ring," Moon said, then her face clouded. "I once promised Lightborn the Griffin Lord I would not go into danger without telling him."

But he's dead. It was the kind of thought I'd learned the hard way to keep to myself. That was why she was wearing his pin on the collar of her shirt. And he was the father of her child, it was his *dra'aj* I'd felt, wrapped around the baby's.

"Okay, I've got it." I raised my hands, palms out, as they both looked as though they'd like to interrupt. "Wolf's the one who should go. He bears *gra'if.* Once he's there, on the ground, he's bound to remember more. Don't you see? Think of all the time that would be saved if Wolf brings the High Prince the Horn." Suddenly, I saw the whole thing clearly. "But I'm the one who should go with him, not you."

They looked at me openmouthed, and I sighed, stifling the urge to roll my eyes again. Sometimes you can be too close to a problem to see the solution. What I suggested would get Wolf away from his brother, and put him farther on the path to saving him at the same time.

"It is too risky." Wolf was shaking his head. *You don't know the half of it,* I thought. My heart was thumping so loudly I could hardly hear myself think.

"Look," I said. "We're depending on your knowledge, and I've already shown *I'm* the key to that."

"Then we will all go," Moon said.

"And who'll explain it to your sister?" I clenched my teeth. I had to find a way to convince them. "How much time have we got? How long do we have to convince everyone else that this is the right thing to do?"

"But once we are gone . . ." Wolf began, eyes focused on something far away.

"It's easier to be forgiven for it afterward than it is to ask for permission first," I agreed.

Moon still looked worried, but now Wolf was slowly nodding

"If we had the Horn, we could bring the Hunt to be cured." His eyes refocused on me. "The *dra'aj* they have taken would be returned to the Lands, as you said mine was." Wolf snatched up his sword from where it was hanging openly in a bracket next to the fireplace. It turned into an umbrella as soon as he touched it. He turned it back and forth in his hand, as if he was examining a blade only he could see. "I had hoped we would not need to force them, but if the time is growing so short?"

Now Moon was nodding, still with a frown, but at least she was getting to her feet.

"Come on," I said. "We have to hit a drugstore.

Nighthawk came out of the revolving doors, shaking his head. Alejandro drew him down the sidewalk to where they would not be interrupted by offers of service from the doormen of the hotel.

"I saw nothing untoward inside," Hawk said. "But if they no longer look like Hounds, how can I be sure?"

Alejandro thought back to his own experience in the train station, when he had followed what he'd thought to be a Rider. "You saw no other Riders?" But Hawk shook his head.

"I am satisfied nothing lurks out here." Alejandro scanned the street with narrowed eyes. "We should join Valory. Now is the time to speak with Stormwolf." Alejandro pulled out his mobile. "Let me tell her we are coming. Stormwolf has done no harm, and we should approach him with courtesy as the emissary of the High Prince."

"Alejandro!"

His phone to his ear, Alejandro turned to see Nik Polihronidis coming out of the revolving doors. He was wearing a tan suit, with a crisp blue shirt and tie, and looked as though he had just come from a corporate meeting.

"I thought I recognized a Rider in the lobby," he said, nodding at Hawk as he joined them. "I've been trying to get hold of you. Where have you been?"

Close up, the Outsider looked tired. "Valory is upstairs with Stormwolf," he said. "She reported seeing a Hound somewhere here," Alejandro gestured at the street. "Have any of your people seen one earlier today?"

Brow furrowed, Nik pulled out his own phone and hit a single button. "Any activity around the station?" As he spoke, he looked over Alejandro's shoulder, and froze, lifting his free hand to point. "Hang on," he said. "There she is, there. Valory!"

Alejandro and Hawk both spun around to look. The girl in the gray linen dress at the far corner was Valory; there could be no doubt. Walking with her was a Starward female, and on her other side, Stormwolf. They had crossed the street at the southeast end of the hotel, and were heading for the entrance to the train station. Alejandro saw Valory glance over her shoulder at the pavement behind them.

But she was not looking in the right direction, he realized.

"Oh, crap." Nik dashed across the street, ignoring the horns and cars screeching to avoid him. Nighthawk, his Rider reflexes so much faster, reached the opposite sidewalk before Nik was halfway across.

The danger was coming from below, Alejandro saw, from the stairs to the subway.

He Moved.

Chapter Sixteen

I COULDN'T HELP MYSELF. I kept looking over my shoulder as we crossed Front Street, checking if Wolf's brother—or some other Hound—was still there, still watching for me. I couldn't see him, or anyone else that looked wrong or out of place, but the hairs kept rising on the back of my neck. I could have called Alejandro back, let him know what I was doing, but I wanted to wait until it was too late for him to stop us. It was Alejandro who'd first told me that it was easier to get forgiveness than permission.

And when Wolf and I came back with the Horn, for sure everything would be forgiven.

The two Riders were intent on getting across the street, Moon shying a little and looking sideways as cars passed in front or behind her. She was between me and Wolf, and every now and then Wolf reached over and took her elbow. She needed the reassurance, I thought, more than she needed a helping hand.

We'd reached the curb when Wolf stiffened. "Walk faster," he said.

I didn't argue with him, and though I looked, I didn't see anything. Moon was doing her best to speed up as well, but she was in front now, and didn't know where we were going. I sped up to get ahead of her and our pace increased a little more.

We were about a third of the way down the departure concourse and the Panorama Lounge was in sight—fortunately in a train station, people running are so common that no one tried to either stop or help us—when I caught movement out of the corner of my eye. Movement that was cutting across the orderly lines of waiting people at an angle that would intersect with ours before we reached the Portal.

"Run," Wolf called, but we were already running. Just as we got to the doors of the lounge, I sensed that Moon was no longer just behind me, and I turned. No point in *my* going on, I wouldn't be able to pass through the Portal, or even the crossroads, by myself. I was frantically trying to get my mobile out—how can *everything* always be at the bottom of your bag?—but except for the hand reaching behind her, Moon was standing still, lower lip between her teeth. Her hand waved at me, and I realized she meant me to take it. If the worst came, she could Move us out of here. I closed the gap between us, though I hesitated to actually take her hand. I didn't think I could afford to be distracted by what touching her would show me. Then I really registered what the glint of metal on her wrist meant. *Gra'if.* I wrapped my hand around it.

Wolf was only a long stride in front of Moon, his back to us, facing a much younger version of the man who'd pretended to stumble on the street. Facing his brother. Now that he wasn't pretending to be an old man, Fox's resemblance to Wolf was more noticeable. Or did I just think so because now I knew?

"Go," Wolf said to us, speaking over his shoulder without taking his eyes from his brother. "Now."

I wasn't sure where he expected *me* to go, and evidently neither was Moon. We both took a step back toward the lounge, but then we hesitated, reluctant to go any farther.

"More may come," Wolf said.

"All the more reason not to leave you alone." Brave words, but even I could hear the tremor in Moon's voice. I tried to tell myself that I had less reason to be worried than either of them. Riders drained of *dra'aj* would fade, their essences gone. The worst that could happen to me was that I'd become an Outsider and I'd have to get regular infusions of *dra'aj* for the rest of my life. Don't get me wrong, I'd touched both Nik and Elaine, and theirs weren't lives I'd choose happily, but at least it *was* life.

Not that I found the thought very comforting. I started to breathe easier when it seemed that no one else, and therefore no other Hound, seemed to be taking an interest in us. At least, until I saw what *might* be others, people heading toward us, cutting through the crowds and lines of passengers, people not carrying bags or luggage of any kind.

Fox shifted to stand apparently relaxed, with his hands clasped together in front of him. If he'd been human, I would have said the look on his face was one of pleasure and anticipation.

"It *is* you, brother," he said. "River wasn't lying."

"That would depend on what more she told you." Wolf held his umbrella as though it was a sword—which of course it was—though it wasn't up in an offensive position, or even a defensive one, but hanging point down in front of him. His shoulders were a little raised, but I thought it was with tension, not anticipation. I'd seen Alejandro poised to attack with his sword many times, and Wolf didn't look like that at all.

"Has *she* done this to you? Is this what *her* touch does?" Fox pointed at me with his chin, and lifted his eyebrows.

"Done what to me?"

I realized that Wolf was stalling, buying time for Moon and me to go. All the time they were talking, the three of us were inching backward, closer to the lounge entrance, but Moon wasn't moving very fast, unwilling, I guessed, to leave Wolf and lose the chance of finding the Horn. As for me, right then I was busy listening to Wolf and his brother.

"Finished the job that the human *dra'aj* starts. Made you whole again."

Wolf was shaking his head. "So she did not tell you all," he said. *Who was* she, I wondered? "Or did you simply choose not to believe her? My condition has nothing to do with any human, not even this one. I am free, and myself once more."

"Free of what?" Fox took another step forward, and we took another step back. We were at the door of the lounge now, and beginning to attract the curious attention of the first-class passengers inside, waiting for their trains. "Why didn't you come back to the Pack if you were free?"

I wouldn't have thought it possible, but there was some genuine hurt in the Hound's voice.

"It is the Pack I'm free of. Free of the hunger, free of need. I am not merely stable, I am whole, and no longer part of the Hunt." Wolf drew himself up slightly. "Once again I am Stormwolf, my mother was Rain at Sunset, and the Chimera guides me."

(flicker) For a second there I glimpsed the Guidebeast I'd only sensed before, and realized that Fox, when he was a Rider, must have been guided by a Unicorn. What I'd seen, in that eye blink, was a limping, twisted, scaly parody of one. Had its front feet even been hooved? Or had they been flippers?

"Who're you trying to kid? That's impossible." Fox's tone was dark.

"It is possible. Here I am." Now Wolf actually took a step forward, reaching out with his free hand. I had put out my own hand to draw him back toward us, but froze when Fox's glance flicked over to me. "Did we not often wish for this?" Wolf continued, as if no one had moved. "An end to our need, to our miserable craving? Miserable we called it, and misery it is."

Fox shook his head and waved Wolf's words away. "*Then*! Maybe in a weak moment. Sure, *then* we might have wanted to end it, but now we don't have to. Now we can control it; we're our own masters." *Funny how all addicts think they're in control*, was the useless thought that spun through my head. "With the human *dra'aj*, everything's changed. We don't need the People." His tone took on a hint of wheedling, just like a younger brother who's trying to coax an older sibling into letting him have his way. "You never wanted this! This *freedom*." His tone left no doubt what he thought of it. "You were Pack Leader, not some errand boy. You never looked for this."

"No, I did not. Not even in what you call our weak moments did I ever allow myself to desire what I never believed could come to pass. Never tortured myself with the possibility. But it is more than a possibility now, it is real. It is before you. A Healing. An end to our long days of hunting."

"Don't be so soft. Why would we want to end the hunting?" Fox's smile was still gentle, though his tone was beginning to harden.

"That doesn't sound like my brother at all, not the brother I knew. Come on, don't be foolish. You belong with us, with me."

Wolf took in a deep breath, and again I wanted to touch him, to find out what was really going on in his head. I thought I knew what he would want, but I wasn't one hundred percent sure.

"You are right," he said finally. I thought my heart would stop. "We do belong together. You followed me before, follow me *now*. Come with me *now*. I can take you to the High Prince. She has promised she will Heal any who come to her."

Now Fox's lip curled back. "Has she now? She promised you? And you fell for it? Is that why Riders have been killing Hounds? Tell it to Stump, to Claw. Tell me, brother, haven't we dealt with Princes before? And how do their promises normally work? Is she even real, this one that's making promises now?"

Moon pushed forward at these words. Wolf put out an arm to keep her back, and though I still had hold of her wrist, I grabbed the tail of her blouse, getting a good grip. "She is more real than you, foul, broken travesty. She is the Dragonborn High Prince of the Lands, of all the People. She is the Sword of Truth and brings Healing wherever she goes. And she would Heal even you, wretch."

"Which you wouldn't, I think. I believe what *you're* saying all right, you call me 'foul' and 'wretch' with such conviction. I spit on you. And I spit on your Prince. As for you, *brother*, I'm sorry you've become so weak, I'm sorry you've let prey rule you. Tell them we don't want their Healing, and we don't want them. We'll take this world instead."

A blur of motion and Alejandro appeared, shouldering Wolf to one side, raising his sword against Fox. Suddenly the other Hounds were there, and I realized they had only been holding off while Wolf and Fox spoke. Just as Wolf and Alejandro were being forced to stand back-to-back, Hawk came out of nowhere, roaring out a challenge and drawing off some of the attackers. But there were other Riders there as well, I saw, not just Hounds, and these new Riders weren't on our side.

"Don't touch my brother!" I heard Fox call out, though I couldn't see him clearly.

Moon's grip on my arm was bruisingly painful, but I didn't shake her off. I wasn't worried at first because none of the Hounds or the other Riders bore *gra'if*, and the brightness of those blades—Wolf's, Alejandro's, and Hawk's—seemed to be everywhere. Then I realized that the points of brightness were farther and farther apart, and that the enemy might overwhelm us by sheer numbers.

One of the Hounds came straight for us, closer than we'd thought one to be, and Moon and I rushed back again to the relative shelter of the lounge doorway. Then Wolf was there, slashing at the thing.

"Go! Run!" he shouted. "Take Valory and go."

I don't know whether Moon would have obeyed him or not. Just as he spoke, two Riders flanked him, one diving for his legs as the other clung to his sword arm. The Hound in front of him looked like he'd forgotten his Pack Leader's order not to touch Wolf. Momentum was forcing them all back toward us. Moon gripped me around the waist with one arm, and took hold of Wolf's jacket with her free hand. The next thing I knew, the air was being sucked out of my lungs, and the blackness roared around me and through me, and I hit the ground hard.

I knew what it was this time and maybe that, along with the Gravol I'd picked up in the drugstore, helped a little, because I thought I was going to be able to raise my own head. There was a new smell, however, a smell of cold, uncooked meat, and a howling, followed by cursing in a language I didn't quite catch, and the brightness of *gra'if* weapons flashing in the incredible light of a cool dawn. Another lurching, a CRACK! a FLASH! and all was still and dark.

At first I thought I'd passed out again, but except for the queasiness in my stomach and the feeling that I was off balance, I seemed to be conscious. I'd heard voices in there somewhere, whispering and urgent, but everything was quiet now. I sat up and my head wobbled. I tried holding it still using both hands, with only marginal success. There were stars overhead. More stars than I had ever seen before in my life. I swallowed and brought my eyes down again, blinking. I wasn't sure whether looking up made my stomach feel better or worse. Still, the Gravol was clearly starting to work. I looked around, trying to move only my eyes, afraid to turn my head. It was another one of those stone rings that reminded me of Stonehenge, or maybe the same one I'd seen before. Great rectangular stones, as big as buildings, set on their ends, with their tops silhouetted against the stars.

Though the temperature was comfortable, the whole place had that kind of sharp beauty that somehow made it feel cold. At least, it would have been beautiful, if only it would hold still, and if I didn't feel as though I was going to be sick again.

"Is this the sickness you spoke of? You were not bitten?" Wolf was kneeling beside me. The moonlight was strong enough that I could make out the colors of his clothes. Black jeans, dark red shirt, silvery tweed jacket. "Are you certain you do not require a Healer?"

"A Healer's not going to help. At least—" I paused to inhale, trying to keep my breathing slow, full, and steady. No need to add hyperventilation to everything else. The grumble in my stomach subsided without turning into a muscle spasm. "At least I'm assuming that if the High Prince can't do anything for me, no one else can. Is there any water?" I normally had a bottle of water in my shoulder bag, but I'd taken it out to refill it, and left it chilling in the fridge. "I'll have to take more of those motion-sickness pills if I'm going to stave off the worst of it."

"We will have to leave the Ring for water, but we would need to do that in any case. You say the High Prince did not Heal you?"

I had to let him help me to my feet, even though it meant I would be touching him. There was just no way my balance would be good enough without his help. I was relieved to see that I wasn't being made worse by the contact, since I had to keep holding on to his arm as we made our way out of the Ring. Either the stones were much closer than they appeared, or whatever it was that bothered me here in the Lands also distorted my sense of spatial dimensions. It seemed that we only took a few steps and we were outside the Ring, standing in brilliant sunshine.

All the while I was getting a running commentary of things from Wolf, almost like the teleprompter that runs along the bottom of the screen on news channels. His feelings were running so hot that I almost couldn't make sense of anything [rage well pushed down but threatening to erupt; the pleasure the others had felt in killing his Pack mates/the vicious predators]. A Hound had come through the Portal with us and been killed by Wild Riders. [Who had it been? Which one?] It wasn't Fox, he was sure of that [but someone he could have saved, given the chance; guilt; relief]. The *dra'aj* it had eaten would be returned to the Lands.

Wolf led me to a nearby grouping of rocks and helped me lower myself onto one that was covered with moss. As soon as he let go of me, I could hear the burbling of water and realized the rocks were on the banks of a stream. Or maybe it was a brook, I know the terminology has something to do with size, but that's all I know. The air was warm, with a light breeze, and this had to be the most peaceful place I'd ever been in. I took a good grip with my left hand on the edge of the rock I was sitting on, and with my right hand on a rock about shoulder height next to me.

"Okay," I said, swallowing. Was I imagining it, or was I actually feeling better?

Wolf turned away and knelt next to the stream. His human clothes were changed now, and he was wearing what looked like silver suede trousers tucked into black boots that came halfway up his calves. What had been a red shirt had changed into a sleeveless tunic worn over a black shirt, long-sleeved, but with wide cuffs held in place by *gra'if* wristbands. The tunic was belted with a web of black leather, from which hung his sword, a long dagger, and a small pouch about twice the size of those folding coin purses everyone has now.

I couldn't be sure, but I thought that Wolf was speaking to the water. *A Natural*, I thought. There might be a Sprite or Nymph living in the stream. Wolf dipped both his hands in as if he was scooping up water for himself. I fumbled the pill bottle out of my bag one-handed. I still needed the other to hold on with. Did he have something to bring me water in? The thought of bending over the stream myself brought on an attack of vertigo so strong I had to shut my eyes and hold on to the rocks again.

"Valory?"

I forced my eyes to open and found Wolf standing over me. He appeared to be holding a shallow crystal cup between his two hands—crystal so perfect, and so clear, it was hard to see where glass ended and water began. I reached to take it from him, but he shook his head slightly and I realized he was right, I would probably drop it.

I put about eight more Gravol in my mouth and leaned forward so Wolf could bring the cup to my lips. He somehow managed to hold it so that I could drink from it without awkwardness, exactly as easily as if I were holding the cup myself. *Definitely not human*, I thought. As if I needed any more proof.

I lifted my head and he dropped his hands. I gasped and shot my own hands out, only to have nothing fall. The cup had disappeared.

"That's handy," I said, after I was sure the movement wasn't going to bring the water back up, pills and all. "Will it come back when you need it again?"

"Will what come back?"

"The cup."

"Oh, there was no cup," he smiled, and this time I saw the same unearthly beauty I'd seen in the faces of Alejandro, and Cassandra. I knew I should look away, but I couldn't. "That was just the form the water took for ease of carrying."

I swallowed again, my mouth dry, and told my eyes to blink. "You could charge a fortune for that trick in the Shadowlands." I never thought I'd be glad to be nauseated, but it was the only thing keeping me from just sitting there staring at him forever.

"The magic is not mine, but belongs to Mountain Stream." He gestured at the water.

Mountain Stream, huh? I would have rolled my eyes if I could. Some parents have *no* imagination.

"Is it appropriate for me to thank her?"

"It is a him in this case, but yes."

I don't know where I got the idea that all Water Sprites would be female. After all, I'd only met one, and that doesn't make for a statistical universe.

"Thank you for the drink," I said, feeling a little foolish now, since I seemed to be addressing nothing whatsoever. "It was much appreciated." I gasped and jerked backward when a slap of water formed and dissolved in front of me, but without splashing me at all.

"He acknowledges your thanks, and invites you to drink again should you require it." Wolf studied my face. "Are you well now? Your color seems to be improving."

I moved my head slowly from side to side. My stomach stayed still. Though I wouldn't know anything for sure until I stood up. "Where to now?"

"Across the Moor of Ravens, beyond the Sea of *Ma'arban*. That is where Ice Tor dwells." His ash-gray eyes narrowed. "Is that not what you said?"

"So that's the Quartz Ring?" I managed to point toward the standing stones I could still see nearby without lifting my hand.

His perfect sloe-black eyebrows drew together. I blinked and this time managed to look away.

"Were you not still conscious then when we came through the Portal? We brought a Hound and two Riders with us, and while the Portal Guards dealt with them, we came here, and Moon went to her sister to report our plans."

"Right." That explained all the noise and commotion I thought I remembered. "We should get moving, then." I hoped I sounded more resolute than I felt. "I won't get better, and there's only so much the drugs will do for me."

Wolf crouched down on his heels and took my hand. His fingers felt cool, and I wondered if that was his natural temperature or whether I was running a fever. "I will take you back if you wish it. You warned us, but I did not realize how ill you would become."

I had to wonder just how bad I looked. "This is the only solution we have," I reminded him. "The only one that helps the Hunt, *and* the Outsiders. The only clean ending for you and your brother."

Wolf searched my face with his eyes. I tried to smile, decided in the last minute to clench my jaw instead. No telling how ghastly the smile might have been. Finally, Wolf nodded and straightened to his feet, laying my hand back in my lap.

"Mountain Stream tells me that there is a hostel along his upper banks. We should go there first." He gestured at my linen dress. "We must find you some clothing better suited for a journey, and shoes."

I looked down at my creased clothing, which closely resembled sheets that had been slept on for a week. And as for my shoes, the less said about their usefulness on this rocky ground, the better. I kicked them off; I was better barefoot, if we didn't have far to go. I braced myself, taking a good grip on my rocks. Wolf put out his hands, but I shook my head—carefully, so as not to upset my balance.

"Better not," I said. "In fact, can you ask that tree over there if it would spare me a walking stick?"

I guess I shouldn't have been surprised when he did.

With the disappearance of three of their number through the Portal, the attackers began to draw off, and Alejandro breathed more easily. He and Nighthawk were still outnumbered, but the Portal was near, and *gra'if* was a terrible thing to face. He thought he knew which of these Riders had been the one talking to Wolf when he'd arrived, and when he saw that one taking advantage of the confusion to make his solitary way through the crowd of screaming humans, he gave chase.

He slowed, cursing, as he entered the food court. He saw nothing that could be his quarry, not even any sign of disruption or confusion among the people lining up for food and heading for exits. People who were now looking at him sideways, and giving him plenty of room. Alejandro grimaced and lowered his sword, sliding it back into the body of the cane he carried in his left hand. He smiled and nodded at the people nearest him, and was not at all surprised when many smiled and nodded in return. They likely thought he was part of a movie shoot and had become lost.

Alejandro took two deep, slow breaths. His heart was hammering in a way it had not done in many years—if ever. Perhaps it was just as well the other had escaped. He walked more slowly through the court, searching now not just for the Rider he'd been following, but for any sign of the type of disturbance he'd caused himself.

Had it, after all, been a Rider that he had seen? And had that Rider simply Moved when the opportunity presented itself?

He took a final look around before turning back. There was nothing to see here, and if the immediate threat was over, he had to go after Valory as quickly as he could.

Besides, he had left Hawk alone with the chaos in the departure lounge long enough. Almost before he had completed his turn, there was a SNAP! of displaced air and his arms were pinned at his sides, seized in firm, painful grips, as a Rider materialized on each side of him.

"No noise," the Sunward one on the right said. "Come quietly and you'll have nothing to fear. We only want to talk."

"Any nonsense, and we'll Fade you right here."

Alejandro did not even bother to turn his head to see the Ward of the other Rider. "On which end of the leash are you?" he asked, pulling his lips back off his teeth as far as they would go.

"Never you mind. You come with us, and no tricks."

There was no point in arguing further, nor any to resisting, the grip on his arms was so tight. Even Moving would have bought him very little else but time, since they would all three Move together. He might as well see who, or what, wished to speak with him. It was not as though there could be a Signed room waiting for him. If none of these even bore *gra'if*, they could not have such a thing.

He could always Move later, if it seemed they would like to kill him.

They took him into one of the stairwells in the Go Bus section of the station. This one looked to be under construction, with new boarding blocking it off from the main concourse.

"Your light doesn't shine very brightly, Old One." This from a Moonward Rider sitting on an upper step.

"I am no Solitary, that you should address me in this manner," Alejandro said.

"Ah, but you're old all right." The other's grin sent a tingle of frost up Alejandro's spine as the face seemed to lengthen and then shorten again. *Hound*, he thought. Not a Rider after all. Alejandro studied the thing's face. It had been a Moonward Rider once, but that was all that he could be sure of.

"You're one of the ones who live here, aren't you? You're the one with the girl. I can smell her on you. I don't see it. How she does fit into this chase? No one seems to be able to tell me what's so special about her?"

Alejandro's grin was his only answer. The Hound stood and came down two steps. "What if I bite you, Sunward Rider?"

The chill spread from Alejandro's back around to his chest, seeming to slow his heart. "Then I would die," he said.

"And your *dra'aj* would be mine, such as it is. It wouldn't return to the Lands."

"That has been true all this long while that I have lived in the Shadowlands," Alejandro said. The chill lessened as he spoke. What he said was true. He had not considered it in those terms before, but his ages-old decision not to return to the Lands, meant exactly that. His *dra'aj* would be forever lost.

So be it. If nothing else, this knowledge freed him of the paralyzing fear of the Hunt. He took a deep breath and managed to stand a little straighter in his captors' hands. *They*, at least, were Riders, he felt certain.

"Then I'm right, you follow no one, you aren't for the High Prince?"

Alejandro would have shrugged, but for the Riders holding him. "What of it?"

The other, the Hound, suddenly thrust his face forward. Only the rigorous training of the bullring, where millimeters might make the difference between life and death, prevented Alejandro from flinching. "Would you do me the great courtesy of standing farther away," he said. "Your breath smells of rotting meat."

The grin on the Hound's face did not fade, but he did move away.

"You're the closest thing to a neutral party I'm likely to find, aren't you? I'm Foxblood," he said. "I'm Pack Leader. I won't kill you, not this time, if you'll agree to take a message for me."

"What message?"

"Tell the High Prince the Hunt has found a refuge in this world. If she leaves it to us, we'll stop preying on People."

Alejandro glanced to his right, and to his left. "And does this Hound speak for you? Do you, also, ascribe to this bargain?"

"It suits us well enough."

"What of those of us who make our home here?"

Foxblood shrugged. "What do I care? If you stay out of our way, we'll stay out of yours." He glanced at the two Riders holding Alejandro's arms and smiled. "Of course, we'd rather you didn't even have the chance to interfere with us, so perhaps you'll want to go home."

I am home, Alejandro thought. "I am neutral, as you say. How am I to deliver this message?"

Alejandro's breath caught as the Hound took him by the throat. A grip that would have killed a human was only painful to him.

"Don't play games with me, Old One. You talk to her followers, you've fought next to them, neutral or not. Either *she'll* listen to you, or *they* will. It doesn't matter to me which." The Hound released him, and Alejandro sucked in a lungful of air. "I'll let you live when you bring back the answer. What happens after that depends on what the answer is, but no guarantees." He looked once more at Alejandro's captors and jerked his head. There was displaced air, and he was alone.

When Alejandro returned to it, the departure area was still in chaos, station and first aid personnel helping the injured, weeping, and hysterical passengers. Alejandro had not noticed him during the fight, but he now saw Nik Polihronidis on his knees in front of a white-haired woman still clutching at her rolling suitcase, holding her free wrist between his fingers as if taking her pulse. Peering through the crowd, he recognized other Outsiders, from the morning they'd trapped the Hound, circulating through the people.

Alejandro began making his way toward Nik when he saw a man signaling him from the edge of the crowd. He was only able to recognize Nighthawk from his coloring and the way that he carried himself, as he now looked entirely differently from a few moments before, a protective maneuver in which they were both well versed. Now the other Rider appeared to be merely another among the crowd who stood idly watching. He even had the same look of curiosity decently covered with concern that showed on the faces of the humans, though Alejandro felt certain Hawk's concern was more than skin-deep. The old Warden had lived long enough among humans to care about them almost as much as Alejandro himself.

Hawk's ruddy face broadened in satisfaction when their eyes met, and he edged around the watchers to Alejandro's side. At that moment Nik straightened from his examination of the elderly woman, and after a quick look around him, circled toward them.

"I thought you might be Faded," Nighthawk said, as he clapped him on the shoulder.

"What the hell was all this about?" Nik's voice was quiet, but his words, and the hard planes of his face, left Alejandro in no doubt of his feelings.

"They have gone through the Portal." Hawk glanced at Alejandro. "I can only assume deliberately, since they were heading here when they were set upon."

"What of your people?" Alejandro turned to Nik. "Did the Hunt create any new ones?"

Nik shook his head in short jerks, though he seemed to be calmer. "No, we were lucky. The Hounds were busy with you guys. We didn't really close in until you ran them off." He blinked and focused on them, as if really seeing them. "We wouldn't need many more to help us, if they were all like you two."

"A fine vote of confidence, for which I thank you, but I somehow gathered the impression that they were not, precisely, trying to kill us." Alejandro exchanged a look with Hawk.

"What now?" Nik was distracted by a signal from one of his people, a tall woman in blue jeans, sandals, and a man's white dress shirt.

"I must go after Valory," Alejandro said. "I must know she is well before I attend to any other matter."

For a moment it seemed that Nik might argue with him, but his face softened, and he nodded. "Sure, but we'll meet up later, okay? Call or text me as soon as you get back."

Alejandro drew Hawk away from the center of the concourse into one of the side lounges where they could wait until the main concourse cleared. "I was lured away on purpose," he told the other Rider as soon as they were alone. "But not to kill me. The Leader of the Hunt spoke with me, saying that he spoke for the Basilisk Warriors as well."

"What did he want with you?" Hawk's brow furrowed.

"With me, nothing. But as a long-term resident here, he sees me as neutral, and he had a proposal, one which he wishes taken to the High Prince."

Hawk drew himself up, his eyebrows as high as they could go. "The *Hunt* has a proposal? *The Hunt* wishes to negotiate?" He shook his head. "It is unheard of."

"Stable Hounds are unheard of. Hounds who can Move are unheard of. Whether it is the human *dra'aj* or no, this is no longer the Hunt of our Singers' histories. Perhaps it is time for us to redefine what we know of them."

"And what, then, is their proposal?" Hawk leaned forward with his forearms on his knees.

"They want the Shadowlands. They say they will stop preying upon the People, if they are given this world as their own."

Hawk was shaking his head. "That did not look like negotiating they were doing with Wolf. And what of that? That was Walks Under the Moon I saw with him."

Alejandro spread his hands. "Perhaps she, also, came to persuade him to return? In any case, the crowd is dispersing." He got to his feet. "The Portal is clear."

Hawk looked at him with narrowed eyes full of questions. "You will carry the Hunt's proposal then?"

Alejandro took a deep breath in through his nose. "You may do so, if you wish. I made no promises, whatever the Hound may think. I follow my *fara'ip*."

"Well, at the least you are not Hounds, nor do you bring any."

Alejandro had automatically raised his hands to shoulder height at the sight of the armed guards who greeted them on their emergence from the Portal, but lowered them again when he saw that Hawk had not raised his. Evidently, his long stay among humans had had more impact on him than he had realized.

There were five guards in the circle surrounding them, all with weapons at the ready. Two of them were Wild Riders, their *gra'if* showing as a glove here, a torque there, bright against the worn leather of their clothing. The Starward Rider who had spoken was smiling, but as Alejandro had long before noticed, weapons cannot smile.

Hawk spoke. "Star at Midnight, you know me. You have been my escort before. I am Nighthawk, my mother is Flyer in the Dusk, and the Dragon guides me. This is my friend and companion, Graycloud at Moonrise."

It took a moment for them all to exchange formal greetings—afterward it was only Star at Midnight's mother, Northern Light, and his Guidebeast, the Basilisk, that Alejandro remembered.

"Do you say a Hound came through here—" Alejandro asked as soon as he decently could.

"Do not be concerned," Star at Midnight, his *gra'if* sword now sheathed, had pushed his helm back from his forehead. "We dispatched the Hound, and the two Riders who brought it—spawn of the Basilisk Prince, as was evident from the company they kept." Star made a flicking motion with his fingers that Alejandro suddenly remembered was the Rider equivalent of spitting in disgust. "As surprised as we were, there are still three of us here with *gra'if*, and as soon as their prey cleared out of the way, we dealt with them."

"This 'prey?' Two other Riders? Walks Under the Moon, and Stormwolf? And a human girl with Sunward coloring? They are safe?" Alejandro looked around him, but the mountain meadow in which the Portal was set on this side was empty except for the three of them, the guards, and their Cloud Horses.

"I thought that was Lady Moon," Star said. "As soon as they were clear of their pursuers, they Moved again."

"A good thing, too," said one of the other Riders, this one a Moonward in flame-colored clothing. "Left us a clear field to kill the Hound."

"So the Basilisk's spawn is allying with the Hunt in the Shadowlands? It explains why so many are trying to use the Portals," Star at Midnight said, flaxen braid swinging with the movement of his head.

"We have news of this and other matters to take to the High Prince," Hawk said.

"I would find the human girl. Valory Martin is her name, and she is friend to the High Prince. Do you know where she was taken?"

"Were you not listening, my friend? They were here and gone before we could even be sure who they were. Perhaps they will return, when they realize the danger is past."

"Perhaps." But would they? Could he risk waiting? Would Valory be worse on her second exposure to the Lands?

"Alejandro." Hawk had taken him by the arm. "They are likely gone to the High Prince. Moon to her sister, Stormwolf to his benefactor. Valory will be with them, and as safe as she can be here in the Lands."

Alejandro nodded. He knew Hawk must be right. And yet the knowledge sat like a stone in his belly.

Cassandra raised her hand and knew that the Riders with her stopped when she did, even though she was not looking at them, her eyes being attuned completely to the tapestry that was the *dra'aj* of the Lands. A new thread had appeared. *Two.* One she knew immediately for her sister, Walks Under the Moon, and the other she knew perfectly, from having Healed it. Stormwolf. And between them a thread so faint, so fine, that even Cassandra could not be certain it existed.

But Moon and Wolf were definitely in the Lands.

Chapter Seventeen

FOX STRODE ALONG the crowded sidewalk, heading north on Yonge Street, and feeling a small pleasure from the way the prey moved out of his way without even noticing they were doing it. They were passing through the milling crowd of shoppers and commuters at Dundas Square when he reached out and grabbed a dark-skinned man by the upper arm. At first the man hunched his shoulders and began to turn toward him, but the aggressive look faded from his face even before he stopped turning and looked down, puzzled.

"Was that necessary?"

Inwardly cursing, Fox flexed his hands, and smiled at the Rider walking next to him. Control. That was what he demanded from the Pack, and what he should practice himself. Not that he would let Sunset on Water know.

"Maybe not, but I thought you'd like it better if I fed from a human than from one of my other options." He showed the Rider his teeth, but this one was made of hard stuff, and looked away only after smiling. He didn't move farther away, either, though he clearly understood what Fox had implied.

Fox didn't want Sunset to know, but the availability of the *dra'aj*, the ease of access, was sometimes more than even he could resist. Like now, for example.

"I'm Pack Leader. I need more than the others." He smiled again. "And I deserve more."

"If Stormwolf's offer changes the stakes between us, you should say so now."

Fox's hands formed fists. How dare he? How *dare* he? A woman shied away, her eyes rolling sideways at him as she crossed the pavement. Like she could feel the heat of his anger. Though he wasn't sure who, exactly, he was angry with.

"Stormwolf's got nothing to offer." It was so typical of Wolf to suggest that there was something wrong with him, something that needed to be cured. Couldn't bear to see Fox in charge. Friggin' know-it-all. Well, not anymore. "The Hunt's the Hunt," he said aloud. "Always was, always will be. It's natural for some to be Hounds and some to be prey. There's no cure for what's natural." Sure there were some among the Hunt who suffered, some who were driven to the point of madness by their condition—but those were the weaklings, the dregs of the Pack. Wolf himself had always been a bit sentimental, but Fox figured his brother's attitude was just a kind of nostalgia for their old lives. All pups looked back fondly on the days when all they did was play. He did himself.

But accepting a "Healing," allowing himself to be ordered around by prey—even when the Basilisk Prince had used the Horn to compel them, it had been *compulsion*. They'd been left unaltered, their Pack intact. Now his brother had become the willing servant of some soft, *dra'aj*-filled Rider.

Fox drew his lips back, unsure whether it was a smile or a snarl. These weren't thoughts he would ever have entertained when Wolf was Pack Leader. Sentimental or not, Wolf hadn't tolerated rebellion. But he wasn't Leader now, was he? With the Basilisk Prince gone, and Wolf stranded in the Lands, Fox had stepped into his brother's position, maintained the integrity of the Pack. A position that he filled much better than his brother ever had, in his humble opinion. It wasn't Wolf who'd discovered the potential in the human *dra'aj*, nor Wolf who'd conceived of the plan to make the Shadowlands their own, to reject the world of the People once and for all. These were Fox's triumphs, and he had no intention of letting them go.

"Not everyone in my Pack has my strength of purpose," he said now to the Rider walking at his elbow. "I wouldn't advise you to go strolling alone with anyone else, and you should tell your own Pack the same."

"There is something I wished to mention, since we are talking of our agreements. That which took place prior to my arrival, that is behind us. But there will be no new turnings. No new Hounds. At least, not from among my people."

Fox stopped, ignoring the humans who parted to walk around them. They were past Dundas, now, and the sidewalks had narrowed again. Some passersby looked like they were going to complain, but something stopped them, and they went on past without speaking.

"We'll assist you. Ally with you against the new Prince. But nothing more. That is my condition."

"Hey, you know perfectly well we didn't start anything." Fox would have given anything to refuse—this Rider was *prey*. But right now he needed allies. "The Basilisk persuaded quite a few of you to follow down the path he was taking himself. What should I do with the ones who are too far along to turn back?"

Sunset shrugged. "Destroy them. I do not need them, and neither do you." The Rider had a toothy smile of his own. "They are just more mouths to feed."

"Okay." It was easy enough to agree. For now. Fox couldn't deny that just now he needed the other's support against the High Prince. But once the Portals were closed, all bets were off. These Riders had no *gra'if*—the Basilisk Prince, not far off becoming a full-fledged Hound himself, had forbidden any of his followers to use it—so those left behind, like Sunset on Water, had no natural defense against the Hunt. It'd be easy enough to deal with them later, if he had to. No way Fox was going to be a subordinate in this new world.

And no way he was going to leave his own brother in the hands of prey—maybe even to be eaten himself, one day. Hounds did occasionally prey on Hounds, usually when fighting over the leadership of the Pack, when the loser literally fell prey to the winner.

But once or twice an injured Pack Leader had just stepped down voluntarily, and stayed a useful member of the Pack, if he behaved himself. Fox grinned. So Wolf could be like that. And the Pack could keep his skills, his knowledge—even his sentiments, so long as Wolf kept them under control. He could be useful. Even if he had to be forced. It could be done.

Fox would take care of it.

A cure. He snorted. Like he needed it.

There were no Cloud Horses under the trees this time, and hardly any armed Riders in the camp, not even the guards around the perimeter.

"I thought they were practically under siege? Anyone could walk in here." Alejandro looked around the almost deserted camp with a frown. Even dealing with Riders—perhaps especially when dealing with Riders, who could Move—guards were of the utmost importance.

"I would not be so sure." Hawk gestured with his right hand, as though he were greeting someone, and the trees nearest them bent their branches in response.

"*Trees.*" Alejandro breathed out the word so softly even he could not be sure he had spoken aloud. He walked toward them with his hands outstretched, not flinching when branches reached out for him, wrapping his wrists, caressing his arms, his face. Trees. Living Trees. It had been so long, he had almost forgotten.

"*Welcome,*" he heard in his head.

"I greet you, Older Sibling. I am Graycloud at Moonrise, my mother was Starwalker, and the Hippogriff guides me."

"We knew your mother. We remember you." The vines and branches clinging to his arms became a woman's hands, a short woman with mottled brown skin, dark green eyes, and hair like cooked leaves. "You will return again, Graycloud. Until then." And the Tree Natural loosened her grip and faded back into the foliage that was herself.

Alejandro took a step back toward his companion, his eyes still on the Trees.

"That was certainly unexpected." Hawk appeared at his side. "What did she say to you?"

"That she knew my mother, that she remembered me."

"And do you remember her?"

Alejandro found himself nodding. "She is *Glinde'in*. She grew to the west of my childhood home." He looked around him. Had the Natural walked here, in the manner of her kind, or was this actually the site of his home? Alejandro saw nothing familiar about the spot in which they stood. "I had forgotten *about* her, but I had not forgotten *her*."

"Well." Hawk's voice was solemn, and he still looked out into the forest. "Now you see why no perimeter guard is really necessary. The Wood Naturals have no love for the followers of the Basilisk Prince, and have an uncanny knack for knowing them, however cleverly disguised." Hawk clapped him on the shoulder. "But come." Alejandro followed, his eyes still turning from time to time toward *Glinde'in*.

They were almost at the Prince's pavilion before they were hailed, and then it was by the Guardian Prince himself, coming forward to shake hands with them both as if they were meeting on the streets of Madrid, and not a few paces away from a Wood.

"Is the High Prince within?" Hawk said, once introductions were complete.

"I'm afraid not," Max said. He tapped the torque at his neck. "But I can get her at a moment's notice, if it's urgent. Why don't you tell me what this is about?"

"Perhaps you should fetch her," Hawk said.

Max raised his eyebrows.

"Nighthawk, you speak to the Keeper of the Talismans, the Prince Guardian," Alejandro said, quietly.

"Relax, Alejandro." The Prince Guardian did not look offended. If anything, he seemed about to laugh. "Hawk isn't being disrespectful, he's just used to me being Exiled—you know, hanging around useless, while someone else did all the work."

"My Prince, it was not my intention—"

But Max was waving away Hawk's apologies. "Never mind, Hawk. For all that Alejandro is being so correct, I can see that he's wondering how long this dance is going to take."

"Forgive me, my Prince." Alejandro inclined his head. "It is just that while we stand about, my *fara'ip* is ill, and possibly in danger."

"Valory? Isn't she with Wolf? MOON!" Max turned into the

opening of the pavilion and called again. "Moon!" A rustle of silks and the young Starward Rider Alejandro had seen with Valory and Wolf at Union Station emerged from the pavilion entrance. There was a more than superficial resemblance to the High Prince, Alejandro saw. Enough that they must have had the same mother, something rare, but not unheard of, among Riders. The Starward one's glance flicked from one face to another, her pale brows drawn together in concern as she looked between Alejandro and Hawk.

"Moon!" Max drew her attention, a note of impatience in his voice that was echoed in Alejandro's heart. "What's this Alejandro tells me? Is Valory ill?"

"She said she would be 'okay.' She purchased 'Grav-all' to take with her." She looked once more at Alejandro. "She said it was medicine for a sickness brought on by the Lands."

"That isn't exactly—"

"Why did she do this?" Alejandro felt his impatience rising. "Why did you not return her at once to her home? To me?"

"What else could we do?" Moon's tone was cool, and Alejandro gritted his teeth. She did not answer to him; that was undeniable. "Wolf has the knowledge we need to find the Horn, but buried deeply inside him. Valory is the key to that knowledge, and only she can reach behind the walls of his life as a Hound." Moon put out her hand, and Alejandro found himself taking it. "She wanted to do this," the young Rider said. "It is her own choice. She said that you would understand."

Now Alejandro did smile. A small thing, a twist of the lips merely that was almost painful to him, but a smile nevertheless. Valory was correct; he did understand. For the first time, she was acting on her own, using her talent as she wished to, even putting herself at great risk, and all from her own choice. From the first time he had seen her, she had wanted freedom. This was what freedom meant.

"I would be with her," was what he said now. "To help her if I can. To help them both. She is my *fara'ip*. Send me after her."

Moon glanced at Max, and Alejandro's heart sank. What was coming would not please him; that much was obvious.

"But Graycloud—Alejandro." Moon stumbled a little over the human name. "We do not know where they have gone. We have no way to send you after them."

Alejandro took a step back, away from the others, and tried to breathe. Why did his lungs feel so tight? He heard the Guardian Prince speaking, but could muster up no interest in his words.

"What did you need Cassandra for?"

From the distance of his own isolated heart, Alejandro heard Hawk explain the proposals of the Hunt, the closing of the Portals, the abandonment of the humans. He knew he should pay more attention, be ready to offer his own arguments—against, never for—but his thoughts still whirled.

He had only known Valory for a pair of years, less than a blink in the lifetime of a Rider, even one separated from the Lands as long as he had been. But he had made her his *fara'ip*. As close or closer than his own blood—none of whom still lived. At the time they met, he had come close to the human emotion of despair, had begun to wonder why he should further prolong his existence. Then he had found her with the Collector, and she had asked his help and given him a reason to go on.

He blinked and drew in a breath. Valory was still alive, and so was he. She would return from her quest—or she would not. In the meantime, it was for him to do whatever he could to further that quest, in trust that she would return. With an effort he returned his full attention to the Guardian Prince.

"What we need more than anything else at the moment is time," Max was saying. "We've got to give Wolf and Valory as much time as we can."

"How?" Hawk's tone was more respectful now, Alejandro noted. Perhaps he had only needed to be reminded once that this was no longer the Exile, his memories gone, but the Keeper of the Talismans.

"Well, to start with, we don't involve Cassandra until we absolutely have to. We tell the Hunt that as High Prince she can't leave the Lands—"

"Is that true?" Moon looked puzzled.

Max shrugged. "Well, the Hunt doesn't know any differently, that's for certain. If she's not available to negotiate, you'll have to do it, and say you have to report back to her. Ask them for precise terms, even let them think you're leaning favorably toward the idea."

Alejandro grimaced. "I am sworn to help the human Outsiders against the Hunt."

"And you *are* helping them. We need information, to prepare. Do what you can to assess their numbers, discover their hideouts. Determine, if you can, how many of the Basilisk Warriors have joined them. See if you can sow discord between the two groups."

Now Alejandro smiled. "That should not be difficult."

Nik let the phone fall into its cradle with a clatter, pushed his chair back far enough that he was clear of his computer keyboard, and rubbed at his eyes. He picked up his coffee cup, took a mouthful, grimaced, and swallowed it anyway. When he poured himself a cup of coffee, he thought, he really should try to remember to drink it before it went stone cold.

After what had happened to Wai-kwong, he'd had Elaine organize a telephone tree, so that all of his people could stay in regular touch with each other, and report to him as well. Her organizational skills were second nature to her; he'd had to learn his the hard way, and even now he'd screw up if he didn't have his lists to refer to. Some had grumbled a bit at first, but the fight at the train station had shown them just how useful a tool it could be. There was no way they could have gotten everyone there to help so quickly, if they hadn't already been in touch. So everyone checked in, and everyone was accounted for.

Everyone except the Riders. Problem was, he had no idea how things worked on the other side of the Portal, and the longer he went without hearing anything, the more nervous he got. Nik picked up his cell phone and used it to call Valory's number again. He'd reached voice mail before, but this time he got no response at all. Nothing. He tried Alejandro's with the same result. Whistling tunelessly through his teeth, Nik crossed the hall into Elaine's office.

His partner looked up from her desk and smiled in her old way. The lost Elaine of a few days before was gone. She'd had to have her *dra'aj* level refreshed again in the interim, but as she became accustomed to her new condition, she'd stabilize and need to be refreshed less often.

"D'you sign the stuff Marg put on your desk?" Elaine finished putting her signature to a letter and moved it from the smaller pile on her left to the larger pile on her right. She was trying to keep up the business of the firm, in between correlating reports. She looked up again.

"Yeah, first thing." Nik threw himself into her client chair and slung one leg over the arm.

Elaine put down her pen. "I know we have all this other stuff going on, Nik, but I have to act as though we'll get through it. As though we're going to have a business to come back to once it's all over. We have responsibilities to our clients."

Nik shut his eyes, nodding. He knew Elaine was right. This is what Outsiders had been doing ever since they organized, trying to live as normally as possible.

"I can't reach the Riders," he said, opening his eyes. "Valory, either. It's like their phones don't exist."

Elaine leaned forward, her smile disappearing. "You don't think they've deserted us?"

"I know a few who would say so." He shrugged. "Maybe I *am* a fool for trusting them."

"I don't know what else we can do, just now," she said.

Nik found himself heartened by Elaine's "we" and "us." She'd always been very quick to assimilate new facts, face new challenges, but what had happened to her was something that had radically changed her life, and changed it forever.

"Did you get into some kind of trouble for helping me?"

Nik gave her his best grin. "We're not running out of *dra'aj* yet," he said. "Don't worry about it, there are still plenty of donors, fortunately—or unfortunately I suppose I could also say, considering that these are people who are dying." His grin faded away a little faster than he'd intended. "But if it turns out the Riders aren't going to help us—" he shook his head. "Rationing might work for a while, but the stability of our community exists because of low population, and careful control of that population."

"So you did get into trouble."

"Like I said, nothing for you to worry about. This is my district, I can make it work out." *So long as I don't help any more new ones, and what happened to Wai-kwong doesn't happen to anyone else.* He put both feet on the floor.

This time Elaine grinned. "Your district? You sound like a sheriff."

Nik shrugged, spreading his hands. "More like a senior adviser. Access to *dra'aj* is regularized, controlled, so everyone gets their share. If there are too many Outsiders in one community, for example, they get help to relocate."

"And with all the new ones? With me? There are too many of us now, aren't there?" His look must have answered her, because she went on before he could speak. "But we have to do *something* to help them." Elaine's tone was bleak, her voice strained.

The phone rang and she turned away, indicating with the lift of one finger that he should stay put. She said "okay" twice, "good" once, and made an entry on a spreadsheet she had open on one of her monitors.

"Elaine." He waited until she was focused on him, looking him straight in the eye. "The restoration of a person's *dra'aj* depends on someone else's death. Do you see what I'm saying? That's a setup for the very worst of worst case scenarios. I've seen it. Our whole system's designed to prevent that from happening again. There's nothing worse."

Elaine made a face. "Not even letting the new ones go on killing themselves, or just dropping dead through lack of interest?"

"Better we should kill people to preserve ourselves? Because whether you intend to or not, that's what you're suggesting. Outsiders in places that aren't being overrun by Hounds are looking at Toronto, and Madrid, and Beijing and Sydney and saying it's our problem, and we can't expect them to help us solve it." He leaned forward again. "That's why it's so important that the Riders stick to their agreement."

"You don't find it a bit ironic that we expect Riders to care what happens to a bunch of humans, when the humans themselves don't care? And I can't believe I just said that." Elaine rolled her eyes. "I'm still trying to come to grips with the fact that we're dealing with nonhumans."

"The Hunt has to be stopped, Elaine. It has to be."

Elaine closed her eyes for a second, and actually seemed to be laughing to herself. "So we're basically looking for Buffy the Vampire Slayer?"

Nik grinned. "I guess so, yeah."

"Nikki, what are you going to do?"

Nik rubbed at his eyes. "What *can* I do? All the Riders I know are incommunicado. Even Valory's gone."

Elaine was quiet for a long time. "You've been thinking about her a lot, haven't you?" she said finally

"I don't know what you're talking about." Nik focused on the pile of folders in Elaine's out basket.

"Come on, Nik, it's me, Elaine." She leaned forward, tapping herself on the chest. For a moment her wide smile and her sparkling eyes denied they had any real problems to deal with. "How long have I known you? You've had 'that look' on your face since you met her. And let's face it, she's solvent, she's got a job, and she's already helped us. That puts her three-for-three on the last girl you liked. If you still had a mother, she'd be thrilled."

Nik covered his eyes with one hand. "Oh, god, I'd already had that thought. Am I that simple?"

"Hell, no. You're a complex guy. It's just that I know you so well. Go. Get out of here. Valory or no Valory, you have work to do."

Nik went back to his own office, but he didn't do any work. He pulled open the same file three times, and three times closed it again when he realized he hadn't registered anything he'd read. His coffee was still cold, and even vigorous face rubbing didn't wake him up. There was no point in going back to the Royal York. That Rider was with Valory—wherever *she* was. He'd just have to trust that Alejandro would call him when they got back. There was nothing else he could do.

Well, actually, there *was* something else. He hesitated, his finger hovering over the button that would connect him with Elaine. No, he could already see the smile she'd give him, if he told her where he was planning to go.

Valory's place on Rhyl Avenue wasn't all that far from where Nik was living off the Danforth. At this time of day taxis weren't the best option, so he took the subway to Woodbine, and then hopped on the Woodbine 92 bus. He checked the GPS on his cell, got off the bus at Kingston Road, walked east to Elmer, and then down Elmer to Rhyl. Number 22 was just in from the corner, a semi-detached not unlike his own, but on this one someone had enclosed the front veranda.

Nik went up the walk slowly; he wished he could stop imagining the smile on Elaine's face.

Valory's right-hand neighbor was pruning bushes in her front yard and nodded at him as he went up to the door of the enclosed porch.

"You may want to go around the back," she said, pushing her light brown hair back from her eyes. "They might not hear the bell if they're outside."

Nik smiled his thanks and headed down the narrow passage between the two houses. The gate was latched, but not locked, and he let himself into the backyard. There was another gate that let out onto a laneway, where there were small garages and parking places for cars. Many of the older neighborhoods in Toronto, including Nik's own, had been set up this way, long before the price of the land made it uneconomical. When Nik had first come to Canada, just after WWII, all these old neighborhoods had been crowded with immigrants, making it easy for him to fit in. Now they were among the most expensive places to live in the city, and a lot of the old garages had been turned into fancy "carriage house" flats.

The back door was closed, but Nik opened the screen door and tapped anyway. It was unreasonable to be as disappointed as he was when no one answered. He sat down at the patio table, and tried to rub away the tightness he felt between his eyes.

"Nik? Nikos?"

Nik lifted his head from his arms and groggily focused on the man peering into his face. Sandy-red hair, dark brown eyes. Plenty of *dra'aj*. He pushed himself upright.

"When did you get here? What time is it?"

"Time for you to come in and have some coffee, I think."

Nik passed through as Alejandro held the door for him. At the Rider's gesture, Nik followed him into a square kitchen, where a pass-through revealed the other ruddy-colored Rider standing next to a dining table made from some dark wood.

"Nik, you'll remember my friend from the train station?" Alejandro had gone to the stove, where an espresso pot was beginning to make noise.

The other Rider stepped forward, his hand outstretched. "Nighthawk, my mother is Flyer in the Dusk, and the Dragon guides me." His voice, deeper and more resonant than Alejandro's, sent a shiver up Nik's spine, but that wasn't anything his own grandmother hadn't been able to do with the right tone, and Nik straightened to look the Rider in the eye.

"What about your father?" Nik couldn't believe he'd just asked that. He must be still half asleep.

Nighthawk tilted his head and looked at him closely, as if he were looking at him for the first time, but with a lift to the corner of his mouth that Nik was sure was a smile.

"What an interesting question," he finally said, and from his tone he meant it sincerely. "It is not our custom to give our fathers' names, I have never realized that before. My father was Rides the Wind."

"I'm Nik Polihronidis," Nik said. "My father was Andreas Polihronidis, and my mother was Christina Angelis. We don't have Guidebeasts, but I'd guess you know that already." He pulled out a chair, stifling a yawn as he sat down.

Nighthawk was grinning at him. "So, you are yourself an Outsider?" The Rider took the chair across from Nik. His voice showed real concern, and Nik warmed to the man.

"That's right." Nik nodded when Alejandro handed him a cup of coffee and reached for the sugar bowl. "I was trying to get hold of you." He looked around. "Did you bring Valory back?" The two Riders glanced at each other, and Nik began to get a bad feeling. "What?"

"Valory is still in the Lands," Alejandro said. "She looks for the Horn of the Hunt."

Okay, not what he was expecting, but at least she was all right. "This is the thing you mentioned before? The thing you can use to make them obey?" Hawk smiled, and Nik found himself smiling back. They were certainly very beautiful, these Riders. Very beautiful, indeed. "So what are we supposed to do in the meantime?" Neither of them bristled, so Nik must have succeeded in keeping his tone respectful. These people meant to help him, but he wouldn't be surprised to learn that they also had their own agenda.

"We are to gather information, under the guise of negotiation," Alejandro said from where he stood in the doorway.

"Uh-huh." Nik put down his sugar spoon and took a sip of his espresso. "What are we supposed to be negotiating?"

"The surrender of the Shadowlands to the Hunt."

"Holy Mother of God." Nik found he was on his feet. By some miracle his coffee was still in its cup. "And *that's* what you want my help with?"

Alejandro was patting the air in front of him with his hands, but it was Hawk who spoke.

"Did you not hear him? He said '*under the guise*.' It is not our intention to do any such thing." The Rider leaned forward, his elbows on the table. "If the Horn is found, we can call all of the Hunt to a single place. But if it is not?" Nik leaned forward, willing himself to concentrate. "Then we must locate as many as possible not only of the Hunt, but of the Riders allied with them." Hawk paused, frowning, a small line between his auburn brows. "We cannot know which way our plans may go. Whatever happens, we must know their strengths, where they are, where they hide."

"And it's my thought," Alejandro cut in, "that you Outsiders can help us with this. For one, you are able to distinguish between stable Hounds and Riders, something we cannot always do."

Nodding, Nik sank back into his seat. "Yeah. I see how this could play out. The more we know about them—well, it's not wasted, even once the Horn's found." Elaine would probably want to start a new spreadsheet. He looked up at the faces above him. "I'm in."

"You can speak for your people?"

Nik thought about what he'd said to Elaine. What had she called him? The sheriff? "Yes, I can." Nik stood, pulled his cell phone out of his pocket.

"Nik?"

The voice came again. Not the first time. He blinked. He was standing up. He was holding a cell phone. Had he been planning to make a call?

"What has happened to him?"

He looked up. Riders. Alejandro. Hawk. He'd come here to get their help. He needed their help.

"Help me," he said aloud.

"What can we do?" Hawk led him to a seat. Took hold of his hands.

"I feel so stupid."

"You must tell us what the problem is." Alejandro sounded far away.

"Here." Another voice. A sharp sting on his cheek. "Look at me."

Nik focused. Why was this so difficult? "A red-tailed Hawk," he said. He felt his mouth smiling.

"Let me show you what I really look like." Suddenly there was a younger-looking man, still square-built, but bigger, taller. Crouching on his heels. Holding on to Nik's hands. His coloring shifted until his hair was the dark red of a full-bodied wine, his skin flushed bronze, and his eyes sienna. Hawk smiled, and Nik felt his heart beat faster.

"Oh," he said. "I've emptied. Damn. I didn't think I was this close." He took a deep breath, though he knew that wouldn't help him to pull himself together. *This has happened before*, he reminded himself. Nothing he couldn't handle. He looked down at his phone. Licked his lips. Felt the phone being taken from his hand.

A voice murmuring in the background. Hawk's eyes, his hands gripping. Nik sighed. *Do I know who this is?*

"Belmont House," the background voice said.

"What's the intersection?" Hawk asked. Hawk. That was his name. "I can Move us there."

"Do you know the place?" Alejandro's voice.

"I've known Toronto since it was a trading post. What's the intersection?"

"Yonge and Aylmer." It took Nik a minute to realize that he'd answered the question himself.

"Stand up. Come now. Put your hand on my shoulder." Hawk again.

He didn't really see the point, but Nik placed his hand on the Rider's left shoulder. There was a POP! in his ears, and they were standing on the southwest corner of Yonge and Aylmer. Tucking Nik's arm under his own, Hawk—who now looked once again like his human self—walked him into the building.

"Nik Polihronidis," he said to the man behind the counter.

"I'll look after this, Carl, thanks."

Nik wouldn't have turned around if he'd been alone, but Hawk did, so Nik did, too. Poco was just coming through the revolving door. He'd been the one who'd spoken. He looked at Hawk and his eyes narrowed. They stayed that way when they shifted to Nik.

"Nik, you okay?"

How did Poco get here? Suddenly Nik knew where he was, and why. *I'm empty.* He swallowed. "I can't do this," he said. He took a deep breath and straightened, no longer leaning on Hawk. The Rider didn't quite let him go.

"Dude." Shaking his head, Poco put his hand on Nik's arm. "Nik, how could you let it get so far?"

"What has happened?" Nik felt Hawk's grip tighten.

"He gave up his turn," Poco said. "To help his friend Elaine. And he hasn't taken any *dra'aj* since."

"I can't." Nik took another deep breath. He couldn't seem to get enough air. "I can't take someone else's place."

"It's okay, there isn't anyone else close enough to be in danger."

Nik shook his head. "That isn't the point."

"It is, man it *is*. Yves organized it. Him and the next two in line, they shared the last donor. So this one's not spoken for, this one's yours."

"Nikos Polihronidis, son of Andreas and Christina, is this how you accept aid? You wish for us to help you, but you will not help yourself?" Hawk's voice was rich, warm. Nik tried to concentrate on it.

"I knew what I was doing." They'd get it, or they wouldn't. "I knew what I was doing when I gave mine to Elaine. I'll be okay in a little while. I've lived through this before."

"But we need you now, not in a little while."

"What difference does it make?" Nik couldn't be sure that he'd spoken aloud. If they'd only leave him be for a minute, he'd be okay. Why couldn't they leave him?

"Nik, look at me." His head was heavy, but there was something in the jewel-like tone of Hawk's voice that made him look up. He saw Nighthawk again. Everything had been dim, colorless, leached of meaning, but that strange, unearthly beauty made everything live again.

"Holy crap."

Nik smiled. That was Poco's voice.

"Come on, man. Come with me. Carl, I'm taking Nik in to see Mrs. Lopez. You stay here."

Nik felt himself being tugged to his left.

"Go, you must go now."

He looked back as Poco led him away. He was seeing Nighthawk's *dra'aj*. So much of it, so beautiful. For a moment, as they turned the corner into the hallway, he thought it wasn't the Rider he saw in the lobby, but a silvery dragon, glowing brighter than the sunlight coming in the windows.

Nik concentrated on breathing, in and out, in and out, as he let Poco lead him down the corridor to Mrs. Lopez's room. When they entered, he could see her *dra'aj* floating in the air around her like particles of colored light almost too small for the eye to register. Not as bright as the dragon he'd just seen, but "Lots more colors," he said.

Poco led him up to the dying woman, and Nik took her hand in his. "Hello, Sylvia," he said.

"Is this it?"

His head felt like lead as he nodded.

"About friggin' time." The twinkle left Sylvia's eyes and joined the *dra'aj* in the air and it swept through him, the feeling suddenly hot as if a million bees stung him at once and then cold. For a moment Nik felt as though he would vomit, and then the nausea passed and he straightened from the bedside. He turned to find Poco regarding him with hard eyes.

"Thank you," he said.

Poco looked down and licked trembling lips. "Just make sure I don't have to do it again. Don't be so stupid next time." He turned away, and Nik let him get a little ahead before following him out of the room.

We didn't just find shoes at the hostel upstream, we found horses. Cloud Horses to be exact, asleep in their stalls and perfectly still, dreaming of the time someone would come for them and they could Ride. They were all the same color, a soft dappled gray, so I could tell where their name came from. Their white manes were long and curling, and they seemed rather delicately boned for horses.

"They are perhaps a little larger than you are accustomed to, in the Shadowlands," Wolf said.

"I'm not used to *any* horses." I stretched out my hand, but stopped short of actually touching the horse nearest me. "I've never seen a real horse. I mean, live, right in front of me." I was babbling a bit; I have to admit I was nervous at the idea of climbing on top of one of these. Their backs looked an awfully long way from the ground.

We had gone into the hostel first, where Wolf had almost immediately found a clothes press. It looked no larger than the armoire that I'd had in my bedroom in Madrid, but he kept pulling clothing out of it until the dresses and cloaks and shoes started to pile up on the floor. Finally, he'd pulled out a pair of breeches not unlike his own, but in a soft brown. They were followed by a long-sleeved, cowl-necked top in some light knit, a golden yellow, and a jacket with a nipped waist of some tougher dark brown material. Short boots matched the jacket, and I was set.

I did find the clothes puzzling at first, until I realized I wasn't getting any read off them, not even dim flashes of the workers who'd made them. When I asked Wolf about it, he looked puzzled for a minute. His response gave me the shivers. Sort of.

"No one made these. It is the function of the cupboard to provide clothing."

I decided not to try touching the cupboard.

The request for him to turn around while I was changing got me another puzzled look, but he did it. I put the breeches on first, and pulled my linen dress off with a quick tug. I slipped the long-sleeved top over my head and shook my hair loose—then gripped the side of the cupboard after all, as the world tilted out of balance and back again. *Right. Note to self. Don't shake head.*

The shirt formed itself around me as if it had been made for me, almost like a second skin. I couldn't tell what material it was made out of, but it was light and airy, and warm and comfortable at once. Likewise, the boots pulled on as though they were gloves, with no socks needed. Everything felt as though it had been made right on me, and if it wasn't for the constant queasiness of my stomach, and the way the world tilted again when I leaned over to pick up the jacket, I would have been enjoying myself.

Now I looked at the Cloud Horses and bit my lip.

"Do we have to ride?" I asked Wolf. "It's just that, the movement of the horse—I mean, I've read that it can be quite unsteady, and I'm not feeling all that hot just standing here."

"We have no idea how far we have to travel." Wolf frowned, looking from the horse to me and back again. "And we have no idea what is required of us to find or create a Horn. We must travel as quickly as we can."

"Can't you just Move us?" The thought of that horse rocking under me while it trotted or cantered or whatever horses did was already making me queasy. Queasier.

"To my knowledge, I have never been to the Ice Tor," he said. "No Rider can Move where they have never been themselves—some can Move to a person, or to a piece of their own *gra'if*, but only those with great skill, or great *dra'aj*. No, I am afraid we must Ride." He took the head of the nearest horse between his two hands and breathed into its nostrils.

"Wake, brother," he said softly. "I have need of you. It is time to Ride."

What had been an incredibly lifelike statue of a horse slowly, very slowly, came awake. Starting at the muzzle, as if Wolf's breath had blown life into it, the animal's color deepened, the small hairs on the coat moved as the skin beneath them tightened, and suddenly the air was warmer, and had the most beautiful smell of cut grass. Wolf had gone on to the next beast in line by this time, and this first one startled me by suddenly turning its head and looking me in the face. I gritted my teeth and managed not to step back.

Like I said, I'd never seen a live horse before, so I had no idea whether they all had this same intelligent, measuring look in their eyes.

"Can you talk?" I asked him. The horse didn't answer, and I caught Wolf looking at me from around the neck of the horse he was waking. "I guess that was a stupid question," I said. "But I don't know how things work around here."

"Not so stupid." Wolf came out from behind the other horse with what looked like a saddle made out of cobwebs in his hands. "Walks

Under the Moon says that some of them do speak. But," he shrugged. "It is not always easy to tell which of them these are. She says Light-born can—could, teach the skill."

He swung the saddle up onto the back of the horse nearest me and stepped away. Apparently, the saddle fastened itself, because Wolf certainly didn't do any of the buckling and tugging on straps and things that I'd seen on television. He put his hand on the horse's nose and spoke again.

"This is a friend to us, and to the High Prince of the Lands," he said. Whether the horse spoke or not, Wolf certainly appeared to think he would understand. "I ask you, give her a sure Ride, a soft Ride, and do not let her fall."

The Cloud Horse nodded, swinging his great bony head up and down, and I almost laughed, it looked so much like someone doing a stupid pet trick on Letterman. The moment the horse turned to look at me, blinking his great dark eyes, all inclination to laugh disappeared.

Wolf showed me how to put my foot in the stirrup, and boosted me up until I was sitting in the saddle. It was unexpectedly comfortable, but I was right, it looked like a long way to the ground. Something of what I was thinking must have shown on my face, because Wolf patted my foot, glancing at me quickly before looking away. Even so, he seemed more relaxed than he had been since visiting me in my bedroom.

"You will not fall," he said. "I have asked the Cloud Horse not to allow it."

"That's all it takes?"

He lifted his eyebrows. "It is part of their *dra'aj*," he said, as if that explained everything. As I suppose it did.

There was only one road running past the hostel, a kind of wide grassy lane, and we took the direction away from the Quartz Ring. I could see the standing stones off in the distance, farther away than I remembered them.

"Have they moved?" I turned my head to watch them, then cursed as the world spun. I grabbed the pommel of the saddle [a black stone from the edge of some bottomless crevasse, I almost had the name, the something Abyss; the saddle had definitely been made] for security.

Wolf turned all the way around to look behind us. "The Rings always look like that from the outside. It would only take us a few minutes to Ride there, and, of course, no time at all to Move there."

"And is it always the middle of the night inside a Ring?" I remembered the stars, and the bright sunshine when we stepped outside.

"Whenever I have been in one, yes."

I nodded, trying to take stock. Apparent distances meant nothing. Apparent time of day likewise. Alejandro hadn't told me much about the Lands, I realized. When he'd first rescued me, my own world was new enough to capture all my interest. Of course, he'd never expected me to be here, and I already knew how people tended not to explain things they took for granted, not even realizing that they'd be strange for a visitor. I'd have to pick up what I could on my own. Luckily, that was easy for me.

"So where to now?" I asked.

Wolf stopped dead in the grassy road. "To the Moor of Ravens, of course. Is this not the way?"

I was glad that my horse had stopped by himself. I stared at Wolf, my eyebrows as high as they could go. "You think *I* know the way?"

"But it was you who set the trail." Wolf wasn't angry—yet, but I could tell from the sudden hardness in his voice that he wasn't far away from it.

I held up a hand, palm toward him. "Wait just a second. I know that the Moor of Ravens and the Sea of, *Ma'arban*, was it? I know that these places have something to do with the Horn, or at least with Ice Tor, but that's all I know. I mean, I couldn't even swear to it that they're *places*. The names could be metaphors."

"Oh, Chimera, give me patience." Wolf covered his eyes with his palms. I sat quietly, with my teeth clenched, until he could compose himself. I had an inkling of what he was feeling. Here I thought he knew the way, and he thought I did.

"I'll need to touch you again," I reminded him. "See if there's any more information, any details you don't know you have." I rested my hand on the pommel again [Eyebright had made the saddle, from the horse's own hair, and had chosen the pommel stone with his cooperation; the horse's name was an unpronounceable sound I could hear clearly in my head], secretly thankful that there were no reins for me to worry about.

"I know the horse's name," I said. Wolf didn't respond, but at least he was now looking at me. "I can't say it, but I can hear it in my head, when I touch this." I indicated the pommel. "I can tell you about the Rider who made it, his name was Eyebright. He brought the stone from someplace where there was an abyss."

"The *Shaghana'ak* Abyss, I know of it."

"Right. Well, that's not the only thing you know. You know the way to Ice Tor, you just don't know you know it."

I really shouldn't have been surprised when he shook his head at me. "And this means?"

"Give me your hand," I said.

Chapter Eighteen

HANDS ON HIPS, Wolf looked along the empty shelves set up against the stone walls of the tower, and frowned.

"What is it?" Valory leaned against the frame of the open doorway, breathing shallowly through her mouth, with her palm against her stomach.

"You are supposed to be resting," Wolf said. They had ridden perhaps half a day since she had touched him and learned what direction to take. Valory had become so sleepy after taking more of her medicine that he'd decided to stop when they sighted this traveler's tower. Her condition had worried him, for all that she'd waved off his concern. He'd gone so far, once he had her settled in a bed, as to look at the package of Gravol medicine, as if it might tell him something. He could recognize some of the letters as things he'd seen before, and that some of the other symbols were numbers, but he had not been able to make out what information was being given.

"You look worried," she said to him now.

She looked ill, her coloring wan, her eyes like great pools of molten gold, underscored by dark circles. Something told him it would be a mistake to mention this to her. He waved at the shelves instead.

"The weapons are gone," he said.

Valory came farther into the room and leaned on the corner of a shelf. She made a beckoning motion with the hand that wasn't on her stomach and Wolf realized she meant him to say more.

"The food containers in the great room are empty as well," he said. "Everything, baskets, flasks, pots, whatever. In a traveler's tower they should all be full. And here," he waved at the shelves again. "There should be swords, daggers, bows, armor, even axes."

Lips pressed together, Valory took a deep breath through her nose and let it out slowly. "Okay. So what does that *mean*?"

"It means that we are lucky I took supplies from the hostel. It means it is not as safe here as I had hoped." He turned toward the door, offering Valory his *gra'if*-covered wrist as support. "These are places of refuge. They should always have supplies, food, weapons. Whatever is taken, something should come to replace it."

"Like the clothes in the cupboard?"

"Exactly. Food in the baskets, wine and other beverages in the flasks. That is the purpose of these towers, to provide for any traveler who might pass. Someone has deliberately tampered with the magic here, so that the tower cannot supply anyone else."

"The Hunt?"

Wolf hesitated, pausing between one step and the next. "No. The Hunt cannot affect this kind of magic. But the followers of the Basilisk Prince can."

"So they've been here? Taken the food and the weapons for their own use?"

"And made sure no others can feed or arm themselves."

"So do we care? You're already armed, and you've got *gra'if*."

"But you have nothing. Not so much as a mail shirt to stop an arrow."

"Oh." Her brows drew downward in a vee. "Well, we'll have to hope it doesn't come to that." She drew him back to the room in which he had left her. "I found something, I didn't know if it was important."

"You were supposed to be resting," he repeated, as he followed her.

"I was looking for a window," she explained. "And I found this. Isn't it beautiful?"

"You arose from your sickbed, when it is of the utmost importance that you rest and regain your strength, in order to show me something beautiful?"

Illness had made her so pale that the flush which spread over her face at his words stood out like a stain. Instead of answering, she turned away and lifted her hand, reaching out to touch the wall. Wolf's eyes followed the movement, and what he had been about to say next faded from his lips.

The walls were covered with lines of onyx and darkmetal, some of them as fine as hairs, some as thick as heavy ropes, with here and there a touch of what looked like *gra'if*. Some great use of *dra'aj* had blasted this pattern into the walls.

For a moment Wolf could not think why he was so frightened, and then he knew. He MOVED and Valory—her hand still reaching out—was in his arms, and they were outside of the room. He held her steady as she retched, until she waved him off.

"It is a Signed room," he said, when she was able to straighten. "I could not take the risk of what might happen if you touched the wall."

Her breathing steadied, and she turned, moving as if balancing her head with great care. Her pallor had increased, leaving green shadows on her cheeks. "What *is* it? Couldn't you have warned me?"

"I did not expect it." He offered his wrist again to steady her. Or to steady himself; he could not be sure. It felt as though his bowels had turned to ice. "There are Songs about Signed rooms, and even buildings. They are Signed against Movement." A wrinkle appeared between her brows. Wolf squeezed his eyes shut in frustration. He tapped his forehead with his free hand. "When Signed, these rooms fall from the mind of everyone except the one who Signed them, and others can Move neither in nor out. They are used to enclose Riders as the only prison that would work against their Riding."

"*That's* a prison room?" One hand gripping his *gra'if* armband, the other braced against the wall, Valory leaned to peer into the Signed room.

"It is likely, though not all of them are. There was a Song that tells of a pair of Riders who entered a Signed room after their wedding, to spend a portion of time completely alone. The Song tells that the Rider who had Signed the room for them was killed in a sudden accident, leaving the lovers trapped forever. The location of the room is long forgotten, but perhaps the lovers love there still." Wolf heard a certain familiar lilt to his voice, and cleared his throat. Valory's caramel eyes shone as if with tears.

"We must leave here, and leave now," he said. "When I think of what might have happened as we slept . . ."

Valory steadied herself, moving a finger to brush against his bare skin. She swallowed, blinking. It was not possible for her to turn any whiter, but she did release his wrist. "Really? *That* could have happened to us?"

Wolf wondered what touching him had shown her. "Before the turning of the Cycle, I would have said there were very few Riders who had *dra'aj* enough to Sign a room. There may be many more now."

"And not just the good guys."

"As you say."

I turned as slowly as I could, trying to walk without moving my head more than necessary; I felt like one of those bobblehead dolls you see in souvenir shops. I'd been so looking forward to getting whatever rest I could, but I certainly wasn't going to argue, not after what I'd seen when I touched him. It was like the song of Ice Tor, except that I got pretty much the whole thing at once, probably because Wolf actually remembered it himself. The tune, the lyrics, and the whole of the sadness and the horror of those two poor people.

I hadn't finished turning toward the door when a sudden blast threw me backward, and I went sliding into the dark corner where the tower's stone staircase led upward. I gasped, dizzy and retching, and clung to the edge of the first stair, just level with my head. There was the loudest rushing sound, like a thousand subway trains in a thousand subway tunnels. The light suddenly brightened, and I realized that Wolf had drawn his *gra'if* sword. The roar of the wind increased, and I was pushed painfully against the stone until I thought the arm under me would break.

The door of the Signed room slammed shut, the light disappeared, and the air pressure increased as a sound I couldn't hear lanced through my head.

Then suddenly everything was quiet, except for a far-off whistling noise, like air through a narrow opening. I swallowed, again and again, waiting for the world to stop spinning, and my retching to stop. The whistling quieted.

"Softly, softly, little one. Thou'rt safe now." The voice was breathy, and in the back of it I could hear wind blowing through trees.

I managed to open my eyes. In the dim light that came in through the smashed door I thought I could see a woman. She shifted, my eyes readjusted, and I cut off a whimper as it tried to force its way through my teeth. There was a bruising force on my shoulder blades and I realized I was trying to push myself backward through the wall. I didn't stop.

It was a woman, if women came around two stories tall, and so perfectly formed that she seemed almost delicate. Her skin was multicolored, like a blanket of leaves in the fall, all golds and reds and browns and yellows and rusts. Her eyes were a piercing blue, and her hair, thick and twiggy, grew straight back from her head as though she were facing into a stiff breeze.

She squatted down on her heels and reached out her hand toward me.

"Please don't touch me." I'm sorry to say my voice was mostly squeak.

"They've hurt thee, then, haven't they? Well, not to worry, my little one. They've hurt me and all, so thou'st nothing to worry thee. I've got thee, and thou'rt safe now, safe as houses." And then she laughed, and the building shook with the wind that roared through it. "Safer than this house, at any rate. I'd knock it down, but for the mouse I've got shut in the box."

I managed to push myself into a sitting position. My mouth was almost too dry to speak. "What happened to Wolf?"

"Wolf, is he? What I thought, then. The wolf's shut away, little one." She tilted her head toward the door of the Signed room, and a sudden shaft of light shone straight into my eyes as she moved, making me blink. Suddenly her index finger shot forward into my face and her blue eyes narrowed. "Thou'rt no Rider. What art thou?"

"Hu—human," I managed to say.

"Human? A Shadowlander? Why, I've not seen one of thy kind

for long and long. What did the evil one's Rider want with you, my little one?"

I'm ashamed to say it still took me a second to figure out that she meant Wolf, and the true nature of what was going on finally filtered through the Gravol, the pain, and the shock. She thought Wolf was one of the Basilisk's warriors, and she thought she'd saved me from him. By putting him in the Signed room.

And if I understood what Wolf had told me, this being was the only thing that could get him out again.

"He's not . . ." I swallowed and tried again. "His name is Stormwolf, that's his name. His mother was Rain at Sunset and the Chimera guides him. He's not with the Basilisk Prince. He's my friend. He, he has *fara'ip* with the High Prince."

She was nodding. "That is what they say, little one. To get you to trust them, and then they try to trap you with Bindings and Chants, and feed you to their Hounds." Then she smiled and her teeth were square, and orange and well-spaced.

I squirmed around until I had my feet under me, not that I thought I had the strength to stand up. "No, he's a good guy. You have to believe me. You have to let him out."

She tilted her head to one side. "Art thou broken, then? Did they turn thee and all? I cannot 'let him out.' He is a plague, an infection. Better he stays shut away, where he cannot hurt anyone."

"No!" I inched closer. My heart pounded in my throat, and I forgot how sick I felt. Wolf would stay in that room forever, longer than forever. Alone for eternity, with only his own thoughts, his own guilt. "Listen to me, you have to—"

She opened her mouth wide and all the air was sucked out of the building. I put my hands to my ears and opened my mouth as wide as I could. Maybe she thought I was imitating her, maybe she only meant to give me a warning to behave, because all the air came rushing back, throwing me against the edge of the stone stairs. *That's going to leave a bruise*, I thought.

I was blinking away tears, and for some reason that infuriated me. Here was another one who was going to look after me, take care of me, do what they pleased with me, take away the people that mattered to me and ruin my life.

I used the stairs behind me to push myself to my feet. I drew myself up as tall as I could, my hands in fists, my face tight. "You listen! You stop that and listen! And you let him out! I'm not stupid and they haven't turned me and you can stop bullying me any time, you stupid bag of wind! I'm telling you the truth and I can prove it."

Before she could move or hit me or anything, I reached out and grabbed her little finger and was immediately swept away on a blast of wind, spun like a top. I clung to the anchor, the one steady, firm hold I had, and then I was moving with the air, not as an obstacle, but as part of it, and everything came clear.

"Little one? Dost thou live?"

I felt a prodding in my side and groaned. Bruises for certain. My eyes blinked open, and there was a huge multicoloured face hovering over me, concern showing in the slant of her eyebrows and pale, sand-colored eyes.

"You're a sandstorm." My voice croaked and I tried to swallow. "You're not supposed to be all fall-leaf colored, you're supposed to be all the thousand beautiful shades of the sand in your desert. You don't belong here, where all there is to blow is grass and leaves, with their ugly, bright, vulgar colors. They caught you with a Chant of Binding you never thought to hear, caught you to stop your storm, and when they knew what they had, some of them fed off you." I patted the back of her hand. Mine looked as small as a doll's. "But they didn't get much, did they? Just enough to make you angry, to hurt you, and you tried to blow them away, but you blew yourself here instead." I blinked. "And now you don't know how to get back."

A tear rolled out of her left eye, splashing me as it hit the stone floor. "Thou couldst guess that," she said. "From what I told thee, thou couldst guess the greater part."

I bit my lip. There had to be something. Something she hadn't mentioned, something I couldn't have worked out by logic. At first nothing came, but then then the images settled, and I had it.

"I couldn't guess about your seven children. Little sand devils. How they create pillars of sand and how you taught them to dance. Their names are Son'iana, Taru'eva—"

"Stop." She sat back on her heels. "Do not say them aloud. No, thou couldst not guess such things. Art thou a Truthreader, then? I did not know that humans could have that gift."

"Not very many of us."

Her head swung round to look at the door of the Signed room. I could see that the outside of the door had the same kind of intricate inlayed pattern that the walls had. I hadn't seen that before. "So what you said of your Stormwolf is also true? He is no brother to the ones who harmed me? He is *fara'ip* of the High Prince?" She got up and leaned toward the door, raising her fingertip to the pattern.

"Yes." I sagged down onto my knees. The room swung sharply to the left and settled again, not quite level.

I squeezed my eyes shut as a high-pitched note pierced my brain and made my head explode.

Wolf left off chiseling the edge of the door with the point of his *gra'if* sword. It would not damage the sword, but just as evidently it would do no damage to the door.

"Chimera, give me strength!" He flung the sword and it stuck point first in the wall next to the door, quivering slightly with a soft musical tone. Wolf rubbed at his face and tried to breathe more slowly. Temper would not free him.

Nothing would free him.

He had thrown away his time, mooning about, feeling sorry for himself and look where that had brought him. Now he would have all the time he needed—all the time anyone would ever need—to do absolutely nothing at all.

And what of Valory? She was only here to help him, and now he had left her, ill and possibly dying, in the hands of whatever being had attacked them, and Signed him into the room. He jerked his sword from the wall and sheathed it. He pulled a chair away from the table and sat down, leaning forward and resting his head in his hands. The baskets and bowls on the table were empty. With luck, he would starve to death.

Sometime later his hearing seemed to fade. He swallowed, and it cleared. The air pressure in the room was changing. Wolf stood and turned to the door. They would pay for locking him away. He would not waste any more time. He pulled his sword free, and when the door opened, he was ready.

"Wolf! Wolf, no! She's a sandstorm, she thought you—" At the last possible instant, Valory's words penetrated and Wolf drew back, the *gra'if* blade trembling in his fist. Valory was on the floor, her back against the curve of the stone staircase. Dust motes floated in the shaft of sunlight that fell across her legs.

Standing next to her, almost over her, was a giantess, all the colors of autumn leaves, but like no Tree Natural he had ever seen. She held up her hands in front of her, and when she opened her mouth to speak, all the dust motes flew from the room.

"I thought thee a follower of the Basilisk, until thy Truthreader gave me the truth of thee." Definitely a Natural, that much was certain, but what kind?

"She is not my . . ." But Wolf let the words trail away. Yes, Valory *was* his Truthreader. "Your pardon, Elder Sister. I thank you for my release."

"She's the storm in the *Todala'era* Desert." Valory's smile was shaky. "She thought we were bad guys."

"I would not have imprisoned thee else, Stormwolf, son of Rain at Sunset, Chimeraborn. It was spawn of the Basilisk, accompanied by the Hunt, made me flee my desert."

"She doesn't know how to get back," Valory said, her voice no more than a whisper. "That's why she was so ready to attack us."

That, Wolf could well understand. A Natural that was so tied to its own space, as a sandstorm must be, could easily be maddened by being torn from its place, though that tearing had saved her life.

"Where is the *Todala'era* Desert?" Wolf had a glimmering of an idea. "What Ring is nearest to it?" He couldn't Move to a place he'd never been, but that was what the Ring Road was for.

"It lies three gusts from the Morganite Ring." There was a tiny note of a lost howl in the Natural's voice, a howl that Wolf felt in his bones.

"And if I took you to the Ring? Could you find your way to your desert from there?" All movement of air in the tower stopped—there was not even any sound penetrating from without.

The Natural tilted her head to one side, and then the other, studying him. "Thou wouldst do this thing?" She turned to Valory. "He would do this?"

"He would," Valory said, before Wolf could even speak for himself. *Does she know me, then, this well?*

"Wouldst thou do it now?"

For answer, Wolf sheathed his sword and stretched out both his hands.

"Farewell, Truthreader."

"Good-bye. Have fun storming the castle." A ghost of a smile flickered across Valory's face.

"Stay here, do not move. I will return in a moment."

CRACK!

The great thing about working with the Riders, Nik thought, blinking at Wolf's darkened living room, is that no time is lost getting from one place to another.

"I'm still getting my head around the fact that you people are living in the Royal York."

"It is where the High Prince lived, when she was Warden to the Exile. Wolf uses it at her command, so it may be a place he and Valory will return to." Alejandro looked around at the room, as if he was wishing Val was there right now. Nik knew how the Rider felt.

"There may be sign outside the door," Alejandro said, moving toward the end of the room farthest from the windows.

Nik followed. "What's 'sign,' exactly, and how will we know it when we see it?"

The Rider opened the door into the same wide, well-lit hallway that Nik had seen once before. Alejandro immediately stepped out and began to scrutinize the carpeting.

Nik stroked the dragon-shaped door knocker with his forefinger, and then examined both door and doorjamb more closely. "Hey, it's not a card lock. I'll bet not very many people have the key." He looked up. Alejandro was examining the nap of the carpet from an angle. "Anything?"

The Rider shook his head. "Marks of the vacuum cleaner."

Nik turned to go back inside, and got about five paces in before he realized Alejandro wasn't behind him.

"What's up?"

"I cannot enter."

"What do you mean? You were just in here."

A line appeared between Alejandro's brows. "Let me try something." There was a small POP! Before Nik's ears had cleared, the Rider was standing next to him.

"Interesting." Alejandro approached the door and, carefully making sure he stayed on the inside, examined the edges, finally pushing it gently shut. He looked back at Nik. "I cannot walk in, but I *can* Move in." His amber eyes sparkled with humor. "Ah. An old Chant, but a useful one. Wolf has used it to keep strangers out."

"Strange Riders, anyway." Nik shrugged. "Shall we get on with it?"

Alejandro nodded, but was still looking around him without moving. "It is hard to know how often we should check this place," he said.

"If all we're doing is checking to see if Valory and Wolf have come back, we could leave them a note."

Alejandro shut his eyes and shook his head slowly from side to side. "Anyone would think I have not lived as a human for all these years. Being with Riders has distracted me too much. Of course, a note."

"What's the big deal?" Nik remembered Wolf toying with the pen and pad of paper that time they were in Alejandro' house.

"It is simply that Riders do not have a written language. Only those of us who have learned to do so can read and write, and then only in one of the human languages."

"Wow." Somehow it never occurred to Nik that the Riders—who seemed as though they could do anything they wanted—couldn't do something as simple as reading. Though, now that he thought about it, there were lots of human who hadn't learned either. He looked around and found notepaper and a pen exactly where he would expect to find them, near the phone.

"Walks Under the Moon is learning to read," Alejandro said, as he watched Nik write the note.

Nik glanced up, his eyebrows raised. "Speaking of which?"

Alejandro grinned. "She said she would join us after riding in the elevator," he said. He looked down at the note. "I notice that you have told Valory to call you, and not me. Have you forgotten that she is my *fara'ip*?"

Nik felt his ears go hot. Yeah, why wouldn't she call Alejandro? "I don't know what that means," he said. "But this way, she knows she can call me, as well." It sounded lame even to him, but somehow, he *did* want Valory to know that she had a human option. That she could rely on someone besides Riders.

Alejandro finally lifted his eyes from the note. "Be very careful, my friend." He smiled, but the tightness in Nik's chest didn't loosen. "I have told you before. She is blood of my blood."

Nik didn't know what to say to that, but luckily Alejandro didn't wait for a response. One second he was standing next to Nik, smiling that not-quite-a-smile, and the next he was at the door, with a sword instead of a walking stick in his hand. Nik's heart thumped in his chest, and his throat felt tight. He took a quick look around and snatched up the poker from the fireplace. Alejandro was standing to the left of the door, and smiled when he saw how Nik had armed himself. With a wave of his blade he indicated Nik should stand over to the right, then grabbed the door and flung it open.

A very tall man, black hair hanging loose down his back, stood with his empty hands held out in front of him, palms toward them. His pale blue eyes narrowed, and then widened again as they fixed on Alejandro.

"Do I not know you?" he asked. He took half a step forward, and brought his hands halfway down. "Did you not once Ride in the train of Lady of the Roc? I am Sunset on Water."

Alejandro narrowed his eyes, and after a bit he nodded but didn't lower his sword. "It was not me you remember, but my cousin. Why are you here? Who has sent you?"

The Rider looked away, letting his hands fall to his sides. "I rode with the Basilisk."

Nik found himself hefting the poker.

"The Cycle has turned," Alejandro said. "The High Prince would welcome you in her court, as she has welcomed others of your following."

The Rider smiled, but it was the kind of smile that Nik thought would break your heart. "I know. I would give anything to bring that to pass, but alas, I have nothing left to offer. I must hold by my pledged word."

"Even when the *dra'aj* of he to whom you pledged has returned to the Lands?"

The man swallowed and looked away again, taking in a lungful of air. He spoke before looking back. "It was a *dra'aj* oath."

Nik didn't know what that meant, but from the way Alejandro suddenly stiffened, it couldn't be good.

"I pledged not merely to follow the Basilisk, but to forsake the Prince Guardian and to fight against him always. I cannot take back my *dra'aj* oath."

Nik glanced at Alejandro. The Rider's eyes were round, and his lips parted. "Certainly you cannot, not now when the one to whom you swore is gone." He swallowed, and inclined his head in a slight bow. "If you are not here to join with us, why are we speaking?"

"There are others like myself, others who cannot retract their oaths, who cannot—" The Rider rubbed at his mouth with his hand. "Who cannot stop. There has been killing on both sides and we . . . we cannot stop." He let his hand drop again. "We could not even *think* of stopping, until we came here, to the Shadowlands. This gives us hope. There may be a way out for us, if someone would carry my words to the High Prince. We may even be of service to her."

Alejandro made an impatient sound that reminded Nik of his grandfather. "You call her the High Prince, you acknowledge her? And yet you ally with the Hunt, the enemy of us all? Is this how you offer your service?"

Nik saw the point of Alejandro's sword rise as his grip tightened. Sunset on Water saw it as well, and took a step back. Nik cleared his throat.

"The enemy of my enemy is my friend," he said. Maybe he was being an idiot, maybe this wasn't the best basis for an alliance, but it was probably the only one they had. He moved closer, but didn't make the mistake of standing between the two Riders. That big an idiot he wasn't. "If there's common ground somewhere between you, isn't it worthwhile to look for it? If lives can be saved?" *Especially Outsider lives.*

Alejandro relaxed. Sunset on Water glanced at Nik, and returned his eyes to the other Rider.

"It is not by choice that we ally with the Hunt, I assure you, Sunward one." The other Rider spread his hands again, as if proving that he didn't carry a weapon. "What I would propose is another alliance entirely."

"Go on."

"Here, in the Shadowlands, our oaths weigh on us less, we can tolerate them, though we are not free of them. Here we could live, build lives for ourselves, escape the poison of the Basilisk Prince. Do you see? There need not be contention between us. Let the High Prince grant us the Shadowlands, and we will destroy the Hunt for her."

Nik's throat closed. Great, someone else who wanted to take over the world. This is what he got for trying to help out. The role of mediator only worked if you were a disinterested third party.

"Why have you not made this offer to her?" Alejandro asked.

"We could not. Not while we remained in the Lands, in the same world as the Prince Guardian. We came to the Shadowlands almost by chance, hunted to a Portal, and found here a sufficient distance from him to think and speak clearly of the matter."

"Hang on; wouldn't you need to destroy the Hunt anyway? I mean, they're a danger to you as well, aren't they?"

Again, the Rider looked at him, but turned to Alejandro to answer.

"We could tolerate them. So long as they have humans to feed upon, we are in no real danger." Sunset made a tossing motion with his hand. "But it is not what we would best want. I would end the killing, even if it means we cannot return home."

"So you would give us your help against the Hunt."

"As you say."

Oh, crap. Nik was torn. On the one hand, this was Rider help against the Hunt—but as far as he could see, this guy wasn't carrying any *gra'if*, so was the help useful? But Alejandro *was* considering it, so there must be *something* these guys could do. Nik cleared his throat, and suddenly both sets of eyes were aimed at him.

"You can't leave humans out of this equation," he said. "The High Prince is looking for the Horn on our behalf so in that sense, we're already *your* allies." Nik nodded in Alejandro's direction. "We need to be a part of this negotiation. We need a—" Nik racked his brain for the words he wanted. "A treaty of offense and defense." He looked between the two Riders. Their faces remained impassive, but not unfriendly. "Mutually," he added.

"Will you speak for your people?" Alejandro didn't sound at all as though he were joking.

Oh, hell, no, Nik thought. He couldn't really speak even for all Outsiders, let alone all humans—but someone had to say something, and say it right now. *Don't screw up, Nikki.* "Sure. I mean, yes. Yes, I'll speak for my people."

"Speak."

Nik took a deep breath, and a tighter grip on the poker he was still holding. Somehow, this simple human tool gave him comfort. "This is our world. The Hunt's no part of it. And neither, really, are either of you. We only have a problem because of you. It's only reasonable that we expect you, at the very least, to clean up your problem."

"And what can you offer in return for our help?" If there was underlying menace in Sunset's voice, at least the Rider was now speaking directly to him.

"I'll remind you that my people are already allied with the High Prince, against the Hunt, and—at the moment—against you. If you make a bargain with Riders like Alejandro—" Damn, what was Alejandro's Rider name again? "Then, you make a bargain with us."

"Is this true?"

When Alejandro didn't answer right away, Nik's heart sank. He was trying to come up with some kind of delaying tactic when the Rider spoke up.

"The High Prince has pledged to rid the humans of the Hunt, so in this much, at the least, we *are* allies."

Nik wasn't the only one who jumped at this fourth voice. Sunset on Water spun around, revealing the tall, very fair woman dressed in black and red standing behind him. Moon must have finished playing with the elevators. She had an umbrella in her hand, and was holding it in the same stance that Alejandro held his sword. Nik had only met her when she came back from the Lands with Alejandro and Nighthawk, but he was pretty sure the umbrella was just an umbrella.

"I have heard what you have said, Sunset on Water. You know me; I am Walks Under the Moon. In this matter, I know what is in my sister's mind, and for her, the humans will always be taken into account in any decision made."

The other Rider gave Moon a shallow bow. "Very well." Sunset on Water didn't seem at all put out by this qualification, but Nik wasn't so sure it was time to break out the champagne. "We would undertake not to interfere in the lives of humans, if we are granted permission to use the Shadowlands as our territory."

"These are only preliminary discussions," Alejandro pointed out.

"We will carry your words to the High Prince," Walks Under the Moon said.

Sunset on the Water nodded, his lips pressed tight together. Finally, he raised his head. "Can there at least be a ceasing of hostilities between us in the meanwhile?"

"I see no reason why not."

Sunset, still nodding, asked, "Then will you carry word to the Rider Nighthawk? He who was once Warden to the Exile? His father and mine were of the same *fara'ip*, and I would have words with him, if he is willing. He might also speak for us."

"I will tell him."

"Let him meet me in some neutral place then, at sunset. He need not come alone," the dark Rider added when Alejandro frowned.

Nik decided to step in. "Inside or outside? Crowded or empty?" he said. "As a place to meet, I mean. 'Cause I'm thinking the Hair of the Dog. It's a bar," Nik added, turning to Alejandro. "Lots of people coming and going. They'd be just another couple of guys. Who's going to notice?" The dark Rider hesitated. "Corner of Church and Wood?"

"I know the place." Sunset was nodding, but he still didn't look very happy. "It is not far from a den of the Hunt." But then he gave a sharp nod, and looked Nik in the eye for the first time. "Not far, but perhaps easier, then, for me to break away."

"Where are you supposed to be now?" Nik asked.

"Watching a building north of here, where there has been a great coming and going of humans of interest to the Hunt, humans like yourself, with no scent."

Outsiders? Does he mean the hospital? Crap, what if he meant Elaine's place?

"Return to your post. I will tell Nighthawk," Alejandro said. "We will speak again."

Moon edged to one side, lowering her umbrella just enough to let the other Rider by. Nik noticed that she watched him the whole time, waiting until he'd reached the far end of the corridor before turning to face them.

"It appears there may be reason for cautious optimism, at least on one front." She shook her head. "*Dra'aj* oaths—did I hear correctly? I have not heard of such things outside of Songs, but it goes far to explain the frenzied attacks my sister has been faced with." She turned to Nik. "You are worried? When Sunset on Water told us where his post was, your face changed."

"I thought he might mean Elaine's place, where our office is," Nik said. "There's been a lot of us coming and going there lately."

"An area of potential danger? Then I have a suggestion." Moon moved closer. "I have need of activity. Now that Valory and Wolf are on the track of the Horn, my work is over, but I find I cannot sit idly by in my sister's court while all around me work. You two have no real need of me. What if I work with this Elaine? I could make myself of use, even if it is only to Move humans quickly to safe places."

Swift River Current was enjoying herself, leaning on the parapet on the northeast corner of the train station, sitting in the sun, eating sausages from the sidewalk vendor. It was amusing to watch the humans walking by.

"What about that one?" Badger nudged River's left arm, indicating a very tall, very slim man with skin the color of ebony. "Think he'd taste any different?"

"Nah, it's just skin color, it doesn't go any deeper." River had tried a few of the darker ones in Australia. Still, it was fun to pick out who might be her next meal, and then come up with reasons not to eat them—yet.

"They're so totally oblivious," Badger said. "They don't even know what danger they're in. Hey, what about that blonde?"

"She'd be good. Okay, why not?"

"Uh . . . skirt's too short for those legs. I wouldn't want the fashion police after me."

The two Hounds laughed until they howled.

River was just wiping away a tear when she glanced across the street and saw Sunset on Water come out of the hotel. She whacked Badger on the arm and pointed, still breathless from laughing. Badger dropped her half-eaten Italian sausage with hot mustard and onions to the sidewalk.

"What's he doing here? This's *our* lookout spot."

"Shouldn't be anywhere near here," River agreed. "Pack Leader's keeping all the Riders away." She didn't know how much the other Hound knew. Didn't know whether Badger knew about Wolf. But for sure Fox wouldn't trust his brother to any of these Rider so-called allies.

Her eyes narrowed and her hand went into her pocket, looking for her phone.

"Just a sec." Badger put her hand on River's wrist. "What say we go see what he's been up to first?"

River nodded, smiling. "Sure. Who knows? We might have something really interesting to report."

It was easy to backtrack the Rider from the door where he'd come out of the building. He'd used the third elevator on the right-hand side of the main bank of elevators, and ridden down from the top floor. The hallway was deserted, and the trail led right up to a plain wooden door with a dragon-shaped knocker.

Badger pressed her nose to the crack of the door and almost immediately leaped back, sneezing. "This is a Dragonborn's lair, someone very powerful." She licked at a line of drool that threatened to escape from her mouth.

River approached the door more cautiously, nose lifted, nostrils spread. "Yeah, but that's not who Sunset was meeting. There's someone else, someone—" River snapped her head back. "The old Rider, the one with the girl! Sun of a bitch! Sunset met with the Old One."

"I don't smell anyone else." Her nose now clear, Badger was using it again. "What's Sunset doing, meeting with the Old One without Pack Leader? Something smells bad about this."

"You think?" River shook her head, mouth twisted to one side. "Well, well, well. You've just made a serious mistake, my Rider friend. A *very* serious mistake."

Badger grinned back at her. "Maybe the last one he'll ever make, huh?"

This time River got her phone all the way out of her pocket before she shoved it back in.

"What?"

"This is too important. We need to tell Fox face-to-face."

Wolf was gone, and then he was back, and then we were outside the tower, and Wolf was helping me on my Cloud Horse. I don't know whether it was the distraction, but I was actually feeling a bit better.

"That's Moon's." I'd meant to get hold of Wolf's wrist where the *gra'if* was, but I'd touched this golden bangle, about as thick around as my little finger, instead. "I don't mean that's her bracelet," I said, letting go of it. "I mean that's her hair."

Wolf had been looking over his shoulder at the tower's broken door, as if worrying that something else might come at us. "Yes. She made it."

"And you made her one." It occurred to me I *hadn't* seen a dark bangle made of Wolf's hair to match this one on Moon's wrist. Only Lightborn's pin on her collar. Anyone could see the significance of that.

Wolf heaved himself up into his own saddle and the Cloud Horse turned so we were facing each other. "After Truthsheart became High Prince, both Moon and I had need of a place of family, a place to rest and finish the Healing she had begun." Wolf stroked the horse's neck. "We were fostered with Honor of Souls, the mother of Lightborn. One day she spoke of this old manner of making a keepsake between members of a *fara'ip*." Wolf turned it on his wrist. "I remembered seeing them on the wrists of some of the Wild Riders, so Moon and I made our own."

I touched the bracelet again. It was like touching Moon, but different. Touching something that belonged to someone often gave me much clearer images, since I didn't have the person's emotional state to contend with.

"She's in the Shadowlands," I said. "With Alejandro. No, with Elaine." I glanced up at Wolf, but his face didn't change. I started to relax, then tightened up again. "Does she have one of these? Of yours? Can it be used to locate you? To Move to you?"

But Wolf was already shaking his head. "Impossible. Only *gra'if* can be used in that fashion, and then only by those with powerful *dra'aj*." He gestured to his throat. "The High Prince wears the Guardian Prince's torque, for example, and he hers. They can use the torques to Move to one another, but—"

"But they're the Princes, okay, I get it. And the bad guys don't use *gra'if* anyway, even if they were powerful enough, which they're probably not. Sorry I brought it up."

I was sorrier that I'd said that. I had to shut my eyes and breathe slowly to make sure nothing else got brought up.

"Valory?"

I swallowed, my ears popped, and I realized I had better take more Gravol. I would have been nodding if it hadn't meant the world would have wobbled. "Okay." I paused a moment to phrase my words properly. "Let's go. A specific question. Concentrate."

Wolf thought for a moment, doing as I'd instructed. "What are the lyrics that will lead us to the Ice Tor?"

I reached out then, and took a firm grip on his arm above both bracelet and *gra'if*. At first, I felt nothing but the warmth of Wolf's skin, the muscles trembling just beneath. Maybe I was too tired after all. Too sick. This had never happened to me before, I always got *something*. I swallowed, and I was looking for the words to tell Wolf we weren't going anywhere, when information started coming. [The scars on his face had come from a clawing he'd suffered when someone else wanted to be Pack Leader; blue had been his favorite color; he'd been annoyed and envious when his little brother had manifested his Guidebeast first.] And then everything else had faded into the background, and all I could see/read/feel was the Song.

" 'Where the sun stands high in the north, never setting;
Where the chill wind creeps down from western crags.' "

I let go and the images stopped. "That can't be right. The western wind is always warm." Wolf raised his eyebrows. "Well, in any poetry I've ever heard anyway."

"Shadowland poetry?"

"I take your point. Anyway, the next bit goes 'Soft footfalls trace the edge of air; A cold snake lurks in the valley.' " I stopped singing and cleared my throat. "That's how it starts anyway. Is it supposed to rhyme? Because this part didn't come out that way."

"Not always," Wolf said. "They are easier to remember if rhymed, but there are many Songs, and passages of Songs, that do not." I took another breath, but Wolf stopped me before I could recite any more. "That is enough for us to begin," he said. "If I Sing, we should Ride to that part of the Road closest to what I describe."

Suddenly I wanted to tell him I couldn't go, that I was too sick, that I couldn't make it. That maybe I should lie down for a while after all. I told myself there was no way to know if lying down was going to make me feel any better. There hadn't been any food for me to eat, but since I could only drink tiny sips of the purest of water without gagging, that hadn't seemed so important. So far, we hadn't really taken that much time; I certainly didn't feel hungry. But wouldn't I feel the lack of food eventually? We had to find the Horn and get back to the Shadowlands—back home—while I was still able to function.

We set off once more. Now Wolf Sang under his breath the whole time. I don't know how he knew the tune—maybe he was making it up as he went along—but as he Sang, he urged his Cloud Horse forward, and we almost immediately left the dense woods for a grassy path where the trees were well spaced and there was little underbrush.

Then, so suddenly it made me blink, we were riding along the edge of a steep hill, with a narrow valley below us, a stream winding along its bottom, far below.

"Um. Are we headed in the right direction?"

"Look." Wolf pointed upward. I shaded my eyes with my hand and looked. "The sun in the northern sky. And do you not feel the wind? Look below, I would wager the water in that stream is cold enough." I directed my eyes downward without moving my head. The stream did sort of look like a snake, now that he mentioned it. "We have begun."

I had to take his word for it. In fact, I had to take his word for most of the rest of the day's journey—if it was a day. I found out for certain why they called the place the "Lands," in plural. From the hillside, we came around the shoulder of a rock and were suddenly in the dark. It was raining, and I would have freaked completely except that we were on what seemed to be a paved road, and the rain was warm. Nevertheless, Wolf passed out short cloaks from a pack he had behind his saddle and as soon as I had mine around me not only did the rain not fall on me, but where it *had* fallen, I was immediately dry. I could see how useful one of these would be at home—not that there was a lot of cloak wearing on the streets of Toronto.

"We'd be rich if we could make umbrellas out of this stuff," I said. But either he didn't hear me, or I hadn't spoken aloud.

The dark rainy road turned into a sandy beach that stretched out for kilometers ahead of us. Between one step and the next, we were in a field of some kind of grain, under cloudy skies, and then in a beautiful mountain meadow dotted with multicolored wildflowers. I went on reciting lines from the Song as we went. Wolf would repeat them after me in his warm liquid voice, and the landscape we were looking for would appear. I started to feel a bit dopey, like when you're falling asleep watching a movie and you only catch glimpses here and there. At one point I wondered whether we were actually traveling into these places, or whether Wolf was calling them into being with his Singing.

Then I wondered why it would matter.

Suddenly, I found myself swallowing a lot, so much that I couldn't get out the next line.

"Do you wish to dismount?" Wolf said. He reached out as if to take me by the elbow, to steady me, but I held up my own hand, warding him off.

"Don't . . . touch . . . me," I managed to say. It really felt as if I was going to puke. Very slowly, holding my head as level as I could, I got down from the Cloud Horse. My foot had no sooner touched the ground, however, than the world began to spin for real, and I had to cling to the saddle to keep upright.

"Wolf," I croaked out. He must have seen what I was trying to do, because he immediately dismounted, and gave me a boost back onto my own horse. He'd only touched me for a moment, and all I got from him was a confused sea of faces and the knowledge that he didn't know how his parents had died—and that he was afraid either he or Fox had something to do with it.

"I know." I was leaning forward, clinging to my Cloud Horse's neck, only dimly aware that I was getting no reading from him at all, and more than grateful for the respite. "How your parents died." I must have been speaking aloud, because Wolf's face was suddenly close to mine. "In the fullness of time," I said. "Their *dra'aj* was returned to the Lands."

"I thank the Chimera who guides me," he said, like he was praying. "I feared . . ." He was just a little too scared to say out loud what it was he'd feared.

"S'okay. I know."

"A little water? Must you take more of the pills?"

"Water." Somehow, now that I was back on the Cloud Horse, my stomach was settling a bit, and I was able to manage a couple of sips of water.

"Should we rest?" There was real concern in his voice, but not just concern for me. Time was passing, and if I couldn't feel it, Wolf could.

"I don't know," I admitted. "Part of me wants to lie down, but if what just happened is any indication, I should probably stay on the horse." I never thought I'd hear myself say that.

"I have asked him not to let you fall." Wolf was nodding. "Perhaps that is helping you. You may be able to sleep if we go forward slowly. Tell me the next ten lines or so, I will find the way, while you rest."

So that's what we did. I dozed, leaning forward, my arms around the Cloud Horse's neck, warm and dry under me, my cheek against his skin, with the most pleasant smell of a recently mowed lawn. Never quite asleep, never completely awake, we followed as Wolf led us through several more landscapes, more than I wanted to keep track of. Eventually, I thought I was feeling a bit better and was thinking about trying to sit up, when the Cloud Horse stopped abruptly. I pushed myself upright.

We were in a valley, treed slopes to our right, rocks and scrub brush to our left. And, directly in front of us, a monster.

I was startled enough that I sat bolt upright, my motion sickness forgotten as adrenaline shot through my system. *That won't help*, I thought. I don't know what would have been worse, the nausea, or constantly cranking myself up to avoid it.

In front of us, blocking the path, was something I had never, in my wildest nightmares, wanted to see. It seemed to have some kind of snakelike body, what looked like a crow's wings, each as big as a kitchen table, a bird's head with a curved beak and a fleshy crest like a rooster's comb, and a spiked and scaly tail. Its eyes were enormous and it kept turning its head, looking at us first with one eye and then the other. I couldn't tell whether or not it had feet, but I guessed not, since it seemed to be thrashing back and forth on the ground. *Hound*, was the thought that gripped me.

The Cloud Horses didn't shy, however, or bolt, which is certainly what I felt like doing, and I was startled to see that Wolf was leaning forward with a look of interest on his face. I was more than surprised. The thing would have made me feel queasy to look at even if I wasn't already suffering from motion sickness.

"What is it?" I think it smelled bad, too.

"A Cockatrice." I could tell from Wolf's tone that I was supposed to have known this.

"Uh-oh, that's bad, isn't it?"

"No cold winds from the west, and now you think a Cockatrice is an evil thing. Where do you humans get these ideas?"

That made me blink. It was true that humans did tend to assign abstract value to things, like dark being bad and light being good. Since I'd been introduced to the world of Faerie—sorry, I mean of the People—I thought I had a pretty good idea exactly where we got some of these ideas. But maybe Riders weren't the best people to explain that to.

I tried to look at the Cockatrice without prejudice. My nose wrinkled up. No, it was definitely ugly, even if ugly didn't mean evil.

At that moment the Cockatrice disappeared and in its place was the youngest Rider I'd ever seen. If human, I would have said he was twelve or thirteen, though he was already taller than me. He was a Moonward Rider, with jet-black hair hanging shaggy and loose down his back and brilliant green eyes. He was dressed completely in black—leather trousers, knee-high boots, sleeveless jerkin. I was surprised to see that he already bore a *gra'if* guard on his left arm.

"Did you see it? Did you see my Guide? I did it! I knew I could. My mother told me I should not try, but I *knew* I could." He was beside himself with excitement, and I pegged his age a little lower. But then I took in what he'd said.

"That was you? The Cockatrice?"

He nodded, still grinning from ear to ear. "My Guidebeast. I am Iceriver. My mother is Tree in Leaf."

Wolf introduced himself and then me, naming me a friend of the High Prince. Apparently, people knew that Cassandra had spent a long time among humans, and it wasn't too shocking for them to encounter one, so long as they thought I "belonged" to their Prince.

"It is an honor to meet a friend of the High Prince," the young Rider said. "I would greatly enjoy speaking to you about the Shadowlands, when your tasks permit it."

"Oh, sure. I mean, it would be an honor to share my knowledge with you."

"Tell me, Iceriver," Wolf said. "Do you know of this place," and he recited "'Far to the horizon the rocks and grasses, Far to the horizon the ravens fly.'"

"Of course. That's the Moor of Ravens. I can Move you there, or do you wish to Ride?"

"By all means Move us, if you are not tired from manifesting your Guidebeast."

Instead of answering, Iceriver stepped between our two Cloud Horses, put one hand on Wolf's left boot and one hand on my right.

CRACK!

"Behold, the Moor of Ravens."

Chapter Nineteen

NIK LED MOON AND ALEJANDRO up the stairs to find the outer office empty, and Elaine ensconced behind her desk.

"I sent the ladies home," she said, without shifting her eyes from the monitor she was watching. Nik looked for any signs of slackness in her face, any shakiness, but his friend seemed fine, her usual poised self. He knew that her last infusion of *dra'aj* should last Elaine a much longer time, now that she was becoming used to carrying it, but he checked her out just the same. *Yeah, and I should be doing the same for myself.*

"Do we still have a business?" Nik approached the desk.

"Sure, or we will have on Monday, once I've got all this organized to run without us." She made a final entry and looked up, looking past him to where Alejandro and Moon stood in the doorway.

"This is Walks Under the Moon," he said. "She's here to help us."

The Rider came forward with her hand outstretched. "Moon," she said.

"Great." Elaine gestured at the monitors. Two still ran news reports, Nik saw. "How handy are you with spreadsheets? I could really use one for—what is it?"

Moon was peering with great interest at what she could see on the monitor nearest her. "Are these 'spreadsheets'?" she said, turning back to Elaine, her gray eyes shining. "We do not read, or at least I do not. The Prince Guardian has been teaching me but," she waved at the monitor, "evidently not enough."

Elaine swallowed. "Okay, no problem. Fieldwork, it is." Her smile faltered. "What's up with you two? You look like you've seen a ghost."

"We have had a most unexpected encounter," Alejandro said, tilting his head to look Nik over. "And I have learned that Nik is a brave man."

"Hey," he said, lifting his hands when both Elaine and Moon raised their eyebrows at him. "Don't look at *me*. I was terrified the whole time."

"But you did not run. You stood your ground, and more, you functioned as mediator."

"Mediator?" Elaine came out from behind her desk. "With whom? Not one of the Hunt?"

"A Rider. A lieutenant of the Basilisk's." Alejandro turned to Moon. "Do you remember him from that time?"

Nik noticed that when Moon frowned, no wrinkles formed on her forehead. "I thought I did. He came to the Basilisk's guard within the last year or so."

Alejandro turned back to Elaine. "He found us in the Royal York, and had a proposition for us."

Elaine made for the door. "Hang on, this sounds like coffee might be needed." As she left the room, heading for the coffee works in the main office, Moon moved to a seat at one end of Elaine's small couch, Alejandro took the seat next to her, and Nik dragged over the upholstered client's chair from in front of the desk. Coffee must have been waiting in the thermal jug, because Elaine returned with jug, mugs, cream, and sugar on a tray before they had even settled in.

By the time they had finished pouring and passing the cream, Alejandro had filled Elaine in on their encounter.

Moon had her lower lip between her teeth. When she finally spoke, her voice was quiet. "I was not there for the beginning of this meeting. Manticore save me, they gave *dra'aj* oaths? There were rumors that the Basilisk had begun some special ordeal for anyone who was not a Sunward Rider, but no one would have thought of this."

Nik leaned forward, his elbows on his knees. "I didn't want to ask, but when Sunset mentioned this *dra'aj* oath, and Alejandro didn't say anything about it . . ."

"It's one of the minor Chants," Moon said. "The Basilisk had a number of People searching out such things." Moon suddenly bit her lip again, and looked away. "There are a number of these Chants, Minors or Smalls as they're known, which manipulate *dra'aj*," she said finally. "Cassandra—my sister—she speculated that the Hunt use a variation of it to take the *dra'aj* of others."

"Even in my day I had heard of such things, of course," Alejandro said. "But I had thought them the stuff of Songs."

"Like so much the Basilisk uncovered." Moon took a deep breath and straightened. "Your *dra'aj* swears the oath," she said, looking down at her clasped hands. "Not merely your heart, or your intention. Your very *dra'aj*. You cannot act against the oath, even if you would wish to."

"Whoa." Nik leaned back in his chair. He'd known it was serious, from the stricken look on the strange Rider's face, but there was something faintly sickening in the explanation. "Still, before I feel all sorry for them, I've got to keep in mind that they're asking for this world, *our* world, as their reward for helping us out."

Elaine set the sugar bowl back on the lacquered tray with a slight click. "When you say they asked for our world, is that such a bad thing? I mean, if these Riders want to live here? *They're* not going to feed on us."

"The High Prince might have to close the Portals to contain them." If Alejandro stirred his coffee any more, Nik thought, he'd wear through the cup. "Their oaths force them to fight against the Prince Guardian, and therefore against the High Prince as well."

"But if the Portals are closed," Nik continued, "What controls do *we* have on Riders? What stops them from just taking over?"

"Really? How many of them are there? No offense," Elaine nodded at the two Riders sitting on the couch. "But how much trouble can you cause against billions of us with your swords?—Oh!"

Nik sat back so abruptly he spilled coffee on his leg. Sitting on the couch, where Alejandro and Moon had been, were perfect replicas of Elaine and himself.

"We wouldn't be limited to swords," Moon said in an eerie but perfect facsimile of Elaine's voice. "We can use any weapons we like."

"And we have many you have never seen." As he spoke, Alejandro resumed his own appearance, but now he had an elegant goatee, and his hair was a darker red.

"'Nuke them from space,'" Elaine said under her breath. But she wasn't grinning, the way she usually did when she used this quote.

"Sure, if they're all in the same spot, but if they're not?" Nik put his mug down on the table and dabbed at his pant leg with a napkin, hoping the others couldn't see his hands shaking. He'd known they were fast, and of course they could Move, but he hadn't known they could change their appearance that much. You could be sitting in a room full of Riders and never know.

Except for Valory. She'd know. Who they were and where they'd been, and maybe where they were going to be. If only people would listen. And how safe would that make *her*?

"Let's not jump into the quicksand before we have to. How likely is any of this to happen?" Trust Elaine to be thinking ahead in an entirely different way. "Is this the kind of bargain that *could* be struck? It feels like the Pope dividing South America between the Spanish and the Portuguese. Don't humans get any say?"

Alejandro looked at Moon, and waited. That's right, Nik thought, she'd already said what she thought the High Prince might do.

Still, he wasn't sure he liked the look on Moon's face.

"Cassandra would wish to include you," she said. "But it is more complex than I led Sunset on Water to believe. It would not occur to most of the People that humans be consulted." She glanced at Alejandro and he nodded at her to continue. "Many regard humans as—well, as mythological creatures—as, I gather, we are regarded by you."

"Great, just great." Nik scrubbed his face with his hands.

"Sunset on Water accepted that Nik had the right to speak for humans. That is significant." Alejandro leaned forward and poured himself more coffee from the carafe. "I would say a bargain *can* be struck. The High Prince would not simply cede the Shadowlands unless the Hunt is dealt with."

But Nik was still watching Moon's face. "You're not so sure," he said.

"The Hunt is an old problem, one we have been living with for Cycles," Moon studied the surface of her coffee. Unlike the rest of them, she was still on her first cup. "As we speak, these forced followers of the Basilisk Prince are being hunted down and killed." She looked around, outer corners of eyes and lips turned down. "There has been no choice."

"But there is now." Elaine was nodding, as though she'd followed a legal argument through to its logical conclusion.

Alejandro was shaking his head. "The whole of the People fights with the High Prince, and eventually the Lands themselves will rise against her enemies." He looked around. "At least, that is what the Songs tell us."

"But it is because she is High Prince that my sister might act to spare the lives of Riders who are, after all, still her People." Moon shrugged. "If they can be forced through the Portals, as Sunset on Water says his squad was, they need not be killed." She contemplated Alejandro, almost as though she were measuring him. "You forget, while you were here, we have all lived through a civil war, and that is something she will work to avoid."

"Wait just a second." Chin in hand, Elaine was tapping her cheek with her index finger. "Right now the High Prince can't send us any soldiers—not unless we come up with the Horn. But these guys, who are already here, are willing to fight against the Hunt? How is this a bad thing?"

"Sure, but once the Hunt are gone, and the Portals are closed, what keeps these Riders honest? Why should *they* keep their hands off us, Ellie?" Nik had a lot more experience in dealing with nonhumans than Elaine had.

"But couldn't the High Prince make them swear to keep their side of the bargain?" Elaine looked from Alejandro to Moon and back again. "That's what they're doing right now, isn't it? Keeping their oaths?"

"But that is a *dra'aj* oath," Moon said. "Even if Cassandra had the

Chant to it, even if she would consider using it, a *dra'aj* oath can only be given once."

Elaine sat back in her chair, holding her cup in front of her, silently whistling through her teeth. Finally she nodded. "Okay. If the Hunt isn't stopped, none of this is going to matter to us. So we'll deal with the Rider problem if it ever comes. We don't even know that the High Prince will agree to speak with these new guys." She waited until Alejandro and Moon both nodded before continuing. "Okay. Now, if these Basilisk Warriors are open to negotiation, is there any way for us to negotiate with the Hunt?"

"No." Both Riders spoke at once.

Nik held up a finger, and Elaine, still blinking from the abruptness of the answer, turned to him. "Valory said they're addicts, that they're actually addicted to *dra'aj*." He glanced at the Riders, and they nodded. "You know what that means, Ellie. They're junkies. They'll do anything, say anything, and then won't feel bound by it. And, in any case, I don't see what *we* could offer them."

Moon looked from Nik to Elaine. "How is it that you have such a quick understanding of this curse? The High Prince has it as well, and the Guardian."

"Addiction is something known and understood in the Shadowlands," Alejandro pointed out. "Humans have lived with it for all of their history."

Elaine frowned. "I was hoping we could offer them controlled access to the *dra'aj* we—the Outsiders—use." She turned to Nik. "People are dying all the time, all over the world, so there must be lots of *dra'aj* we're not using. Surely we could offer them that? An orderly and organized use of the available resources?"

"You mean like in some countries where you can register and get your heroin or whatever from the government?" Nik said.

"Exactly."

Moon leaned forward, frowning, searching all their faces. "But why would they agree?" she said. "You speak as if you *could* control this access, as if you could stop them, or as if they needed you to find and provide *dra'aj* for them. Why would they care about controls? They believe the *dra'aj* here is limitless, they will not stop." Moon held her cup close to her, as if using it like a shield. "They cannot stop."

"Cows don't negotiate with us to provide milk," Nik said. His voice sounded hallow to his own ears. Elaine turned to him, the distress on her face replaced with determination.

"So some kind of treaty with these other Riders may be a smart move, if we can't negotiate with the Hunt." She nodded. "But if we also help to destroy the Hunt . . ." Her voice trailed off, and her eyes grew distant.

Nik brought his hands down on his knees. "Look, if we can destroy them without an assist from the Basilisk Warriors, so much the better. If we can't, we accept their help and hope we'll find some way out of that quicksand when the time comes."

"'Sufficient unto the day is the evil thereof,'" Elaine said. This time her smile was real.

"Yeah, exactly. So this new offer doesn't affect us, not really. We're still waiting to see if the Horn gets found." Nik paused, his thoughts still turning. "The Hunt can only be killed by a Rider—and a Rider who has *gra'if* at that." He looked at Alejandro. "What about injuring them? Slowing them down?"

The Rider was shaking his head, but as if he was thinking. "The Troll, Mountain Crag, drove one off with his hammers. So they *can* be injured." He looked at Nik. "Can you use a gun?"

"I have, sure. And with the newer ones it's fairly simple." He made a pistol shape with his hand. "Point and shoot. The trick is to get hold of one, not so easy in this country."

Alejandro waved this away. "For someone who can Move?"

"All right. Now we're talking. If Wolf and Valory come back with the Horn, we've got a weapon against the Hunt. Remove the threat of the Hunt, and we don't need any help from the other guys." The two Riders exchanged another look. "Or am I missing something?"

"Wolf's goals may not be identical to ours," Moon said.

"Wolf's okay—" Nik started to respond, but Elaine put up a hand and he subsided.

"What do you mean?" she said.

"Wolf means to offer the Hunt a chance to be Healed, as he was."

Nik was on his feet. "You mean *Wolf* is a Hound?" He leaned across the table toward Moon. "And you let him take Valory?" Alejandro was also on his feet, but froze when Moon clapped her hands, once, sharply.

"Sit down, both of you." She waited until they had. "Yes, Wolf was once a Hound. But he was cured by the High Prince herself. Cured, trusted, and made part of her *fara'ip*. Is it so surprising that he wishes to offer the same opportunity to those who stand in the same mire that once dirtied him?"

"What if they refuse Wolf's offer? They'd be destroyed then, wouldn't they?" Elaine asked.

"Like mad dogs," Nik said.

Moon frowned. "They are dogs, and they are mad." She looked up. "Wolf agreed."

Nik's cell rang—he didn't remember programming it with "Dance of the Sugar Plum Fairies"—and he fished it out of his pocket. "It's Hawk," he told the others. "We're at the office, but—"

A SNAP! of displaced air, and Hawk and Poco were in the room.

"Gee, lucky I already had company," Elaine said, getting to her feet.

"Your pardon, *señorita*." Hawk was suddenly next to her, kissing her hand. "I presumed—"

"Relax, I was joking, mostly."

Hawk, Elaine's hand held between his, searched her face. "You do not look as though you are finding much at which to laugh."

Poco nodded at Nik, his eyebrows slightly raised. Nik rolled his eyes, and was answered with a shrug. He supposed he would have to put up with everyone checking him over for the next little while. Poco propped himself against Elaine's desk, leaving the other client chair for Hawk.

Both Hawk and Poco switched their attention to Alejandro and Moon, but, after retrieving her hand from Hawk and sitting down, it was Elaine who spoke up. She'd had plenty of practice summing things up for courtroom digestion, and had the newcomers up to speed in no time.

"Which of us will take this Sunset's offer to the High Prince?" Alejandro said. Nik joined everyone else in looking at Moon and Hawk.

"When we are ready, I could easily go," Moon said. "But I suggest we delay. This Rider wants to meet with Nighthawk." She raised her eyes to look at the Sunward Rider. "You knew his father, and it's likely you would be able to make an assessment of him, and his offer."

Hawk nodded. "Then I should be on my way. I would like to get to the meeting point early."

"I'll come with you." Poco straightened to his feet. Poco was more relaxed than Nik had seen him in days. The time he'd spent with Nighthawk must have done something to improve his opinion of Riders.

Hawk, however, was shaking his head. "Better I should go alone. Whatever he may have said, Sunset on Water may speak more freely to me if there are no witnesses."

Poco shrugged and leaned on the desk again, crossing his arms.

Alejandro, however, got to his feet. "I shall return home, in case Wolf brings Valory there."

"Then I'll go with you," Nik said.

"It's just that I'm not sure how long it's been since I've eaten." I rubbed at my forehead with the thumb and fingers of my right hand. My left had a grip on the pommel that was making my knuckles numb. "I feel faint, but how much of that is the motion sickness, and how much is lack of food?"

"Whichever it may be, you are getting worse. Should I take you back to the Shadowlands so that you may at least eat?"

"Can you remember any more of the Song without me?" I knew the answer, but Wolf needed to know it, too. As it was, I'm pretty sure he started to say yes before doubt shadowed over his face. Fact was, he remembered every lyric perfectly once I gave it to him, but he couldn't remember what came next, no matter how hard he tried.

"I could bring you back. We would use another Portal, one where we could be somewhat sure that the Hunt does not await us, and return here, directly to this spot, with no time wasted."

I took a firm grip on my lower lip with my teeth. The temptation to agree was enormous. I was beginning to forget what it felt like not to be dizzy and nauseated. "What if I didn't make it? I'm a lot sicker this time." I remembered that Cassandra had said my illness could get worse each time I was exposed. I suppose I should have been thankful that on top of everything else I wasn't swelling up and itching. "Then where would you be?"

"Then we must find you some food that you can keep down." Wolf frowned. He looked around us, eyes narrowed, lips pressed together. We'd ridden across the Moor of Ravens, and were now on a rocky hillside covered with scraggly pine trees. It was autumn here; there were oak leaves on the ground, blown in from who knew where, and the grasses and plants between the trees were dry and browning. Where we were standing, in the sun, it was warm, but there was a not unpleasant chill to the air, as if winter was on its way.

"Is there a Solitary within sound of my voice?"

I was startled enough to almost let go of the pommel. Wolf waited a minute and called again.

"I am Stormwolf, on a task of the High Prince. Is there any who can hear me and answer?" Still nothing.

Wolf looked at me, frowning. "If there is a spirit in these trees, it is too young, or too wary to speak with us. And it appears there is no Troll or Ogre nearby."

I admit I felt relieved. The Cockatrice, cute as he'd turned out to be, had used up all the energy I had left for strange beings. "What did you want one for?"

"Riders usually find a Healer if they are sick or injured," he said. "The Wild Riders are an exception, but there are none here. Solitaries often suffer from the same kinds of illnesses and injuries that Riders do, but have other ways to treat them. I thought, if there was a Solitary near us, they could advise us what to feed a person who suffered as you do."

What do you give a person when there's a danger of vomiting, I wondered. Aside from a glucose IV. "Liquids," I said.

"But you are drinking water. Would you prefer ganje? Or wine?"

I remembered just in time not to shake my head. "No. I meant a clear broth, like you use for a soup. Beef, or chicken broth."

"That is not food, it is a flavoring."

"There's enough food in it, at least the way it's made in the Shadowlands."

Wolf pulled a dark green flask from his pack. "A broth? Made from a chicken? What else should it have?"

I tried to remember what Alejandro had told me. "Onions, carrots, celery. Peppercorns. Parsley. Rosemary. Thyme." What else? I remembered I was going to drink it, not use it for as a base for something else. "Salt, but not too much." Alejandro put in other things, I knew, leaves and stems and pieces of veggies that he saved in a bag in the freezer, but surely I'd covered all the essentials. I was afraid to ask for vitamins, since Wolf might not know what I meant—and frankly I wasn't so sure myself. I thought about my queasy stomach. "Skim most of the fat out. As much as you can manage." I swallowed. "That's all I can think of."

All the while I was talking, Wolf had the flask in his hands, turning it over in his strong fingers, humming, tapping it with his fingers almost as though he was playing a tune on it that only he could hear. "Fascinating," he said. "We do not cook here, we ask for what food we desire, and the container provides it. I would not have known what ingredients to ask for, to make sure it would be effective."

Finally, he turned the flask upright again, pulled the stopper out, and handed it to me. It was now about the size and shape of a soup thermos, made of some kind of stone, or opaque ceramic. It was cool on the outside, but the contents steamed, just enough to show that it was warm. I must have got the ingredients right, because the smell was astounding, taking me right back to the first time I'd smelled it, in Alejandro's kitchen in Madrid. I took an experimental sip. My stomach turned over and I swallowed again, two or three times, but then everything settled down once more. I managed six more sips before I handed the flask back.

"You have not taken much."

"Let's see if this stays down before I use up any more."

"There is as much here as we may need," he said as he replaced the stopper and tucked the flask away again.

Whether it was the broth itself, or just having something warm inside me, I did start to feel a bit better—enough so that after a while I asked for the flask again and drank more. I felt functional again, but I didn't get my hopes up. No one with seasickness has a career as a sailor; they either get over it, or they go ashore. Staying in the Lands wasn't something I could do for very long, no matter how good the broth was.

We had come to the end of the pine wood by this time and to the edge of what looked to me like pictures I'd seen of the prairies in

Canada. Tall grass as far as the eye could see. Though we couldn't feel anything here under the trees, there must have been a breeze, as the grass was moving, fitfully as though the wind was gusting.

"What are the next lines again?"

"'Green the waves are, gold and white. Clear the sky and the hot yellow sun,'" I said.

Wolf repeated the line and his Cloud Horse took a step forward, with mine following at its side.

Nothing happened. There was still nothing but grass in front of us. Wolf turned to me. "Have we missed a line?"

Gritting my teeth, keeping my grip on the pommel, I touched his wrist again. At first I thought I wasn't going to be able to concentrate, but finally I heard the Song once more, softly as though Wolf were singing it to himself. I found myself relaxing.

"No," I said. "Those are the next lines. We haven't missed any."

"This is no sea." Wolf breathed out through his nose and looked around, eyes narrowed, lips pressed tight.

I saw what he meant. "I could see green and white, or blue and white, but how can waves be golden—oh, for heaven's sake. 'Amber waves of grain.'" I rolled my eyes. I waved my hand at the prairie stretching out in front of us. "This *is* the Sea of *Ma'arban*. Not an ocean, not water, a sea of grass."

Now Wolf was smiling. "First green, then gold, then white, as the grass matures and dies. Very good, then we are still on the correct path. The Mountains of Ice Tor should be very close now. What are the next lines?"

"There are only four lines left," I said.

"Then give me them all."

"'Winter skies are icy dark,
Rocky hills around us lie.
Shadows born of Ice Tor fly
The caller of the Hunt.'"

This time Wolf sang the lines back to me, a strange tune, the music changing the emphasis of the lines a little bit.

"This is the fragment Moon knew," Wolf said. "Was it . . . Do you know if it was *my* Song?"

"No." I licked my lips. "But you learned it from the person who first Sang it."

He nodded, his eyebrows lifted slightly as if my answer hadn't been of any real importance, but I wasn't fooled. He'd been hoping the Song was his—his creation, his work. It would have meant he had something from before he'd become a Hound.

To the eye the Sea of *Ma'arban* stretched out to the horizon, but with Wolf Singing it took us only a few steps to leave it and find ourselves on a rocky plateau, bleak in the meager light. It was night, but the clouds obscured any stars that we might have seen, though a brighter spot showed where the moon was. A cold wind made our clothing flutter.

"I was expecting more snow," I said.

Wolf was looking around and now he nodded. "It certainly does not seem like an ice tor."

"Who speaks my name?"

Sunset on Water walked slowly along King Street, mentally reviewing the encounter he'd had with Graycloud and the human. He could have Moved back to his post, but he needed time to think, and the sidewalks here were strangely empty, something that matched his mood.

The encounter had gone well, he thought, due very likely to his great luck in meeting with a Rider who had lived here throughout the reign of the Basilisk Prince, and not one of the others. Someone who had suffered at the hands of the Basilisk, or who had always been loyal to the Prince Guardian, might not have listened to him, but Graycloud had chosen no sides in the recent conflict. Even the human had seemed disposed to consider his offer. There was more to the creatures than he had been led to believe, and Sunset began to hope that he and his fellows could find refuge here in the Shadowlands after all.

Who knew? Perhaps one day a way might even be found to free them of their *dra'aj* oaths, so that they could once again go home, perhaps even serve the Guardian—

Sunset stayed bent over until the terrible stabbing pain in his head eased. His lips were pulled back from his teeth when he straightened, though the smile had no humor in it. If even *thinking* of following the . . . person in question brought on such a reaction, how likely was it he and his fellows could be helped?

"Headache?"

It was all Sunset could do to stifle the startled jump he had almost given. When he turned around to see the Hound standing behind him—what was her name again?—he judged from the smirk on her face that she knew anyway.

"Pack Leader wants to see you," she said.

Sunset glanced at the angle of the light, hoping she couldn't hear his heart rate increase. "It's early."

"Yeah, well. I just got sent with the message, like."

Sunset shrugged. Now that he was over being startled, his stomach settled back down. He'd seen all he needed to see of what the Hounds were like before the Basilisk Prince fell. Not very quick, mentally speaking. Nothing to worry about for someone like him.

"Where?"

"At the den."

"I can Move us there." As Sunset expected, the Hound shook her head. The Hounds had made it clear they did not want Riders to Move them, though Sunset had yet to find out why. Still, the Hunt was swift, and he anticipated no trouble in keeping his appointment with Nighthawk. The Sunward Rider had been part of his father's *fara'ip*, and as such had to be given his father's last words.

Memories of his father—however had he become *fara'ip* with a Sunward in the first place?—occupied Sunset on the way back to Fox's den. Just as well, he thought, as he followed his guide inside through the boarding and then up the massive staircase—torn open along one side—of the building. There would not have been any point in making conversation with the Hound. Even though they mostly kept to a Rider form now, and mimicked the ways of real Riders, they were still little better than animals.

So when he was knocked to his knees and held, facedown in the grime and dust of the human-made rock floor, Sunset was too surprised at first to even speak.

"Who'd you meet with?"

Sunset shut his eyes, concentrating, before he realized that the clamps that held his hands, elbows and ankles were not rope, but hands—misshapen but strong. If he Moved, his captors would Move with him. Another hand grasped him by the hair and pulled his face around until he could see Fox, squatting on his heels, and looking down at him. The Pack Leader was smiling, his forearms propped on his knees. Sunset said nothing.

"Really? That's the way you're going to play it? You think we can't tell you were talking to Riders, and one of their scent-free stooges? You think we can't smell them on you?"

"I would have told you, given the chance."

"Have I already said 'Really?' 'Cause if I haven't, right now I'd be saying 'Really?'" Fox glanced at the female Hound who'd come in with Sunset, and she shook her head.

"Heading entirely the other way," she said, with a toothy grin of her own.

"So, *not* on your way to tell me what you talked about." Fox pressed his face closer to Sunset's. "Not that I really need to be told, do I?"

Sunset fought not to shut his eyes. Fox's breath was cold, and smelled of meat just beginning to go off. *Say nothing*, he told himself. *Say nothing*.

"Tried to make a deal with the High Prince's Riders, didn't you? What did they say?" Fox blinked at him. "Cat got your tongue? Would this loosen it any?"

When Fox moved out of his field of vision, Sunset could see what the Pack Leader had been blocking. There, sitting in a row, trussed with living bonds exactly like his own, were three of his men. Three of the seven who'd come through the Portal with him. And the others?

"Same deal." Even as the words left his mouth, Sunset inwardly cursed. He should have kept silent. "To leave us the Shadowlands. Same thing you asked for. Show them we are allies." He had to force the words out. Was it worth trying? He was certain Fox would kill them anyway.

"You asked for the same deal? To prove to them that we're allies?"

Sunset nodded his head as best he could.

"Tell you what. Let's make sure we really *are* allies." Fox got to his feet and made a gesture Sunset could not make out from his position. Then the Hounds holding his men dragged them forward, and the Hounds holding him shifted their grips—not enough to help him, he very quickly discovered.

"Don't knock him out!" Fox said. "I want him awake for this."

Hands, cold hands, hands with long claws, and scratchy scales, loosened his clothing. Other paws pushed the hands of his men flat against Sunset's bare skin. They felt warm, callused. He smelled jasmine, spring water, and diamonds.

He heard Fox's voice. The Pack Leader was Singing, but Sunset could not make out the words he used. As the Song continued, the hands pressed to his skin grew colder—no, Sunset realized it was the patches of his skin that grew cold. Very cold. Fox Sang, and the coldness spread, and the hands that had been struggling to pull away no longer struggled, and the coldness spread, and the shhhhhhhh of noise in his head did not disguise the growls and the howls that arose around him and the last thing he heard before the coldness claimed him was the clear notes of three new howls.

Nighthawk waited at the bar in Hair of the Dog until the sun was well and truly down. *Fara'ip* with his father or not, it was clear that Sunset on Water was not coming. Hawk finished his glass of beer, tipped the young man behind the bar, and walked out into the street. The shell of Maple Leaf Gardens sat across the street. Sunset had said something about the Hunt having a den nearby, was that it? Had something occurred to make the other Rider think the pub was not, in fact, a safe place to meet? Where might he have gone instead? Hawk checked the angle of the sun, and Moved.

Fox pressed his face against the doorjamb and inhaled. Here in the hallway there were plenty of smells. The stuff they used to clean the carpets and walls, plus traces of the cleaners themselves. Behind everything, coming from inside the door, was Wolf's scent, unmistakable, even though his brother wasn't here, and hadn't been for some time.

And out here in the hall, here Fox could smell Sunset on Water, and the old Rider, Graycloud, along with another Rider he didn't know, and the weird absence of smell that was one of the scentless humans, just like River and Badger said.

Not that he hadn't believed them—the proof was in the den. One

Faded Rider, and three new Hounds. He'd told River and Badger to bring humans in for them. They were too new to be trusted in the streets by themselves.

He turned back again to the door, got a good grip on the handle, and twisted. That had broken every lock he'd found so far in the Shadowlands. The handle broke off with a satisfying snap, but the door didn't open. Fox peered at the edge of the door. He fitted the (flicker) tips of his claws into the gap between door and jamb and heaved.

Nothing. (flicker) He breathed fire, scorching the wood, but still the door wouldn't let him past.

"Lost your key?"

Fox whirled around, the fires still burning hot within him. Something had to be broken. Something had to pay.

"You are not Stormwolf." The Sunward Rider's eyes narrowed.

This was a Rider. A Rider surprised to see him—and with a *gra'if* blade in his hand. And the smell of *dra'aj*, thick, luscious, and heady. Rage ignited in his belly. (flicker) Fox let his smile stretch out, displaying teeth that could not fit in his original mouth, and leaped, but the *gra'if* blade swung, faster than fast, and he barely managed to dodge it in time. His tail lashed. (flicker) "Did you come for him, the traitor?" he asked. "You're too late. He's paid his price." The Rider's scent burned him further, churning the air in his lungs. Nighthawk, this was Nighthawk.

The bright point of the killing blade hung in the air between them. "Traitor to whom? Who would ally with such as you?"

"I'm Foxblood, Leader of the Hunt, I'm your death, Sunward one." Fox flickered, lunging for the Rider's legs, but it was a feint only, and he regained his position by the door. "Are you one of the ones holding Wolf's leash? Are you? Are you ordering him around? Using my brother like your hunting dog?"

"Your brother?"

"My brother. You might have him tricked and docile now, but I'll get him back. You wait and see." Fox could not stop his voice from rising until he was almost shouting. This time he flickered in mid lunge, diving under the blade and pinning the other against the wall.

The Sunward shrugged him off with a great heave of his shoulders, and the blade flashed. Fox stifled a shudder at the shimmering of *gra'if*. It could follow him, the only metal that could, through any change, so the wound wouldn't flicker away. (flicker) He restored his Rider form and Moved behind the prey, putting it between him and the impassable door. As the Rider spun to face him once more, Fox debated whether he should simply Move away from here. But the scorched door still laughed at him, taunting him. And the smell of *dra'aj* still pulled at him. (flicker) Fox's shoulders took on heft and his hands and feet became clawed. His neck elongated and darted in for a bite at the Rider's unprotected flank. The prey moved, but not quite fast enough to strike back before Fox withdrew.

He couldn't Move in this form, any more than he could talk. (flicker) Smaller, winged, he took to the air to dodge another thrust from the blade, this time landing a blow of his own with a (flicker) heavy tail the Rider did not expect. The other was quick, very quick. (flicker) Hooves struck face and shoulders, blood spattered. Whose was it? Fox thought he was okay, it wasn't his blood. (flicker) Coils of scaly hide thrown around legs but not quite knocking the other down before a (flicker) change to rear back from the deadly glimmering blade.

Closer. Dodge. He could taste the other's *dra'aj*. Closer. Duck. He flickered through three more changes, and still the *gra'if* was there, always, always in front of him. He threw back his head and howled.

Three of his Pack appeared, one behind Fox and the other two behind the Rider. As soon as they saw the trouble, they lost the Rider forms that had let them Move and closed in for the kill. One—who was it?—drew back immediately, the stump of a severed leg dripping blood on the carpeting. The other dove for the Rider's legs, and Fox rushed in, shouldering him up against the door that would not open, casting the barbed whip of his tail around his arm and binding the blade still. And looked the prey in the eyes.

At that moment Fox would've liked to talk, oh, how he would've liked to, to tell this Rider how wonderful his *dra'aj* smelled, and how exquisite it tasted. But to speak he'd have to become a Rider again, and the prey might escape. Slowly, as slowly as he could, Fox squeezed, and squeezed, and squeezed. Until the *gra'if* blade fell to the floor.

Humming, Fox sank his razor teeth into the Rider's chest and inhaled, groaning as a wash of light passed through him, lifting him on a radiance of color, of warmth, of utter contentment and joy.

All too quickly the body in his upper limbs was a body, indeed. Fox hooked the wristband from the limp arm and let the body drop to the floor, watched it as it Faded completely, and the deadly blade with it, until not even the blood was left on the carpet.

The others of his Pack, Badger was one, were Riders again, helping the injured one, who still bled from its severed arm.

"Pack Leader?" Badger knew what had to be done, but she also knew enough to ask for permission. He nodded, and the other two fell on the injured one.

Fox turned his head to focus one of his eyes on the item caught in his claws. He knew just where this could be left. Let the other Riders know there'd be no separate bargains. That treaties would be made only with him. Only with the Hunt. Fox shifted, his (flicker) form growing larger and then smaller as he thought. He couldn't take the form of a dog; he would lose the wristband. He must regain his own form. It was the only other way to avoid notice. The *dra'aj* of a human would fix him.

Fox wondered if the other doors in this building would prove to be as hard to open as this one.

Once again the rush of adrenaline settled my stomach and cleared my head. If only I could tell who, or what, had spoken, and from where, my happiness would have been complete.

"I am Stormwolf," Wolf said, speaking slowly and distinctly. I was impressed that his voice didn't shake. It was all I could do to draw in a steady breath. It was hard to tell where the inquiry had come from. "My mother was Rain at Sunset, and the Chimera guides me. My companion is a human from the Shadowlands, a Truthreader, and friend to the High Prince."

"Did Truthsheart send you?"

Wolf hesitated, catching my eye before answering. "We are on a task she has set, which has brought us here."

There was slow movement in front of us, as if the ground itself was heaving. *What kind of beast is* this *going to be?* I thought, trying to keep an open mind. *Ugly doesn't mean evil.* A rasping sound, a flare of brightness, and I blinked at the sudden light.

It wasn't a beast holding the torch, however, but a man. Sort of.

He wasn't in the sandstorm's league, but when he finished standing up, he was fully tall enough to play basketball anywhere in the world, though it was unlikely any professional team would have taken him, seeing that he was almost as wide as he was tall. No matter where you looked—hands, shoulders, face, nose—the word "massive" kept coming to mind. His hair was long enough to touch his shoulders, iron gray, and bound around his forehead with a black ring that shone like metal in the light of the torch. His beard was short, as if he hadn't been growing it for very long. Rather than trousers, he was wearing what in the human world would have been called a kilt, though it wasn't pleated, and had no tartan pattern to speak of.

"And your task is to me, Younger Brother?"

Wolf dipped his head in what was very close to a bow. "Elder Brother, I look for Ice Tor, where the old Songs tell that the Horn of the Hunt was once made."

His laugh was loud enough to make the Cloud Horses snort. "I am the dwarf Ice Tor," he said. "A 'who' and not a 'where,' Young One, so your task is indeed to me."

"You're a dwarf?" I swallowed hard when they both turned to look at me. "It's just that dwarf means small where I come from."

He laughed again, but this time I was prepared for it. "I must go there sometime, and see if I can change their minds. But what is it you require of me, Younger Brother?"

"The Horn of the Hunt."

"The Hunting Horn?" He sat down on a nearby rock and I saw how it was we hadn't seen him in the first place. Without the torch in his hand, he could easily be mistaken for one of the many boulders that surrounded us. "There was one made, nine Cycles ago, or more. I cannot make another, if that one still exists."

"We believe that it does not," Wolf said. "The Basilisk Prince was wearing it around his neck when he was killed on *Ma'at*, the Stone of Virtue."

"Not very virtuous, then, was he?" The huge Solitary laughed again, but more quietly this time. My head thanked him. "But come, I will have to check what you say. It is convenient that you brought a Truthreader with you."

He turned and led us away into the dark. I never realized before that a torch is not a very efficient lighting tool. You can't aim it, and you can't focus it. This one was large enough to illuminate quite a piece of ground around us, but that's all it illuminated, we were walking in a circle of light that moved with us, gaining ground to the front, while losing it in the rear. Finally, we seemed to be walking down a passage that may have seemed narrow to Ice Tor, but was nice and wide for Wolf and me, even with the horses. The rock walls grew higher and higher, but it wasn't for quite some time that they roofed us overhead. Ice Tor doused the torch, though I didn't see how, and walked on, using it now as if it were a walking stick.

I could still see, as the walls around us seemed to be covered with a kind of velvet moss that gave off a warm green glow. The light was restful, and my headache faded a bit. I was wondering what I was going to do when we got to where we were going and Ice Tor expected me to get down off the Cloud Horse. My thighs and lower back would have been quite happy to feel the ground under them, but I remembered how awful I'd felt the last time I tried it.

At last we arrived at what looked like a workshop for giants, or maybe the god Hephaestus' foundry, take your pick. There was a half-finished statue of what might have been a Water Nymph, and a huge wooden wheel with the rim off and a spoke missing—and that was just what I could recognize as we swept past. He took us through doors at the far end into a room that was smaller only by comparison, and furnished, oddly, like a reading room in a library. Though the shelves seemed to be stocked with toys, not books.

"Bring your horses this way, Younger Brother, they will be happier waiting here, I think." We followed him through yet another archway to the right of the entrance we'd come in by and found ourselves standing outside in a meadow in the early morning under an April sky. The air smelled pleasantly of a recent rain, and the Cloud Horses signaled their delight with head shaking, and pawing at the ground with their hooves.

I eyed the same ground with trepidation. Wolf explained my situation to our host. "Being on the Cloud Horse calms her condition."

"Come, Young One." The dwarf stood next to my Cloud Horse and held out his arms. "I will carry you back inside."

"I'll read you," I said. "When you touch me." I wasn't sure who I was warning.

"I care not for that. We Dwarves are not frightened by the idea of truth."

I swallowed, nodded, and reached out for him. He guided my arm around his neck and lifted me from the horse's back. For a moment I was a small child again, in my father's arms. Images swept over me, but slowly, as if I were being lowered into a warm bath.

[Great age. Great humor. Greater curiosity. Insatiable curiosity. The items on the shelves are copies, some of them miniature, of all the artifacts he's made; armor, jewelry, houses, mountains, shoes that could Move, a comb that you only needed to use once and your hair would be perfect forever.]

I was nervous when he put me down, but the world stopped its yaw and spin. I actually had to put my hand to the back of a chair—a perfect size for me. I had become so used to the feeling of motion that now the stillness seemed strange. Welcome, but strange.

"Wow," I said. "You fixed me."

"Yes, in a manner of speaking. You are now fixed in place."

"So, will I be all right from now on?" I was thrilled, not only that I felt comfortable for the first time in what seemed like days, but at the thought that now I would be able to come back and forth—but he was shaking his head.

"Stormwolf tells me it is the Lands themselves that give you this sickness, by their very nature. You are not Healed, rather this place is not, in the normal sense of the word, part of the Lands."

Wolf paused halfway to sitting in his chair. "Where are we, then?"

Ice Tor tapped himself on the forehead. "In my home and workshop. It is the only place I can make you comfortable."

Wolf shot a quick look at the doorway we'd come in by. "How is this possible?"

"We are the artificers of the People. We Dwarves and the Trolls. It is Dwarves and Trolls who make the *gra'if* you Riders bear, and your bowls and jars and baskets and containers. It is told, in Songs older even than I am myself, that it was Dwarves who made the Talismans—Sword, Spear, and Cauldron—from the rock of the Stone of Virtue."

"You can bend space and time," I said. I turned to Wolf. "Didn't you say that the Hunt would answer the call of the Horn, no matter where they are? Even though they can't Move? This is how, because

Ice Tor made it." I turned back to our host. "You made the Portals," I said. "Oh! And the Rings. Not you, personally, but someone close to you, like a parent or a grandparent. Someone like you."

"You *are* a Truthreader, good. That will make my work much easier, then. What else did you see? What else have we made, my People and I?"

"You made—oh, no," I almost couldn't say it. "You made the *Shadowlands*?"

"Cassandra? What is it?" Max rolled over and a light came on over the bed. "Bad dreams?"

Cassandra shivered and allowed Max to draw her into his arms. "No. At least . . . you know that I told you I could feel Moon's *dra'aj*, and Wolf's, and even to some extent, Valory's?"

"Sure."

"Well, now I can't. Wolf and Valory, they're gone."

Max sat up. "Back to the Shadowlands, maybe?"

"No, they're just gone."

Chapter Twenty

"ALEJANDRO, THERE'S A WATCH on the deck." Frowning, Nik leaned closer to the window, squinting through glass and screening.

Alejandro appeared in the doorway from the kitchen, a bottle of wine in his hand.

"It wasn't there a minute ago, when the cat wanted in."

The Rider's eyes narrowed, and he set the bottle down on the marble-topped table. There was the barest shush of air, and he was standing next to Nik again, this time with the watch in his hand. "It is not mine," he said, as he set it down on Nik's palm.

Nik turned it over. "This is a really old Seiko," he said. "See the dark face?" The metal was cool. Nik weighed it in his hand before handing it back. "I think it's Hawk's."

"How can that be?"

Nik shrugged. "I noticed it particularly. I used to have one like it, and when I saw Hawk wearing it, I was reminded."

"Hawk would not have returned to leave this trinket and go again without a word." Alejandro turned the watch over. There was engraving on the back, but Nik couldn't read it from where he stood. "It must have been taken from him."

"And then brought here? What for?" Nik swallowed. "Some kind of message?"

"But from whom? Even if there had been a confrontation, if Hawk somehow enraged Sunset on Water and was killed, why would it be revealed to us in this way?"

Nik eyed the bottle of wine. He could use something stronger. "Could it be the Hunt? Maybe they captured him and this is some kind of message? Their way of letting us know?"

Alejandro, head tilted to one side, set the watch down and picked up the bottle of wine again. Nik followed him back into the kitchen, watched as he took a corkscrew from its hook among the other kitchen utensils. The cork was out, and the wine poured almost before Nik was ready to take the glass handed to him. Before he raised it, Alejandro had already tossed his back, and was pouring himself another.

"I hope this isn't the good stuff," Nik said.

Alejandro grimaced and refilled his glass. "The People have always thought of the Hunt only as unreasoning beasts, a living hunger." Alejandro took a more careful sip of his second glass, and this time Nik joined him. "It is hard to keep in mind that we must think of them as rational creatures, capable of planning. But if leaving this watch here is somehow a message, an opening of negotiations, even if only for ransom, why would there not *be* a message?"

Nik thought of Moon, and the computer monitors in Elaine's office. "*Can* they write?"

Alejandro looked down at the wine in his glass. "Hawk can, if he were still alive."

Nik's mouth was suddenly dry, and somehow he knew the wine wasn't going to help. "Yeah, but they wouldn't trust what he'd said, would they? So they wouldn't let him write anything." The hope on Alejandro's face was almost as painful to see as it was to feel. He reached out and tapped the watch. "If Valory were here, she could tell us what's going on."

"Ah, no, we did not make the Shadowlands. Not exactly." Again there was a deep rumble of laughter in the Dwarf's chest. "We make *things*, we Dwarves, objects, even doors, like the Rings and the Portals. *Places* we cannot make, that takes other skills, other talents. Though we did help to make the Shadowlands what they now are. So the Songs told, at least, and I am gratified to have it confirmed in so far as you can do so. These events took place so long ago that even the existence of the Songs that tell of them has been forgotten, the Singers who Sang them long gone, remembered only vaguely by some of us very Old Ones. And the Songs tell that the fixing of the Shadowlands in its place was not done by Dwarves and Trolls alone, but by all of the People, Riders, Solitaries, Naturals. All of us."

We were in that strange sitting room, or study, Wolf leaning forward in his chair, his clasped hands hanging between his knees, me sipping on my chicken broth, taking advantage of the steadiness of my stomach. I thought about asking who I had to kill for a bacon and tomato sandwich, but I knew I shouldn't risk it.

"I had always thought the Shadowlands to be exactly that," Wolf said. "A *shadow* version of the Lands."

Sheesh, I thought. No wonder humans weren't very important to them. Who cares about the welfare of their shadow?

"Not at all," Ice Tor was saying. "What we call the Shadowlands always existed, separately from the Lands. But the two, separate, were unstable. Together," he moved his hands as if they were the plates on a scale.

"Yin and Yang," I said. "A balance," I added when they both looked at me. "Black and white, light and dark, male and female."

"Exactly. Each anchors the other. Each contains some part of the other within it."

"*Dra'aj*," I said. "That's why human *dra'aj* works differently for us." I'd read some of this when he'd picked me up in his arms; I just hadn't understood what I was seeing. "My world is like the foundation of a building. It was crumbling, and *dra'aj* was poured into it, like humans would pour cement, or put rebar in." I thought about it. "So if we're the foundation, is the Lands the building?"

The Dwarf waggled his massive finger at me. "Now you see the problem with trying to take an analogy too far."

Ice Tor was grinning, but Wolf was frowning intently at his

clasped hands. "All this is very interesting, and I would love to hear more about the Songs that tell of these events, but we are here for another purpose."

"Ah, yes, the Horn." Ice Tor rose to his feet and led us through a doorway I hadn't seen before into a different section of his home. Not that any of the doorways actually contained doors, I noticed. The new room looked much more like a workshop than the first one we'd passed through, though now that I looked more closely, the unfinished statue and the broken wheel were in here as well. It was more like the room itself had changed. There were tools and objects I thought I recognized from seeing them on television. Hammers and sledges, cutters, clamps, carving tools. Other things looked familiar, like the forge fire that glowed to one side, but I couldn't have sworn to what they were.

Ice Tor went first to the shelves on the far side of the room, returning with what looked like a piece of tree branch in his hand. I saw, when he laid it on the table, a piece of a deer's antler. *Horn*, I said to myself.

"Really?" I said aloud. "Just that simple?"

"Just that *symbol*," he said, laughing the way punsters always do. I wrinkled my nose and stuck out my tongue in the approved manner of those receiving puns, and the Dwarf laughed louder. "Go on, touch it and tell me what you feel."

Wolf put out his hand as if to stop me, but when I raised my eyes to look at him, he lowered his hand again.

"We've got to know," I said, and he nodded, but his lips were pressed tightly together.

I laid the tips of my fingers on the piece of antler and, as I suspected, felt only the cool, slightly uneven surface of bone. I didn't move my hand at all, I didn't have to. This wasn't a symbol anymore. It wasn't anything.

"There's nothing there," I told them, lifting my hand away, and jumped back, startled, as the antler suddenly disappeared. It was like it had never been there in the first place. Even my fingers didn't remember the feel of it.

"So you are right, Younger Brother. The Horn is no more, and another may be made."

Ice Tor went to a clear area on a central bench, and began pulling objects toward him, among them a hammer as long as my arm, and some tongs. Directly in front of him, he placed what looked like a mortar and pestle made of some pale gray stone.

"The more elements an object contains," he said, sorting through a number of lids until he found one that would fit the mortar, "the stronger it is, the more often it can be used without wearing out or breaking." He turned to look at us as he strapped on an apron. I was immediately reminded of Alejandro in the kitchen. "The first Horn had many elements, so many that, from what you tell me, it took the Dragon fire of the new High Prince to destroy it—that and the use to which it had been put."

"It was used to summon the Hunt." Wolf was clearly puzzled. He had pulled up a couple of high stools for us to sit on. Obviously, Ice Tor was used to having an audience. "What other use has it?"

"It gathers the Hunt, yes. And who holds it can lead them. But what use was then made of the Hunt by the Basilisk Prince?"

I could tell by the look on his face that Wolf wasn't following, and I have to say I wasn't in much better state. "But did he not use them to hunt?" Wolf said. "To find and kill his enemies?"

"Ah, but was that the true use of the *Horn*?" Ice Tor said. "Such a Horn is used to call, and to direct, as are the horns of war. Some say this Horn is older than the Hunt, some say it was originally conceived as a tool to control the Hunt. In either case, it was used to lead them to a place where they would not be a danger."

Wolf looked at me, but I shook my head. "I can't know," I said. "Not without touching the Horn itself, or at least someone who's touched it."

"And no such person is available to us." Ice Tor gestured with his tongs to underscore his point.

"Why was the Horn not used to destroy them?" Wolf was completely flummoxed. I had to admit, having seen them in action, that I agreed with him. Besides, locking an addict away somewhere, with no cure and no access to the drug they craved, didn't strike me as the best kind of solution.

I was reminded once again that Riders—and perhaps the rest of the People—didn't always think in humanitarian terms.

"That I cannot say. Some discord, perhaps, some disagreement? No record remains of the Horn's use. It was lost for many Cycles, and the Hunt dormant, until the Basilisk Prince located it and called them. The details of its original purpose may well have been lost to us."

"But not how to make one," I said.

He grinned again, clearly happy at the thought of building something, and I noticed how square and even his teeth were. "No, not how to make one. That knowledge is still with us."

"So you are . . ." Wolf cleared his throat. "The Song that led us here told that Ice Tor made the Horn, so . . ."

The Dwarf laughed aloud, so infectiously that even Wolf smiled. "No, no Younger Brother. I am not *that* Ice Tor, otherwise I could answer all and any of your questions about the Horn. I am *this* Ice Tor." He thumped himself on the chest. "Any who lives here," the sweep of his arm indicated the whole of his living space, but I noticed he kept his other hand on his chest. "Any who occupies this space is Ice Tor."

But manipulating space—and time—was what Dwarves did, I thought. Was it possible that this huge Solitary, this old/young giant Dwarf both was and was not the Ice Tor who had made the original Horn? Perhaps without being aware of it himself? I wanted to touch him again, to find out, but I was also afraid, not sure that the answer wouldn't overwhelm me.

He clapped his hands together. "So, what elements did you bring me?"

Wolf and I looked at each other. "Um, what elements were you hoping for?" I said.

"For a Binding, or Summoning, object—such as this one—a piece of the thing or Person to be bound or summoned is customary."

"Where would we get a piece of a Hound?" I said. "And if we were able to fetch one, why would we even need a Horn?" I glanced at Wolf and the look, bordering on despair, that sat on his face was heartrending. "Oh, no, Wolf. That can't be what he means."

"Stormwolf is not a Hound," Ice Tor said warily. "He would not have been able to enter here if he was."

I wondered if they knew what DNA was, and if they didn't, whether I could explain it to them. "I know, but he *was* a Hound," I said. Wolf stiffened, but instead of looking away, as I expected him to, he kept his head up, and looked the Dwarf in the eye. "And I'm maybe the only person who knows it and isn't freaked out by it." My voice sounded sharp even to me. It was so easy to be frustrated by people who couldn't *know*. I turned to the Dwarf. "If I can read the things that Wolf knew before he became a Hound by touching him, then the part of him that was a Hound is still there as well. So won't something of his do?" I thought about the things I'd read about spells and enchantments. "Hair? Fingernails?"

The Dwarf nodded, scratching his chin. "There is only one way for us to know." Was his smile a little toothier than it had been a few moments before? "But other elements, similar in nature, are also needed. Those who require the artifact must contribute also. For the original Horn, contributions came from each of the People: Rider, Solitary, and Natural. Have you a piece of live wood from a Tree Natural? Voluntarily given, of course. Or water from a living spring or fountain?"

I was wondering what I'd done with the walking stick Wolf had got for me when he spoke.

"Water we have, in my pack." He started to get down off the stool, but Ice Tor held up his palm.

"Allow me." He lifted a small trapdoor I hadn't noticed on the surface of his workbench and reached in, pulling out a blue ceramic bottle I recognized as part of the supplies Wolf had picked up at the hostel where we found the Cloud Horses. When he saw us both staring, he grinned again. "Doorways, my Young Ones, doorways. Always a specialty of mine." He unstoppered the bottle and poured the water drop by drop into the pestle, counting under his breath as he did.

He restoppered the bottle, placed it back into the opening in the table, and closed the trapdoor. This time I looked, and there was definitely no sign of a door on the tabletop. He dusted off his hands.

"Have you anything else?" When we shook our heads, he gave a sharp nod. "Well, we have a Natural here," he tapped the pestle, "and a Hound." He pointed at Wolf. "I am myself a Solitary, but what shall we do for a Rider?"

"What about—" but just as I was about to say "me," Wolf's hand flashed out and closed on my wrist. *That's going to leave a bruise*, I thought.

"This comes from Walks Under the Moon," Wolf said. He took

off the bracelet made from Moon's hair and set it down in the center of the Dwarf's enormous palm. Ice Tor placed the bracelet into the mortar and looked at us again.

"And now you, my houndling."

Wolf's sloe-black hair, cut fashionably short when we were in my world, had reverted to its natural state here, hanging halfway down his back, partly loose, and partly made up of small braids used to restrain the loose part. He sorted out a braid a little thicker than a pencil and held it out.

"Have you scissors?" he asked.

"Younger Brother." Ice Tor's voice was solemn and deep. "We used the Rider's hair because that is all we have of her. From ourselves we must have something stronger, or the magic will not work."

Wolf's eyes narrowed, and his lips thinned. I remember something Alejandro had told me, about there traditionally being a level of distrust between Riders and Solitaries. That distrust was clear on Wolf's face. "Something stronger?" he said, his tone full of skepticism.

"He's not lying," I said. "Or trying to trick us. What he says is the truth."

"Thank you, Young One," he said. "I knew it would be good to have a Truthreader with us, and so again I am proved right." He turned to Wolf. "But to offer my own proof, to show you that what your friend says is correct, I will give first."

He picked up a tool that was half wooden handle and half metal so bright I couldn't focus on it. It had a familiar shape, however, and when I realized what it was my heart went cold in my chest. I opened my mouth, but my protest came out at the same time that the blade flashed down. I shut my eyes, my hands jerking up to cover them, but I couldn't prevent myself from looking.

Not his hand, not his hand. The words kept racing through my brain in relief. At first I didn't see anything at all, and then I noticed something that looked like a sausage, and my hands came up again, this time to cover my mouth.

His finger. Ice Tor had chopped off the pinkie finger of his left hand. There was very little blood, though I don't know what I was comparing it to, since I'd never seen anyone chop off a finger before.

"It is a *gra'if* tool." Ice Tor's voice was so calm that my escaping breath came out in a giggle. Both of them immediately looked at me with concern on their faces, and I clamped my hands tighter. "It will heal quickly. See?" He held out his hand and I couldn't look away, even though I desperately wanted to. He was right, though, the wound was already shut, scar tissue had grown over it, and was already fading to a pale color.

"Chimera guide me," Wolf breathed next to me.

"So this would be why so little *gra'if* is made? And borne by so few people?" I said.

"Something like this, yes." The Dwarf's voice was gentle.

I thought of Alejandro's sword, and Wolf's. I thought of Cassandra, in her *gra'if* mail gloves, with their tiny scales, the shirt that showed in the neck of her top, and the torque around her neck. I shivered. "But people don't lose their, their body parts to make *gra'if*," I protested. "At least . . . do they?"

"It is usually blood," Wolf said, his voice sounding stronger now.

"The *gra'if* uses blood, of course, and not body parts. Nor is there any guarantee that there will be regrowth of the blood while, for this, a Healer could put me right if I require it."

"And that is why many do not survive the process of making *gra'if*." Wolf wasn't asking.

"That is why, Younger Brother. Not," he turned to me, "as many believe, because we Solitaries are not to be trusted. There is no way to know who will survive the process until it has begun."

"Truthsheart." Wolf's words were just a whisper.

"Sword of Truth, High Prince of the Lands and the People, bears more *gra'if* than any other living Rider." Ice Tor shrugged. "She is High Prince."

"But she had the *gra'if* already, when she went to be Warden of the Exile, she has borne the *gra'if* since then."

"She is High Prince," the Dwarf repeated.

Wolf looked at him quietly, steadily, before finally smiling. He got down off his stool and took the two steps that put him right against the edge of the table. It was far too tall if he'd been wanting to use it as a worktable, but it was just the right height for him to rest his bent arm comfortably along the flat surface. He could have been leaning on one of those little serving ledges that go along the walls of pubs, at the right height to hold your pint or your elbow.

I slipped off my own stool to stand beside him. I started to slip my arm around him, to comfort and support him, but he shied away.

"No, Valory, no." He smiled and there was gratitude in his eyes. "You cannot. Think what you might see, what you might feel."

I licked my lips. "If you need me—"

"No, you cannot. Please."

I'm ashamed to say I was mostly relieved by Wolf's decision. I'd thought I was pretty brave, but evidently there was a limit to my courage.

"There are Healers," Wolf said. "The High Prince, for one." But whether he was telling me or himself, I couldn't say. When he smiled again, I managed to smile back.

Ice Tor put his own hand down on Wolf's wrist. I couldn't help noticing that it was the same hand that was now missing a finger. I took a deep breath to steady myself, but I'm afraid my eyes were shut when the blade came down.

When I opened them again, Wolf was cradling his injured left hand in his right, but I could see that the scar was already forming, and that his face was not set in an expression of pain. Ice Tor was hunched over the mortar, pounding away with the pestle. I expected to be totally horrified, but the sound was not at all what I anticipated. There was nothing soft or liquid about it, rather it was as if he was grinding nuts or hard spices.

He stopped the grinding motion, peering into the mortar, his gray brows drawn down in a vee, and his pursed lips lost in his beard. He looked over at Wolf, at me, and then at Wolf again.

"It is not enough, the elements are too few."

Then they were both looking at me.

"No," Wolf said. But his ash-gray eyes said something different.

"Wait," I started to say, but no sound came out of my mouth. I licked my lips and cleared my throat. Yeah, I was real brave. "I'm not one of the People," I said. "I've got no magic. My *dra'aj* . . ."

They were still looking at me.

"You are a Truthreader," Wolf said. "And you have more *dra'aj* than the usual human. Perhaps even the fact that you are human is significant." I was grateful for his matter-of-fact tone. He was stating facts, not trying to convince me.

"The number of the elements can be as important as their nature," Ice Tor said. He gestured at the mortar. "We simply do not have sufficient diversity."

"And for sure it would work? If you add something from me?"

Now he looked sad. "Your gift must be voluntary, so I will not lie to you. I cannot be sure, no, but what is our alternative?" He looked at me with his head tilted. "You need not fear us."

"And you would be Healed," Wolf said. To be fair, I'm sure he believed it.

But would I? Even Cassandra hadn't been able to cure my motion sickness, what guarantee did I have that she could regrow my finger? Maybe it wasn't the same thing, but did I want to take the chance? Even Wolf had been reluctant, and he had much better reason to believe he could be Healed. I looked from one to the other, their identically injured hands reminding me of a Japanese man who'd once had dealings with the Collector. He'd been missing a pinkie finger. A matter of honor.

I shut my eyes tight, giving myself a mental shake. *Come on*, I said to myself. *Grow a spine.* Was I really, even for a minute, thinking about refusing? When I thought about what was at stake—Wolf and the Outsiders, the whole world if what I'd read from Fox was true . . .

I put my arm on the table.

Wolf was not surprised when Valory fainted as her finger was taken. She had been very ill indeed during the Ride which had brought them here.

When Ice Tor had braced his hand on Valory's wrist, the girl's face had taken on that look of concentration that it assumed when she was reading the truth about something. The touching could not be helped, the Dwarf had to be sure that Valory did not flinch—and who knew? Perhaps the distraction had been beneficial. If nothing else, the touch would have reassured her that the Solitary was not in any way trying to trick them.

The finger once in the mortar, Wolf picked Valory up in his arms and carried her to a settle Ice Tor showed him against the wall near the banked fires of the forge. For a moment he stood, cradling the girl in his arms. This was the first time he had truly been able to hold her, and would perhaps be the last, her gift made her so shy of being touched. He breathed in deeply. What if he did not put her down?

Would this moment last forever? She would be in his arms, and her vanilla scent would fill his nostrils, and there would be no Hunt, and no brother and no Horn.

But there would be a Horn. Valory had given a piece of herself for it. To brave her illness was one thing, but Wolf had seen true fear in her face when she had offered Ice Tor her hand. He laid her carefully on the settle.

"I must get her home, to the Shadowlands, as quickly as I can," Wolf said. He sat on the edge of the settle and touched Valory's cheek with the back of his fingers. She seemed somehow less fragile to him now.

Ice Tor breathed into the mortar before looking up. "You will not take her for Healing?"

Wolf shook her head. "It is the Lands themselves that weaken her so."

"You will use the Horn there? In the Shadowlands?"

Wolf hesitated. He could take the Horn to the High Prince, of course. Draw the Hunt away from the Shadowlands entirely. But that is not what they planned. He could not be sure that if the Horn were used in the Lands, even by the High Prince herself, he would have his chance to save his old Pack. Foxblood. The voices of many, if not all, would be raised against them. And what of the tale the Dwarf told? That the Hunt might not be killed, but sent away, to suffer the torments of their hunger where they could cause no harm?

Once he was there, in the Shadowlands, he would call them, his old Pack, his brother. And he would be able to save them, all of them. But especially Fox.

Taking care not to disturb Valory, Wolf edged around to watch Ice Tor. There was now a light coming from the interior of the mortar, as if the contents were glowing. The mortar itself had altered slightly in shape, its rounded bottom now coming to a point. Just as Wolf was wondering how he planned to set it back on the table, the Dwarf turned to the forge fire, and pushed the mortar down into it.

"It must heat of itself a short while," Ice Tor said. "Then we shall see." He drew up a short, three-legged stool and sat upon it.

"Younger Brother," he said. "I saw you hesitate, what gave you the courage to give me your hand?"

Wolf glanced down at Valory. The girl had turned on her side, her injured hand curled half-closed, and sheltered in her good hand.

"I was with the Prince Guardian when he faced the Basilisk Prince," Wolf said. He inspected his hand. "Having seen what he gave? Even if it does not grow back, this is nothing."

"What gave *her* the courage?" Ice Tor nodded his head at the human girl.

"We must ask her when she awakes."

"This is it." Nik looked up at the familiar building. "This is where they were holding Wai-kwong."

"Why? What is this place?" Alejandro took a step back to get a better sight line on the top of the building.

Nik found himself smiling. "Maple Leaf Gardens." Alejandro looked at him with his eyebrows raised. "They used to play professional hockey here, hold concerts, that kind of thing. They've been working on it for a while, converting it to other uses, though I'm not sure exactly what."

Alejandro looked at Nik. "How does one enter?"

Nik tapped his upper lip with his tongue. "Let's try something." He set off up Church Street and Alejandro followed. When they were almost at the corner of Wood, Nik stopped in front of an overhead door, large enough to allow the entrance of just about any size of equipment. A movement across the intersection caught his eye, and he waved at Yves, standing outside the Hair of the Dog, holding the heavy door for Wai-Kwong. They were all traveling in pairs now. Yves signaled, and Nik nodded back.

"No sign of Hawk inside," he said, turning back to the construction doorway. "This is the entrance people have been using lately—workmen, trucks, and that kind of thing." He glanced at his watch. "Though the workers are likely long gone by now." And didn't that give him an unpleasant thought. "If the Hunt's been living here, I wonder what the suicide rate is among the workers? There've been no reports."

"It is possible that they have been left unmolested," Alejandro said. "Most beasts will not feed too close to their dens."

There was a padlock on the overhead door, the kind that was fastened to the door itself and had a number pad rather than a keyhole. Alejandro took the box in the fingers of both hands and simply snapped it off. Nik felt his mouth go dry. *On my side*, he reminded himself. *Friend.* He put his hand on the Rider's arm.

"There might be some kind of security cameras inside," he said. "Motion detectors or something."

But Alejandro was shaking his head. "I would wager they have been turned off, though no one will have told the insurance company. The coming and going of the Hunt will have set the alarms off constantly. If the dogs are always barking, one stops paying attention."

Even so, Nik noticed that Alejandro lifted the door only far enough to let them duck under it and closed it again behind them. Nik had expected the place to be dark, but not only did some of the daylight filter in from openings high up on the walls, lights had been left on inside. The Rider's sword, which had looked like a walking stick as they were standing outside, became a sword again. Nik couldn't be sure, but he thought it had a faint glow to it as well.

Near the entrance the place looked like any major construction site—piles of materials, everything from concrete blocks to bags of cement to sand and lumber—and those were just the things Nik recognized. There was also the kind of equipment you usually associated with the outdoors: a crane, a scissor lift, a backhoe. Farther away, deeper into the building, there were piles of debris, rubble, and chunks of concrete, some as large as cars.

Nik looked up and gasped. He'd been in the Gardens dozens, perhaps hundreds of times in his life, and he had never, ever realized just how vast the interior space was. Almost all the interior walls had gone, though he could see where some of the offices—and even the concrete bases for the raked seating—still clung to the ceiling, six stories up. Funny, when he'd been sitting up there in the nosebleeds, as Torontonians called those seats, he hadn't really thought about how high up he'd been.

Most astonishing of all, however, stranger even than seeing the scoreboard still hanging in the middle of nowhere, was the great pit dug into the ground, where once the ice and boards had been, so deep that the dump truck sitting at the bottom looked small.

"Something wrong?" Alejandro asked.

"No, not really. It's just so different, so changed." Nik waved his hand at the scoreboard. "I still see these little remnants of what used to be here, but everything else has been," he gestured at the pit,"destroyed." From the way the Rider patted him on the shoulder, Nik had the feeling Alejandro understood the kind of change he was talking about. "You want me to wait here?"

The Rider looked at the space immediately around them as if he were checking for tracks before answering. "I think not. If there is danger, better you should be with me than to face it alone."

"No argument here." Nik found he was grinning, but was pretty sure that bravado, rather than bravery, was behind it. Coming along had seemed like such a good idea when they were standing in Alejandro's kitchen.

Once again, he let the Rider lead. This was definitely a work boot and hard hat area. The footing was secure but not even, and once they were farther in, there was less feeling of the vastness of the space, as they had to concentrate on their footing, and on getting around immediate obstacles.

"What, exactly, are we looking for?" Nik dodged between another scissor lift and a smaller backhoe.

"Any sign that Hawk might be here." Alejandro was standing on a small rise created by the piling up of chunks of concrete floor, perhaps even the concrete that once lay under the ice itself.

"We've been watching the place," Nik said. "And no one's reported seeing Hawk." *So maybe you and I can get out of here right now.* Nik remembered Alejandro's praise of his courage and kept his thoughts to himself.

"Which tells us nothing, unfortunately." Alejandro was frowning as he looked around. "Valory says the Hunt can Move."

They had only made their way across about two thirds of the space when Alejandro froze, holding up his hand. Nik narrowed the space between them, until he was within arm's length, but kept to one side, leaving the Rider room to use his sword. He badly wanted to ask what Alejandro had seen or heard, but bit down on the question, reminding himself how scornful he always felt of idiots in movies who asked dumb and noisy questions at the worst moments. He'd be a little more forgiving of the idiots from now on, he thought.

"Come forth," Alejandro said, addressing, so far as Nik could see, a pile of debris the size of a convenience store. "I will not harm you."

At first there was no response, but then a small scurry of dirt and pebbles rattled down, followed by a heavier crunching of actual footsteps. Nik braced himself, jaw clenched, but what walked around cement blocks and cracked flooring was just an ordinary man, his clothes worn and dusty, his hair brushed up on one side as though he'd slept on it funny.

Nik inched closer to Alejandro, whispered to him out of the corner of his mouth. "Some homeless guy." If there was a way into a place of shelter, the homeless would find it.

"You think so?" The Rider held up his sword, and it was glowing, no doubt about it now. He pointed at the space in front of him. "Come here," he said to the homeless man. "Stand here in front of me. Now."

Nik blinked and backed up a step before he even knew he was going to do it. The man moved way faster than any homeless guy Nik had ever seen. Not as fast as Nik had seen Hawk or Alejandro move, but still. Now that he was closer, Nik noticed other things. For one, that he couldn't smell anything. Any homeless person as scruffy as this could usually be smelled from much farther away.

And was there something odd about the guy's eyes?

Eye? No, eyes, definitely two eyes. And the quality of energy around him—*Hound*. For certain. He was about to tell Alejandro when the thing spoke.

"You're the Old One who talked to the Pack Leader." The voice was rough, but in no way a growl, though the hairs on the back of Nik's neck did stand up.

"I am. Do not make the mistake of believing me prey." Alejandro gestured with the *gra'if* sword. "I have here teeth and claws enough for you."

The other cringed away, and for an instant Nik thought he saw claws where the hands should be, and rough feathers in place of clothes.

"No, no. That's not what I meant at all. Do you, do you know anything about Stormwolf?" Now the tone was wistful.

Seeing Alejandro take a step closer to the thing, lowering his sword, Nik relaxed and did the same.

"He's been cured," Nik said. "He's not a Hound anymore. You could be cured as well." The thing nodded violently, and Nik moved closer still, but Alejandro barred his way with the *gra'if* blade.

"No, please, don't touch me," the creature said. "I won't be able to resist. The hunger's always hungry, you know?" Nik swallowed and allowed Alejandro to push him back. He couldn't afford to be drained again, not now.

"It is well, Hound. The Portal is nearby, can you follow me if I Move there?"

"Sure. Of course. Then what?"

Nik knew exactly what was making Alejandro hesitate. These were the things that had preyed on him, on Poco and Elaine—on all the Outsiders. And they'd done the same and worse to Riders over who knew how long. But surely there had to be more to them than this? Wolf had been one, and now he was different.

"We should help him," he said aloud. "If he wants it."

"I will take you to the High Prince myself," Alejandro said. "She will Heal you, as she did Stormwolf."

The Hound inclined his head, turned it slightly to one side to expose his throat. "Go. I'll follow."

Nik was standing very close now, almost between Alejandro and the Hound. "Where do you want me to wait for you," he was beginning to say, when he caught a movement out of the corner of his eye. The Hound's hand snaked out toward him, and the *gra'if* blade swung, and the hand, the paw, the taloned foot, lay on the ground and became a hand once more.

The sword flashed again, the head came free from the body, and Alejandro was pushing Nik back out of the way of the fountaining blood.

Chapter Twenty-one

ELAINE SHOOK HER HEAD and closed her phone. "Still no response," she said. "It rings seven times, and then goes to voice mail."

Moon looked around the intersection where York Street crossed King Street. There was a widening of the sidewalk here, and tables set out where people were sitting drinking coffee, some reading large sheets of paper, others books, and some studying flat black rectangular squares. It looked peaceful. Fun.

"What does David's phone sound like?" she asked. "I thought I heard something."

Elaine manipulated her own phone until it showed her a different display. "Chingon," she said. "It's a piece of music called 'El Pistolero.' "

"Try it again," Moon suggested.

Elaine changed the display again and pressed one of the buttons now revealed. Moon studied the Outsider woman. She could neither see nor feel the quality in her that made Elaine an Outsider and not an ordinary human, but she had been warned what signs to look for.

At the moment, the slight line that formed between the woman's brows indicated concern, so all was well.

Except, of course, that this David was missing.

"Did you know him well? David?"

Elaine was shaking her head, and clearly about to speak when Moon held up a finger. "There," she said. "This way." She led the way east. "Call him again. Keep calling until I say."

Elaine complied. "I don't know him at all," she said. "But it's like being adopted and suddenly finding your real family. All these people you've never met, who you now have so much in common with."

"But this is a good thing, is it not? You have gained, not lost." Moon concentrated, but the sound had faded again. "Again, please."

"Sorry." Elaine pressed the button again. "In a way I've gained, but Nik . . . Nik's forgotten that he told me this, but—well, I'm going to live longer than usual, apparently, but I won't be able to have children, so—" Here, Elaine gave a small sigh that, from her smile, was meant to be laughter. "I guess I win some and I lose some."

Moon placed her hand on her womb. "Yes, I guess we do."

They had proceeded almost halfway to the next intersection and Elaine's eyes widened, as she, too, heard a faint sound of music, the same phrase repeated again and again.

"Here." The sound came from a round bin made up of metal mesh, lined with a thin green bag. Moon tilted her head, listened as the phrase of music repeated once more, stabbed her hand into the bin, and came up with a phone that looked much like Elaine's.

"No way." Elaine snapped hers shut, turning her head to look first one way, then another. "No way David or anyone else dropped that in the garbage by mistake. That's a $600 phone."

"Do you see him?" But Elaine was already heading for a nearby building. A low stone wall surrounded the entrance, enclosing a small section of grass and flowers. A man was leaning against this wall, holding one of the sets of wide papers in front of him. His eyes lifted as Elaine approached him, and he smiled. The hairs rose on the back of Moon's neck.

"Excuse me," Elaine was saying. "Have you seen a man in his fifties? Blue jeans? Tattooed forearms? He—"

The man put his papers aside, and his smiled widened. Surely he had far too many teeth.

"Elaine!" Moon was at her side in an eye blink, and as soon as her hand closed around the Outsider's wrist, she Moved.

Half-closed blinds shielded Elaine's office from the afternoon sun. Most of the light came from the computer monitors they'd left running when they'd gone to find out why David wasn't answering his phone.

"Was that—"

Moon never found out what Elaine meant to ask her. She was abruptly pushed to one side by the rough scaly back of a monster.

For a time I wasn't sure where I was. There was an odd quality to the light, as if it glowed and flickered at the same time. Then I realized that I was looking at the coals of an open fire, a fire that burned without smoke, since I couldn't smell any. A murmur of voices turned my attention in another direction, and when I saw Wolf and Ice Tor standing next to the workbench, it all came flooding back to me. I grabbed my left wrist, and lifted my hand to eye level.

There was more than enough light, even in this darkened corner, to show me the new shape of my hand. At first my mind refused to acknowledge it, it didn't even feel like my hand. There was no pain, no numbness, and no, I was glad to say, phantom feeling. It was, strangely, as if my finger had never been there. *Maybe I'm in shock.*

The other two hadn't seen I was awake. They were still by the workbench, still looking down at something.

The Horn.

I sat up, fully expecting the room to spin around me, but again, nothing. Not even a trace of the motion sickness that had been troubling me so much on the way here. Whatever the Dwarf's magic was, it was still in place.

I must have made some sound, however, because Wolf was at my side before I saw him move.

"Are you well?"

"I think so," I said. "Is it ready? Did it work?" I gathered my feet under me and Wolf held out his forearm for me, hesitating only when I shook my head. I pushed myself up using my right hand only. Even though there was no pain, even though it didn't, yet, feel any differently, I couldn't bring myself to use my left hand, not even to touch Wolf's *gra'if*-covered wrist. My eye kept being drawn to it, as if to check that the missing finger was still missing.

Ice Tor stood aside, and I approached the workbench. He had laid out a piece of black felt, and on top of this rested what looked like a miniature flute. It was about the length of my hand, had a raised hole for the lips, just like a real flute, and air holes as if for notes.

"I was just saying that it is much larger than the one the Basilisk had," Wolf said.

"Different elements, perhaps," the Dwarf said. "Or simply the other was more finely made, by artisans of more skill than I."

"But will it work?"

"That I cannot tell you. It is made, made well, with the best elements I had to hand. It should work." He paused here, fixed his eyes on Wolf and then on me, making sure we were both looking back at him. "But those elements, however good, were not many. The Horn is less stable, more fragile than it would have been had we many parts to draw upon." He looked back at it, then nodded his head firmly. "It will work, but I would not depend upon it to work more than once."

"If we only have once . . ." I turned to Wolf. "Does this mean we should give it to Cassandra?"

He had his eyes fixed on the artifact. "It is what we have," he said finally. "We will make it work for us."

That wasn't exactly an answer, but I figured we had some time yet to talk it over.

Ice Tor folded the black felt over the Horn, bringing in the edges like an envelope. He pulled a hair out of the tangle on his head and tied the package closed before presenting it to us. I looked at Wolf, but he shook his head.

"You carry it, Valory. You keep it safe."

It wasn't until after I'd tucked it into my shirt that I realized I'd picked up the Horn with my left hand.

"If we're going," I said to Wolf, "can you make me another flask of chicken soup? And give me a half hour or so to digest it. I wasn't prepared before, but this time there's no reason for me to Ride on an empty stomach." With luck, I had enough Gravol left to help me keep the soup down.

Wolf brought the flask out again, but slowly, and all the while with a puzzled look on his face. He paused with his hand on the stopper. "The flask is ready to provide more broth," he said. "But why not wait until we are back in the Shadowlands, and you can eat anything you like?"

"But that's going to be a while, isn't it? I mean, even though we know the way now, it'll still take us at least as long to get back to the Quartz Ring and . . ." He was shaking his head, smiling. It wasn't that easy to make him smile. I wondered what I'd said.

"We only Rode here because I did not know the place, and could not Move here. Now we have only to take the Cloud Horses where they would like to be, and I can Move us directly to the Portal, and then through to your home. The sooner we bring the Horn, the better."

Ice Tor escorted us back to the meadow where the Cloud Horses waited, patiently cropping grass. Because of the nature of the space Ice Tor inhabited—or created, we still didn't know which—Wolf didn't want to Move from where we were, and the Dwarf took us all the way back to the rocky hilltop where the boulders were. It was still night there, the full moon making a bright spot behind the clouds.

"Farewell, Stormwolf, son of Rain at Sunset. May the Chimera guide you well. Farewell, Valory Truthreader. Come and tell me of the outcome, if you live."

And with those ominous words, we were alone again.

Instantly, I broke out into a sweat, and the world spun to the left before wobbling back to the right. Wolf took my elbow and guided my hands to the pommel of the saddle. As if the touch of something familiar steadied me, or maybe it was the nearness of the Cloud Horse, my head cleared and my stomach settled.

Shallow breaths, I told myself. It had all seemed so easy. Persuading Moon and Wolf back at the Royal York—that felt so far away. I glanced at my left hand and quickly looked away. Nothing seemed easy now.

Wolf was staring off into the distance, shaking his head in short, shallow arcs. The thin sloe-black braid he'd pulled loose to give to Ice Tor moved back and forth. I almost reached out to tuck it back into place, but let my hand fall without touching him.

"We're not going to the High Prince, are we?"

"Valory, this is my chance—it may be my only one—to make my brother listen to me. If I give the Horn to another, they will not see this as I do." I patted Wolf on the shoulder as he continued to speak. I heard his deep voice, and could almost feel it in my bones, but I didn't make out any more words. Cassandra had warned me that human drugs wouldn't work as well in the Lands, and it looked as if the Gravol was beginning to lose its effectiveness.

"Wolf." I'm pretty sure I interrupted him, but at that point I didn't much care. "It's okay. I'm with you."

I think he spoke to the Cloud Horses and got some kind of answer before he boosted me up into my saddle. He said something about a short delay, and I think I nodded, but I can't be sure. In a moment he was in the saddle himself, and put out his hand for me to take. It was his left hand, I saw, and somehow, seeing his missing finger, and the way he paid it no attention at all, made me feel a little better. Our hands touched. [I saw the Basilisk Prince, a Sunward Rider dressed in magenta] and then CRACK! my ears were popping and we were outside the hostel once more. I managed to get down from the Cloud Horse on my own without falling, and held it together long enough for Wolf to run them into their stable. He was back out so quickly I wasn't sure whether he'd taken the time to remove their saddles, but to be honest, I was too far gone to ask.

"Asleep again," Wolf said, holding out his hands. Again, I took hold of his wrists and WHOOSH! I was on my hands and knees and Wolf was arguing with someone over my head.

"You know me, Cloud of Witness," Wolf was saying. "I must get this human girl back to the Shadowlands before her illness kills her. If this was something one of us could Heal, it would have been done already." I couldn't hear the response, but I could guess it from what Wolf said next. "Of course the High Prince knows about this journey. Do you think I act without her knowledge and permission?"

Riders aren't so different from human beings after all. I saw that these guys weren't going to question Wolf's authority, even though they probably thought they should.

The next thing I knew I was being lifted to my feet and Wolf was walking me forward, murmuring under his breath to brace myself. The Gravol seemed to have worn off completely and, frankly, if he'd told me at this point that he was about to walk me off a cliff, I would have nodded and kept on walking. Somebody said once that people didn't die from seasickness, they only wished they could. That was the state I'd reached.

Again, the blackness, the feeling that my breath was being squeezed from my lungs, and we were someplace very hot [Mexico City, what happened to Toronto?], then I was on a cold terrazzo floor, and people were helping me to my feet [*he* was going to propose to his girlfriend tonight; *she* had a winning lottery ticket in a jacket pocket at home], and Wolf was saying. "My friend slipped. I am sure she is well now. Thank you."

All I knew was that the world was level again, without even the wobbly edges that I'd had at Ice Tor's place. I was home. And starving. Fortunately, there was a convenience store right there on the departure level, and I made Wolf stop while I grabbed myself a chocolate bar and a Diet Coke.

"That does not smell like food," he said, nose wrinkling as he leaned closer to me. "Nor drink, for that matter."

"And I'm sure it would kill me eventually, if this was all I ever ate, but for now, I'm just getting a bit of an energy boost. Then we'll see what you have in your fridge."

There were too many people on the concourse for us to risk Moving from there, but Union Station has a lot of back corridors and deserted alcoves, and it didn't take Wolf long to find us one empty enough that he could Move us into his apartment. We'd learned from the last time that it wasn't a good idea to walk across the street when we didn't have to.

The place was exactly as I remembered it. The temperature just cool enough for comfort, the air lightly scented with saffron. The drapes and blinds were open, but the sheers were drawn, giving the otherwise unlit room a quiet, misty feel. I could see the red message light blinking on the phone, and I moved toward it. As I did so, my mobile began to vibrate and rang twice.

"You've got a message," I said, as I pulled my mobile out. Seven missed calls. One from Alejandro, six from Nik.

"It is unlikely to be for me." Wolf was at my side looking down at the blinking light.

I put down my mobile, lifted the receiver with my right hand, and pressed the message button. I disturbed a sheet of notepaper as I did. "Valory, call Nik," it said. I put my finger on it. Nik had been here with Alejandro. They'd Moved. I handed the note to Wolf just as the message played back.

"Dr. Kennaby," the voice said. "Sorry to disturb you, this is Jonathan down at the front desk. You must have seen the damage to the hall outside your door—and well, the door itself. The lock still works, as I'm sure you've noticed. The carpenters will return to finish on Monday. It looks as though someone tried to break in, and when they couldn't, they set fire to the hallway." The voice hesitated and then continued. "I'm afraid the police would like to speak with you when you have a moment."

Wolf was already heading for the door, the note from Nik still in his hand. The door swung open without any difficulty. There had obviously been a clean-up attempt, but anyone would have known something was wrong. The table that had stood outside the door was gone, and a whole section of the green, red, and gold carpet had been replaced, but they hadn't been able to do much with the wood trim around the door. There was a still faint smell of scorched wood, as well as something much less pleasant. I looked at Wolf, but he was studying the hallway, brow furrowed, nostrils flared. His almond skin paled to bone, the scars around his eye standing out, and his eyes moved to my face. He looked as though he had something to say, but was afraid to say it.

I lifted my shoulders and let them drop again. I took a step out into the hall and deliberately put my hand on the doorframe.

My knees buckled as the sounds, the smells, washed through me. I could dimly feel Wolf's hands, his arms around me, holding me up. But over it, like a cold, slick fog, lay Nighthawk's despair. Fox's triumphant feeding. I clapped my hand over my mouth and turned my face into Wolf's chest, thinking maybe I should sit down, thinking that if I were going to faint, I could at least do it from closer to the floor. My stomach was sorry I'd eaten the chocolate bar. Tears ran down my face onto my hands. Maybe I hadn't known Hawk for very long, but I'd touched him. I knew things about him even his mother didn't know.

And it could have been Alejandro. I don't think I really understood until that moment that these long-lived, inhuman People could actually die.

Finally, Wolf's baked-cinnamon smell grew stronger than the blood and the smoke. I straightened, got my hands up between us. The way I felt, I knew that if I didn't push him away right then, I might never be able to do it.

"It is as I fear. Tell me."

I cleared my throat, wiped my eyes with my *right* hand as I straightened my back and raised my chin. "A Rider—Nighthawk." My voice trembled on his name, but I needed, and he deserved, that I say it out loud. "Hawk was killed here." I indicated the floor we stood on. I'd meant to tell him everything, but in the last minute I couldn't do it. "A Hound," was all I said.

Wolf looked at me then, his pale gray eyes boring into mine. I wasn't going to say I knew who the Hound had been, not unless he asked me outright. He lowered his eyes again, and I saw that he didn't have to.

"And Graycloud? Alejandro?"

I was touched that Wolf's next thought had been of the person who was most important to me. Though it wasn't much of a stretch to figure out how he'd gone from thinking of Fox to Alejandro.

"Wasn't here," I said. "He's still okay." I wrapped my arms around myself.

"Nighthawk's *dra'aj*?" Wolf asked then, but his voice was just a whisper.

At first I didn't know what he was getting at, but then I did and my heart sank. "He took it." I coughed to open my throat a little so I could say it. "Fox took it."

Wolf swallowed, but he didn't look away. "Nighthawk is Faded. I will have to tell the High Prince. They are of the same *fara'ip*." The muscles of his face had firmed up again, and his voice was stronger. "You are certain it was Fox." It wasn't a question. He'd known from the scents before I ever touched anything.

"I can't be wrong."

He nodded. By the look on his face, I was guessing Wolf had already turned his thoughts away from the hall, trying to think of something else. He gestured, and I walked back into the apartment ahead of him. I'd only taken two steps into the entry when I realized Wolf wasn't right behind me. I turned to find him still at the opening, frowning. I went back to see what he was looking at.

"What is it?"

"I cannot enter." He was frowning, his black brows drawn down. "I do not understand. The Binding I put on the room, the door, it should not keep *me* out as well." He raised his eyes to mine. "For you to enter, and for me not—this is beyond my experience."

"But you *were* in." I turned away from him, looked around without moving, but nothing appeared out of the ordinary. All the furniture was in the same place it had been when I last saw it. Then I had an idea, and I ran my hands over the walls near the door.

"This is your doing, all right," I said. "When you Sang, something changed in the walls." I bit off a laugh that felt as painful as it sounded. "Looks like you were a bit too general in your Binding. Riders who have been here before can Move into the apartment, but Riders—and I'd guess any others of the People—can't just walk in." I looked back at him and tried to smile. "So the only Riders who can come in, are the ones who have been here already. One of us."

Wolf looked past me into the apartment, then down the hall toward the elevators. I saw that the note from Nik was sticking out of his jeans pocket. "We must go."

"Take me home," I said. Suddenly I needed to see Alejandro.

Wolf Moved us to the backyard, and it seemed odd, somehow, to run up the steps of the deck to the back door, almost as though I'd been away for months. For the first time, however, I felt as though I was actually coming home. The house was so ordinary, so human, and the sight of the pieces of furniture that Alejandro had brought from Spain, and a pair of my shoes lying under the table in the sunroom where I'd kicked them off, were almost enough to make me cry.

At the sound of our entrance, Alejandro appeared in a flash from the kitchen, his sword in his hand. For a second I knew what the bull must have felt like in the bullring, back in the day when Alejandro Martín had been the name that appeared on posters all over Spain. He folded me into his arms, and I was happy to be held there, clinging to him, his familiar smell of ripe cherries in my nostrils, the warm familiar buzz of him against my psyche.

Finally, he held me away at arm's length, looking from me to Wolf and back again. "You are safe, almost I cannot believe it. *Querida*, where have you been?"

I caught his hands between mine. "Alejandro," I said. "We have the Horn."

His eyes lit up, he brought my hands to his lips and kissed them.

I'd forgotten my left hand, at least until I heard the intake of Alejandro's breath when he saw it. He held my hand gently, careful not to touch the place where the finger was gone.

"A Solitary?" he said, distress written large on his ruddy face. When I said yes, he closed his eyes for a moment, resignation clear in the way his lips pressed together. Somehow, his acceptance of my injury without lamentation made me feel warm, as if he were really treating me, for the first time, as an adult able to make her own decisions, and bear her own burdens.

"Come," he said. "Nik is here, and we have dire news."

I stopped him. "If you mean Nighthawk," I said. "He's Faded. We already know."

Alejandro shut his eyes tight. "You are certain." It wasn't a question, but I nodded. He shook his head and kissed me on the forehead.

It's against my normal practice, but I gave Nik a hug when Alejandro led us into the front room. After what I'd been through, even his fragmentation felt familiar and homey—though different. Nik responded immediately to my hug, even tightening his grip when I tried to take a step back. He wasn't as tall as Wolf, and I looked almost directly into his deep brown eyes.

"You need to be more careful," I said, my hands pushing against his chest. His *dra'aj* was different, and I knew why. "Both of you," I added. I'd gotten some of the same images from both of them. "You shouldn't get that close to a Hound."

Nik blinked at me, looked at Alejandro as he stepped away. "Wow. It's true. She's really psychic. How did you get used to her knowing things without having to tell her?"

"The problem is that the rest of us do not know exactly what she knows, unless *she* tells *us*." Wolf was looking at me sideways, reluctance strong on his face. "I take it they have had an encounter with a Hound?"

I bit my lip. But it *was* hard to remember that Wolf wouldn't feel as triumphant as everyone else when a Hound was killed.

"You see," Alejandro said to Nik. "You must tell your tale in any case. What Valory knows about our encounter may not be what Wolf, for example, wishes to know."

"Does anyone mind if I eat while you're doing it?"

Alejandro hustled away into the kitchen. I sat down in my own wing-backed chair and Wolf perched on the arm. Nik smiled with half of his mouth, his head tilted to one side, prodded the footstool over with his toe, and sat down to my left. I kept my face as straight as I could.

"At first it seemed the Hound would come to be cured," Alejandro said, as he came in from the kitchen with cheese and bread, beer and sangria on a tray, setting it down on the end of the coffee table, where I could reach it without difficulty. "But it was only a ruse to get close enough to Nik to take his *dra'aj*."

Nik took up the tale from there. Now that the worst was over, I knew he was feeling pretty good, happy to have escaped, but his elation faded as he spoke, and he grew more and more serious as he told us how the Hound almost tricked them, and how Alejandro had ended by having to kill it. By the end he was compressing his lips, sobered.

"Thank you for giving him every chance," Wolf said. His voice was so quiet I twisted my head round to look at him. His face was remote.

"One never knows when one might need such a chance oneself," Alejandro said. He hesitated, studying Wolf's face a moment before continuing. "I did not ask his name. I did not think he would give it to me."

Wolf became very, very still. I moved my hand over and touched him. *Of course.* He'd actually known the Hound Alejandro had killed. It had been a Pack mate to Wolf, not just a monster to be killed. And all the *dra'aj* it had taken over its immeasurably long life was lost now, never to be restored to the Lands. My breath hitched in my throat. Lying under Wolf's sorrow was disappointment deep enough to drown in. This was the third Hound who hadn't wanted to be cured.

I had no idea what the statistics were about drug addicts, how many got cured. "People don't always go to get help right away, the first time it's offered," was what I said. "Sometimes you have to keep offering. Give them a second, maybe even a third chance."

"But can we afford to give them these chances?" Alejandro said. "Lives are being destroyed even as we speak."

Wolf took a deep breath, his head lifting as his chest expanded. "What do we know?" he said.

Alejandro looked at Wolf for a long moment before nodding. It wasn't a change of subject. "They have been seen coming and going from this Maple Leaf Gardens, and it is clear that they have denned there." He turned to Nik.

"My people have been keeping a watch out, and I've asked them to report to Elaine. She's been acting as clearing house for the latest, up-to-date information."

"Walks Under the Moon has been helping her," Alejandro added.

"Then they should be here." Wolf glanced around as Nik pulled out his mobile phone. "Has Moon been to this house?"

Nik looked up, his mouth open. "I'm not sure."

Wolf stood up. "Then I will bring them." And CRACK! he was gone.

It was almost comical the way Alejandro and Nik turned to me, the identical look of uncertainty on their faces.

"What?"

Nik rubbed at the bridge of his nose. "Using the Horn isn't going to be all that easy for him, is it?"

I didn't know what I should say. "He wants to save them," was what I said finally. "He was saved, so he figures he owes them the chance."

Nik frowned. "I'm sorry about his friends, but the Hunt's going to destroy us, if we don't destroy it first. Doesn't *that* have to be our priority?"

"Maybe it won't turn out the way he hopes, maybe none of the Hounds will accept Healing, not even . . ." I hesitated. Had Wolf told anyone else about Fox? I mean, he hadn't really told me, had he? I turned to Alejandro. "But the Horn might give Wolf a chance. He won't be able to live with himself afterward if he doesn't even try . . ." I shivered as though a dark, cold cloud had passed over me. I was missing something. I knew it, but what?

"So, now that we have the Horn . . ." Nik began.

"It's possible we can only use it once," I said. I refrained from mentioning the chance, slim though it might be, that the Horn wouldn't work at all.

"Then we will not be able to summon individual Hounds, as the Basilisk Prince did," Alejandro said. "We must summon them all at once." Alejandro stroked his chin, his gaze turned inward. "Nik's people have been invaluable. We know where the Hunt gathers, and are starting to make some estimate of their numbers. I have three other Riders who have sworn to help us, as soon as I tell them when and where." Alejandro looked at me. "The High Prince has said that she could not spare anyone, to search the Shadowlands for the Hunt, but if we had them all in one place . . . once we blow the Horn . . ."

I put my hand on the felt packet that was still under my shirt. When we'd come back from the Lands, the clothes that I'd been wearing had changed into a pair of jeans and a tight T-shirt with a ruffled front, perfect for hiding things. Alejandro made an aborted gesture with his left hand, and I slipped mine off the arm of the chair and put it down next to my thigh. Not carefully enough, obviously, since Nik caught it.

"What is it," he asked. "What's wrong with your hand?" He was on his feet, already reaching for me, and I could read the determination in his face. Alejandro flashed to Nik's side, and was pulling him away before he could touch me, when I raised my hand, effectively answering his question and putting a stop to any possible struggle at the same time.

"Valory." I saw the same thing on his face, and heard the same thing in his voice as I'd seen and heard the first time I'd met him. Horror. Grief. Then his eyes narrowed, and his face hardened with accusation. "How did Wolf let this happen?"

My mouth suddenly dry, I looked at Alejandro.

"Wolf has suffered the same loss," Alejandro said. "I have seen it with my own eyes, and you could have done so as well, if you had cared to." He looked back at me. " 'Those who come asking favors of Solitaries have always a price to pay.' "

"It was a voluntary price," I added. "The Horn wouldn't work without it."

"Oh, Valory," Nik said, sinking back down to his stool. He put his hand on my knee, and this time no one stopped him.

"Hey, it's not like I played the piano or anything," I said, hoping they couldn't hear the flatness in my voice.

Wolf could smell his brother the instant he arrived in Elaine's office. Elaine herself was lying facedown in a corner, as limp as though she were nothing more than a pile of empty clothing.

"Step out, brother," Wolf said. "I can smell you. Step out."

A shadow moved, and suddenly Fox was leaning against the wall just inside the door. His form—his own form, his true form—startled Wolf, even though he'd seen it at the train station. Almost, almost, Fox looked as though the Hunt had never existed. Still, Wolf knew better than to look his brother in the eyes.

Clearly, Fox had fed from humans since taking Nighthawk's *dra'aj*. Wolf glanced at Elaine, and gritted his teeth.

"Where is Moon?"

"What do you care?"

Wolf turned back toward his brother. "She is my *fara'ip*."

"Your *fara'ip*?" Fox took a step toward him; Wolf held his place. "What about me? *I'm* your *fara'ip*. Your brother, your *Pack mate*. Or has this Healing you keep telling me about made you stupid as well as soft?"

Wolf moved his head slowly from side to side. "You are the stupid one, if you believe me soft. Where is Moon?"

"I got tired of waiting for someone to get back to me. I don't like being ignored. Maybe your precious High Prince'll listen better now. Tell her that her sister's safe for now. But I'll kill her; I'll *Fade* her, unless our demands are met. Leave this world to us, close the Portals. You have until sundown."

"*Where* is she?"

Fox grinned. "In a safe place."

Wolf's hands clenched, and he wished he'd arrived sword in hand. "In what place could she be safe?"

"I'm Pack Leader now." Fox's satisfaction was plain. "They'll do whatever I tell them to. Besides, they don't need her anymore." He flicked his fingers as if removing a speck of dirt.

"I wish I had your faith in their good behavior."

Fox lounged on the arm of the couch, his elbow propped on the back. He crossed his legs, swinging one foot. "Maybe I should get back to her, then. Make sure she's okay."

"What do you want?"

"I've told you." Fox didn't move. He'd delivered his ultimatum, but he was not in any hurry to leave. Wolf knew his first concern should be for Moon, but it was impossible not to think of his brother. Impossible to keep the hope that had sprung up, a warm note in his chest, from spreading. But he had to move carefully—it appeared Fox remained contrary and stubborn, whatever form he took.

But it was just possible that the taking of Nighthawk's *dra'aj*—when Fox had sworn so scornfully that he did not need it, would never touch the *dra'aj* of a Rider again—had been enough to show Fox his last shame. Might he be ready to listen? Even his boasts and insults might be the last show of bravado before he gave in.

"What if I said I wanted *you*?" Fox smiled his old smile, and Wolf's heart turned over. "To bring you back to my side? We can run the Pack together. With this new world to live in, we can finally be free of the Lands and the People."

"But not free of the craving, of the hunger."

Fox waved this away. "It's only shortage of supply that makes the craving a problem. There's so much prey here—enough for all of us—that shortage isn't something we'll ever worry about again."

"And never to see the changing Lands again?"

His brother fell silent and Wolf risked a quick look at his face. Fox's eyes, the brilliant green that he remembered so well, were focused in the middle distance. "There's change here." But the voice was not so sure now. "And now we can Move."

"It is not the same. Sun and moon in the same hour, in different skies. Landscapes as many as the leaves on a tree, as grains of sand on a beach, each unique, each itself." Wolf reached out, turned his hand palm up. "You say you can Move, but where to? Everywhere the Shadowlands are the same. We will not see here the *tabo'or* waves of the Sea of Storms."

"The stars beneath the *Shaghana'ak* Abyss," Fox said, his tone soft and far away.

"Hunting the white stag in a forest of living Trees." Wolf felt a tune stirring in his throat, in one minute, in two, he would remember the Song.

But Fox shook himself, straightening to his feet, and the Song was gone. "You're still the same, brother. Always looking back."

"I am not looking back now," Wolf said. "I look forward. I look to the life I now have before me. The life you, too, could have before you, if you wished it."

"It's that easy, then?"

Was there a longing in Fox's voice? Was his brother finally listening to him? He'd listened once before, long ago. Wolf had to take this chance that Fox would listen again.

"I will not hide from you that there was pain," Wolf said, remembering the tearing agony, the dragon fire as it burned through him. "But pain is something we know well. Pain is nothing that we fear."

"No, we don't, that's so." Fox straightened until he was no longer leaning against the back of the couch, and Wolf allowed the small flame of hope to grow. "And the others?"

"Will they not be led by you?"

Fox grinned, his mouth, for one heartbeat, too large and too full of too sharp teeth. "That they would be," he acknowledged.

Wolf stayed silent. Now was the time to let his brother think over all that he had been offered. Push, and Fox would push back. Finally, Fox tilted his head, looking up at Wolf from under his eyebrows. Wolf focused on his brother's left ear.

"I'll give that some thought. I will. I'll think about what you said. In the meantime, you think about what I've said. You've got until sunset." He pointed at Elaine with his chin. "*She* knows where."

A rush of air, and Fox was gone.

Chapter Twenty-two

SOMEHOW THE DINING ROOM felt like the safest place to show them the Horn. It probably had something to do with the lack of windows. It seemed important that no one be able to see us. I pulled the well-wrapped package out of the front of my T-shirt and laid it on the table, slipping off the tie and flicking the edges of cloth aside. Viewing it for the first time here, in my own world, I saw that unlike my clothes, or Wolf's—or the cloth it was wrapped in, for that matter—the Horn itself looked exactly as it had on Ice Tor's workbench, like a tiny flute made of old ivory.

"Ice Tor told us ours is made from fewer elements, and maybe won't be as strong." This time I added what I hadn't been able to say out loud until now. "It might not work at all."

Alejandro was shaking his head. "It is unlikely that it would take on the form, without also having the function. But have you touched it, *querida*?"

I licked my lips, looked from one face to the other. Nik scrubbed at his chin, his look of determination overlaid with curiosity. Alejandro looked at me, not at the Horn, concerned, as if he thought I might somehow be hurt by it.

I stretched out my left hand and laid my index finger on the breathing hole. [A sound I couldn't hear; cavernous darkness; howling; a horn; a unicorn; flash of *gra'if*.] "It *will* sound," I heard myself say. "But only once." Alejandro shifted, as if he'd like to touch the Horn himself, but I now knew that he wasn't the one, so I folded over the thick black felt and once more tucked the artifact away in the front of my shirt, hoping that no one saw my hands shaking, and asked me any more questions. I couldn't share everything I'd read.

I was saved from further questions by a *whoosh* of displaced air that made the papers on the kitchen corkboard flutter. Alejandro went immediately to investigate, his sword in his hand. He was waving me back with the other, but I knew it could only be Wolf, so I was right behind him, in time to see Wolf laying Elaine down on the daybed in the sunroom. Nik made an incoherent sound behind me, pushing past us to Elaine's side.

"Where is Moon?" Alejandro's voice was quiet but sharp.

"The Hunt has her."

It felt like there was something stuck in my throat.

"Elaine knows," Wolf was saying. "She knows where we must go to regain Moon."

"Is she . . . ?" Nik was trying to take Elaine's pulse. Instead of pushing his fingers up under her jaw, he had her by the wrist, which even I knew is the most difficult way to do it.

"Here," I said, taking hold of his sleeve with the fingers of my right hand. [His shirt was made in Germany by a left-handed man.] Nik licked his lips, and held out Elaine's wrist, stepping back to give me room.

I didn't feel for a pulse, but instead took a firm grip on Elaine's hand and lower arm. Her skin felt elastic and cool and, better still, she felt [a laundry basket full of potatoes?] strange, but *whole*, her pieces gathered and tidy.

"She's okay," I said, and I heard Nik let out a breath, and felt it on the skin of my neck. "He didn't take her *dra'aj*."

"Who, *querida*?"

"Fox," I said. I didn't look around, not even when someone hissed. Touching Elaine was easier than usual, and I wondered if that was because she was unconscious. What I was reading was clear, but that didn't mean it made any sense. "Why do I keep getting Maple Leaf Gardens?"

I turned around in time to see Nik and Alejandro exchange looks. Wolf caught it as well.

"You know the place?"

"We do." It was clear from the tone of Alejandro's voice that Wolf wasn't on his good list any longer.

"You'd better tell them, Wolf." I folded Elaine's arm across her chest in what I hoped would be a comfortable position and covered her with the lambswool afghan that lay at one end of the daybed.

"Fox says he will return Moon to us at sunset," Wolf said. "If we meet his demands."

"And Maple Leaf Gardens is where he'll meet," I said.

"Where is she now? Is that where he is holding her?" Alejandro turned to me.

I shook my head. "That's more than Elaine knows. They've Moved together, and to some extent imprinted on each other, but . . . Moon's alive, that much I can tell, but not where."

"We have badly miscalculated," Alejandro said. "I thought we would have more time. Does he have new demands?" Somehow his cool question made everyone relax just enough to listen.

"What he has already asked for," Wolf said. "The Shadowlands, the closing of the Portals."

"He wants to exchange Moon for this?" It didn't make any sense to me.

"She is the sister of the High Prince. Foxblood believes Truthsheart will be more likely to listen to him now."

They all looked at me, but what could I tell them? "I've never had a good reading from Cassandra, not after she was wearing all her *gra'if*." I thought about it. "But I have touched Moon, and I'd say Cassandra would sacrifice her sister, if it would mean saving or helping the most people."

"Valory is correct. Truthsheart would not give the Shadowlands to the Hunt, not even for her sister." Wolf had his eyes squeezed shut, but his voice, though faint was firm.

"This may turn to our advantage."

We all looked at Alejandro, but he was focusing inward on his own thoughts. All at once he blinked, as if he realized we were staring at him.

"We need a place to call the Hunt. The time is not of our choosing, but why not this place?" Alejandro looked around at us. "We can have our own allies there. If Fox has Moon with him, we can blow the Horn. He will be unprepared to have the rest of the Hunt suddenly appear. Whatever plans and provisions he has made will be completely overturned. We can take them."

Wolf shook himself. "I ask that you delay in using the Horn, even if Moon is there," he said. "I have spoken with Foxblood, and it is possible that he has listened."

Nik had more color in his face, but from the way he was rubbing the bridge of his nose, he wasn't entirely happy yet. "And do you think he'll listen to you this time?"

"I was Pack Leader; he has had to listen to me in the past. He may do so again."

"You're going to have to tell them," I said. Wolf looked at me, his lips parted. He knew I was right, but the habit of protecting his brother was so strong he couldn't bring himself to speak. I had to say it for him. "Foxblood is Wolf's brother."

"And that is why you have not killed him, though you have had the opportunity." Alejandro's voice was so deadly quiet, it was worse than yelling.

"I have not killed him, and he has not killed me."

Alejandro stood, his hands in fists.

"Oh, come on." To my surprise, Nik spoke before I could. "Would *you* trust someone who could kill his own brother just like that?" He snapped his fingers. "Even if he's only some *thing* that used to be his brother? I mean, he *knows* there's a cure." Nik fell silent. He took hold of Elaine's hand again and was looking at her when he spoke. "This is his brother. All he has left. He'd want to give him every chance."

Wolf put his hand on Nik's shoulder.

Alejandro blinked slowly, amber eyes clouded as he looked inward. His shoulders relaxed, and his hands opened. I'd thought it was safe to tell him the truth, and I was glad to see that I hadn't called it wrong. Finally, he nodded. "Still," he said, "you have not explained why this should delay us in using the Horn."

"I know my brother well," Wolf turned away from Nik and leaned against the edge of the table. "Always he could be led, but never pushed." His throat worked as he swallowed. "I have offered him the chance of Healing that the High Prince has promised to the Hunt." He looked around at everyone. Alejandro was in the doorway, arms folded in front of him. Nik was half-turned toward me, sitting on the edge of the daybed. "He listened to me, I know that he did."

"But he didn't agree," Nik said.

Wolf swallowed again, forcing the muscles of his jaw to loosen. "No." He held up one hand before any of us could speak. "But it would not be his way to agree quickly. Always he must be courted and persuaded. But he will agree in the end, as he always does." Wolf looked away, and I thought I knew what he was hiding. "And when he agrees, as Pack Leader he will bring the whole of the Hunt with him."

"It is a weighty consideration," Alejandro said and Wolf looked back with hope. "We would succeed without bloodshed. And further, without the element of the Hunt to complicate matters, the Basilisk Warriors can be dealt with more straightforwardly. Guards at the Portals should be enough; they would not need to be closed."

I had to say something, though I hated to. I'd been hoping all along that maybe Wolf was right about his brother, and Fox could be persuaded. But that was before I'd touched the Horn. Before I could put the images I'd received from it together with the ones I'd just gotten from Elaine. Now I had a definite, disturbing, picture. Once again, I had to say it.

"But it won't happen," I said. "Fox won't agree. He never meant to."

Wolf rounded on me, lips pulling back from his teeth. Nik stood up between us, but it was Alejandro who, with his hand on Wolf's shoulder, made him sit down.

"You cannot know this," Wolf said, as if he and I were the only people in the room. I could also see the heat in his eyes. He felt betrayed—and why not? When we'd talked about this in the Lands, I'd been on his side. I wished I'd been able to explain in private the difference between then and now.

"Of course I can know it." My hands had formed fists, and I had to force them open. Did he think I *wanted* to tell him this? "I don't just know the things you want to hear," I reminded him. "I touched

Fox—and now I've touched Elaine. I know what his plans are. He won't give it up. Not the Hunt, not the *dra'aj*. Not now that he has his new dream. Now that he believes he can have this world. Whatever it is we know about Cassandra and what she will and won't do, *he* doesn't know it."

I reached toward Wolf, but he turned his head away.

"Look," I said. "If I wasn't sure about your brother, I would have said so. I'm sorry, Wolf, but he won't change." My breath hitched as I took it in, and I pressed my lips together to stop them trembling. Last thing I wanted to do was cry. "I wish we had time to let you try, to prove it. You'll just have to trust me."

"Valory is right," Alejandro said. "What she knows, she knows. We have believed her about you, Stormwolf, and we must believe her now. If there was cause for uncertainty, she would say so. I say we do not wait."

"I agree." Nik held up his hand. "I vote with Valory," he said.

We were all looking at Wolf now, waiting for him to speak. To decide. "You will blow the Horn regardless," Wolf said as though he were thinking aloud. "My saying 'no' will not stop you." He brought his head up, his gray eyes, now stone cold, boring in on Alejandro. "Will you trust me to be there?"

When Alejandro hesitated, I put my left hand on the table, my missing finger on display. "I trust you," I said. Wolf would try to save his brother, I knew that as well as I knew anything, but I put as much certainty into my voice as I could.

"Then I, too, vote with Valory," Wolf said.

"We will wish to be there early, so let us make what plans we can." Alejandro looked around the table, waiting until all of us, including Wolf, had nodded. Elaine, looking pale but otherwise calm, was now sitting at the head of the dining table with Nik beside her. Alejandro had given her a stiff brandy, which she'd managed to sip at.

"I've got an idea, something Moon and I talked about," she said now. "You know the Hunt calls us 'scentless ones'? What if a group of us hid in the construction area?" She turned to Nik. "It would be like what you told me about the train station. They might not even know we're there. Maybe we can't kill a Hound, but Alejandro says they *can* be injured. If we arm ourselves as well as we can, at the very least we can distract them—you know, drop things on them, trip wires, that kind of thing."

"Some of us have got guns—not many, mostly long guns for hunting, but some," Nik said. "But what about the Basilisk Warriors? Are they for us or against us? We don't know what happened to Sunset on Water, so how do they fit in?"

"If they are against us, we need worry only about those actually present," Alejandro pointed out. "Blowing the Horn will not summon *them*." He grinned suddenly, but there wasn't any humor in it. "And guns will kill a Rider, if he is hit in the right place." He tapped his forehead.

I'd been trying to avoid looking directly at him, so it took me several minutes to notice that Wolf wasn't with us, though I knew he hadn't Moved anywhere. Alejandro saw me trying to glance into the living room without drawing attention to myself, and made a slight motion of his head toward the back door. Sure enough, I found Wolf on the patio, leaning against the table, with his arms folded in front of him.

"They're figuring we should be in the Gardens before the sun sets, get ourselves set up," I said, using the shortened version of the place's name that Nik and Elaine had been using. Wolf nodded but didn't speak.

I sat down on the edge of the deck. "I'm sorry, Wolf," I said. It wasn't much, and I knew it was a lot less than he needed, but I had to say something. Apparently, it was the wrong thing, or maybe it wouldn't have mattered what I'd said. The next thing I knew I was pinned up against the side gate, Wolf with his teeth bared, and his hand around my throat. His left hand.

I told myself it was the suddenness of it, and the speed, that started me shaking. Not fear. He was so angry [the Chimera's lashing tail] that I could barely see anything else. But he wasn't going to change what I knew about Fox, not even if he ripped my throat out.

"You are wrong about my brother," he said, his voice hard.

"I wish I was," I said. I wished my mouth wasn't so dry. "You think you always persuaded your brother, but you didn't. It's easy to think you've won someone over, when they agree to something they decided to do anyway. Do you understand me? It's not just that you won't persuade him now, you never have. He just let you think so.

You didn't talk him into becoming a Hound. [It wasn't the Hunt, that's not what Fox was joining, but nothing clearer came.] He jumped at the chance. Fox wanted what you had, what he hated you for having. Always. You're punishing yourself for nothing." I waited, but he didn't speak, didn't move. It was like being held by a warm, breathing statue.

"Fox has always acted in his own self-interest," I said. Part of what I was saying I was getting from Wolf, part I'd gotten from his brother, that time on the street. "Even wanting you back, it's so he can be Pack Leader instead of you, *over* you. To show you up, command you." I swallowed. "I wish I was wrong," I said again. "I wish I could give you your brother back. Maybe some other time, some other place, I'd lie to you just to make you feel better, but there's too much at stake right now."

"I could kill you," he said, his breath warm on my face.

"Not today," I said.

That startled him, and his grip on me loosened. I'd still have bruises.

"Not today?" he repeated. "But one day?"

"One day you'll do something that could get me killed," I said. "You won't kill me yourself, but you'll put me where I might be killed."

This time he stepped back completely, and the jumbled flow of information I was getting from him stopped. He shook his head in short, slow arcs. "No. You cannot know these things."

"I wish I didn't," I said. I'd have to be careful of him now, and that saddened me. I'd have to watch what situations he put me in. Unless what I was reading was the present situation? I almost smiled. Nothing seemed more likely than that what we were planning to do would lead to the death of one of us.

"Alejandro and Nik are the ones who know the inside of Maple Leaf Gardens best," I said. "But you know the Hunt. Come in and give your opinion."

Nik looked up from the surface of the table when Wolf and I came in. His eyes went from me to Wolf and back again, and the corners of his eyebrows drew down, but he didn't say anything out loud. I took the chair at the far end, and Wolf stayed nearer the door. I tried to give Nik a reassuring smile.

Alejandro had fetched a large pad of paper, the kind I'd seen used on a flip chart, from one of the storage boxes in the basement. I couldn't remember seeing it before, so I wasn't surprised to learn, when I snagged a corner of paper between my thumb and index finger, that it was part of the tidy pile of things the previous owners had left. Apparently, they'd replaced it with a smart board.

Nik had been sketching out the inside of the Gardens with Elaine looking over his shoulder.

"This is a good big cleared space right here," he said, tapping a spot on the paper. "We've counted about thirteen Hounds, so we'd get them all in there for sure. Wolf?"

His voice came rumbling. "Thirteen is too few. Fives of five? I cannot be sure. The numbers have changed, over time." I risked glancing up and saw him frowning, his gray eyes narrowed, as if he was trying very hard to remember something that was just on the tip of his tongue. Had anything I'd seen be useful now?

"Twenty-seven? No. Maybe twenty-nine?" I said. I could hear people breathing in the silence that followed. Maybe I could even hear their heartbeats. "More have been killed since the Basilisk called them than in the whole of the previous Cycle." I looked around. "They're not all here, of course; some are in the Lands."

"But if the Horn blows, they will all come," Wolf said. "That is what Ice Tor told us."

Crap. I'd forgotten that. Master of space and time. Great.

"How can there be so many?" Alejandro wondered. "The Songs speak of single Hounds." He looked at Wolf. "Fives of five, you said."

"There have been more," Wolf said. "But even a Five of Hounds is not always together. Perhaps that gives the impression of smaller numbers."

"People who have met the Hunt and lived have only met the one they killed," I said. "Anyone who meets more than one generally doesn't survive." I thought about Nighthawk and shivered.

"So, the only Songs that tell of the Hunt convey the idea that there were not so very many," Wolf said.

"But it *is* too many. Twenty-nine?" Alejandro was shaking his head, upper lip between his teeth. "Even if the others arrive in time, we will be only four. Three swords, a wrist knife, and a dagger? Even if we have killed Hounds before? Even with the Outsiders to distract and injure them?" I could hear the despair in his voice. Then he looked up. "We must approach the High Prince. We would not be asking for a long-term commitment of Riders, but a short, surgical strike. I am sorry." Wolf had flinched at Alejandro's words. "Wild Riders," he continued, slightly less animated. "They all bear *gra'if*, and even a few would make all the difference."

"Isn't it their job?" I asked.

"It is not so simple," Wolf said. "It is not the way it was before the Cycle turned, and the Wild Riders were exactly as their name describes them. They are pledged to the High Prince now."

"Then she must give her permission," Alejandro got to his feet. "Come. We will find the precise spot to take our stand, and I will go for reinforcements."

Walks Under the Moon brought her left wrist up just in time to jam her *gra'if* armguard into the mouth of the Hound pushing her to the ground. It yelped, and for a moment Moon thought it would change to something from which an armguard—*gra'if* or not—could not protect her, but the female grabbed the thing by the scruff of its neck and pulled it away.

Moon was not fooled. She already knew that the ones shaped like Riders—such as the one holding on to her right wrist—were no different from the others, the doglike ones, the twisted ones. There were three holding her, two that looked Moonward and one Starward. They were all too thin, the sinews standing out in their hands, and they all smelled wrong somehow, of dust, dried blood, and putrefaction.

The chair was set upright once again, and Moon grimaced as she was pulled back to her feet and shoved into it. The Starward one holding her wrist—Rider-shaped or no—pushed its nose into the curve where her neck met her shoulder and inhaled noisily.

"You can't blame Hook," it said, clearly speaking to the female. "She absolutely *reeks* of *dra'aj*. It's like she's been dipped in friggin' chocolate."

"Keep a civil tongue," the female said. This one appeared to be in charge; at least, the other three obeyed her.

"I wish I could understand you," Moon said. "It seems you are speaking to one another, but all I hear are growls and barks."

Moon's head was yanked back by the hair, as the female was suddenly beside her. "Don't think you can make us angry enough to kill you, Rider bitch. You wouldn't even know how to begin insulting us." The female grinned, showing pointed teeth. "I can see from your eyes that you understand me."

Moon pressed her lips together, tight. Her eyes might give her away, but she had no intention of saying another word.

Something licked the inside of her ankle and despite herself she stiffened and tried to pull away. She already knew that with them clinging to her, she could not Move away from her captors. She would have taken the chance, but once they knew that she would try it, they kept distracting her—licking her, sniffing her, pinching her limbs–till she lacked the necessary concentration to Move at all. If she had been at home, in the Lands, where there were so many places she knew better than the inside of her own head, she could have managed it. But here? What would be the point in Moving to Elaine's home, or Wolf's, if it meant the Hunt would come with her?

"She smells so ripe." This was the one who'd been sniffing her neck. "Are you sure we can't eat her?"

Moon swallowed, trying not to show any reaction—not because she was pretending not to understand, but because she knew she would lose by it if she showed them any fear.

Let them not guess about the child.

"Pack Leader says we keep her safe," the female said. There was a little growl in her voice, but she sounded as though she were laughing.

The Moonward Hound holding Moon's left ankle tickled her foot. "Pack Leader's not here," he said.

The female cuffed him across the back of the head, but again, Moon had the feeling it was done almost affectionately. "Good thing, too, or you'd have paid for that remark."

"What we mean is," this was the one holding her right ankle, the one who'd tried to bite her, and whom she'd beaten with her *gra'if* armguard. "We're *your* Five, River. *You* decide for us."

"And Fox decides for me, Hook," the one called River said.

"But you're his favorite, everyone knows that. He listens to you."

"Make your point, Hook."

Moon jumped as the one holding her left hand twisted her thumb enough to make her squeak.

"She's got so much *dra'aj*, like as much as three or four Fives of humans. And while we're here, guarding her, we can't feed."

"Go on."

"So just a little taste," the Moonward one said. "Just, like, a human's worth."

"Each," cut in the other Moonward.

"Yeah, each. That still leaves her more than half, so she'd still be safe." He grinned and, leaning in, licked Moon on the cheek—and pulled away howling when she struck him on the ear with her *gra'if*.

Very likely she would be safe, if they actually could control themselves enough to take only some of her *dra'aj*—something Moon very much doubted—but she would lose the child, and what would become of Lightborn's *dra'aj* then?

River leaned her hip against the Hound on the left and trailed her fingers through Moon's hair. "Well, it's true we can't hunt."

You could go out one at a time. Moon was very proud she had not said that aloud. The temptation to save herself, to buy time for herself and Lightborn's child, time with the lives of others, was so very great. But she could not save herself at the risk of others, not even humans. Not if she expected to face her sister again.

Stop it, she thought. So long as she thought she might live through this, her hope gave the Hunt leverage over her. She took that advantage away from them if she was not afraid to die. What was it Max and her sister had said once? "The way of the warrior is death." It was some old human philosophy. The idea was that you knew you were going to die, so you stopped being afraid of it, and once you had stopped being afraid, no one could use that fear against you. No one could make you do something you would despise yourself for, merely to live.

But the child. Moon flexed her right hand. The Hounds were still talking.

"We don't know how long this is going to take," one of them was saying. "I know Pack Leader said sunset, but what if there's negotiations? What if there's bargaining?"

"He can't mean us to starve, that's for sure," the one called River said.

Moon licked her lips, her hands forming fists despite her intention to relax them.

"We can't Fade her," River said. "That's all. We need her as a hostage. We have to give her back when the agreement's made."

"What if the agreement's not made?" The Moonward one on the right almost sounded hopeful.

"Well, then it won't matter," River said. "We can have her for sure then." Her brow furrowed as she thought. "No, the thing is this, she's so tricky, that if we're not strong enough to hold her, she could still Move, and we'd lose her entirely. So we've got to stay strong and alert, to keep her." She smiled around at her followers, who all smiled back at her. "Get it? If we damaged her a little, just a little, like you said, Hook, she'd be less likely to escape as well. So, damaged is okay, so long as we don't Fade her. We'll take just enough to stay alert ourselves—not even as much as a whole human."

"Dibs!" The Starward Hound sank its teeth into Moon's left arm. Even through the pain, Moon could feel a slight vibration, as though the beast was howling, or humming as it bit down. Almost immediately, Moon's wrist and hand turned cold, until she could not feel her fingers. She tried to pull away, but it was like trying to move a Tree.

A different sensation made her look at her right wrist, where she saw her *gra'if* armguard glowing bright, like a flame of metal, hot, almost too hot to bear. But that heat suffused her, rushing through all her limbs, burning away the cold that had claimed her left hand, burning away even the smell of the Hound, and the feel of his teeth.

And he was not biting her any longer. He had fallen away from her as if thrown by a Troll, and even before hitting the ground he began changing, flickering through so many shapes—and so quickly—that it was too fast to follow. Once Moon thought she saw a unicorn's horn, and once claws that could have belonged to many a Guidebeast, but nothing more. A horrible keening sound began, like the highest note of a damaged flute, and the Hound settled into its Rider shape once more, its lips burned black and peeling away, skin flaking, bones collapsing in on themselves until there was only a small pile of dog-shaped dirt on the floor, and even that Faded completely away.

Only those who bore *gra'if* could kill a Hound, Moon realized. Or at least that was what so many of the old Songs told. Moon's heart thundered within her. She had not thought of her armguard as a weapon in that sense, she had not known *gra'if* would stop the Hunt from feeding, no Song spoke of it as a defensive weapon. Would she live long enough to tell anyone else?

Suddenly Moon realized she was free. In the confusion, her captors had released her. She closed her eyes, subtracted the floor with its oil stains, the hardness of the chair under her, the smell of dust, and dried blood and putrefaction. Added the silk and linen upholstery of Elaine's couch, added the sea mist scent of her air freshener, added—

Searing pain in her left arm as her elbow seemed to explode. She was cheek down in the dirt of the floor, skin abraded on the concrete.

"Oh, no, you don't, *prey*. No. You. Don't." River was kneeling on Moon's shoulders, grinding her face into the concrete, her left arm with its broken elbow hauled up behind her back.

"Okay, okay. Settle down, you two!" Whimpers in the background faded almost to silence. "Get her feet, again. Now!" Moon felt long, hard fingers take hold of each ankle.

"All right. Okay. We can't drain you. Fine. But that only buys you time, prey. And not much of it. We can still kill you, you know. We could tear your arm off."

Maybe it was the new knowledge she had. Maybe it was the note of annoyed fear in the female's voice. Maybe it was only hysteria. But Moon began to laugh.

Chapter Twenty-three

I PROBABLY WOULD HAVE FOUND the shell of Maple Leaf Gardens impressive if I hadn't just been to the Lands, and in the halls of Ice Tor—if they really were halls. After that, even the grand scale of deconstruction inside this downtown landmark couldn't move me much. It was cold inside the building, all that stone and concrete insulating us from the warm summer afternoon outside. It smelled of wet cement, and dust. I was careful to keep my elbows and hands tucked in, especially around the machinery. I didn't want to be picking up on any of the workmen.

Alejandro had already gotten as far as the spot Nik had described as the cleared central space when he turned around, looking at Wolf, eyebrows raised. Wolf nodded, his head up, his nostrils spread wide. "They have indeed been denning here, though they are not here now."

This cleared spot in the center of the construction didn't look very large to my eye, but like I said, my perspective had become a little distorted. Alejandro walked a little farther away from us, his steps sharp and precise, chin up, left hand in a fist propped on his hip as he looked around. It took me a minute to remember where I'd seen that particular posture before. In the bullring. That was how Alejandro Martín must have stood, many hundreds of times, looking up at the cheering crowds.

"What's he looking at?" I hadn't realized that Nik was standing so close to me.

"The crowds," I said. "The crowds in the stands of the *Plaza de Toros*."

"He was a bullfighter?"

I shook my head, my eyes still on Alejandro, and the invisible *corrida*. "A *matador*."

"Same thing, isn't it?"

I blinked and turned to face Nik. "No. A bullfighter is a *toreador*. *Matador* means killer, the one who actually kills the bull. *Un matador de toros*. A killer of bulls. *Un matador de hombres*. A killer of men."

"He's done both, hasn't he?"

"Yes, he has."

Nik was quiet for a few minutes, watching as Wolf joined Alejandro. The two Riders started pointing around them and gesturing at the small hills created out of the construction debris, and the hiding spots afforded by the equipment. Alejandro pulled out his mobile and started talking into it. I wondered if the Riders he was calling would get here in time.

Nik turned to face me, taking my right hand in his. It was late in the day, and his beard was coming in. It suddenly struck me that the Riders I'd seen were either bearded or not; none of them ever needed a shave.

Alejandro and Wolf turned their heads suddenly, looking behind us. I spun around, but Nik's touch on my arm steadied me.

"It's Poco," he said. The thin man had brought along about a dozen other Outsiders, four of them carrying either shotguns or rifles, don't ask me which. I recognized the guy I'd seen in the lobby of the Royal York, on the day I'd met Wolf. Yves, that was his name. He had a crossbow.

"Hey, Nik. You must be Val." Poco gave each of us a nod before tilting his head back to stare at the space around us. "Sure is something, isn't it? Didn't look anywhere near so big when the Leafs were still playing here." He brought his eyes back down to us. "You figured out where you want us?"

"We've got some ideas, yeah. Follow me." Poco signaled the others, and Nik led them away.

Once they'd gone, I settled down on a chunk of concrete. It had been part of a stairwell at one time, but so many feet had used it over the years that it was the inanimate equivalent of the living city around me. Nothing but buzz and white noise. I was glad to be sitting down. My heart was pounding, my palms damp. I thought about Moon and her child. I hoped they were going to be safe, and I wished there was a way for me to know. The Horn would be blown. Right now, that was about all I could be sure of.

I took a deep breath and let it out slowly, watching Alejandro and Wolf. They were a study in contrasts, and not just because one was Moonward black and the other Sunward red. Alejandro looked like his normal human self—even when we'd been in the Lands, I now realized, he'd retained his Hector Vega suit. But now that he was distracted, Wolf's clothing looked less human. His jacket was longer, the material was more silver-gray than blue, and it looked as though it was brocaded with some kind of animal. His *gra'if* glowed slightly in the dimness.

What was coming would be harder for Wolf to face than anything he'd come up against before, even his Healing. That, as he'd said several times, had been forced on him. Sure, he was happy about it now, but it wasn't as though he'd planned it—he'd never even had the chance to say no. Now, on the other hand, he was deliberately planning to ambush his own brother, and he had plenty of time to think about it, to second-guess the plans—even to wonder if he could trust himself.

Alejandro still stood with his head up, eyes narrowed, thin lips pulled to one side in an ironic smile—just as if he was hearing, somewhere in the distance, a glory of trumpets. As if imagining the crowd on their feet, and their "*¡olés!*" echoing off the rafters far above us. Was he *feeling* it, too? The fire in the blood, the imminent danger, the possibility that, today, it would be the bull that walked away?

I'd seen a glimpse of this fiery being in the days after Alejandro had rescued me from the Collector. Maybe once or twice since, like when he'd come back from Granada that time, after killing the Basilisk Warrior. But more in the last few days. The spark, the glint in his eye, told me a part of him was enjoying this very much.

He seemed so alive, almost glowing. In that moment I wondered what would happen if we all lived through this. I wondered whether Alejandro would be able to find something to give him this zest for living again. Maybe living with me in our nice house in the Beaches would be too tame? Could he go back to the *corridas*? Turn himself into a younger man and start again from the bottom, with a new face and a new name? Or maybe he could go into the military once again.

I also wondered whether any of us *would* live through this. I knew what I had to do, but I still wasn't sure *why*. There was so much at stake that, for the first time, it was actually hard for me to trust my ability. And there wasn't anyone I could ask for advice.

"You are very serious." I'd been thinking so hard I hadn't noticed Wolf come up beside me.

"I'm thinking about what Alejandro will do when the adventure is over," I said.

"It's a way of distracting oneself." I turned to him in surprise, and not only because this was the first time I'd heard him use a contraction. "To think about what one will do afterward makes the present seem less full of danger," he added.

"People have the habit of living," I said. "Even the Outsiders, who literally deal in the deaths of others and see it all the time, even they plan for tomorrow."

"Riders, too," he said.

"Ah, but then you all have so very many tomorrows."

He turned to look at me directly, and I felt the impact of his ash-gray eyes. "None of us—Rider, Solitary, Natural, or human—is promised any tomorrow. Any of us can be killed."

"And who kills us, unless it is we, ourselves?"

Suddenly the breath was knocked out of me, and Wolf was pushing me to stand between him and Alejandro. We hadn't Moved, but Wolf had covered the ground at top Rider speed, bringing me along with him. I staggered, but managed to keep my feet, then turned around and looked back at where we'd just been.

There, sitting right on the chunk of cement I'd been using, was Fox.

"Did you really think I wouldn't know if you came early?" He shook his head, upper lip ever so slightly lifted. "Did you think coming now would give you some kind of advantage?"

Alejandro, just on my right, hissed in his breath. It was only the second time, I realized, that he'd seen one of the Hunt looking like a Rider—and the first time he knew what he was looking at. Even now that he was wearing ordinary clothes—jeans, and a black T-shirt that said Red Dwarf—there was no mistaking the height, the perfect symmetry of the features, and the clarity of Fox's coloring. He was a Moonward Rider, of course, like Wolf, and had almost exactly Wolf's shade of color, the almond skin, the ash-gray eyes. Fox's hair was, if anything, darker, the kind of sable black that seems almost blue in certain lights.

"I wish I knew where you fit in." Fox focused his attention on me, and I remembered just in time that I'd been warned not to look into a Hound's eyes. I assumed that held true even if he looked like a regular Rider. "Are you the piece that wins the game? Or are you already off the board?"

He dismissed me again, looking between the Riders, as if weighing up which one was leader. "So. Do you have an answer for me?" he said finally, looking at Alejandro. "I'm assuming you're the one empowered to tell me, since it can't be my brother." Fox laughed, but I was glad to see that Wolf didn't react to the jibe, except to grip his sword more tightly.

Alejandro didn't step back, exactly, but his stance subtly shifted, as if he'd been at attention and was now at ease. Somehow, something about what was happening was making him more relaxed.

"And if I said I was not the one?" Alejandro's lips twitched as if he was about to smile. "As you say, we are early. We await the arrival of the High Prince's herald, with her instructions. You have given us until sunset."

Fox's eyes narrowed. "I got a feeling you're not taking this very seriously. Maybe my brother gave you the idea I'm a nice guy." He smiled, and he was so beautiful I could feel the sting of tears in my eyes. "That's too bad. The sun'll set soon, but I'm in the mood to end this right now." He lifted his hand and waved his fingers in a "come forward" gesture.

With everyone's attention elsewhere, I started to get the Horn out of the front of my shirt, reaching in from the bottom with my left hand. I was going to need it soon, and I didn't want to be fumbling for it. Fox's words froze me momentarily

"You have given us until sunset," Wolf reminded his brother. "It was you who set the time, Foxblood. Will you break your word already? Why, then, should we treat with you at all?"

I had managed to get my fingers into the folds of cloth until I had the end of the Horn between my thumb and index finger. Once again I had the image of the person who was going to blow it, but since I'd had that already, I also saw beyond it, to Wolf, and to Ice Tor, and even to the Water Natural who had supplied the liquid in Wolf's flask.

"Hey, I don't care if we don't speed things up. It's just that Walks Under the Moon makes such a tasty mouthful. It's hard for my people to resist her. Even when they want to preserve what human *dra'aj* gives us." He swept his hand down, indicating his own form. "Did you know we can Move now, *brother*?"

"That and more would be possible with Healing," Wolf said. "Can you not see how your own words condemn your choice? Even with what you see as the benefit of human *dra'aj*, the Pack is still drawn to feed on People. You have no control."

"Hey, it's *you*, you're causing the trouble." Fox's voice, his whole *face*, sharpened. "Go. Away. Close the Portals. We can control ourselves just fine without you around. Leave controlling the Pack to me." His eyes shifted momentarily to me. "Take your pets with you. We can spare them."

Both Wolf and Alejandro shifted their eyes to look at me. At first I thought they'd noticed me getting out the Horn, but then I realized they were reacting to Fox's suggestion. Both of them had the same oddly wistful look on their faces, and I suddenly knew that either one of them *might* have considered Fox's plan, if I'd actually been able to go. But I wouldn't live very long in the Lands. I wondered if I would have been brave enough to tell them to go. I was glad I would never have to know. Even if I had been willing to sacrifice myself to save everyone else (oh, how I hoped I would have been), it wouldn't have mattered. If we didn't stop Fox and the Hunt, no one would be safe.

"You can even take the ones up there. Hey, just because I can't smell them doesn't mean I can't hear them." Fox pointed up and to the left, for all the world like a tour guide pointing out the CN Tower.

I held my breath as every one of us looked up in the direction Fox was indicating, but it was only Nik who came out of the shadows at the top of the open flight of concrete stairs. He was shrugging, but his jaw was clenched. I think we all waited, holding our breaths, for Fox to say something more—and stifled our relief when he didn't. Maybe he bought it, maybe he thought it was only Nik he'd heard.

With eyes off me once again, I drew the Horn all the way out of its wrappings, gripping it tightly in my left hand. That hand still didn't feel any different, and there still wasn't any pain. That's when another piece of the puzzle fell into place. It was almost as if the Horn itself was compelling me to speak.

[I saw Ice Tor, and the Portals; the *dra'aj* it took to make them work, to keep them stable in space and time; the *amount* of *dra'aj* and the *kind* of *dra'aj*.] What was it I'd been told? The Portal in Australia had collapsed during the Exile. Now the one in Toronto wasn't working. What did this mean?

"Take your pets and go," Fox said again. "And I'll give you Moon back into the bargain."

"You can't." Now they all turned to look at me. Alejandro and Wolf had almost identical looks of concern on their faces. Fox only narrowed his gray eyes.

"You can close the Portals, I don't mean that. But if you," I made it clear I was addressing Fox. "If you take the *dra'aj* from this world you'll destroy it. And this world anchors the Lands. Yin and Yang," I said. Nik, Alejandro, and Wolf all nodded, while Fox just frowned. "*Dra'aj* doesn't naturally exist here, like it does in the Lands. It had to be brought here." A flicker of images cascade through my brain. Something about how the transport was done—but then it was gone. "And the place itself won't support *dra'aj*, only the people can." And some other living things, I suddenly knew, but I wasn't going to say that aloud. "How long will it take you to eat all the *dra'aj* here? A thousand years? Two? Not very long for Riders." I edged forward until I was standing just in front of Wolf. "And the supply of humans won't last that long. You think you can organize yourselves? Figure out some kind of rationing system? You're *addicts*, no matter what you say, you can't control yourselves."

Fox stood up and took a few steps closer to us. "I can control them. I am Pack Leader."

"Until they turn upon you, and make you prey," Wolf said.

"You can't even control yourself," I added. "Otherwise, you wouldn't have taken Nighthawk's *dra'aj*—you could have passed along this proposition to him. A Warden of the Exile? Are you kidding me? The perfect person to approach. But you couldn't stop yourself." I took a deep breath. "By the time you figure out you'll have to breed more humans, it'll be too late. Humans don't breed fast enough, and humans without *dra'aj* don't breed at all."

Now I turned to Alejandro and Wolf. "And don't think you can let this happen. Because when they've used up all the *dra'aj* here, they'll be coming to you for help, except you won't be there anymore. Without the anchor of the Shadowlands, the Lands will break up and disappear."

"How do you know this?" Fox did his best to sound skeptical, but I could hear the belief underneath.

I held up the Horn. Fox hissed, but there wasn't anything I could do about that. They all needed to see where my knowledge came from. "Ice Tor knows about the forging of the bond between our worlds. The Dwarves built the Portals. The knowledge is part of them, passed down through the Cycles." I held up the Horn again. "This is part of him. It knows what he knows." I tucked the Horn into my shirt again, but this time just into the neckline, where it would be easy to reach.

Fox laughed. I saw Wolf flinch out of the corner of my eye. I wondered if his brother had laughed the same way when they'd been boys together. I hoped not. "You listening to this prey? 'Course she's not gonna want us to come to terms."

"She is a Truthreader," Wolf said, and the slightest flicker of concern passed over Fox's face.

"We will trust her, before we trust you," Alejandro added. I was a little shocked to hear an undercurrent of laughter in his voice. Was he *enjoying* himself?

"So that's it, then?" Fox looked from Wolf to Alejandro and back again. "Basically what you're saying is we've got no agreement? So I don't need a hostage, do I? We're through here." He began to back away, for some reason not Moving this time. I wondered. Was it maybe not as easy for them as it was for real Riders?

"No," Wolf spoke up. "Fox, think. Listen to me. If you choose to be Healed, it would resolve everything. Think, Fox. You are Pack Leader, and where you lead, they will be sure to follow."

It was flattery of the worst kind, and just for a second Fox did look undecided, and I could see that Wolf was beginning to relax by the way his shoulders lowered. Even though he knew the truth of what I'd told him, he couldn't help hoping I was wrong. But I knew what would happen. Fox waited until the hope was clear on Wolf's face, and then he laughed, with that little "gotcha" gleam in his eye.

"Still whining like a little puppy? Brother, *you* listen to me. I will *never* accept this so-called cure. I will *never* become the lackey of Riders, of *prey*. How does it feel? Do you enjoy it? Is this your new Pack? Two of you and a couple of humans and you're not even the leader?" His laugh was almost a bark. "You think I'll go back to that? Never! And you *are* right. Where I lead, others *will* follow, and I'll forbid any other to accept."

"Then I challenge you for the leadership of the Hunt."

"No way. You can't—you're the one who says you're not a Hound anymore."

"Wolf! What are you playing at?" Nik went to grab Wolf by the sleeve, but Alejandro pulled him back, still with the same sparkle in his eyes that he'd had during the whole exchange.

Wolf spoke directly to me, as if I'd been the one to speak. "You were right. He will not change his mind and rejoin us, but if I beat him, he will have to submit to me, or the Pack itself will turn on him. If I win, the Pack will do as I say."

"And if you lose?" This was Nik, saying the words my tight throat stopped me from saying.

"We are no worse off than we are at this moment, and I will buy time." Buy time for what, he couldn't say aloud.

"Hey." Fox raised his hands and waved them at us. I could swear he was laughing. "I still say *I* have no reason to agree."

"Well, gee, I guess I could always *use* this." I pulled the Horn free again. "I think this little trinket makes *me* the one in charge of the Hunt, doesn't it?" Wolf started to say something, but then fell silent again. He'd just remembered that Fox didn't know the Horn could only be used once.

You wouldn't think someone so pale, someone so black and white, could show so much heat, but Fox was suddenly blazing with rage.

Eventually, a calculating look came into his eye. "Okay." He gave a short nod. "Okay, then. I'll accept the challenge." He smiled again, this time showing too many teeth. "But I want conditions." He pointed at me. "First, that human will not blow the Horn." I nodded, tucking the Horn back into my shirt. "Second, you, *brother*, since you say you don't want to kill me, won't use your *gra'if* blade. And last, if I win, you come with me. You rejoin the Pack."

Both Nik and Alejandro were shaking their heads, but anyone could see that Wolf was going to agree.

"If you do not bear your *gra'if*, he will kill you," Alejandro said.

This time Fox laughed out loud. "Kill my own brother? No more than he'd kill me. Have your Truthreader test me; see if I lie."

"I won't touch you myself," I said, before either Alejandro or Nik could object. "But I will touch Wolf while he touches you." That was acceptable. Wolf, his *gra'if* blade in his hand since we hadn't yet agreed to the conditions, took my hand and led me across the rubble-strewn floor to where Fox stood. He sheathed the blade and took hold of his brother's hand.

"He's telling the truth," I said. There was something else, something still just out of my reach. With Wolf between us, I reached out with my free hand—my left hand—and brushed the back of Fox's wrist with my fingertips. His skin was hot.

There. I had it, clear. Maybe because Fox still had all the *dra'aj* he'd ever collected, when Wolf didn't, but now I saw the *why*, where touching Ice Tor had only shown me the *how*.

"He's telling the truth," I said again. "He will abide by the agreement—in fact, he's got to."

I shifted around, beginning to straighten up, more relaxed now that was sorted, and even Wolf was breathing more easily, when Fox struck. So fast that I couldn't see his hand move, he reached into the gaping neck of my T-shirt and snatched out the Horn. Before Wolf could react, Fox had the Horn at his lips, and blew.

At once we were struck with a blast of cold air, bringing with it a sound so low it shook my bones. Where there had only been the clean smell of concrete and dust, I smelled old blood and rot. Suddenly there were new forms and shadows around us, but before Wolf could even draw his sword—CRACK!!

In the dim light filtering through the green glass doors, I saw enough high-backed, padded chairs and long, low tables to recognize the Panorama Lounge at Union Station.

We'd been Moved.

The sound, horrible and jarring, seemed to pass right through Moon, making her bones shiver and her blood hurt. She'd become used to the old meat smell of the Hounds around her, but now it seemed fresher—if that was not a contradiction in terms. The sound died away, or at least became obscured by the howling and the baying that now arose around her, all the more horrible because only a few of the Hounds had changed into dog shapes; more retained Rider form. As she watched, the Hounds began disappearing, popping out of existence one by one.

Moon braced herself, trying to be ready for whatever might come. The light changed suddenly, and she found herself in a cavernous building, dimly lit and filled, apparently, with ruins. Her wrist and one of her ankles were suddenly freed as two of her captors abruptly became dogs and lost their grips. She swung her fist at the third, striking it repeatedly about the head with her *gra'if* armguard. As soon as she was free, other hands, different hands, grabbed her and, despite her struggles to resist, dragged her away.

"Rider, we're on the same side." It was a voice she hadn't heard before. The people around her, she realized, were humans.

"Let me up," she said. "They cannot feed from me, let me up. Give me a weapon."

A warm piece of metal was shoved into her hand, its handle feeling strangely comfortable to her grip.

"Point this end," one of them said. "Pull this part."

The thing went off with a most satisfying noise, and Moon had the joy of seeing a Hound go down with part of his head missing.

The sound, the horrible teeth-shaking sound pushed Nik to his knees, but before he could even think about his danger, Alejandro yanked him to his feet, and thrust something cold and metallic into his hands. About to protest that he hadn't used a sword or dagger for years, Nik was relieved to find he was holding a handgun.

The first thing he did was laugh out loud. "You know it's illegal to have one of these?" he said, but all the Rider did was smile wider.

Nik had never shot this type of handgun before, but like everyone who owned a TV, he'd seen it done thousands of times. He braced his right wrist with his left hand, took aim and fired. Luckily—or unluckily—some of the Hunt were presenting fairly large targets. Even those not in Rider shape were more-or-less Rider—that is to say human—sized. *Easier to get a bead on than a dog.*

"It's working," Nik called over his shoulder as a lucky shot spun a Hound right around, crashing him into another and knocking them both down.

"Does not kill them," Alejandro yelled back.

Right. Nik remembered now. Torso shots might knock them down, but they wouldn't stay down.

Alejandro seemed to be everywhere at once, and yet somehow never in Nik's line of fire. The *gra'if* blade, blindingly bright, flashed like a bolt of lightning.

Something grabbed him by the ankle and while Nik tried to twist to get the gun aimed at it, he was pulled down before he could safely take a shot. Only the fact that the thing wasted time getting close enough to bite him saved him from having his *dra'aj* drained on the spot. Nik was still trying to get the gun positioned so he wouldn't shoot his own foot off when a chunk of concrete the size of a soccer ball glanced off the Hound's head, knocking it off balance and loosening its grip. Now that he was aware of it, Nik heard other guns firing, and the blasts of shotguns, and grinned again as more concrete missiles banged down into the group of Hounds around them.

All at once, a flash of bright silver sliced through the limb that was still wrapped around Nik's ankle. The thing howled, blood fountaining from its cut wrist. *Not a light saber*, Nik thought, trying not to giggle as he turned to fire point-blank at something else that was getting too close.

This isn't a movie, was the next thought he had. Alejandro's sword wasn't a light saber, and his gun was going to run out of bullets. If someone didn't come to help them soon, he and Alejandro were goners.

In a moment Moon was able to stand back with those around her and take stock.

Below them, and to the left, she could see two figures fighting, back to back. The *gra'if* blade one held was so bright, and moved so quickly, that even her Rider eyes had difficulty following it. The other figure had a weapon like the one she held herself. It did not stop the Hounds around them, Moon saw, but only slowed them. If something was not done, and soon, these two would be overwhelmed.

"Wolf?" she asked.

"Lady, no idea. Gone, you know?" The one who answered clapped her hands sharply, and Moon understood this was the sound of Movement. That gave her an idea.

"I will go for help," she said. "Be steadfast."

The cuts and scratches on Alejandro's arms were too numerous to number. More serious by far was the slice along his left calf, and the puncture, low in his belly, close to his right hip, that had missed the abdominal artery only by virtue of his quick reflexes and the long training he had had in the bullring. And it was that training, along with all his years in arms, that allowed Alejandro to ignore the pain—and the knowledge that while the injury would not kill him quickly, a slow death was the best he could hope for if help did not come soon.

Out of nowhere a rock struck the flank of the twisted Chimera that menaced him, throwing it off its stride, and allowing Alejandro the opening he needed to slash its throat while its scaly lion's head turned to seek out the new menace. Rocks and debris were dropping and falling all around them, flying out of the darkness—darkness which slowly increased as the day outside darkened into night, and the few windows left unboarded became nothing more than pale shadows.

Without this distraction from the Outsiders—their rock throwing punctuated with the sharp pop of a pistol, or the boom of a shotgun—he and Nik would long ago have been overwhelmed. He knew exactly where the boy stood at his back, could almost feel with him the recoil of the gun as he fired. Almost the first thing Alejandro had done was to take off his jacket and he now held it in his left hand, shaking it sometimes gently and sometimes with force. When the eyes went to the jacket instead of staying on him, he struck.

On the defensive as they both were, they would lose this battle soon. Only the *gra'if* blade could kill, and Alejandro was expecting at any moment that one or both of them would be bitten, he to Fade forever, and Nik to be emptied. He was doing his best to keep them off the boy, but why he had not succumbed himself was more than he could guess at. It was important to defend the boy. Valory would wish it. They did not need to win, only to die on their feet.

Alejandro's blood sang and in the distance he could hear the crowds cheering him. He looked around him for the bull.

Moon lost too much time finding a working Portal to allow protocol to delay her further. She Moved directly to her sister's pavilion.

"Max," she said, her sides heaving. "Where is Truthsheart?"

"Take a breath." Max came round the table with hands extended. "What is it?"

Moon tried, but her throat was still too tight. She coughed, her lungs painful as she dragged in air. "Max, I must have a squad of Wild Riders, now, immediately." She was afraid he would waste time with questions, but she should have known better.

"Wings of Cloud," he called. The Moonward Rider appeared in the doorway, with a smile for his Prince that faded when he saw Moon. "How many Wild Riders in camp?" Max asked.

Frowning, Wings thought for what felt to Moon like several minutes. "Five, perhaps six," he said finally.

"Any more who bear *gra'if*," Moon asked. "Anyone? It is Hounds we must kill."

"Perhaps one or two more," Wings said. "But—"

Max held up his hand. "Have them in front immediately." He turned to Moon. "Where's the problem? Can you Move everyone there directly?"

Moon shook her head and held up her hands. "The Shadowlands." She coughed, and braced her hand on her belly.

"The Shadowlands? Moon, you know that Cassandra isn't sending anyone there." Max turned away from her, as if to recall the orders he'd issued.

"Wait." She took him by the sleeve. "We have the Hunt, all in one place. The Horn was blown."

Max stared at her, blinked, and smiled. "Now that, as they say, is a horse of a different color." He began running for the exit.

The Wild Riders, accustomed to sudden alarms, were already

gathered in front of the pavilion when Moon followed Max out. Other Riders, most in the colors of someone's household, began to appear. All three Wards mixed together freely: Star, Moon, and Sun, and all bore *gra'if* of one kind or another.

"*Gra'if* weapons only, if you please," Max called out. "Those of you who don't bear actual weapons can stand down."

Moon waved her hands in the air. "By no means," she said. "Those who bear *gra'if* cannot be eaten by the Hunt, so any and all will be useful."

Max looked at her, brows raised. "We'll talk about this later," he said, turning back to the troops around them. "Everyone," he said. "Gather round."

Wings of Cloud appeared at Max's elbow. "That is everyone," he said. "And I am myself the senior Wild Rider present."

Max patted him on the shoulder. "Riders," he called out. "I have need of you, and of your *gra'if*. I ask that you follow Walks Under the Moon to the Shadowlands, where you'll find a nest of the Hunt."

"A Hound hunt!" called out a voice from the back of the group, and there were grim smiles, but little laughter.

"Moon says even those of you without weapons can help, as the Hunt cannot Fade someone who bears *gra'if*." The smiles became slightly less grim.

"Can you tell us anything more, Lady Moon?" called out a Wild Rider, pushing her way to the front of those assembled. She was a Sunward Rider, her red-gold hair cut short and shaggy around her head, and kept in place with the crownlike circlet that was her *gra'if* helm. She leaned against the long spear that was the favored weapon of many among the Wild Riders.

"There looked to be at least thirty," Moon said. "The Fourth Portal has collapsed, and so we must use the Fifth, and then a crossroads. Once at our destination, I can Move us directly to the location of the engagement."

"Any allies we should look out for?" Wings of Cloud asked.

"Stormwolf is there." Moon said. There were nods and murmurs among the Wild Riders. "As well as Graycloud at Moonrise, a Sunward Rider who has been living these long years in the Shadowlands. There may also be several humans," she added. "But you will know them as soon as you see them, from their dress if nothing else. You may kill any other."

Now there were more smiles, straightening of shoulders, and hefting of weapons.

"They are not many," Moon said, almost under her breath.

"Then the glory will be greater," Wings said. "Come." He clapped his *gra'if*-covered hands. "Spear Circle, with Lady Moon as our focus."

With the Wild Riders to show them how, the troop formed a tight circle around her, two deep, each with one hand on the next Rider, and one hand on the Rider behind. Those in the outermost circle kept a free hand for their weapons, those in the inner circle reached in to take hold of Moon herself, touching her on shoulder or arm.

"When you are ready, Lady Moon," Wings of Cloud called out from his position in the outer Circle.

Moon took a deep breath, focused her concentration, and Moved.

Fox still had hold of my wrist [giddiness; the kind of nausea you get from eating too much; he'd wanted to be a Wild Rider when he grew up] and swung me around behind him as he turned to face Wolf, and I went limp, thinking I would drag his arm down and keep him off balance. The ploy might have worked on a human, but my weight was nothing to a Rider. Fox jerked me back into an upright position so sharply that my teeth snapped shut and I bit the inside of my lip. He probably could have held me in the air for a couple of hours without feeling the strain.

Too fast to follow, Wolf spun in, his *gra'if* blade flashing bright, but Fox was just as fast, swinging me forward again, and Wolf had to hold off, or cut me instead of his brother.

"Good, now we know how important she is." Seeing he could use me as a shield, Fox curled his arm around me, keeping me close up against his chest with his hand on my throat. Maybe I could flail my arms a little, but I found myself reflexively hanging onto his wrist, though I was in no danger of choking. Yet. Keeping his eyes directly on Wolf, Fox dropped the Horn on the ground and stamped on it, crushing it under his heel. Pain flared in my left hand, leaving me gasping as the heat of it passed through my entire body. For a second, I thought it would actually choke me, and Fox's grip was the only thing that kept me upright.

"Is this why you won't come back to me, brother? This human thing? So how can I change your mind? What might persuade you, I wonder?" Fox turned his face into mine and breathed in, as if he was trying to inhale me. Somehow I knew his eyes were still fixed on Wolf's. "What if I say I'll kill her if you don't come back? Or maybe I should promise she'll live if you do? Hmmm? What do you think? Which would work better?"

Wolf looked at me. My head had cleared, though my hand still felt as if it was burning. I could taste blood from where I had bitten myself. I moved my head from side to side, just a centimeter or so each way, but Wolf was looking for it, and caught it. To be honest, I didn't know whether Fox was lying or not. Apparently, sufficient pain was enough to dampen my talent—temporarily, I found myself hoping. I shook my head not because I knew Fox was lying, but because I knew that it didn't matter, that Wolf would have to deal with him regardless, and I didn't want to be the thing that stopped him.

"Let her go." Wolf said. "You will do what you will do. Whatever may happen, may happen. But if you do not let her go, I will kill you myself, right here and now." I couldn't be certain, because of the angle my own head was at, but I was pretty sure Wolf wasn't looking Fox directly in the eye. *Do not look them in the eyes, and keep striking, no matter what.* I didn't know where that thought came from; I only knew it wasn't mine.

"No, I don't think so." I could feel Fox's voice rumbling in his chest. Suddenly I was choking as Fox's grip on my throat tightened. Wolf stepped forward, his blade up, and Fox must have seen the determination in his eyes because he relaxed again, not letting me simply drop to the ground, but tossing me to one side. I tried to curl, to protect my hot and throbbing hand, but I landed hard against the arm of a chair, and felt something give in my side.

"I don't need that," Fox said. "You won't kill me. You're still a Hound." From his tone you would think we were all sitting in the lounge, having a nice conversation as we waited for our train. "That's your only value to them, and they're using it, *and* you. How does it feel to be the thing of no account? The unimportant one?"

"I am of the High Prince's *fara'ip*."

"Oh, sure, along with every bird in the sky, every fish in the water, every mouse and every rabbit—every *vegetable*. Everyone and everything in the Lands belongs to the High Prince, and the High Prince belongs to each and every one of them." Fox took a breath, spreading out his hands like he was welcoming Wolf in. "And not a single one of them is ever going to let you forget that you once ran with the Hunt. Come back to us, Wolf. Come back where you belong. I'll let you be second to me. That's got to be better than what you are now. They all see you as tainted, and you'll *never* be one of them."

Wolf's face had been calm, assured, waiting for his moment to speak, right up until Fox said the word "tainted." Then I saw Wolf's face change, and I knew that Fox's words spoke to him in a way maybe no one but me would understand. And not only because I'd felt this in him, this fear that there *was* a taint in him, never to come clean. That was the real chink in his armor, not just his love for his brother—you can kill the thing you love, if you really need to—and not just the guilt Fox made him feel.

It was the fear that he might never belong anywhere else but the Hunt. That's what was stopping Wolf from speaking. The fear that Fox was right.

"You don't need to be one of them," I managed to gasp through my bruised throat. "This isn't the only choice you've got—either Ride with the Riders, or Hunt with the Hunt. There's another option."

"Oh, really? Now dinner has an opinion?" Fox was letting me speak because he didn't believe anything I could say would influence Wolf more than he could himself. But Fox didn't realize that I knew Wolf better than he knew him. I knew Wolf better than he knew himself.

"You can wolf with the wolves," I said. He needed to belong—something I understood all too well. Would he be brave enough to stop looking to belong to someone else, and start asking people to belong to him? I shifted until I was sitting up, hissing at the stab in my side, sharper now than the dull ache of my maimed hand. "You don't need to be one of them, either a Rider or a Hound. You can be one of yourself. Hell, start a new Pack, a *fara'ip* of your own. So you have a talent that other people value and use, and maybe without it you would have been left to yourself, living an uneventful life, and that makes it hard for you to accept it." Again, I knew that I was speaking for more than Wolf now. I was also speaking about myself, and about the life I might have had if I hadn't been Collected.

"But your talent also made you important to people, kept you alive and safe when circumstances might have overwhelmed you." Still talking about myself. "Sure, other people use the talent, but don't you see? *You* can use it, too. It's yours. It's valuable to *you*. You can make it work for *you*."

Wolf was looking at me now, and his face changed again, as I had hoped it would, and it seemed that my pain faded away as his gray eyes grew warm and his lips began to smile. But I wasn't the only one who saw the change, and knew for certain what it meant. With a howl of the darkest rage and despair, Fox struck.

Nik had gone down to one knee, and Alejandro found himself almost leaning against the boy's shoulder, unsure which of them was propping the other one up. *How many bullets can he have remaining?* Alejandro thought. As he parried yet another slash, he became aware of the numbness down the right side of his body, the burning in the muscles of his arms, and the growing weight of his sword. The end was here. Now. Help would not arrive in time.

The noise of the other gunshots, the falling of the rocks, was already fading away. The number of the Hunt around them increased, notwithstanding the ones he had killed. Some of these—in Rider shape—had gone up into the higher sections of the arena, attacking the Outsiders. There would be empty humans now, emptied again.

Alejandro gripped Nik's shoulder just as a monumental CLAP! of air rocked them both, followed by an astonishing brightness, brighter by far than the beams of sunlight that had earlier illuminated the darkness. The space around where Alejandro and Nik stood gripping each other in a failing attempt to remain upright, was suddenly filled with figures in black, in greens and reds and purples, and with bright, swift *gra'if*. Alejandro sank to his knees, and Nik went down with him, barely softening his fall until he was lying on the cement floor.

"Healer!" He thought he had bellowed the word, bellowed it in the voice he would have used in the bullring. The voice he had many times used to call "medic!" in other battlefields. He looked around and thought he saw Moon running toward him. Nik, the gun still in his hand, was saying something, but Alejandro could not hear him.

"Bring them," he told the boy. "Bring your friends. I have *dra'aj*. Let them take it."

He smiled and saluted the cheering crowds. He would get both ears today, and perhaps the tail.

I should have been terrified, but I think all my terror circuits were burned out. Either I was just too tired, and too hurt, or too many things had frightened me too recently for me to feel very much more. Like Wolf said, whatever was going to happen, was going to happen. *Que será, será. That's* what the song meant. I'd wondered. I rubbed at my forehead with my uninjured hand, as if that would make my thoughts more orderly. I knew I should be feeling more, but every time I tried to take a deep breath, my side stabbed at me.

There wasn't a lot of room in the Lounge, and they were circling each other in a narrow aisle, Fox with a chair he had grabbed up, and Wolf with his *gra'if* blade poised, left hand raised for balance. I looked around me for a weapon, something I could use to help, but Wolf and Fox moved so fast that they were mostly a blur, with every now and then something coming suddenly clear, like watching bad stop-motion.

—the chair was on the floor and Wolf slashed at a unicorn covered with sores and scraps of scales, its horn broken off.

—Wolf ducked under the belly of a dragon with hairy wings, cutting upward as it tried to grab at him.

—a bank of chairs exploded into shards of metal, bits of wood, and upholstery smeared with blood and ichor.

—they stood chest to chest, Wolf's sword arm trapped under Fox's arm, each gripping the other in a fierce hug, Fox's teeth growing out to bite Wolf in the throat.

Wolf was trying *not* to kill him, I realized. Did he still think that somehow he could force his brother to be cured?

—Wolf, bleeding from a wound in his shoulder, with a thick green snake looped around his body, left hand holding its head away with a grip on its throat, right hand with blazing sword raised.

—a table shattered as Wolf staggered away from a towering kraken, slashing off a tentacle at its root.

—Wolf stood with his foot on his brother's throat, Fox limp, eyes rolled up, bleeding from the stump of his right arm.

I staggered to my feet, gasping as the sharp pain of my broken ribs stabbed freshly, trying to breathe shallowly. Using the backs of a couple of the chairs that still stood upright and in one piece, I managed to make it around to where Wolf could see me without having to move his head. I touched him.

"Go ahead," I said.

"If I kill him here, his *dra'aj* will be lost forever. All the *dra'aj* that he has taken in all his time." He shut his eyes tight. "Nighthawk."

I shook my head. Fox didn't have Nighthawk's *dra'aj*, but I couldn't take the time to explain that now.

"Go ahead," I said again. I already knew what he was planning. "Go. I'm okay here. Someone will come and help me."

And they were gone.

I looked around me and swallowed. There would be water and who knew, maybe even food in the fridge.

Though it would take more than the cleaning crew to fix up what had happened to Union Station's Panorama Lounge.

Chapter Twenty-four

"ARE YOU READY?" Wolf raised his hands as if to place them on my shoulders, but lowered them when I flinched. Everybody was being very careful not to touch me, and normally I would have really appreciated that. But just now it reminded me of how alone I was. I managed to nod.

"Ready as I'll ever be." I was hoping I'd imagined the flatness in my voice, but I doubted it. I sighed. I'd been doing that a lot lately.

"You don't have to do this," Nik said. He and Wolf exchanged glances. They'd been doing *that* a lot lately.

"Yeah, I do. You know I do." It's not that I'd been putting it off, but a part of me had definitely been relieved at the week or so it had taken to set this up.

Wolf undid the buttons of his shirt, exposing the dragon tattoo. The colors were so rich that they made the furniture in my living room drab. Wolf nodded at Nik, and the two of them clasped each other's wrists. Nik had argued hard that another human should go with me, and even though Wolf had maintained that, first, it wasn't necessary and, second, Nik wasn't a regular human, he'd given in.

I swallowed and placed my hand flat on the center of the dragon.

At first, all I felt was the warmth of Wolf's skin, and then I heard Ice Tor's chuckle, and Wolf's warmth became the heat from the forge, but before I could become afraid of the fall of the hatchet, the room around us dropped away and was replaced by one about half again as big. Soft light came from all directions, even the floor, diffused through what looked like the silk walls of a tent.

Cassandra, the High Prince of the Lands, was standing to one side of a table set with four armed chairs, plates, goblets, and platters of food.

"Where are we?" I said as both Nik and Wolf backed away.

"I'm not sure, exactly." Cassandra was examining my face, her eyes huge and gray. "It's a space Ice Tor arranged for me, when I explained that I could not go to you, and that you could not come to me."

"I . . ." Suddenly my lips were trembling and my tongue wouldn't work. Cassandra made a "tsk" sound and then I was in her arms. I stiffened, but instead of a cascade of smothering images I got nothing. Exactly nothing, except the strength and warmth of her arms around me, her hand patting me on the back, and the smell of saffron as I buried my face in the crook of her neck. I'd been unable to take this comfort from anyone else, afraid of what I'd read when I touched them. I wrapped my arms around her so tightly that I could feel the tiny scales on the mail she was wearing under the fine cloth of her shirt.

All of a sudden I was weeping. These were the tears that hadn't come when they'd told me what had happened to Alejandro. I hadn't even been able to say good-bye; he'd Faded while I was still waiting for help in the Panorama Lounge. His *dra'aj* was spread through most of the Outsiders who'd been in the Gardens that day, but it hurt me to touch them. The arms around me tightened.

"He was your *fara'ip*." The liquid tones of her voice seemed to swirl around me, warm and comforting as a hot bath. "He honored us all with his life, and with his death. It was a proud ending, and he was ready."

I nodded. *But I wasn't.* I didn't say the words aloud, but somehow I knew that Cassandra heard them.

What I did hear was a shuffling of feet behind me. I drew in a ragged breath, and Cassandra's arms loosened but still supported me as I straightened.

"We have all the time we need," she said, shooting a glance behind me. "This space is apart from all things."

I heard her, but I was focused on the shoulder of her shirt. The material was perfectly dry and unwrinkled, not at all as though I'd just been wiping my snotty nose on it.

Come to think of it, I didn't have a snotty nose. Cassandra caught my eye and smiled. The smile I gave back to her was shaky, but real. She lifted my left hand and touched the scar with her *gra'if*-covered fingers.

"Valory, I do not think I can heal this without removing my *gra'if*, and that might do you more harm than good."

I took in a deep breath, all the way in, something that, until now, I hadn't been able to do without a sob catching me in the back of the throat. "That's okay," I said. "It . . . it reminds me that everything is real."

"I understand. Come." Holding me now by the arm, Cassandra turned me toward the table and indicated a chair. "Take some food, and some drink, and then we will talk."

I took the nearest chair, and Cassandra sat down across from me. Wolf sat down in the chair to my right, and Nik to my left. Nik perched right on the front edge of the chair, and looked from the food to Cassandra's face as if he didn't know which was more marvelous.

"Is it safe to eat?" he asked, his voice pitched low.

Wolf frowned, but Cassandra only smiled again. "I know what you're thinking of, and yes, it is. The food is charmed—all food in the Lands is—but not to keep humans here." Her smile changed a little, and Nik swallowed. "We use other charms for that." Then she laughed, the spell broke, and Nik was able to lean back in his seat. He shot a quick look at me, raised the center of his eyebrows and half shrugged. Even a few hours ago that shrugging would have reminded me painfully of Alejandro, but now the pain was gone.

Cassandra truly didn't seem to be in any kind of hurry, smiling as she let Wolf and Nik pour the wine and offer meats and breads from the platters and baskets, but I was feeling so much better I was ready to begin. As if she sensed this, Cassandra put down her goblet.

"Valory, when did you know that the Horn would be blown by Fox?"

Nik moved as if he was going to reach toward me, but let his hand drop. Wolf put down the roll he'd been layering with cheese and looked up. His eyes were a little bit like Cassandra's: gray, with fire behind them. Though his fire was oddly dampened. I was suddenly reminded that I wasn't the only one who'd lost somebody. He inclined his head ever so slightly, as if acknowledging my thought.

"I knew when I touched it in my dining room," I said. "Not just that it *would* be him, but that it *had* to be."

"When I told you that you would not have an easy time of things, I had no idea." Cassandra sighed, shaking her head slowly from side to side. "And the relationship between the Lands and the Shadowlands, how sure are you that it is as you described?"

Here we go again. Was this going to be my curse? Would people only believe what they wanted to hear?

"It is certain." Wolf answered before I even opened my mouth. "Like so many of the memories of my life before the Hunt, I did not remember this until Valory spoke it aloud. But it is true. The Lands will not survive without the anchor of the Shadowlands."

"It's like a double solar system," Nik said. I'm afraid we all blinked at him. He shrugged and went on talking. "Or a binary star, whatever they're calling it these days. Two masses revolving around each other, each dependent on the other." He moved his fists around in front of him to illustrate. I nodded. "Take one star away," he put one fist under the table, "and there's nothing to keep the other one in place." He let the other fist drop.

"And in order to create this anchor, *dra'aj* was taken from the Lands and stored in the Shadowlands?" Cassandra looked around at all of us, as if she wasn't sure who would answer.

"That's what I got from Ice Tor," I said. "The Dwarves and the Trolls were the ones who created the doorways between the two worlds."

Cassandra narrowed her eyes and began to nod. "Now I know who to ask to fix the broken Portals."

"They were the ones who figured out that the anchor could be made by spreading out *dra'aj*," I said. "And how much needed to be moved."

"And Wolf was involved with this project?"

Now we were all looking at Wolf again, and I could read the respect, and even the awe in the face of the High Prince. Wolf had been born into a time before any history that any of them could even remember. Not just lifetimes ago, but Cycles.

Wolf looked up from the piece of bread he was crumbling, turning his head to me. "He was a courier," I said. "Wolf and others, all of them Riders."

"Did they all become Hounds?" Nik asked. "So all the ones we killed –?"

"No, some of them came along later." Cassandra made a movement with her hand, and I looked at her.

"Couriers," she said.

"Well, the *dra'aj* had to be transferred somehow." I glanced back at Wolf, and he was still looking at me, his gray eyes cold and bleak in his pale face. I cleared my throat. "I didn't know until I was touching both of them at once," I said. "Both Wolf and his brother. Then I could see it. How they had started out the same way."

"The High Prince—not you, Truthsheart, the High Prince of that time—was a Natural and he could give us the *dra'aj* to carry." Wolf reached out for his goblet of wine, but he only turned it around, without picking it up. "There was a Chant—there *is* a Chant—that draws *dra'aj* out of the Lands." He looked up. "And also, as we later learned, out of the People. It was important work, it carried much prestige and honor." Wolf dropped his eyes again. "I asked for my brother to be made part of the group—"

"You mean he nagged at you until you gave in," I corrected. "Fox couldn't stand that Wolf had something of importance that he didn't have himself."

Wolf shrugged. He knew I was right, but that didn't make it easier for him to acknowledge. "We did not know our danger—no one did—until it was too late."

"Only the High Prince can be exposed to so much *dra'aj* without becoming addicted." Cassandra had the air of someone who was putting some pieces together herself.

Wolf grimaced. "I do not know how it was done, but when the danger was discovered, the *dra'aj* of the Lands was cut off from us, to keep us from glutting ourselves."

"But not the *dra'aj* of the People." Cassandra poured herself another goblet of wine. The food on her plate was untouched.

"No, that was not possible."

"But they had the Horn," I said. Wolf looked grateful to have the focus taken off him. "And they used it to put the Hunt to sleep—like hibernation," I added when Nik made a noise in his throat. "So that the couriers wouldn't be a danger to anyone or to themselves while they figured out the problem."

"But they did not figure it out," Cassandra said.

"Well, no." I shrugged. "Later on, much later, maybe even after another Cycle, someone found the Horn who didn't know what it was for, and blew it."

"And we awoke, and became the Hunt." We all heard the whisper of a growl in Wolf's voice.

Somehow I wasn't surprised that it was Nik who finally broke the silence. "I can see it's good to know all this, the history of how our worlds connect, and how important we are in the larger scheme of things, but what happens now?" he said.

"I understand that some of the Hunt escaped?" Cassandra said.

"Seventeen were killed outright, including Foxblood." Wolf didn't raise his eyes from his own clasped hands. I wasn't the only person feeling alone just now. "Five submitted and have been Healed," he continued. "They have been placed with the Wild Riders for their own protection and security."

"A safe enough haven while we see if the Healing takes," Cassandra said.

"So that is twenty-two, leaving five unaccounted for."

"And they are scattered, no longer a Pack."

I cleared my throat. "That's if we go by how many there were when Wolf was Pack Leader," I said. "There may not even be a whole Five left. We know some were killed before. Wolf and Nighthawk killed one in Spain. Alejandro killed one outside Union Station." I was proud of the way my voice didn't change. "But our count may be off just the same. Something I picked up on when I touched Fox," I said, turning to Max. "I think some of the Basilisk Warriors got hooked." I looked at Cassandra. "I know you killed one once," I said. "I don't know if that one was part of the original count."

Wolf shook his head, once, still not looking up.

"We can try to create another Horn, but Ice Tor is not optimistic about our chances." Cassandra picked up her goblet and put it down again without drinking from it. "The danger is not great, with so few left, but we cannot ignore it. Wolf. I fear to ask this of you."

"If we had nets, made of *gra'if*, I believe they could be captured. I will not hunt them, unless the attempt is made."

Nik looked as though he might say something, but he glanced at me and stayed quiet.

"I will ask for volunteers," Cassandra said, "and speak to the Solitaries about the possibility of such artifacts."

She'd get most of her volunteers from the Wild Riders, I thought. That was a bunch willing to try out new things.

"But I must do something more. Now that the Hounds are stable, and can Move, I must consider that they may also be able to use the Portals. For that reason, I must order them closed."

Wolf looked up, startled.

"I hope this will be only temporary, until a Horn is made, or the nets that Wolf suggests," Cassandra was still speaking. "I acknowledge our responsibility to deal with the Hunt. But I still cannot spare any large force. Any Rider or Solitary who wishes to stay—Mountain Crag, the Troll, has already returned—may of course help the Outsiders. But any who choose this may be stranded there—at least for a time—as you may be yourself, Stormwolf." It was clear from her expression that Cassandra had asked a question, and was waiting for an answer.

Wolf was silent for a long time, looking at Cassandra. I couldn't tell what passed between them, but some kind of communication did. Wolf put out his hand to me and I reached for it, figuring that he wanted me to confirm something, or to answer some kind of question. Then I saw it was his left hand, and that, like me, he was still missing a finger.

As he took my hand, he looked across the table at Nik. And Nik grinned, shrugging with just his right shoulder, and nodded. So I knew what Wolf was going to say before he said it.

"I stay in the Shadowlands," he said. "I stay with my *fara'ip*."

I let out a breath I didn't even know I was holding.

Violette Malan lives in a nineteenth-century farmhouse in southeastern Ontario with her husband. Born in Canada, Violette's cultural background is Spanish and Polish, which can make things interesting in the kitchen. She has worked as a teacher of creative writing, English as a second language, Spanish, beginner's French, and choreography for strippers. On occasion she's been an administrative assistant and a carpenter's helper. Her most unusual job was translating letters between lovers, one of whom spoke only English, the other only Spanish.

Join Violette on Facebook and read her blog on her website: www.violettemalan.com